The Swing of
the Pendulum

by

Frances Mary Peard

The Swing of the Pendulum
by Frances Mary Peard

ISBN: 978-93-60469-57-3

Published by

DOUBLE 9 BOOKS
2/13-B, Ansari Road
Daryaganj, New Delhi – 110002
info@double9books.com
www.double9books.com
Tel. 011-40042856

ABOUT THE AUTHOR

Between 1867 and 1909, Frances Mary Peard wrote more than 40 story books for kids and adults. She was born on May 16, 1835, and died on October 5, 1923. Most of them were books or collections of short stories set in the United States. Many of them were historical and took place abroad. Commander George Shuldham Peard (1793–1837), a navy officer who went to the Arctic to look for Sir John Franklin, and Frances Cooke (née Ellicombe, 1805–1895) had five children; two of them died young. She was born in Exminster, Devon. Joshua Peard was her grandpa, and John Whitehead Peard was her uncle. Her brother George Shuldham Peard (1829–1918), who was also an artist, had served in the Crimean War. Since she comes from a family of famous soldiers and sailors, it's not a surprise that fights and military themes show up a lot in her stories. She seems to have traveled a lot, maybe even as far as India. But in her later years, she lived with her mother in Torquay, Devon. French author Frances Peard wrote books for kids of all ages, including fiction for adults. She got ideas for her books from her trips, especially in France and India.

CONTENTS

Chapter One
Dislike.. 7

Chapter Two
A Man's Judgment... 15

Chapter Three
We Start Ourselves and Cry Out that Fate Pushes............................ 25

Chapter Four
At Six in the Morning... 38

Chapter Five
The Skittishness of Fate.. 49

Chapter Six
And the Pitfalls of Cupid... 63

Chapter Seven
How a Letter got Written.. 73

Chapter Eight
Eden.. 82

Chapter Nine
Tongue-Tied 90

Chapter Ten
The Inconvenience of Two Heroes....................................... 102

Chapter Eleven
Catechisms... 108

Chapter Twelve
An Air with Variations 117

Chapter Thirteen
Persuasion.. 125

Chapter Fourteen
  "Over the Water wi' Ane" 135

Chapter Fifteen
  The World is Stuffed with Sawdust 141

Chapter Sixteen
  Straws 148

Chapter Seventeen
  The Result of Incoherence 159

Chapter Eighteen
  Bergen Again 171

Chapter Nineteen
  Will She Leave Him? 178

Chapter Twenty
  Not for Two Months 186

Chapter Twenty One
  Farewell 194

Chapter Twenty Two
  A Name in the Air 201

Chapter Twenty Three
  A Walk 210

Chapter Twenty Four
  Doubt and Pride—Which Wins? 222

Chapter Twenty Five
  Fire and Cold Water 232

Chapter Twenty Six
  On the Watch 240

Chapter Twenty Seven
  The Hour—and the Woman 249

Chapter Twenty Eight
  A Note of Interrogation instead of a Full-Stop 261

Chapter One
Dislike

The shallow North Sea had been fretted by a northerly gale, and the voyage from Hull even more than usually unpleasant, when the passengers on board the *Eldorado* struggled up to see the low-lying land which forms the entrance to Stavanger. The vessel was crowded, but hardly any one had appeared at meals, and the groups on deck had been too much occupied with their own discomforts to do more than take a languid interest in each other. Now that the worst was over, this interest quickened.

Two ladies, a mother and daughter, were standing a little apart, when a gentleman strolled up to them. They greeted him with a smile.

"I have not seen you since the night you came on board; where have you been all the time?" he began.

"Don't ask," said the elder lady, with a shudder. "For the first time in my life I have suffered the pangs of actual remorse, because I persuaded Millie to come. However, we are never going home again, that is quite decided."

"Unless we walk," said Millie firmly.

"Do you mean to land at Stavanger?"

"How can you ask? I would land anywhere, even on a desert island. Besides, we have been reading somebody's Best Tour, and according to that it is the right way of going into Norway. Once adopt a guide-book, you become its slave."

"Then we shall be likely to jog along together, unless you object?" said Wareham, with a smile.

Millie looked at him with frank delight, her mother gave a quick glance, in which more mingled feelings might have been read. She made haste, however, to express her pleasure.

"I am not likely to object to an unexpected piece of good fortune, but I give you fair warning that, although I can get on by myself as well as most women, if there is a man at hand, I am pretty sure to turn over exacting carriole-drivers, or anybody making himself disagreeable, to him."

"I am not alarmed. There are no exacting carriole-drivers in Norway, and you are more likely to over-pay than be over-charged. You will like the country."

"I am going to enjoy it immensely," said Millie, "when once I am there. This doesn't count, does it? because, though I believe we are staring at lovely mountains, and there are rose-red sheds standing up against them, I feel too much humiliated to be enthusiastic, and my one longing is for tea. Besides, I am dreadfully cold."

"Come to the other side of the ship," said her mother briskly. "We shall see the town better, and be nearer our luggage."

Wareham followed, he hardly knew why.

He liked the Ravenhills very well, but he had not intended to attach himself to any fellow-travellers, and when he spoke of jogging along together, it was rather an allusion to the inevitable gravitation of Norwegian travel than to that deliberate companionship which their words seemed to accept. He told himself, however, that this was a natural mistake, born of inexperience. It would be easy enough to break away when he found it desirable; he would not worry his holiday with excess of caution. Mrs Ravenhill was charming, and Millie might turn out to possess the same delicate quality. As she stood before him with her mother, he was struck with the prettiness of her hazel eyes and her dimples, and with that swift rush of thought into the imaginary future which we have all experienced, and from which we often return with a flush of shame, he saw himself falling in love with Millie, and coming back to England an engaged man. The thought was so vivid, that when at this moment she turned to speak to him, he had scarcely time to call himself back to the actual condition of things, and something of his mental picture was perhaps betrayed in his face, for she glanced quickly at him a second time, and coloured slightly.

"Norway may be as delightful as you all declare," she said, "but when I set up a delightful land it shall have no custom-house. Here we shall have to wait, I suppose, while great big men amuse themselves with rummaging among all my most nicely packed corners. Oh, it's absurd, it's barbarous! And mother wouldn't bring a maid."

Mrs Ravenhill had moved a little forward, to speak to one of the stewards who were carrying up the cabin packages. When next Wareham looked at her, she had apparently relinquished her intention, and was talking to a gentleman who up to this moment had stood aloof, and who, even now, showed no great conversational alacrity, as Wareham remarked with a little amusement.

"Who is that?" he asked Miss Ravenhill.

"That?" Millie's eyes began to smile. "Oh, poor Colonel Martyn. It is really wicked of mother, for she knows how frightened he gets when he hasn't Mrs Martyn to protect him. But here she comes," and Millie stopped suddenly.

Wareham did not notice the break, for his eyes had passed Mrs Martyn, and fallen with a start of annoyed surprise upon the face of a girl who followed her. The girl was young, and unusually tall, though, owing to an extraordinary grace and ease of movement, this only became evident when you compared her with the other women who stood round. She looked neither to the right nor left, and with the sun shining brightly behind her, it was difficult to see her face distinctly, but Millie, who was watching Wareham, perceived that he recognised her, and that the recognition was, for some reason or other, unwelcome.

"You know Miss Dalrymple?" she asked curiously.

Wareham's expression had stiffened.

"No," he said briefly.

"No? But you have seen her? You must have seen her this season?"

"Yes, I have seen her."

Millie's mouth opened as if she were going to put another question, but if it were so her intention changed. She said with enthusiasm—

"She is very beautiful."

Wareham did not answer. He had turned his back upon the group, and was looking over the water past some brilliantly red-roofed barns to a broken line of tender amethyst-coloured hills.

"Are those people going to get out here?"

"What people?"

"Miss Dalrymple and her friends."

"No. They told us at Hull—we all dined together at the Station Hotel, you know—that they should go on to Bergen."

"Oh, good!" said Wareham, with unmistakable relief.

Millie began to laugh.

"You don't know her, yet you have a dislike to her!"

"Yes. I dislike her."

The Swing of the Pendulum | 9

Something in Wareham's tone checked further questioning. It was grave, outspoken, and the least little bit in the world haughty. Millie flew away from the subject, though her thoughts crept back to it again and again, with, it must be owned, a secret glee.

Slowly the vessel steamed into the harbour. The sun had broken out brilliantly after the gale; clouds, blown into strange shapes, struck across the sky, and glittered whitely behind a cleft in the distant mountains; the indigo blue water was full of dancing movement, and gave everything an air of gay exhilaration which it was difficult to resist. Into Millie's pale face colour returned, and her eyes brightened as she looked about her at the vividly-painted boats, the white houses, and the cream-coloured ponies standing on the quay. Thanks to Wareham, they were among the first to leave the vessel, and to make their way through a gently interested crowd towards the inn. Mrs Ravenhill was more enthusiastic than her daughter. She sketched, and all she saw resolved itself into a possible effect on a square of white paper, and breathed the joy of creation. She was possessed, besides, with the fancy that her coming to Norway in a spirit of warm good-will should be warmly reciprocated, so that she looked at the people smiling, ready to shake hands with them all, since she had heard that was the form of greeting they liked. Millie, who had not her mothers buoyancy, found it more difficult to forget the impressions of the voyage. She began to pity those remaining on board.

"Unfortunate people who go on to Bergen! Weren't the Martyns very sorry for themselves, mother?"

"Oh, didn't you hear? They have given up the idea, changed their plans, and are landing here. Mrs Martyn vowed she couldn't stand another hour."

Millie shot a quick glance at Wareham, and told herself that his face spoke annoyance, but at this moment Mrs Ravenhill's alert attention to the unusual was caught by a pony standing in a little cart, hobbled by reins twisted round its fore-feet, and she broke into exclamation. Then they left the harbour by a short street, and presently found themselves at the entrance of the comfortable inn which calls itself the Grand, where the two ladies vanished up-stairs, while Wareham, who had a telegram to send, went up the hill to the post-office.

Already he repented of the rashness which had allowed Mrs Ravenhill to suppose that he was ready to join her. He had known them long, but not well, and to a mail used to self-disposal, there was horror in the bare thought that they might make undue claims upon his attentions. That was bad enough, but the Martyns lay behind—worse, and that they should be worse was annoying. The best friend in the world cannot adopt the misfortunes of his friend as though they were his own, least of all, as Wareham reflected, with a half-laugh, when they are the misfortunes of love. As Dick Wareham with Hugh Forbes opposite to him—seen through a cloud of smoke, and the mist of years—sympathy bound him to denunciation of the woman who had ruined Hugh's happiness; but as Richard Wareham in a holiday land, old surroundings behind, only folly would allow disturbance because this same woman was under the same roof! What was she to him? He reflected impatiently that he had been a fool to tell Miss Ravenhill that he disliked her. Wareham was hot-headed, and hot-headed yet fair-minded men must often wade through deep waters of repentance. He owned that he had behaved ill, and as his opinion of himself was of more importance to him than that of the world, the judgment annoyed him, and Miss Dalrymple, the cause of annoyance, became more obnoxious. He sent his telegram, and it was to Hugh Forbes.

If he had indulged in a hope that the Martyns might have betaken themselves to another inn, that hope was promptly dispelled, for after making his way back, followed by children shyly inviting him to buy paper screws, containing each four or five strawberries, he found their names largely scrawled across the black board in the entrance-hall, where the good-humoured burly porter was still arranging rooms for white-faced arrivals. Then he jumped at another chance of escape. Had the Sand steamer gone?

It had. The *Eldorado* was some hours late, and the steamer left at two. No other was due for twenty-four hours. Wareham went to his room, ashamed of the impulse of retreat. A bath and increasing hunger braced him, and he came down to the meal which in Norway does duty for late dinner, caring nothing as to whom he might encounter. He was not surprised to hear that Mrs Ravenhill had already made intimate acquaintance with Stavanger, its streets, harbours, and boats, but he was appreciatively grateful for the tact which had led her to abstain from asking him to accompany her; evidently she intended him to understand that travelling with them was not going to interfere with his liberty. Millie, like the rest of the world, had been sleeping; now she was quite herself again, and announced that she meant to go out immediately after supper.

"Meanwhile I intend to try everything that is on the table. Isn't that the properly unprejudiced spirit in which to dine in a strange country?"

"Oh, praiseworthy!" said Wareham. "Do you mind how they come, or will you follow hackneyed routine, and start with salmon?"

"Please. I don't wish to go in too strongly for emancipation. I shall begin with salmon, and be much disappointed if you don't provide me with reindeer collops—isn't that the proper word?—and cloudberries and cream."

"You are born to disappointment," Wareham announced. "Cloudberries are not ripe much before September, and we are in July." Millie looked at him, laughing and frowning. He admired her dimple.

"Spare my delusions," she said. "I shall not listen to you. I know what to expect. Cloudberries and cream I shall feast upon, if not to-day, another day. Pirates will be in the fjords, at a safe distance. There will be islands, and if we look long enough, we shall see a man swimming, and flinging up his hands; while up by the saeters we shall come upon a little Lapp, carrying away a cheese as big as himself. That is my Norway," Millie continued triumphantly, "not the miserably complicated country of Ibsen and Bjornson." She lowered her voice to an "Ah!" and said no more, as the Martyns and Miss Dalrymple appeared.

Three empty seats opposite the Ravenhills had been reserved for the new-comers. Colonel Martyn gave a nod to Wareham, expressive of the sympathy of a fellow-sufferer, and dropped into the chair corresponding with his. Mrs Martyn came next, a large fair woman, with hardness in her face and brusqueness in her manner. Wareham passed them and looked at Miss Dalrymple, hostility in his heart, and admitted; as well as a curiosity which he would not have so readily acknowledged.

She faced the level light of many windows, a position against which Millie had rebelled, and she had just gone through a trying sea voyage; but her beauty defied what would have affected others. Her skin was warmly tinted, her hair a lovely brown, growing low on the temples, and lighter than is usual with brown beauties, some shades lighter than the beautiful eyes. Wareham, looking at her, pelted her with all the detracting epithets he could light upon; he called the poise of the small head on the slender throat arrogant, yet to most people it would have seemed as natural as the growth of a flower, and as perfect. As for the line of her lips, it was hard, hard, hard. Sitting down, she swept the table with a swift glance, half closing her eyes as she did so, to her judge a sign of sinful vanity, though really due to near-sightedness. This done, she turned and talked almost exclusively to her neighbour, a small old lady, shy, and a little prim, who had also crossed in the *Eldorado*. She was often, however, silent: once Wareham encountered her half-shut glance resting upon him. She showed no confusion at meeting his gaze, and he had to own, with a little mortification, that her look was as impersonal as that which she turned upon others of the unknown company.

Millie had grown silent, perhaps because her neighbour spoke less; and the link between the two sets was Mrs Ravenhill. She knew many people and could talk easily; at one moment in her conversation with Mrs Martyn, who had not yet stepped back into her usual assertive mood, she leaned across her daughter, and introduced Wareham. It was only an act of courtesy; after the interchange of a few words, his talk drifted again to Millie.

The motley meal ended, it broke up abruptly.

"Mother and I are going out," said Millie, with careful avoidance of pressure.

"I will come, if I may." He added heedfully, "That is, if you are to be alone?"

"Alone, of course." The girls eyes danced. Triumph had not often come to her, and to find a man, a man of distinction, who preferred her society to that of the beautiful Miss Dalrymple, was intoxicating. She swept her mother to her room, and implored her to make haste. .

"Why?"

"Why? Because it is pleasanter to be alone."

"Shall we be alone?"

Pinning on her veil, Millie admitted that she believed Mr Wareham would come.

"Oh!" Presently Mrs Ravenhill added, with a little intention—"Millie, don't spoil Mr Wareham."

The girl laughed frankly.

"The bare idea makes you fierce, mother, doesn't it? But I do think it is nicer to have a man with us than to trail along by ourselves, and if he comes, he will expect things to—to—well, to go as he likes."

Mrs Ravenhill emitted another "Oh!" She added—"In my day a man would have thought himself honoured."

"So he would in mine, if I had the arrangement of things," Millie retorted. "But I haven't, and all that can be done is to make the best of them. Perhaps you haven't found out that Mr Wareham detests Miss Dalrymple, and evidently wishes to avoid her. We needn't force them upon each other."

"I thought he did not know her?"

"Nor does he."

"Well," said her mother, with impatience, "have it as you like, Millie, only, for pity's sake, don't let us plunge into a cloud of mystifications and prejudices! We didn't come to Norway for that, and Mr Wareham isn't worth it."

To this the girl made no answer, and the subject dropped.

So they went out, all three, in the cool clear daylight, which had no suggestion of evening about it, except that the shop-doors were locked, and people strolled about with leisure which seemed unnatural. The streets were not beautiful, but all the boarded houses had clean white faces, red roofs, and cheerful windows crowded with flowers. Presently they came upon the old cathedral with its two low spires; on one side an ancient avenue of storm-stunted sycamores, dignified a grave little cluster of houses at its end. Millie wanted to go into the church, and professed herself injured at finding it closed.

"Mayn't they ever shut up?" said Wareham, holding out his watch with a smile.

"It is a quarter to ten!" she exclaimed, but refused to return. A lake glimmered through the trees—they went there, and afterwards along stony ways round the harbour. Something—was it the pure light air, the kindly sensible-faced people?—set the girls heart, throbbing. She had suddenly caught her mother's simple power of enjoyment, and Wareham owned that her quick intuition gave originality to the commonplace.

By the time the harbour was reached, lights were golden, colour ran riot in the sky. There was too much ripple on the water for reflections, but the green boats bobbed gaily up and down; while far away the mountains lay faintly blue against the eastern sky, out of which light paled. Beyond the streets are public gardens, the houses are left behind, and the wide water-mouth stretches broadly. Now there was nothing but the lap of waves, distant islands, more distant mountains, and the sunset sky above.

They lingered, and silently watched the pomp fade, found a boat, and rowed across the harbour in the last afterglow.

Chapter Two
A Man's Judgment

Strange, indeed, that Wareham should have been thus shot into the society of Anne Dalrymple! Never personally acquainted with her, he had heard more about her than of any other living woman, could have described her positively, and believed he knew her mind. Heart he denied her. Had he been in England during the past year or two they must have met, but he had first been ordered abroad after a narrow escape of breakdown from over-work; then, bitten by the charm of the south, let himself drift lazily from Italy to Greece, from Greece to Egypt, from Egypt to India, all lands of enchantment.

During the latter part of this stay, letters had been showered upon him from his chief friend, Hugh Forbes, letters crammed with enthusiasm, with hope, with despair, a thundering chord, with the beautiful Miss Dalrymple for its root. Wareham pished and poohed, and sometimes pitched away as much as half a letter—unread—with a word. But he was a man with an unsuspected strength of sympathy. Probably it belonged to his success as an author that, once interested, he could project himself into another mind, and feel its sensations. Especially where his affections were concerned was this the case, and it may have been fortunate for him that his affections were not easily moved, perhaps because he feared what he counted a weakness, and was reluctant to let himself go. Once he had loved a woman, but this happened before he was famous, and she married a richer man; since that time his heart had apparently remained untouched, although he never avoided women's society.

The dark time of disappointment drew him nearer to his friend. Hugh was three years his junior, but they had been at school together, and the habit of befriending the younger boy had stuck to Dick. When this happens, the strength of the tie is scarcely calculable, at least on the side of the elder. Hugh knew and acted upon it almost unconsciously. He would as soon have expected the Funds to collapse, as Dick to fail him in case of need.

After a time his letters announced the unexpected to Wareham. The affair was serious, and Miss Dalrymple had accepted him. Rapture filled sheets of paper. Then letters ceased, and Wareham, who was in India, smiled, recognising the inevitable; and waited without misgiving, until a cooler time should bring back the outer manifestations of a friendship which he could not doubt. They came in the form of a cry of misery. Within six weeks of the wedding Miss Dalrymple had broken off the engagement.

He read the letter in amazement, and rushed back to England, snapping the small ties with which he was lazily suffering himself to be entangled, and knowing that in the blackness of a lovers despair his was the only hand to bring the touch of comfort. Under his own misfortunes he had been dumb, but this reticence did not affect his sympathy with a more expansive nature. Hugh liked to enlarge upon his sorrows, unfailing interest lurked for him in the question how they might have been avoided, and the answer was never so convincing as to suffice.

Wareham gave a patient ear to the lengthy catalogue of Miss Dalrymple's charms—until he could have repeated them without prompting—and offered one suggestion after another as to the causes which had induced her to break off her engagement. For there had been no quarrel, no explanation. Hugh had merely received a letter saying that she had discovered it to have been a mistake, and could not marry him; she accepted the whole blame, and asked him not to attempt to see her.

It was a preposterous request, and he battled against it with all his might, only to find that the fates were on her side. For, although he wrote stormy, heart-breaking letters, although he battered at her doors, his letters remained unanswered, and all that he could hear was that Miss Dalrymple was ill and would see no one. This made him worse. Her father was dead, brothers she had none; Lady Dalrymple, her step-mother, an inconsequent careless woman of the world, who had shrugged her shoulders when Anne announced her intention of marrying Hugh Forbes, admitted him to her boudoir, and told him, with another shrug, that she could neither interfere nor offer an explanation. Anne had acted throughout on her own responsibility; as she had not opposed when she disapproved, he could not expect her to take part against her judgment.

"How was I to fight such an argument?"

Hugh asked Wareham, not once but twenty times. The first time he was answered by a question whether he had never met the girl anywhere? "Was I going to insult her in public!" groaned Hugh, and his friend liked him the better for manly self-restraint when he had reason for being distraught. He had avoided society and nursed his misery, exaggerating it, perhaps, but acting gallantly. Wareham could not but reach the conclusion that he had been abominably treated. Yet where lay the remedy? Patience had to be offered in draughts, and was turned from with loathing. This went on until even Wareham grew weary of repetition, and was not sorry when Hugh's sister came up to town, and appeared eager for confidences. With the belief that his friend would be the better for a change of consolers, Wareham resolved to carry out a vague plan, and go to Norway for three or four weeks. And there, as has been seen, he at once found himself confronted with Miss Dalrymple.

Naturally, she now occupied his thoughts. He had sent a telegram to Hugh on arrival, in compliance with a promise he had made to let him know if he at any time became acquainted with Miss Dalrymple's movements; a promise made idly, and already regretted. To-night he pieced together his impressions.

They were as unfavourable as might have been expected. The signs in her face he had already read against her, and her composure almost shocked him. He was certain, from the exuberance of Hugh's friendship, that his own name must be familiar to Miss Dalrymple; and, considering her tacit acknowledgment to Hugh that she had treated him very ill, a woman whose heart was what a womans should be, must have felt and betrayed uneasiness at finding herself face to face with the dearest friend of the man she had jilted. Miss Dalrymple, however, had shown no symptom of feeling. She had treated him as if he had never so much as touched her thoughts, and to do Wareham justice, it was friendship, not vanity, which resented the indifference. He thought it horrible that a woman should be so cold.

Pride, also, he read accusingly. In his own mind he believed Hugh to have been flung over because she had grown discontented with his position. That she had yielded primarily, Wareham interpreted as due to the young fellow's strong personal charm, perhaps to weariness of other men. It was an impulse, not love; and it was not powerful enough for a strain. He depreciated her beauty; who cares for half-shut eyes? He was not sure that Millie Ravenhill was not prettier; at any rate, he was certain that she was more attractive.

When conclusions stand up before us in such mighty good order, the chances are that we have always kept them ready made. This did not strike Wareham, sifter of causes though he might be; he set them down to acuteness of observation, and credited them with impartiality. It vexed him the more to be thrust by circumstances into a sort of companionship with Miss Dalrymple, whom of all women he would have avoided. He would take the first opportunity to break away, but when? For in Western Norway, where there is but one short railway, it often happens that you must leave when you can, not when you will, and at Stavanger this means once in the twenty-four hours. Imagine the sensation, nineteenth-century Englishman! What annoyance! what repose! Whether he would or no, he must make up his mind to journey as far as Sand, perhaps Osen, perhaps even Naes, with all the others who had landed from the *Eldorado*. After, he might go on by himself, and this consolation sent him off to bed.

When he met the Ravenhills in the morning, he found that Mrs Ravenhill's inexhaustible energy had carried her out sketching, and brought her back hungry. She vowed that the place was charming, and after they had breakfasted—waited upon by a girl in Hardanger dress, cut-away scarlet bodice, beaded stomacher and belt, with white chemisette, sleeves, and apron, and fair hair hanging in a long plait—insisted upon bearing them off to prove her words. And, indeed, though there is nothing striking in the town itself, it was impossible not to feel its bright pleasantness. The sun shone gaily, the sweet pure air made every breath delight; even in July there was a fragrant freshness abroad, such as only comes to lands where spring and summer flutter down as fleeting visitors, and we cannot do enough to welcome them. All the houses are painted, whitened, and decked with flowers; they have not the lazy, sunburnt, picturesque charm of the south, but under the delicate northern sky there is a quiet yet vigorous cheerfulness about them. Wareham, who had seen Eastern splendours, was conscious of this gentle quality, and liked it.

They wandered round the busy harbour, into the cathedral, with its Norman pillars, and great impressive barbaric pulpit. The minister came out as they went in, a long black figure with a tall hat, a Puritan ruff, and a kind face, who looked as if he had stepped out of a story-book. Afterwards they strolled on, not much caring where, between hedges of sweet-briar, past boggy places waving with cotton rush, and climbed a hill to see the interlacing fjords, and the distant mountains veiled with advancing mist, and the women making their hay in the fields. Millie, who had not cared very much for Norway before she came, having something of a girl's indifference to the unknown, was discovering delightful things around and before her—were they not rather blossoming in her heart? As for Wareham, he, too, became sanguine. So far, the Martyns were avoided, and with good luck the annoyance of their presence might be reduced to a minimum.

Three people content! What good sprite was here, and what mischief lurked behind? The three, equally unconscious of their luck and their danger, looked at all they could see, went back to the inn for more salmon, and steamed away down the fjords towards Sand.

An hour afterwards they were on the upper deck of the little steamer. Grey mists had gathered in their scouts, and swept up, chilling the air and battling with the sunshine. Now one, now the other gained the day. Miss Dalrymple walked about with Colonel Martyn. Wareham believed she shared his own disinclination to meet, and, under the circumstances, disinclination was more creditable than indifference. His hard thoughts of her softened slightly—very slightly. Mutual avoidance would prevent difficulties which might otherwise prove awkward in the coming days. Meanwhile, as yet nothing had been said or done which foreboded trouble.

It pleased Millie to treat Wareham as if he were responsible for anything lacking in the beauty of the country, and as the wide entrance to the Sand fjord is uninteresting, and a cold wind, nipping in from a bleak sea, chilled the landscape, he became the butt of many mock reproaches. Wrapped in a fur cloak, and barricaded behind an umbrella, she vowed there was nothing to see. Perhaps there was not much. But Wareham found a never-failing attraction in the small scattered villages at which the steamer stopped. A dozen or more white houses, a little stone pier, against which, under the crystal-clear water, seaweed of a wonderful green clung and floated, and a stir of human interest among the people who came down to the water's edge to meet the steamer. At one of these landing-places the crowd was more than usual—a pink, green, and blue crowd—and there was concentrating of eyes upon one young girl, to whom the vessel had brought a bouquet—a white bridal bouquet. The pride with which she received it, the eagerness with which she read the note accompanying it, and allowed the children to admire and smell it, the interest of the other gazing girls, and the dignified air she assumed after the first few moments, made up an idyll which Wareham watched, smiling. He was sorry when the steamer backed away from the busy pier, and left the girl with her hopes, her triumphs, and her awe-smitten companions.

Going back to tell the idle Millie that she had missed something, his eye fell upon a tall slight figure in a long cloak, standing near the spot where he had stood, and talking to a shorter man with a grey beard. It was Miss Dalrymple, and she had apparently been occupied in the same way as himself. Her face was turned towards him, but she made no sign of recognition.

"Well?" demanded Millie gaily.

"Well, you would have found it interesting."

"How do you know?"

"Listen to what were the accessories. A note and a nosegay."

"Go on. No more?"

"A young woman. Beyond question, a wedding near at hand, and I have remarked that all women are interested in weddings."

"Distantly viewed they are tolerable; but looked at closely, one's pity becomes painful. And I am too cold to cry comfortably."

"You must be super-sensitive. I saw no promise of tears."

"The actors conceal their feelings; only the spectators may suffer theirs to be seen. Look how grave Miss Dalrymple is!"

Wareham glanced. Anne stood where he had last noticed her, apparently listening to her companion, and it was true that she appeared to be grave and preoccupied. Hers was a face in which beauty played capriciously, and at this moment the lines justified his charge of hardness.

"Merely bored, I should say, and not troubling herself to hide it."

Millie put a sudden question.

"Wasn't there some story, some engagement, in which Miss Dalrymple was mixed up? I am sure there was something one ought to remember."

Wareham did not feel himself called upon to assist in this mental examination.

"With her beauty she is likely enough to be talked over," was all he said. But Millie persisted.

"I am certain there was a sort of sensation—I must ask mother, for I am suddenly seized with curiosity. What was it? Wasn't there—?" She broke off, and in a moment looked up triumphantly. "Of course! How stupid of me! Now it comes back. She was engaged to a son of Sir Michael Forbes. Didn't you hear of it? Oh, I am sure you did! The wedding day was actually fixed, and everything arranged, and the next thing one heard was that it was at an end. How could I have forgotten!"

Wareham was silent. She looked at him in surprise.

"It is impossible it should not have come to your ears?"

His face changed a little. If she had known it, she was irritating him by her persistence, although he acquitted her of intention.

"One may as well leave the idle talk of the season behind one," he said gravely.

"One can't, with the chief subject before one," retorted Millie. "Confess. Haven't you thought about it since you saw her?"

He hesitated, then allowed the fact, adding that thoughts might remain one's own.

"Ah, you think me a chatterbox," she said good-humouredly. "How tiresome! Here is another shower sweeping across."

"Shall I get a cloak?"

"No. I really want to hear more. I am sure you can tell me." She added with eagerness—"Which was to blame?"

"What a question!"

"Why, is it strange? Somebody was, I suppose. I have very little doubt myself that Mr Forbes was the sinner."

Wareham was startled from his impassive attitude.

"What has given you that impression?"

"What? How can I tell you? If I were to say it was a woman's intuition, you would laugh. So that I imagine it is owing to vague recollection of what I may have heard."

"If that is all, I think you should disabuse yourself of the idea. Whoever was to blame, it was certainly not Mr Forbes."

She looked at him mischievously, and remarked that he spoke so gravely of an indifferent matter that one might suppose he had an interest in it.

"I have not said that it was indifferent."

"Oh!" Millie coloured, and said hastily—"I beg your pardon. I am very sorry. If I had dreamed that there was anything to make you care, I should not have tried to find out your opinion. Do you know, I should be really glad of a mackintosh."

Wareham went to get it, but when he came back he reverted to the subject.

"Let me explain why I care. The man to whom Miss Dalrymple was engaged is my friend, and knowing as I do the circumstances of the case, I can't stand hearing him reproached. I can't explain the facts, simply because they are inexplicable, but I will ask you to take my word that no blame rests with him."

"Oh no, I understand, I quite understand," Millie stammered, wishing herself anywhere else. She was frightened, and could not find a jest with which to swing herself out of the difficulty. Her embarrassment made him think more kindly of her again.

Presently Mrs Ravenhill, who had been talking to Mrs Martyn, came to carry Millie to a more sheltered corner. Wareham, seeing that they were approaching another fjord village, went to the vessels side. This time there was a contrast—no crowd, no happy throng of girls: a few children, a few older people gathered on the pier; the baker came to receive his sack of flour, the postmaster his letters; next, out of the steamer another burden was lifted, an empty black coffin, studded with silver nails; the children—and the children only—stared curiously at the label, then they too ran off. And, so long as the steamer was in sight, there lay the strange black deserted thing, a blot on the green, unclaimed, and to all appearance uncared for. Some prick of the universal humanity kept Wareham's eyes fixed upon it. He felt as if the dead man, whose home it was to be, was wronged by this callous desertion; as if he had been bound to all of them by a tie they were ignoring; and while conscious of the unreasonableness of his blame, he could not shake off the feeling that he shared in the common cruelty. Suddenly, by his side, a voice exclaimed—

"It is horrible!"

He turned abruptly, and saw Miss Dalrymple. Her eyes were fixed where he had been looking, and she went on—

"One has no right to resent a mere accident. They may have to come from a distance, and it can't be known exactly when the steamer will call. Still—"

"It offends one," said Wareham.

"It is heartless."

He kept his eyes on her face.

"Happily the dead are not hurt by heartlessness."

"Happily," she returned, after a moment's pause. She glanced at him, half closing her eyes, in the manner he disliked. Already the conversation had taken an edge, of which, even had it been unintentional, neither could have been unconscious. But Wareham wished to wound. He asked whether she had noticed the group at the landing-place before this last? She made a sign of assent.

"What did you think of it?"

"I?"

"Was it more creditable to human nature? Was heart there, or was the girl merely pleased with her power?"

A smile made him more angry.

"What makes you or me her judge?"

"Dismal experience as to motives," Wareham replied. "One lives and learns."

"Not so surely," Anne returned coolly. "Half the time our pretence of reading motives is sheer affectation. What we are really after is the making our conclusions fit our theories." She suddenly shot away from the subject. "Are you travelling with the Ravenhills?"

"Yes—no," said Wareham, surprised. "It was a chance meeting, and we have all to go the same way."

"All?" She frowned. "Do you mean that we are irrevocably bound together?"

"Practically. Naturally there may be small deviations."

"Oh, hateful!" she said frankly, and apparently mused over the information. Having bestowed it, Wareham was silent until she put another question. "May I inquire where you are all going to-night?"

"I can only help you so far as the Ravenhills are concerned. They will push on to Osen."

"And you?"

"Oh, I, of course."

"You were mistaken, then," said Anne triumphantly, "in supposing that we follow the same route. We stop at Sand."

He laughed. "Pardon me. Sand or Osen are practically the same thing. We meet on the same steamer to-morrow morning."

"Oh!" She reflected again. "There is no help for it, then. Except—"

Wareham waited.

"I trust to you not to take advantage," she said, in a hurried tone, and with a movement of the head which he interpreted as his dismissal.

Instead of rejoining the Ravenhills he stood solitary, and thought over the conversation. What ground had been won or lost between two antagonists'? He had made it plain to Miss Dalrymple that he was on his friends' side, and she had let him know that the meeting was disagreeable to her. So far there was equality. But though he had not disguised his feelings, he could not flatter himself that he had caused Anne the slightest embarrassment. And there was vexation in the thought that their first movement had been towards sympathy, so that he remembered a throb of satisfaction on hearing her exclamation by his side. He remembered, too, and dwelt upon, the expression of her look—which said more than words—the brow slightly contracted, the eyes fixed, the strong pitiful curve of her lips. In spite of his prejudice, she was beautiful. Hugh's raptures had inspired him with contradictory views, but he told himself now that there was no reason to be unfair, and that a lover might very well lose his head over fewer charms. Disapproval, contempt, perhaps, were as strong as ever, and proof against a woman's face. Yet something in his own thoughts irritated him, and he turned from them to talk to a tall German, whose wife and children were ensconced in the warmest corner of the deck.

Chapter Three
We Start Ourselves and Cry Out that Fate Pushes

All the skydsguts, and all the owners of vehicles for miles round Sand, stormed the steamer on its arrival, and out of the struggling crowd Wareham with difficulty extricated Mrs Ravenhill and Millie, and started them in a *stolkjaerre*, while he himself followed in a second with a young Grey, who had, of course, crossed in the *Eldorado*. (Stolkjaerre pronounced stolkyerrer. Skydsgut pronounced shüssgoot.) In all there was a string of nine or ten little carriages, each drawn by a cream-coloured or light dun pony, its two occupants in front, and its skydsgut perched on the luggage behind.

Now that they had left the open fjord, wind-swept by a north-westerly gale, it had grown calm and warm; and, driving up to the mountains by the side of a hurrying river, the charm of the country began to reveal itself. Mrs Ravenhill would have liked to have broken away from the procession, and enjoyed it alone, but this was impossible. The ponies trotted in regular file, walked up the slightest incline, and raced wildly downhill; nothing would have induced ponies or drivers to part company, and, indeed, after all, something in the small cavalcade was refreshingly different from ordinary modes of travelling. Colours glowed and softened in the clear air, crimson sorrel turned the long grass into ruddy fields, waving and shimmering in the breeze, the river, narrowing, dashed itself into milky whiteness. In parts, trees growing singly out of the green, made the country park-like; elsewhere a wilder character prevailed, with a background of grey hills, on which grey clouds brooded. It was ten o'clock before they reached Osen, but so lingering was the day, that even by that time the surrounding outlines were scarcely touched with uncertainty.

Throughout the drive importunate skydsguts had petitioned on behalf of a new inn, but Wareham had decided to stop at the Suldal, known to him of old. Of all the procession only the two stolkjaerres halted there, the rest whisking by to the other and more pretentiously illuminated building; it seemed to Millie that the very landlord met them with surprise. The whole house was at their disposal; no one, he explained, was there, because the other house was very liberal to the skydsguts, and they persuaded their employers in its favour. There was something pathetic in the sad resignation with which he made this statement, and Mrs Ravenhill, whose face had fallen at realisation of the solitude, which appeared to point to something obnoxious, became enthusiastic. The quaint box-like little bedrooms, all pitch-pine, unbroken by paper, plaster, or carpet, delighted her; and as every sound was audible throughout the house, she and Millie in their separate rooms could talk as easily as if they had been together. Presently, however, other voices mingled themselves, and it became evident that some of their fellow-travellers had retraced their steps. When they came down to the meal which had been energetically prepared, they found half-a-dozen others. If it was not a very elaborate repast, there was plenty and good-will, and a homely hospitality which was pleasant. Besides, they were all hungry, and all sleepy, and neither the careful warnings against fire, with directions how to get out of the little passages, and where to find the "safety ropes," nor the rather loud confidences of two travellers on the upper floor, could keep Mrs Ravenhill or Millie long awake.

Wareham, on the contrary, was not drawn to sleep. A paper in hand, which he wanted to think out by the help of a cigar, gave an excuse for strolling along the quiet road, where all was still except the unresting swirl of the river. His will forced concentration upon the matter which was in his mind, but it was like driving unruly horses, and the moment he relaxed his hold, his thoughts bolted to the words Anne Dalrymple and he had exchanged. It was difficult to explain why, except that her talk, her manner, and, above all, her face, had interested him. They possessed a certain quality distinct from the words and faces of others. That he thought of her with an ever-increasing disapproval did not interfere with the interest, but served for an excuse for returning to its contemplation, since nothing is more absorbing than a problem. It was doubtless this attraction which led him to fill out their conversation with imaginary words and incidents, such as might have led to an altogether different result. Jilt or flirt, Anne Dalrymple was no mere brainless woman, and he found himself on the verge of a wish that he had not been Hugh's friend, so that he might have talked to her without prejudice. A man's anger against a woman leaves him uncomfortable, with a sense of his own unfairness, whether deserved or not.

He began to resent his position. He had dropped into it unknowingly, but the bare idea that it might suggest to Hugh a thought of his friend's disloyalty, cut like a lash. Kicking at pebbles in the road, or staring up at the dominating height rising blackly on the other side of the river, would not help him, and for the moment there seemed nothing else. He must make the best of it. Why on earth trouble himself with what could not be helped? Was he by ill-luck becoming morbid? He walked back to the inn, disgusted with himself; pitched away his cigar before entering the inflammable box, and slept, resolved to accept ordinary intercourse as if he and Miss Dalrymple were strangers.

It is difficult to adopt any course of action which does not involve others in unexpected ways. His last intention would have been to make marked advances to Millie Ravenhill, yet, treating her as a haven of refuge, meant being much by her side on the following day. The morning was all summer, full of light and freshness, and as the little carriages began to arrive from Sand, Wareham was very willing to get out of the way by joining half-a-dozen of their fellow-travellers in a stroll over the grassy hill behind the inn. Then Millie and he drifted away together, and she wanted a flower plucked out of a marshy bit of land, and when that was gathered a daring stone-chat enticed them, and the frank innocent beauty around beguiled Wareham, so that when the steamer sent up a warning shriek they were forced to run, and reached the vessel breathless. Mrs Ravenhill flung a look of reproach at Wareham, while she scolded Millie.

"How could you be so imprudent! I have been waiting in terror, not knowing where to send. Osen is all very well, but to be forced to spend another twenty-four hours here! I am really very angry."

"Blame me," said Wareham penitentially. "It was all my fault."

He pleased himself by observing that the Martyns and Miss Dalrymple were in possession of seats, and as there had been a certain intention—on his part—of delay, it is doubtful if he were really sorry. Millie was radiant.

"I should not have minded staying," she remarked, when breath had come back; "it is a dear little place, and it would have been a real crow for the landlord. He loved us so dearly for driving straight to his inn, instead of being forced there by want of room in the other! But what an odd state of society must exist in this place, when out of half-a-dozen houses two are rival inns! Do they speak? Do they fight? Human nature could not allow them to be friendly!"

"Oh, I'm not so sure," said Mrs Ravenhill; "you forget the strength of nature here, and that the human part of them would have to combine against snow and darkness and solitude. Once we are gone, I dare say they are good friends together."

As they were carried along over the green waters of the Suldal lake, it seemed to some of those who were looking, as though they were entering a solemn and enchanted region.

The sun, which blazed upon the great granite hills, could not rob them of their supreme gravity. They were mighty Titans resting after labour and conflict; earth-forces up-heaved and left to lie and bleach, exposed to the more subtle forces of air and water. For the lake crept in and out between them, always softly pushing through, although often the tremendous cliffs closed so menacingly round, that the boat appeared to be making for a wall of sheer rock against which she must be ground. At such moments those on board watched almost breathlessly for the passage to declare itself, sometimes splitting a sharp angle, sometimes stealing through a sinuous curve, once urged between two colossal barriers, which bear the name of the Portal. It is the gateway into a shadowy, mysterious, yet radiant world, which lies as God's Hand has left it, untouched by man. On either side the mountains rise precipitously, or melt away into ethereal distances; out of their soft purples and greens an occasional raw patch marks where the frost-giant has split off a vast fragment from the rock and tumbled it into the green waters below. Birch and oak clamber up and down the cliffs; a sharp white line shows a slender waterfall leaping from the heights, and re-appearing here and there, but, too far off for movement to be perceptible, it looks a mere scratch on the shadows. More rarely, where there is the suspicion of a valley, or, at any rate, a flatness, the steamer screams to some half-dozen—or fewer—scattered houses, tying in a scarcely-endurable solitude, a little amphitheatre of silence; each with its tiny patch of emerald-green rye, its square of half-cut grass, its small potato-ground, its boat lying on the shore. Some rough track may exist, but of visible roads there are none, nor any cattle, except, possibly, a few goats away browsing on the hills. Such forlorn habitations only deepen the brooding solitude, by forcing on the imagination dreams of these alone, self-dependent lives, but for the call of the steamer as alone as though they were a knot of sailors shipwrecked on a desert shore.

Wareham, for whom they had a strange attraction, watched them from the forepart of the vessel. While he was there, Colonel Martyn joined him. He was a tall sad-looking man, with a mountainous nose, devoted to sport, and hating society. He grumbled a disconsolate question.

"How much longer does this sort of thing go on?"

"The lake? Three hours, from end to end. Doesn't it please you?"

"It would please me well enough if I were pulling up in a boat. Cooped up with a lot of other fools, it makes me sick. Do you mean to tell me you find any pleasure in the business?"

Wareham laughed.

"Evidently I haven't your energy." He went on to ask whether with these sentiments his own free will had brought Colonel Martyn abroad?

The other turned a melancholy eye upon him.

"Good heavens, that you should put such a question! My wife insists upon going through an annual period of discomfort. I don't much care where it is. This year she and Anne Dalrymple took a craze for Norway, and here we are." It was as if his last words meant "Poor devils!"

Wareham had no thought of letting fly his next words. They escaped him.

"Has Miss Dalrymple travelled with you before?"

Colonel Martyn again looked at him.

"Never. She is my wife's last friend. A former acquaintance of yours?"

Wareham hastened to repudiate.

"I have never spoken to her until Mrs Martyn introduced me." Some unaccountable impulse made him add — "But I have often heard of her."

"No good?"

"I did not say so."

"Never mind me," said his companion, seating himself on the bulwark, and swinging one long leg. "Women are frauds — most of them."

"Well for you that your wife is not within earshot!"

"She would vow that it showed I was enjoying myself. That's a delusion she holds on to. Keep your liberty — there you have my advice. As for Anne Dalrymple, I've an idea there was something on with her this season, but I don't listen to society crams, and I've heard no particulars."

The red rag was irritating Wareham.

"This was not a society cram. We'll leave it alone, however. Miss Dalrymple is your wife's friend."

For the first time a smile flitted across Colonel Martyn's lantern visage.

"My dear fellow," he said, "say as much or as little as you like. So long as you don't hold me responsible for the freaks of my wife's friends, I'm indifferent, profoundly indifferent, as to what is thought of them. Only wish they'd carry out this sort of amusement without me. I'm no use. Can't speak a word of the lingo. Miss Dalrymple's handsome, that I'll own — there she has the pull over most of Blanche's cronies—but I don't doubt she behaved badly—"

"Mrs Martyn wants the key of her bag," said a voice at his elbow. He swung round guiltily to face Anne Dalrymple.

"Eh?—what?"

"The key of her bag."

"Oh, of course!—yes. Shall I take it or will you?" His embarrassment was pitiable, while she stood cool.

"You, I think."

He bolted.

Wareham, annoyed with his position, stood confronting her. Her height nearly reached his own, her eyes, dark with anger, swept him scornfully, she drew a deep breath.

"Honourable—to set my friends against me!"

He remained silent. Her tone grew more scathing.

"Do not imagine that I take exception at your opinions—your attitude,"—a stress on the 'your'—"to them I am absolutely indifferent. Think what you please—judge me as harshly as you like—influence your own friends if it amuses you to do so. When—not satisfied with this—you attempt to prejudice the people under whose care I am travelling, then, Mr Wareham, you are taking advantage of my being a woman to offer me an unpardonable insult."

Wareham stood like a statue, while she scourged him with her words. Indignation gave such beauty to her face and gestures, that his own anger grew soft.

"You are right," he said. "I am not conscious of having said anything to which you could take exception, but it is true that Colonel Martyn gathered that my thoughts of you were not friendly, and I acknowledge that I was to blame in permitting myself to mention your name."

Her look had been full on his, now she dropped it reflectively. Anger still burned in her eyes, but she was not so composed as she had been. Her breath came and went quickly, and when she spoke her voice was slightly shaken, yet abrupt.

"Be more careful in future."

"You may trust me," said Wareham, bowing gravely. He was not surprised at her turning to leave him, what astonished him was that she came back.

"I don't know whether it is because I am a woman, and have no means of defending myself except by words," she said coldly, "that I think you owe it to me to tell me what you said to Colonel Martyn."

"Anything is owing to you that lies in my power. But this is exceedingly difficult."

"Do you take refuge in an imaginary failure of memory?" she asked, scornfully again.

"On the contrary, I can trust my memory."

"Then?"

"It is just because the words were so trifling, that I shall find it difficult to convince you that I am keeping back nothing."

She hesitated, but her eyes met his frankly. "I imagine that you will endeavour to give me a true impression."

"Thank you. What happened, then, was that on Colonel Martyn's mentioning your name, I asked whether you had travelled with them before?"

"And what was that to you?"

"Nothing. I have already expressed my regret at having put the question."

"Go on."

"Colonel Martyn, on his side, inquired whether I knew you, and from my answer jumped hastily at a conclusion which I imagine you will not require me to excuse?" She made an imperious gesture.

"I have told you that your own opinions do not concern me in the least. Come to something more definite."

"But there was nothing more definite," said Wareham, lifting his eyebrows. He let memory travel slowly over the conversation, picking up threads. "Colonel Martyn, in a discursive review of his dislike to travel, made an allusion to a matter in which you were concerned, and I replied that, as you were his wife's friend, we had better drop the subject. Evidently he likes to emphasise the idea that he and his wife are two, and I imagine this led him to make the unfortunate remark you caught. Pray assure yourself that you have heard all there was to hear, and permit me to repeat how deeply I regret it."

She did not at once answer. The vessel was passing through a marvellous cleft, precipitous rocks arose out of the clear water on either side. Wareham saw Mrs Martyn approaching, curiosity in her face. He waited for Anne to speak.

"I suppose I ought to thank you," she said at last, slowly. "I suppose you tried to be fair. If you did not succeed, perhaps it was beyond your powers."

Mrs Martyn arrived.

"Anne, did you ever see anything so remarkable? I hope you noticed how sharply the steamer turned?"

"Did it?"

"Did it! You are as bad as Tom. What have you been doing? Talking?"

"I suppose so."

"Was it interesting?" asked Mrs Martyn, glancing from one to the other.

"Hardly," said Anne, before Wareham could speak. "We only took up a legacy of conversation left by your husband." She walked away.

"Poor Tom!" Mrs Martyn uttered a laugh. "It must have been a legacy of grumbles. He is miserable because he has to sit still, and submit to be carried from point to point, without the possibility of using violent exercise to accomplish his purpose. If he could only pull up the lake, and tug the steamer behind, he would be happy again. Can you take life with less play of muscle, Mr Wareham?"

"As lazily as you like."

"All the better. It is enough to endure growls from one's husband, without hearing them echoed by others. Please do your best to induce him to enjoy himself."

"I!" said Wareham, with surprise. He added that it was unlikely that he would find an opportunity in the short time they would be together.

"I thought you travelled with the Ravenhills?"

"Accidentally."

"Have you fallen out?"

"No, no," he protested, half amused, half provoked. "But chance having thrown us together, does not bind us."

"It might. Chance might have much to answer for," she went on rapidly. "While it keeps you near us, do be good to my unlucky Tom! I thought he and Anne would have amused each other, but they do not. I hope,"—she reached the point to which he had divined she was tending, and adopted a careless air—"I hope that Tom did not try to run down Anne? He has a deceptive way of saying more than he means, and saying it in his melancholy way produces a stronger effect than if it came from an ordinary person; as I always tell him, I don't think he is in the least aware of the impression he makes. Anne is the dearest girl in the world!"

Wareham felt as if fate were determined to force his opinion about Miss Dalrymple; he answered cautiously—

"I understood from Colonel Martyn that you were friends."

She looked at him.

"I don't believe that either he or you stopped there!"

He gathered that her husband had confided the unfortunate remark which had caused his flight, and thought it hard that she should come to him, instead of applying to her friend, for particulars. He was resolved not to be drawn a second time, experience having already proved sufficiently embarrassing.

"I am not aware of having gone beyond it," he said indifferently. "How should I? Until five minutes ago I had scarcely exchanged twenty words with Miss Dalrymple."

She persisted.

"But of course you had heard of her? Every one who is anything is heard about now-a-days."

He agreed to the general remark, and she tapped her foot impatiently.

"How cautious you are! Now, I always speak my mind, even if it offends people. Life would be unendurable if one had to weigh one's words like so many groceries."

It is difficult to answer the people who present you with themselves as an example. Wareham laughed, and assured her that she had only to choose an impersonal topic.

"A hint for a hit. Well, I don't think you're acting fairly towards Anne, because you won't say what has prejudiced you against her."

So far Wareham had kept his temper, but at this point annoyance made a sudden leap to the front, and with the smile still on his lips, he felt savage. It seemed to him that they wouldn't leave him alone, that they wanted to force his hand, and oblige him to say something that was either offensive or false.

"If you mean that I object to discussing Miss Dalrymple with her friends," he said coldly, "you are right."

"Ah, you would prefer doing it with her enemies," she returned with a shrewdness perhaps unexpected.

"I should prefer changing the subject altogether," said Wareham. "Do you know that we are nearly at the end of our voyage? Behind those grey elephantine rocks lies Naes, and there it is ordained that we dine."

"Dine! At two! Poor Tom! But how good for his health!"

Wareham did not feel himself called upon to express an opinion on this point. He went back to Mrs Ravenhill and Millie, landed, and walked with them up to the little inn, from which a red flag was gaily flying.

It is between Naes and Haare that the Bratlandsdal lies, one of the most beautiful secrets of Norway. Secret, indeed, only by comparison, since the road has been carved out, but as yet not so freely tourist-ridden as other parts. A hard-worked clergyman and his wife, flinging the energy of work into their holiday, at once set off on the long tramp; the other travellers, more respectful to comfort, waited to engage stolkjaerres and carrioles, and to go through the routine of salmon and stringiest mutton; so that it was three o'clock before the Ravenhills, Wareham, and young Grey—wrenched from remote homage of Miss Dalrymple—set off leisurely to walk to the head of the gorge, stolkjaerres and luggage at their heels.

Grey was an enthusiastic fisherman, and his talk of flies, many of which festooned his hat. His companions were careless as to their merits, but Millie had a charm of simple sympathy, which all along Wareham had recognised and liked, and she let him expatiate upon them without giving a hint that she was bored. Almost at once they were in the shadow of the great gorge, the road mounted; down, far down, cleaving its way between thousand-feet rocks, dashed a wild river, beryl-coloured when not churned into whiteness, leaping, laughing, flying from rock to rock, curving into green pools, flinging foam at the growing things which bent to kiss it, an impetuous, untamable, living force. To think of it in storm with a hundred angry voices crying out, and mountain-echoes hurling back their rage, was to shudder. But now, under a brilliant sun, there was a lovely splendour abroad; feathery beds of moss and fern hid away the menacing crevices of the grey rocks; streams tinkled, drop by drop, from the overhanging heights; shadows were soft, tender, and wavering, radiant sunlight changed harshness into beauty.

"And we have it to ourselves!" sighed Mrs Ravenhill thankfully. "The others are ahead, and are welcome to the better rooms. But what of the Martyns?"

Young Grey was eager in his knowledge.

"They were tired, and waited another hour. I promised to arrange about their rooms. It was Miss Dalrymple who said she was tired."

He spoke with an unmistakable touch of reverence.

Mrs Ravenhill thought it a pity they should risk losing the lights.

"The days are long enough," Millie put in. "And how delightful to have this delicious place to ourselves! Let us enjoy it."

"Let us," said Wareham. "How do you begin?"

"Oh!" cried the girl indignantly, "there is no beginning. You must *do* it."

"Ah, that is feminine impracticability. You issue a command, and we are anxious to obey, but every act has a beginning and an end."

She broke into a smile.

"Well, then, put away the wish to be anywhere else."

"Done," said Wareham, after a moments consideration. "But don't you see Mr Grey eyeing the river?"

The young fellow excused himself. He was only wondering how a particular fly which the landlord had bestowed upon him would work in the pools.

"Precisely," said Wareham, smiling at Millie. "In our advanced civilisation, enjoyment has ceased to be spontaneous, and has become an art. It can't be treated so unceremoniously as you suggest. Stalk it as you would a deer, and, even then, ten to one your prey escapes you."

She cried out—

"I should think so! You had better pretend that an epicure who has made up his mind what to have for dinner is the only person who knows what enjoyment is!"

"I suppose so—yes, I dare say you have hit on the best definition," returned Wareham reflectively. "What is very certain is that he should not come to Norway."

"I think you are hateful! Do you mean to tell me you are never pleased?"

"Oh, pleased!—yes, certainly. Enjoyment is something more important—more all round."

"Well, that is what we feel now." She swept in her mother with a comprehensive look. "We like the beauty, the air, the solitude—and our companions," she added, with a smile. "Isn't that all-round enjoyment?"

"I really believe it is," said Wareham, glancing at her kindly, "and that you know more about it than I do. Long may it be so!"

He thought he had never seen her look prettier. Her eyes danced, the dimples in her cheeks gave her face a sweet child-likeness, she was as fresh as the young summer which ran riot all about them. The idea took him that Miss Dalrymple's beauty would have faded in this world of laughing colour, of flashing waters, too much of the other world belonged to it. Millies was heightened, and it pleased him to dwell on the discovery. Her merriment was contagious. When the stolkjaerres overtook them, she fed the good ponies with barley-sugar, and aired her attempts in Norwegian upon the men, who answered in excellent English. Afterwards—when they had climbed again into the little carriages, the skydsgut perched behind upon portmanteaux, as the clever ponies trotted cheerfully along, requiring no touch from the whip, but quickening their pace under an encouraging chirrup, and stopping at a long-drawn Pr-r-r from the driver—they overtook the clergyman and his wife, tramping unweariedly along. And here Millie had her triumph. For in their hands they carried a bunch of red and yellow berries, and held them inquiringly to a skydsgut, who answered "Multer." Now, *multer*, as Millie had taken care to ascertain, is Norwegian for cloudberry, and here was what she had determined to see and taste, and been told she was too early for. Two or three were at once made over to her, but she would not eat them there, preferring to taste them with the dignity of cream at Haare. And it may as well be added, that these were the first and last cloudberries she saw in Norway.

Watches told them that it was early evening when they made their last climb to Haare. For some time past the grandeur of the gorge had been smoothed into tenderer lines; the river broadened—driving young Grey into distraction when he looked at it—and presently a lake opened, lying quiet and shadowy under sheltering mountains. They passed a waterfall, and mounted slowly to the inn, perched obtrusively on the hill-side, red flag flying, stolkjaerres and carrioles crowded about.

Supper ended, they strolled out; golden lights lingered in the sky, and the mountains rose against it in royal purple. The roar of the *fos* reached them brokenly, and as they crossed the zigzagged road, by grassy cuts, to this sound was joined that of advancing wheels and voices. Two stolkjaerres passed along the road below, two people walked, a word, a light laugh, came up.

"The Martyns," said Mrs Ravenhill.

No one answered. They stood and watched the little cavalcade slowly mounting. Shadows deepened, the clear air was fragrant with newly-mown grass, a star trembled into sight. It was very solemn and peaceful.

Chapter Four
At Six in the Morning

By fits and starts Wareham was an early riser, and the next morning he was out between five and six. By that time the sun was high in the heavens, dews were dried, life—insect and plant-life—was in eager movement. A cottage with a wonderful roof, lying not far from the foot of the *fos*, had attracted him the day before; he crossed the zigzags, made out a narrow path over short grass, and reached it.

It was a tiny cottage, built partly of stones heaped roughly one on the other, partly of boards of many shapes and sizes, a hut full of odd cranks and changes, deep eaves on one side, a perched-up window on another. But what had attracted Wareham to closer inspection was the roof, lovely with waving grass, sorrel, starlike daisies, and a mass of lilac pansies. It was the subject Mrs Ravenhill would pounce upon to sketch, and he felt a gentle gratitude towards the Ravenhills for the small demands they made upon him. An extraordinarily stony little path flung itself headlong towards the lake, through tall emerald-green rye; he stumbled down a few yards to look back at the hut, standing out against a violet mountain, all the colours sharply insistent in the clear morning air. To his extreme astonishment he saw Miss Dalrymple appear on the crest of the hill, and make her way down towards him. She came lightly and firmly, stepping from stone to stone without hesitation. She wore a white dress, and the impression she gave was of some one younger than he had fancied her. As she drew nearer the impression strengthened by her calling out gaily—

"I have just discovered what it is all like; Sunday morning, the freshness, and the enchanting air. Do you know?"

"No." He added in spite of himself—"Tell me."

"The opening to the last act of *Parsifal*."

"I dare say. But I am no musician."

"Nor I. But I suppose one need not be a painter to be reminded of a picture. However, I did not come after you to talk about *Parsifal*." She stood in the narrow pathway looking down upon him, and spoke with extreme directness. "I saw you from the window, and, as I wished to say something, I followed—"

He bowed. She looked beyond him.

"I have known you two days, but of course have heard of you enough, and though you may not believe it, no one wanted you home from India more than I. I fancied from what I gathered that you might understand."

He steeled himself against the flattering softness of her voice.

"Because I was Hugh Forbes' friend?"

"Yes," she returned quickly—"for that reason. You might have saved him suffering. For I am afraid he has suffered."

"You are afraid. Do you doubt?"

"Not now."

"Compassion has awakened tardily," he said, with a laugh, which brought her eyes upon him.

"Wait a moment," she said suddenly. "The grass on this bank is dry. Let us sit down. Now go on."

Seated, she was still above, and her dark eyes rested on his face. He found it difficult to say what a moment before had seemed easy. "He will feel his hurt all his life."

This time her eyebrows went up.

"Oh, no!"

"I know him," persisted Wareham.

"So I thought. But you are mistaken. His feelings cry out, and are quickly consoled. In a year he will have forgotten them."

"Your doctrines are convenient."

She breathed quickly, but appeared to wait for more.

"To break off your engagement without so much as a word as to the why! To refuse even to see him! Caprice could hardly show itself more cruelly."

Anger leapt into her eyes.

"You allow yourself strong expressions, Mr Wareham!"

"If you do not like them it appears to me that I am the last person to whom you should speak. You may not know what Hugh is to me."

"If I did not, I should not be talking to you at this moment," she retorted, flinging back her head. "Should I discuss the subject with an indifferent person?"

It had been good to him to feel the impetus of his own anger, he courted, encouraged it. A secret fear made him dread a softer mood. He kept his eyes upon a butterfly, balancing itself on an ear of rye. As he did not answer, she went on—

"Taking it from your point of view only, for I suppose you would be incapable of a broader outlook, do you consider a lingering end more merciful than one which is short and sharp? I have never for a moment regretted the manner of the doing."

"You have regretted something," said Wareham quickly, recognising that she laid a scarcely-perceptible stress on one word, and beginning to think that she intended him to undertake the mission of reconciliation. A drag of reluctance he believed to belong to disapproval.

"Perhaps," she said, with hesitation.

"Isn't it a little late?"

It struck him that his question had an offensive air, but she appeared not to have heard it; she was looking beyond him at the glowing lake, and the mountains which bordered the green waters.

"I am ready to own that I was to blame," she went on, still slowly; "but I shall always think that he ought to have understood."

"What?"

"What can't be put into words. Why, I did not care to marry him."

"You are enigmatical."

She made an impatient movement.

"At any rate, it should be enough for you that I did not like him well enough."

"And that is your explanation?"

"What; else?"

"It had occurred to me that the match might not have been considered sufficiently brilliant for the beautiful Miss Dalrymple." She did not reject the supposition with anger as he perhaps expected, merely shook her head.

"You are like the rest of the world," she said resignedly, so that he immediately felt shame for his own stupidity, but had nothing to say against it. He took refuge in pointing out that they had placed themselves in the line of a procession of caterpillars, all apparently on their way to the lake, and that several were at that moment on her dress. She brushed them off with indifference. "Why should you have fastened on that motive?" she asked.

"Was it so unlikely?"

"Your friend rejects it."

"Yes. He believes—still believes—nothing of you but what is good."

"Dear Hugh!" she breathed softly. Wareham started with amazement.

"You like him still!"

"I have never ceased to like him."

For the first time in their talk he had turned his eyes on her face, and met her look full. Sitting there, the lovely lines of her figure curved against the waving rye, the warm brown tints of her hair caught by the sunshine, eyes in which the fire was veiled by long lashes, a mouth slightly drooped and softened; all this close to him, and seen in the divine freshness of the young day, sent an intoxicating throb of delight into his heart. Clinging to a bending purpose, he stammered—"Then—then—"

"I shall not marry him. Make him understand this."

He looked away—closed his eyes, reckless whether she saw the movement or not, only conscious that the momentary madness had passed. It sharpened his voice as he said—"Do not expect me to succeed. I told you that you were enigmatical, and I repeat my words. Nothing that you have said alters the cruelty of dismissing poor Hugh in the sudden and unexpected manner you adopted." She rose, without at first speaking, but stood in the same place until she said slowly—"Perhaps. But it was difficult to act."

The words that were on his lips seemed glued there; by an effort he succeeded at last in bringing them out.

"May I tell Hugh to hope?"

"Oh, no," she said composedly. "Certainly not. My mind is absolutely made up. Urge him to think no more of me; above all, not to try to see me. It is quite useless."

Wareham smiled.

"He will thank me."

"If he does not, I shall," she said softly; and again he was conscious of the strange throb which had surprised him before. This time it was slighter, and he did not look or speak, while in another moment she turned and began to climb the stony path.

Wareham followed slowly, more perturbed than he would have cared to own. He had failed in discomfiting her, as he had never doubted his power of doing, once they met; and though no blame had been cast on Hugh, he had an angry and unwilling feeling that if it was want of love which had broken off the marriage, the lover himself should have been the first to realise it. Hugh had never suffered him to suppose this could be the cause. He thrust away the feeling irritably. Was he to blame Hugh for the act of a heartless girl?

At the top of the path, a very poor old woman stood outside the hut, holding a goat by a cord. Anne, perhaps glad of the interruption, began to talk to her. Wareham stood a few feet off, and she presently came back to him.

"She is not so old as she looks. I thought her a hundred, but that was her husband who went down the path just now. I would ask her about the caterpillars, only I haven't an idea what is Norwegian for caterpillar. Have you?"

He was as ignorant.

"She is not begging," Anne continued, "though I am sure she is dreadfully poor, and in spite of all the laws of political economy, I shall give her a krone."

He neither objected nor encouraged; and his self-respect was partly restored by standing aloof in a position of indifference. Anne, smiling, glanced at him between half-shut eyelids, and went off again. He followed. The old woman, almost beside herself with delight, seized her hand, and shook it with rapturous gratitude. Blessings of every kind were invoked, and showered also, undeservedly, upon Wareham. Then she made vigorous signs that Anne was to stay where she was, while she herself hobbled into the hut.

"What is to follow?" asked Wareham.

Anne shook her head. "I shall certainly wait and see. What can come out of that poor little place? Not!" She turned upon him a horrified face — "Oh, no!"

"What?"

"I believe—I am sure—she is bringing me a tumbler of goat's milk! Of all things that I loathe—"

Her face was tragic. Wareham was prepared to see her decline the gift, but had to own to injustice. She took the tumbler, drank to the end, and thanked the old woman with a sweet courtesy. If, after it, she moved quickly away, she told Wareham that it was to rescue him from a similar fate. He owned that he could not have been so heroic, and that she had surprised him.

"What else was there to do?" she asked simply.

Her mood had changed. All the way back to the inn she talked gaily and lightly about the country, their fellow-travellers, and the children they met. He found his conception of her lost, not to be called back, and between this and that grew bewildered. There was nothing for it but to follow her lead, and to set Hugh's wrongs on one side. They went there easily, and left the ground more pleasantly open, so that he reached the door in eager talk, and, what was worse, with desire for more.

He kept silence to the Ravenhills as to his morning, never even telling Mrs Ravenhill of the little cottage with pansied roof, which he had ostensibly sought for her. Something in him, something which he did not choose to admit, but which secretly controlled him, made him averse from admitting any one to the place where this morning he had met Anne: he told himself that he wished to put away the recollection of a painful incident. Painful it should have been, and must be.

It was Sunday; a little service was held in the salon. Afterwards, except at meals, Wareham saw no more of Miss Dalrymple. He went out and walked far over the hills with the clergyman, whose wife was at last tired, but whose own energy was unfailing. He carried it into botany, and though Wareham knew nothing of the subject, the triumph with which a rare discovery was hailed gave relish to the walk. Would Millie have liked something different? She made no complaint, but at supper chatted cheerfully of the cottages into which she had penetrated; the children's shake of the hand for "*tak*" when she gave them sweets; the strings of fresh, kindly-faced women coming back from their walk of miles to the nearest church. Millie had won the children's hearts, and the next morning, when, under a sky of tender northern blue, they started on their walk up the pass, they came smiling round, no longer in Sunday scarlet skirts and green aprons, but in work-a-day clothes, to wish her good-morning and farewell.

The air was pure and sweet, soft yet exhilarating. The stolkjaerres were to carry only luggage to the head of the pass, Mrs Ravenhill declaring herself ready for the five miles walk. The clergyman and his wife were ahead of them. . .

They went up gradually towards the heights. The mountains fall away on either side, and it is a wide desolate-looking expanse through which the road to Odde curves and zigzags. Patches of snow lie in sun-forgotten gullies, or crown the higher summits. All along the road tall posts are set at intervals to mark the track on those gloomy days of winter when the light of stars shines on one vast sheet of snow, filling the broad valley cup, and smoothing every rough outline. Something of this melancholy solitude remains throughout the year; not a tree breaks the sweep, not a building asserts itself. Walk for hours, and it is unlikely that you meet a human being; the only trace of his activity is the white road which twists upwards. But on a July morning the world under your feet is astir with gladness; the springy turf is starred with myriads of tiny flowers; shrubs of the dwarf cornel peep at you with white brown-eyed blossoms, and the boggy land, through which melting snows are making their way, feed the bright green succulent winter chickweed, or the delicate bells of the false lily of the valley.

And it was across this beautiful upland world, making short cuts from zigzag to zigzag, that Millie, as young as the summer and as happy, went her way. Young Grey had, without deliberate arrangement, become a sort of hanger-on of the party, and he was here. From such small adventures as sticking in a bog, or being forced to wade a stream, merriment flowed joyously. Now and then they sat down, rather from wishing to linger than from need of rest; and it was in one of these halts that, their own carriages having reached a higher level, they beheld two others crawling up the road, and presently a shout reached them from a long spindle-legged figure striding towards the group, and waving a stick to arrest attention. Young Grey sprang to his feet and waved energetically in return.

"It's Colonel Martyn, and there's Miss Dalrymple in the carriole!" he exclaimed. "What a shame that she isn't up here!" He was darting off, when reflection brought him back with—"You don't mind my trying to persuade her to come with us, Mrs Ravenhill?"

"How should I? By all means persuade her."

He was off like an arrow from a bow, and Mrs Ravenhill praised his good-nature. Wareham chimed in; Millie sat silent.

Miss Dalrymple did not leave the little carriage, and young Grey did not return. Colonel Martyn was a melancholy substitute. Naturally it fell to Mrs

Ravenhill to cheer him, and Wareham and Millie wandered on together. She avoided touching Anne's name: he repeated it more than once to himself, that he might impress on his mind a stronger sense of his relief in not having her there. All Millie's little prettinesses he made an inward note of, and extracted admiration, telling himself that here was a sweeter charm. If such a thing had been possible, it might have seemed that he fashioned them into a shield. But why? And against what?

It gave Millie great pleasure to reach the snow-beds, though their edges were little more than crusts, under which trickled out the melting water; and when a sudden shade came between them and the sun, and looking up, they realised for the first time what a bank of cloud was sweeping down from the north, she professed a strong desire to see a storm in these desolate regions. At the top of the pass, where lies a sullen lake, slaty grey now with menacing shadow, the stolkjaerres were waiting, their own and the Martyns'. And, as there opened before them a vast faraway whiteness of snow, unbroken and eternal, a driver, pointing, said the word which they had long expected—"Folgefond!"

"Where is Tom?" Mrs Martyn demanded hastily.

Mrs Ravenhill reported that he had left her to make his way up a hill, from which he foretold a view. "He said he would overtake us."

"And I am in mortal terror already!" cried his wife. "The skydsgut says we go down a tremendously steep descent, and that a dreadful storm is coming. Thunder frightens me to death."

Consolation was offered, but failed to soothe. A livid shadow which touched the snow set her trembling. She desired Miss Dalrymple to take Colonel Martyn's place by her side, then looked imploringly at Wareham.

"I am ashamed—it is wretched to be such a coward—but Mr Grey is with Mrs Ravenhill—*would* you mind coming close behind in Anne's carriole, Mr Wareham? The comfort that it would be!"

Wareham perceived that his attendance was resolved upon. He made a slight demur.

"Of course if I can be of any use—"

"The greatest! You would not condemn me to stay on this dreary spot until Colonel Martyn has finished his survey?"

"Ought we to leave him behind?"

"Ought he to have deserted us? Pray let us start. Anne, beg Mr Wareham not to delay. There, I am sure I heard thunder!"

"One moment." Wareham made a quick step to where Millie stood, a little aloof.

"You bear?" he said, in a low voice. "Are you alarmed?"

If there was effort, Millie did not show it. She said cheerily —

"Not in the least."

"The woman is absurd, but I suppose one must humour her."

"Of course. Besides, as she says, we have Mr Grey."

"Why couldn't she appeal to him?"

His reluctance contented her, and pacified himself.

Waterproofs were hastily pulled on, for the storm advanced rapidly; clouds, black as ink, brooded on the mountains, blotted out the sky, and before they had gone far, poured down torrents of rain. The turmoil was magnificent, and Wareham could not but excuse Mrs Martyn's fears, when he noted the acute angles of the steep descent, and heard the thunder crashing overhead. He could see her grasping her companion's arm, and looking round in terrified appeal, but in the hurly-burly, voice was mute. Yet so swift was the rush of the storm, that by the time they reached more level ground, it was fairly over, and, drawing up, Mrs Martyn was able to bewail herself under an outbreak of sunshine.

Wareham sprang out of his carriole, and went to theirs.

"Safely through it," he said, smiling.

"But it was awful, awful!" moaned Mrs Martyn. "I have just told Anne that my one comfort was in knowing that you were close behind."

"A lightning conductor!" Anne said mockingly. "I believe I should have preferred you at a greater distance, for if we had come to grief, you would certainly have been on the top of us."

"I am afraid you are very wet?" He eyed her anxiously.

"Nothing to mind. But the others? Ought they not to be in sight?"

He felt a twinge of shame.

"I think they ought. I will go back and see."

Mrs Martyn called after him that she was sure they would be here in a moment, and that it was only because their ponies were not so good that they were behind, but he was already running back. She shrugged her shoulders discontentedly.

"Manners!" she exclaimed. "Tell the man to go on, Anne. I don't mean to wait in the road for Mr Wareham's pleasure."

Anne said coolly—

"Why should you? Besides, he belongs to them."

"Belongs? Nonsense! Do you suppose he thinks of marrying that child?" She took off her felt hat, and shook the wet from it.

"Why not?"

"Absurd! An insignificant little creature, with no attraction except a dimple, which she doesn't know how to show off. You have only to lift your little finger, Anne, and he would be at your feet."

Anne showed no surprise, and made no disclaimer.

"And it would be better than that last foolish affair from which you were only just saved."

She repeated the word slowly. "Saved? And what saved me?"

"Oh, don't be vexed! Nothing, my dear, but your own worldly wisdom, which came to the rescue in the nick of time, as I always knew it would." Mrs Martyn laughed.

The girl had pulled the hood of her coat over her head to protect it from the rain. She let it slip back, and it showed her face grave.

"Why must you all talk of my worldly wisdom!" she exclaimed. "Am I so hateful that you can't give me credit for a good impulse?"

"Oh, I think you have impulses—it was no doubt an impulse which landed you in the entanglement to which I was referring—but then, happily, you retract in time. Recollect, you can't do this all your life. I wish you were safely married."

Anne drew a deep breath, then laughed.

"When I am, the somebody, whoever he is, will have to sweep me away like a whirlwind—"

"Why: What do you mean?"

"I can't stand the hesitation, the thinking about it. I invariably begin to repent, and if *he* hesitates—he is lost."

Mrs Martyn opened her eyes roundly.

"So that is your theory? I hardly thought you owned one."

Anne went on as if she had not spoken.

"I mean to marry, and it appears that I have not the power of falling in love. If I take the leap I must do it at a gallop. Now do you understand?"

"A little. This last man, did he represent a whirlwind? My dear, you let it go too far with him, and he could not be expected, poor fellow, to see the absurdity as we all saw it."

Anne's eyes darkened.

"There was no absurdity. If I had cared a little more, I would have married him."

"If he had happened to have twenty thousand a year instead of one, you mean. No, Anne, no. Nothing short of a brilliant marriage will satisfy you."

Anne looked as if she were going to reply, but checked herself, and turned her head in another direction. Mrs Martyn yawned.

Chapter Five
The Skittishness of Fate

Before Wareham reached the companions he had deserted, it was evident that something was amiss, for both Mrs Ravenhill and Millie were on foot, and their skydsgut led the pony. Millie, however, called out to him that no harm had happened, and he then saw that Colonel Martyn was with them.

"What has gone wrong?" he asked, as he came up. "There's a very disorganised look about you."

"We were nearly disorganised altogether," said Mrs Ravenhill gravely, for she was not well pleased at Wareham's leaving them. "We might have been, if Colonel Martyn had not come to the rescue."

Wareham asked what had happened.

"I suppose the man drove too fast, and that fierce clap of thunder startled the pony, for he went over the edge."

"Good heavens!"

Colonel Martyn interposed to explain that fortunately the descent was not sheer, and the ground was soft. Moreover, the skydsgut jumped off, and held on like death.

"Mr Grey too. And cut his hand," Millie broke in, with a grateful glance at the young man. He turned red.

"Oh, that's nothing."

"Well, as nobody will accept the honours of the situation, I shall take them myself," said the girl, laughing. "Know then, Mr Wareham, that mother and I showed immense presence of mind in refusing to be shot out when the jerk came, and in scrambling over the back when we realised that we were still there."

"Then?"

"Then the pony was unharnessed, the stolkjaerre dragged back, and — here we are!"

She spoke lightly, but she was white and trembling. Colonel Martyn inquired where his people were.

"I left them in the road below," said Wareham briefly.

"Then we'll sort ourselves again, and I'll go on."

As he strode away, Mrs Ravenhill called after him, "Thank you for your help."

"He enjoyed it," said Millie. "It was the nearest approach he could have had to a steeplechase, and has quite raised his spirits." Wareham felt so unconscionably guilty, that it might be supposed something else was really scourging him, and using his small neglect for a lash. He murmured—

"I am thankful he was here. If I had dreamed of real danger—"

"There was as much for the others as for us," said Millie reasonably. "Besides, I believe Mr Grey and the skydsgut were equal to the emergency. Poor Mr Grey was the only sufferer."

"Oh, I'm all right," said the young man. "I say, Mr Wareham, was Miss Dalrymple frightened?"

"Not that I know of," answered Wareham shortly.

Mrs Ravenhill raised her eyebrows at the tone.

"Now, if you and Mr Grey like to drive on before us," she said, "Millie and I are quite equal to taking care of ourselves on level ground."

"I see no reason for changing."

His voice was sharp, and he knew it and was vexed by it, the truth being that he was out of sorts with himself and the world. Fate, he felt, had played him a skittish trick, in thrusting him into companionship with the one woman whom he would have avoided; nor, spur his steed as he might, could he get away into the old track. He recalled his deliberate judgment of Anne's character, but it rose a bloodless ghost, behind a living, glowing, dark face, with a look of reproach in the beautiful eyes. Avaunt, sorceress! How should beauty outweigh friendship? Can a fleeting fancy shake solid foundations? The very thought pricked, scourged him. Even if he extricated himself from his false position by the simple method of breaking away from his companions at Odde, he was wroth at having to admit that he could not easily regain his self-respect.

Young Grey babbled youthfully about Miss Dalrymple's charms, as the two men drove along, but this was a mere outside accident to which Wareham was indifferent. Barring Hugh, what others thought mattered nothing; it was himself he arraigned with the reluctance of a strong character. He answered briefly yes and no, happily sufficient for his companion, who was content to talk.

The storm had vanished, leaving an added beauty, on either side a land flashing light from raindrops on which the sun shone brilliantly, a land of bold heights, leaping torrents, and sweet recesses of bedded moss, out of which peeped wild strawberries and a hundred delicate flowers, while far up against the soft blue of the sky gleamed the unbroken whiteness of the snows.

The others were overtaken at Seligsted, a small roadside inn, crowded round with unharnessed stolkjaerres, and besieged by ravenous travellers. Willing but inefficient hosts lost their heads under press of custom, and tourists stormed in vain, while the young girl-waiters grew sullen under their reproaches. The Martyns, arriving earlier, had managed to secure some food in a balcony; the others, resigning themselves to a long wait, strolled to the river, sat on the grass, and looked at the blue cleft in the hills through which they had passed, or in the opposite direction, where the country broadened into tamer beauties.

When they got back, the most irate of the tourists were driving away in a carriage and pair, a red-faced father, and two or three black-eyed girls, half ashamed, half proud of his brow-beating. "Hurry up! Why the devil can't they understand plain English!" he was shouting. The men standing by looked at him with calm disapproval; an old man, with a grave, refined face, shrugged his shoulders silently.

There is extraordinary variety in Norwegian roads, variety which is beyond word-painting, and, to a large degree, depends upon the cultivation which the eye brings to bear upon it. Admiration rushes easily after vast outlines, and these are lacking, for in Norway the mountains are of no great height, and when you are among them the lower masses block out the summits. Subtler charm lies in the variety, the infinite multitude of tints and shadings with which the sun is always painting hill and sky, the colours which the granite yields to its radiant touch, so that on these summer evenings the barest piece of rock is a wonder of soft and rich colouring. Then, perhaps, where the shadow deepens, a *fos* flings itself down, an aerial spirit, here spreading like a veil, there cleaving the purple gloom with a silver flash. Hardly had the Espelandfos been passed, when the ponies instinctively stopped, and the skydsguts, springing off, announced the Lotefos.

They climbed a steep path, and, passing a small summer inn, a great roaring mass of water, broken into three falls, and rushing and seething in an indescribable tumult of beauty, was before them. Clambering from point to point, whichever way the eye turned, it fell upon clouds of spray, upon swift giddy leaps made by the clear beryl-coloured water before it was churned into foam by the force of its descent. Great wet rocks, shining metallic, stood erect in the midst of racing waters, waving grasses caught in the eddies were washed relentlessly, never a pause allowed in which to straighten themselves, and over the magnificent turmoil a rainbow arched serenely. Young Grey sprang into perilous places; Millie gathered trails of the delicate Linnaea Borealis, slender northerner which the great botanist chose for his own; Mrs Ravenhill and Wareham strolled down to the carriages, and leaving the Lotefos behind by a road which soon began to edge itself along a lake, they drove on to Odde.

"Civilisation and late dinners!" sighed Millie, as they got out at the cheerful door of the Hardanger.

"Shops!" groaned young Grey.

"Excellent things, each of them," retorted Mrs Ravenhill cheerfully. "I wonder how long it will be before you all find yourselves in that shop?"

It was not long. Every one is attracted by the furs, the carvings, the silver buttons, the soft eider rugs with their beautiful green duck-breast borderings. In the sweet summer dusk it is pleasant to stroll about the little town, buy cherries from the men who bring their baskets of ripe fruit, and turn into this store of Norwegian handiwork. It is more enchanting to go to the front of the hotel, where the fjord runs up between snow-flecked hills, and ends. Grave evening purples steal over the land; in the sky, and reflected in the faithful waters, daffodil and primrose tints melt into each other. A yacht lay in a sea of gold, her fine delicate lines repeated below. A light shone out. Some one stood at the top of the landing steps, looking at the water. Wareham hesitated, then quickly walked up to her.

"I expected to overtake you at the Lotefos," he said abruptly.

She did not turn her head.

"Are you grateful to me for having spared you the encounter?"

"If I were, should I be here?"

"Very likely. I do not know why you have come."

"I venture to bring a suggestion."

"More likely a reproach," she said. "I believe you are determined to force a quarrel upon me."

"You misjudge me—indeed you misjudge me!" He spoke warmly, then hesitated. "Certainly we need not quarrel," he said slowly. "The fates have flung us together, and it appears to me that for a time at least we might leave the past behind us. Forbes is my friend. I cannot think that he was well treated—your friends, doubtless, would take another view. But if we are not likely to agree on this one subject, there are, happily, others in the world to talk about. Come. Do you agree?"

She did not immediately answer. He found himself speculating anxiously what her words would be. When they dropped from her at last, he hung on the low tones—

"I don't think that two can talk with comfort on even the most indifferent subjects when there is total absence of trust between them."

"Is that our position?" he asked uneasily.

"Is it not? I have taken trouble to give you an explanation, and you do not believe a word of it."

"Do not let us discuss that matter."

"It is there," said Anne.

Both were silent. A boat came towards them, shattering the tranquil golden lights of the fjord; a few strong strokes brought it up to the landing-place, and half-a-dozen English sprang out, two young girls among them. They looked tired, carried alpenstocks, and called out a gay good-night to the rowers. They had just come back from a hard climb to the Skjaeggedalsfos, and were almost too weary to be enthusiastic. The boat pushed away again into the shining waters, the sound of the oars died into silence. Presently Anne spoke, ignoring their last words.

"The difference between north and south is curiously strong—forgive a truism! What I meant to remark was the different call they make upon oneself. Here there is a good deal of enjoyment to be met with, and it is exactly the opposite kind of enjoyment to what one finds in Italy or Greece. Do you feel this? Since we landed, I believe I have hardly thought a thought or encountered an idea."

"My own sensation," Wareham answered eagerly. "It has been like taking out one's brains, and leaving them with one's plate at the bankers. The odd thing is, that I don't miss them." He laughed.

She went on—

"I have wondered more than once how long it would take to settle down to existence in one of those isolated little villages of two or three houses each which we passed on the Suldal lake?"

"With some of us I suspect the savage would take the upper hand more readily and more rapidly than we suppose possible."

"The brain would not rebel?"

"You would have to admit glorious physical excitement."

Anne shivered.

"I cannot realise the possibility of any excitement at all in those desolate homes."

"Can't you? I, on the contrary, picture a good deal. Chiefly gloomy, I allow. Think of living for ever next door to your worst enemy—or your best friend! Which would be the most unbearable?"

She took no notice of this cynical speech.

"I could understand the life being endurable in summer, but in winter—winter! And such a winter, with its snows and darkness!"

He demurred.

"So far as I can make out, winter is the most sociable time of the year. You forget that lakes and fjords become the great means of communication; in summer, houses are isolated, owing to the want of roads, but in winter the frozen water serves in their place. No, depend upon it, they have a good time when once they can skate, or strike away on the great snow-shoes you saw by the roadside to-day."

"But the darkness?"

"Well, one gets used to that in London. I don't know that we can talk. Besides, they have a great pull over us in the stars. I assure you that all the men who have said anything about it speak of the winter with evident satisfaction."

"They know nothing better," Anne said incredulously.

"The root of all satisfaction," Wareham observed.

She glanced at him quickly, bit her lip, and walked on. He found himself admiring her tall slender figure, and the poise of her small head thrown into relief by the glassy water. He had dropped the fiction that she was not beautiful, and retreated behind a yet feebler barricade, the pretence that hers was not the beauty he extolled. He had ceased to wonder that it served for Hugh.

At the end of the landing-place Anne turned. Wareham was immediately behind, and she faced him as she had not yet done. She spoke, too, more softly —

"You leave to-morrow?"

He flushed and hesitated.

"I — I am not sure. Possibly."

Her eyes rested on his for a moment, and moved away. She said, indifferently — "Here is Colonel Martyn."

Colonel Martyn was charged with hope. He had met the party from the Skjaeggedalsfos, and report of certain difficulties owing to a fall of rock had fired his athletic soul. Wareham added that the *fos* itself was worth a visit, but this idea he rejected.

"See one, see all," he declared. "A hurly-burly of water, and no fishing — there you have it. But there might be a chance of a climb getting there, and at any rate it must be better than loafing about this wretched little hole. Anne, will you come?"

"No, thank you. I prefer loafing."

"Will you?" — to Wareham.

"I don't mind. I've been once, and should not be sorry to see it again."

"Eight. And if you know the lingo, perhaps you'll make the arrangements. Better change your mind, Anne."

"No. My mind is set upon easier pleasures. Where's Blanche?"

"You needn't ask." Colonel Martyn's gloom returned. "Buying Brummagem goods in the shop."

"I shouldn't wonder if you believed the fall came from Brummagem too," Anne retorted. "Well, I'm going to help her. Good-night."

"You'd better be sure you know how to work your fire-escape before you go to bed," he called after her. "It's a common occurrence for the hotels to be burnt down once a month."

Young Grey, torn between Anne and adventure, felt as if adventure might possess a qualifying power, and went off with the other men early the next morning. Millie tried to get her mother to slip away to the Buarbrae glacier, but Mrs Ravenhill was tired, and disinclined for a long climb. She agreed to go with Millie to a spot which they had remarked the day before, where a river flung itself out of the lake, but she promised Mrs Martyn to join her after luncheon. They captured a stolkjaerre, and drove to their point; then, dismissing it, and leaving the dusty road, turned into a wood that belonged to a fairy tale, where low trees stood singly in the grass, and where every now and then they saw through a break the blue Hardanger hills, rising out of the fjord, and topped with snow; or, on the other side, a silver lake, with mountains stretching, fold after fold, into the solemn distance. Here and there a great rounded granite boulder cropped up, tossed out of its place by Titan wrath; one little farm nestled amid cherry-trees, but the silence was profound, and hardly a living creature passed; only a child or two, then a quaint old couple with a dog. The woman was tall, with a sweet dignified face; the man, bent and aged, carried a Hardanger fiddle. They stopped and chatted readily, and after they had talked awhile, at a sign from his wife, the man began to play his fiddle. It was an odd jangle with no tune, but somehow the old couple, the granite rocks, the wild peasant music, seemed to belong to each other, and to the country.

Mother and daughter slowly walked home, past a picturesque saw-mill, bringing sighs from Mrs Ravenhill, and through fields where hay-making filled the air with fresh fragrance. Each field has its hurdles on which the flower-scented grass hangs drying. When they reached the first outlying house, Mrs Ravenhill put a question which had once or twice fluttered on her lips.

"When is Mr Wareham going to leave us?"

There was a moment's pause before Millie answered—

"Is he going?"

"I suppose so. From what he told me I believed he intended going off on his own account as soon as he had landed us at Odde."

"Well, he hasn't gone," said the girl, looking straight before her.

Her mother glanced, but could not see her face.

"I shall have a talk with him to-morrow," said Mrs Ravenhill, in a decided tone. "He may consider himself bound to us, and I am sure I should be vexed beyond measure if he imagined anything of the sort. It would be most annoying. You see that, don't you, Millie?" she added incautiously.

"What am I to see?" asked Millie, with a laugh. "Mr Wareham bound with cords to you or to me, or to Miss Dalrymple—which is it?—and unable to extricate himself? I'm not sure that the picture is as pathetic as you imagine, but what will you do about it? Implore him to consider himself a free man? You should get Miss Dalrymple to speak for you."

Mrs Ravenhill was a little offended.

"What has Miss Dalrymple to do with it? You told me he disliked her."

The girl did not answer the question; she began to talk to a pony standing in a cart by the roadside. Then came a shop, and doubt as to the purchase of an ermine purse; after that, hurry for the *table-d'hôte*. An English yacht lay in the fjord; her people had come on shore, and were lunching at the Hardanger, next to the Martyns. Millie, who had for her neighbour a clever young Siamese prince who was travelling with a Danish tutor, hoped that Miss Dalrymple might select them for her afternoon companions. But, luncheon over, she made straight for Millie.

"You and I will escape from all these people," she said, with a smile which would have sent young Grey to her feet. Millie was unaffected.

"It is very hot," she said.

"Here, very. But I have a cool plan in my head. Please come."

It would have been ungracious to refuse, and pre-engagements were not to be pleaded in Odde. In an hours time the two girls were sitting in one of the light boats, pointed at each end, and being rowed across the fjord to the opposite side, where a slender waterfall is seen from Odde, dancing down through purple and green woods. The fjord was still as glass, each line of the English yacht repeated itself in the opal waters, two children with scarlet caps hung fishing over the side of the vessel. Anne lay lazily back, looking at everything through half-closed lids. Everything included Millie.

Millie asked at last where they were going.

"To a farm. Does that please you?"

She did not answer the question.

"I can't see anything like a farm."

"Nor I," said Anne, idly turning her head. "We must take it on trust. Old Mr Campbell tells me such a place exists, and hinted at cherries and milk."

"But the *fos*?"

"To be crossed by a bridge. You see I have got my bearings."

Apparently, indeed, she and Millie had changed natures, for she rained talk and laughter upon the younger girl. And she showed no sign of being daunted by the steepness of the climb when they had landed and were struggling up the bank. The path they sought eluded them; presently they found themselves in a thick-growing grassy wood of low trees, through which they pushed a devious way. It was green, fresh, lovely; the roar of the waterfall was in their ears, now and again they met some impetuous little stream, which had rushed away from the greater fall to make its own wilful way to the fjord. Delightful assurance of solitude, cool deepness of grass, stones sheeted with moss and wet with spray, clear dash of waters, interlacing boughs through which sun-shafts shot down, lured them to breathless heights—lured Anne, rather, for Millie dragged. It was Anne who made the ventures, Anne who held aside hindering branches, Anne whose voice came laughing back to vow that the labyrinth grew more tangled, Anne who at last dropped by the side of a baby stream babbling over its stones, and bade Millie rest. She could not say enough of the fascinations of the spot.

"They will come back boasting of their fall with the hopeless name, only because it is big. What has size to do with beauty? This thing is perfect. Look at its curves, and its swirls, and its pools, and its grasses, and its small airs!"

Millie roused herself to admire.

"You are tired?" Anne asked.

She owned that she had walked far that morning.

"And this place doesn't rest you as it does me?"

"I don't know."

Anne settled herself against a sapling.

"I feel as if I had reached the one breathing-place of my life. You don't know that sensation."

"Do you think you would like it—often?" asked Millie.

"Certainly not. It is liking it so much which is so unexpected to me. I am of the world—worldly. And to find myself exhilarated and delighted is like growing young again."

Millie had to smile.

"You are not so old!"

"Aged!—in experience. As for years, they don't count, or I dare say we might find that I am not so much older than you as you—as every one— would imagine. But I have lived." Did that mean she had loved? Millie coloured at the charge of inexperience, galling to youth.

"You can know little about me," she protested.

"Next to nothing. Tell me. You live alone with your mother?"

This was admitted.

"You are not engaged to any one?"

"Oh, no!"

"And have never tried that position?"

"No, oh, no!"

"That shocks you," said Anne, with a laugh. "My dear, it often happens to me."

"Not seriously?"

"Quite seriously." She leant back and watched Millie's face with amusement. "Are you disgusted?"

"Why—why do you do it? I can't understand."

"It comes somehow, often really without my intending. It's the way of my kind, I suppose. For one thing, how is one to know a man at all until one is engaged? And so often I can't tell beforehand whether I like them well enough or not. As you see, it has generally ended by my discovering that it would be intolerable. I don't pretend that there have not been other reasons," she added frankly. "Riches sometimes fly away on nearer approach."

"And that would be enough?"

"Oh, yes."

"You think nothing of your promise?" Anne was looking at her through half-closed eyes and smiling.

"I am not sure that I don't think too much. It becomes unendurable. When I am married it will have to be in a whirlwind. No hesitations, no hanging back. So much I can tell him. The rest he will have to find out. Stormed, really stormed, I should be afraid of myself."

She fell into silence. There was no sound except the rush of the water, not so much as the chirp of a bird. At last she looked round again.

"So you see—*me voici!*—Anne Dalrymple."

Millie cried out—

"I am glad I am not a London beauty!"

"There are more disagreeable positions," Anne said reflectively. "Now, if you had said a London beauty with a heart—"

"Have you no heart?" Millie asked impulsively.

"Not I! What does duty for it is a poor little chippy dried-up thing, which may be reckoned on never to give me an ache or a pain." She sprang to her feet. "Come! The farm! I am not going to let you off the farm."

No bridge could they find, and there was nothing for it but to retrace their steps. Down the hill-side, through the entangling greenery, they plunged, breathless and laughing, and found themselves at last overlooking the fjord, without any means of crossing the *fos*. Anne, undaunted, spied a boat on the fjord rowed by a boy; her signals brought it to shore. The boy readily agreed to row them to a higher point, but, this carried out, he refused to wait for them.

"Never mind! We are here!" Anne cried, springing out. She followed a rough path, and presently pounced on wild strawberries.

A man was digging. Seeing them gathering strawberries, he made signs that they were welcome to the cherries which hung temptingly from his trees. He bent the boughs down; Anne picked and brought crimson handfuls to Millie lying on the grass. The warm sun shone, a little stone-chat scolded from a rail, it was all calm, restful, and fragrant with hay. They went up the narrow path towards the farm; the way was overhung with cherry-trees, and a vagrant stream of water, which played truant from the fall, dashed down, flinging lovely spray over the waving grasses. The farm dominated the fjord; fold after fold of blue hills stretched away, the white water at their feet, and desolate-looking islands staring up at the sunshine, which scarcely softened their black outlines. Anne's mood changed, she grew silent, and silently they went their way down the little path, till they reached the man still digging his patch of ground.

Millie, tired, inquired how she proposed getting home.

"He will take us in his boat. I asked him as I picked the cherries."

Going back, it appeared as if the waters had grown yet more still and glassy. Each patch of snow, each outburst of green, each violet shadow, sent a lovely repetition of itself into the world below. The boat slipped dreamily through them, only the lap of the oars, and the faint and distant murmur of the waterfall, breaking the silence. One after another the little green promontories dropped behind, the white church of Odde and the clustering houses took form, a boat passed them. Anne looked up.

"This is not the time for commonplaces, yet they haunt me," she said impatiently. "I—I—I—I am the commonplace, and I have stumbled into a thick mist of doubts and questionings. Tell me, are you always direct? and certain that right is right and wrong wrong?"

Millie coloured, hesitated. Such an appeal confused her. Anne went on—

"My rules are not so ready. Something else steps in and hoodwinks me, though I dare say it is true that I offer my eyes for the bandage. What I complain of is that when I do my best to walk straight—according to my lights—I am the more cried out upon. Your Mr Wareham, now, acts Rhadamanthus, yet what does he know? How can he pretend to judge what motives influenced me, and whether they were bad or good? Has he discussed them with you?"

The question came like a bolt; the answer was a brief "No."

"No?" Anne's eyes were fastened on the girl; Millie's honesty gave unwilling explanation.

"Never your motives. He said once that Mr Forbes was his friend, and that the breaking off of your engagement was not his fault. He said this before—"

"Before?"

"Before he knew you."

Anne meditated. Her eyes softened.

"I suppose it is the everlasting I—I—I, again, which makes me imagine that people talk when they are not even thinking of me. However, it is true that he misjudges me, I had it from his own lips, and I am sorry, foolishly sorry, because he is a man—" She broke off and laughed—"Somehow my vanity would make me wish to appear at one's best before him. Does that shock you again?"

"Why should it?"

"I couldn't say why, but I am for ever shocking people unintentionally. You have not got over my talking of my engagements, yet—*they* don't judge me harshly, any one of those men would marry me to-morrow. Yes, even Mr Wareham's friend, in spite of Mr Wareham!"

Women, however unsophisticated, possess the gift of intuition. Millie divined that Miss Dalrymple wished her to talk of Wareham, and was ready to profess a spasmodic anger for the pleasure of hearing him defended. She was reluctant and ashamed of her reluctance. The shame stung her into crying—"Why do you talk of Mr Wareham's judging you harshly? You must know very well that if it ever was so, he has forgiven you."

A smile began to play about Anne's mouth.

"Do you think so?"

Millie flung her a look.

"Well—I hope you are right. He has been so stiff that it would be a victory to bring him round. We shall see. Meanwhile, here we are at Odde; and what am I to offer to our boatman?—boat-master too, I suspect."

"Ask him."

The man smiled, shook his head, wanted nothing. The equivalent of a sixpence was all he would at last consent to receive.

Millie dragged a heavy heart up-stairs, and Anne went in pursuit of Mrs Martyn.

Chapter Six
And the Pitfalls of Cupid

Once more a shifting of sunny lights and purple shadows, of ever-varying colours, of small hamlets nestling by the water-side, each with its pier, its boats, and its many-hued little crowd, as they steamed down the Hardanger fjord towards Eide. Contempt for waterfalls was balanced by joy in the effort of reaching them, and, by dint of swearing to travel night and day until he overtook them again, Colonel Martyn obtained leave from his wife to go off to the Voringfos, and young Grey he dragged reluctantly with him. This threw the others of the party more together, and it seemed necessary for Wareham to offer his services to those who were bereft of their nominal protector. The mid-day meal was taken at the excellent "Mellands" at Eide; afterwards they strolled about in the meadows, and sat under hay-hurdles, in order to allow the great noonday heat to subside, before mounting the steep hill which lay between them and Vossefangen. Anne, indeed, vowed she would not walk, and chose a carriole, as a lighter conveyance; but Mrs Ravenhill and Millie soon jumped out of their stolkjaerre. And what a road it was! High up, a great waterfall hurled itself into a chasm of foam, and while the carriages crawled round zigzags, those on foot could cut off green corners, clambering ever higher into the sweet elastic air, until at the top they rested, breathless, until the cavalcade of patient ponies pulled slowly up, then merrily along the level road to Voss.

Voss is ugly, but friendly. It has a good inn and a well-known landlord, an ancient church with a brown timber spire, a few shops, and a little train, which leisurely trots backwards and forwards to Bergen. Between it and Stalheim lies one of the most beautiful roads in Norway, a road constantly changing, with every variety of river and lake, of waving sorrel-tinted grass, now red, now green, now grey, as the wind kisses it; of distant snowy heights, and nearer sterner hills; here and there a fall, a water-mill, a group of cottages with turf-roofs starred by ox-eyed daisies, and always before you the road running, white, into the far away.

No zigzagged hills, however, and no opportunities for talk except in the halts which come occasionally for the hardy ponies. And once, from Anne's skydsgut, a little gill of eight or nine years old, with the usual white handkerchief over her head, there rose an agonised wail of "Toi, toi!" Wareham drove up rapidly. Anne's portmanteau, which also formed the seat of her infant driver, hung threateningly over the edge; there was much hoisting and roping before it was restored to equilibrium.

"No more carrioles for me," said Anne. "It is too dull. Think of not being able so much as to inveigh against the dust! Apparently it would cause a revolution in the country if you, for instance, were to drive by my side?"

"I don't pretend to cope with a Norwegian pony and its skydsgut," answered Wareham, laughing.

He said no more; but, after these words of hers, it might have been noticed that he contrived to keep sufficiently close to exchange remarks, if only in pantomime, and when they halted at Tvinde, it was he who was at hand to help her down from her dusty perch. There was, as usual, a *fos* to be visited.

"Not worth seeing," announced Mrs Martyn. "Some one, I forget who, said so."

"The more reason for going," Anne insisted. She invited Wareham to accompany her, Mrs Martyn watching their departure with expressive lifting of her eyebrows.

"There is Anne at her usual pastime, making fools of the men," she said to Mrs Ravenhill. "I thought she had had a lesson, and might be trusted for a time; but it's in her, it's in her! If there is no one else, she sets to work upon my husband. Fortunately he's wood, not wax."

"What was the lesson?"

It was irresistible to Mrs Ravenhill to put this leading question.

"Don't you know? London was full of it. She was engaged to a Mr Forbes, a son of Sir Martin's, and broke it off with outrageous abruptness. I never expected her to marry him, it was the way she put an end to it which incensed people. We thought the best thing for her was to get her abroad. And here—you see!"

"Why was she so abrupt?"

"She is ambitious. Only a brilliant position will capture, but a fancy will sway her."

Thankfulness sometimes goes oddly askew. Mrs Ravenhill breathed a sigh of relief that Millie's innocent inclination had been checked in good time. Still, a touch of hostility towards the man who had roused it was in her tone.

"Possibly Mr Wareham is of the same kind, and can take care of himself?"

"Oh, poor fellow, poor fellow!" ejaculated Mrs Martyn, rejecting the possibility.

The last thing in the world that would have entered Wareham's head was that he was already the subject of comment. He allowed that there was a change in his thoughts of Anne, but would have scouted the idea that it implied change in his attitude towards Hugh. He now told himself that her conduct was probably capable of explanation. That meant pardon. He even indulged in dreams of reconciliation under his auspices. That included friendship. Hugh's infatuation no longer amazed him, he was only surprised that he had not held her more strenuously; for it seemed to him that had he been in such a position he would not easily have been ousted. Thinking this, the rash man also watched her, noting the delicate side-lines of her face, the short curve of the upper lip, the soft growth of hair where it touched the neck, and the dainty ear; details which only stepped into prominence when, as now, her eyes were turned away, for their dark depths drew, and held captive, other eyes. They gave the impression of offering much to one who could interpret what they said, and in face of them it was useless to moralise upon the untrustworthiness of woman's beauty. This was what Wareham had presumed to do, and now, when she suddenly turned them upon him, something startled him.

"Have you got over your prejudice?" she asked, smiling.

"Prejudice?"

"Against me? But I should not have asked you, I didn't mean to do anything so imprudent, only that you are changed, and wonderfully pleasanter, and women never know when to let well alone. They want words to quiet them, and I want you to tell me with your own lips that you don't dislike me any more."

Again that momentary feeling of intoxication. He murmured almost inaudibly—

"I can't."

She slackened her steps.

"Why not?"

"Say that I don't dislike you any more? Had I ever known you to dislike you?"

"No, no, but you had imagined me, and it was not a pretty picture you evolved. Tell me whether the picture still exists, or whether it is blotted out?"

Protestation was on his lips, when the recollection of Hugh's misery rose up and checked him. She was still watching him, but now she turned away her face.

"It is not, I see," she said quietly. Wareham clutched at a feverish memory.

"How can I forget his suffering? But," he hastened to add, "since I have known you, I can't believe that caprice or heartlessness caused it. There must have been something I don't understand, and I am certain you could explain it if you would."

Among Cupid's pitfalls there is no occupation so dangerous as for two persons to discuss each other's sins and virtues—none perhaps more attractive. Wareham would have pointed this out in his books, yet here he was floundering. And Anne? Was she playing Will-o'-the-Wisp? She looked at him again.

"I suppose you expect me to drop a curtsey, and offer a meek thank you?"

"I don't expect the impossible."

"Impossible?"

"I can't imagine the meekness."

"Your own fault. You don't inspire it. You try to ruffle my temper."

"What is that but giving you an opportunity to display the virtue? You can't display meekness without cause for it."

"Cause for it?" Anne struck back. "You offer cause freely!"

"Oh!"

"Can you say you have not been harsh in all your judgments?"

"Before I knew you."

Hugh was forgotten. He had ceased to be anything but a peg on which to hang banter, and, perhaps strangely, it was Anne who recalled him with a sigh.

"Did he—did Mr Forbes blame me so much?"

"He never blamed you."

"Yet his friend was unmerciful."

"What could I think? I came home to find Hugh dashed from his heights to lowest depths of wretchedness. He neither slept nor ate, but talked immoderately. From his talk I gleaned my own impressions. He was devoted to you, he was miserable—you must forgive me if I became unjust."

Apparently she had forgotten the compassion which had made her sigh, for she repeated his words demurely—

"Talked immoderately! And your patience held out all the time?"

"I believe I can be patient."

"And I can't. There's the mischief!"

He did not ask her to what mischief she alluded. They were close to the *fos*, and had been looking at it with unseeing eyes. Now some pause in the flutter of their thoughts made them turn with relief to an outward object. Wareham muttered a platitude about its beauty. He thought Mrs Ravenhill would have liked it for a sketch, while Anne scorned the thought.

"Sketch a waterfall? As well sketch a disembodied spirit."

Silence again, spent apparently in dreaming of the delicious freshness of the leaping water. Really, Wareham was looking at her, and wondering how he could ever have been such a prejudiced fool. He had made up his mind, that she was a creature of the world, adept in its wiles, knowing how to torment poor Hugh, and using her knowledge remorselessly. Here, by the flashing waters, she was young, frank, imprudent, perhaps, but cruel—never! Whatever had happened, hers was not the fault. So far on the primrose path Wareham had strayed, and was certain of his footing. Presently she spoke again.

"Some day perhaps I shall tell you. Not yet, for I am not sufficiently sure of my ground. If I have gained anything, it would be humiliating to see it all melt away, as it might. I was vexed at your prejudging me, because it was not fair; all your sympathies were heaped on one side, and I really believe if you could have crushed me with them, you were quite ready to have done so. Now I start on a better footing. Now if you blame me, as you will, it will not be in that hard, unreasoning fashion."

"Why say that I shall blame you?" His voice was not quite steady.

She turned and walked down the hill. "Because you cannot yet judge fairly."

He remonstrated.

"You need not be displeased. It is not your fault. No man is capable of placing himself in a woman's position in such a matter."

"Try me."

She laughed merrily.

"There is another thing which no man can do—imagine that he is not an exception to the general rule!"

"I wish you would find something which a man can do, instead of crushing with negatives!" He was growing impatient, and she said abruptly—

"I believe I will tell you."

He waited, eagerly desiring that she should look at him.

"But I risk a great deal, because you are Mr Forbes' friend, and you will not believe it possible."

Alas for friendship when it is first confronted with love! Afterwards it may recover its footing, but in the, as yet, unacknowledged whirl of head and heart, the poor thing gets swept into the vortex. At that moment Wareham could have believed much.

"And it sounds so little when one puts it into words!" the sinner went on hesitatingly. "It must have been that I did not like him well enough— ever. I thought I did. I assure you I was quite glad to discover that I could feel so much, but—"

She paused so long that Wareham repeated the word.

"But?"

"I got tired of him, of it, of all!" She turned her eyes on him. "You have never tried, have you, being adored from morning to night?"

"Never."

"It is sickening. Like living upon sweetmeats. I used to try to provoke him, and if once I could have got him out of temper, there might have been some hope. If he had contradicted me! I longed for a breath of fresh air. And dragging on—oh, he made a mistake all through. Of course you can't understand—" She ended abruptly.

He felt a burning desire to assure her that he could, but his muttered words struck him as absurdly inadequate. Silence became more eloquent. Anne broke it at last—

"It was a hundred pities," she mused, "and rough on him, for what could I say? What reason could I give? Tell him that he bored me? I couldn't, I couldn't! I can't lose my friends. No, no, no, poor fellow! Here we come upon all those people, and Blanche is beckoning wildly, and I can't think how I have had the face to talk to you. Forget it!"

With a sudden movement, for which he was unprepared, she sprang from him, and ran down the steep slope. He restrained the impulse to quicken his own pace, and by the time he reached the road, the carrioles had started, and Mrs Ravenhill and Millie, the clergyman and his wife, were moving off in a cloud of dust. Wareham, in spite of the impatience of his skydsgut, held back until carriages and dust had rolled away in the distance.

Tumultuous thought made it at first impossible to grasp a single idea, and to hold on to it as a centre for others. Anne's face, the flutter of a small curl on her forehead, softly outlined arch of eyebrows, all manner of idiotic fancies, hustled and jostled each other in his brain; and he presently became aware that instead of sending the airy traitors to the right-about, he was encouraging them to stand, wall-like, between himself and the truth about himself. Too strong a man to keep up the mask when once he discovered it, he proceeded to chase the busy throng. From behind them Anne's face peeped again.

He dragged out a hiding fact, and held it bare to his own scorn. He loved her—loved her; and though but a day before the amazement of it would have struck him mute, it had already ceased to look strange. All had led to it. The inconceivable would have been his failing to love. So far his heart with easy swing.

But judgment stood stubborn in refusal to go with it. Judgment it was which held the scourge. With Hugh Forbes in the background, what might be acknowledged natural became also offensive. As Wareham jogged along the white road, unheedful of bold outlines or lovely verdure, he found himself mentally writing to his friend, and recoiling with a start. How could he word such a dispatch—"I have seen the woman for whom you are breaking your heart. I love her myself, and shall try to win her"? The very thought was brutal.

Yet—to resign her for a dream, even for an ill-placed devotion, what could be more foolish and morbid? What fresh chance could come to Hugh? His had passed when, sooner than carry out an engagement, she had broken away abruptly, and faced the talk and jibes of her world by venturing on a course for which blame was the more unsparingly heaped on her because it was inexplicable. Hugh was young, handsome, ardent. Until this moment Wareham had fancied him the very man to catch the fancy of a woman, and it was only since Anne had lifted the curtain which friendship held tight, that he could admit that possible something—was it the power of boring?—which had driven her from him. This was what she meant when she said she had no patience. That patience should be wanted!

Here was his heart once more racing smoothly, until judgment caught the reins again, and tugged at the runaway steed. What boy's work was this! A woman but a few weeks ago betrothed to his friend, and still beloved by him—crazily it might be, but with all his heart—a woman of whom he knew next to nothing, and that little, up to now, not in her favour—and here, at a word, a look, he was at her feet! Shameful! Yet—worst shame of all—not to be parted with at any price. Already the world without Anne's figure in the foreground looked cold and unendurable. His eyes tried to pierce the whirl of dust ahead, and to distinguish her amid its folds; he fancied he could do so, and straightway his thoughts were occupied with nothing but foolish longing to know what her eyes were saying at this moment. The confidence she had given surely pointed to a touch of sympathy, a budding liking? Happy, happy he! In another hour or two they might be again together, and he would show better than he yet had done, how much he prized her frankness. The next moment these thoughts turned upon him with scourges. Honour stood by, and scornfully directed the flagellation, and he felt himself a miserable traitor. Here was friendship! Here was a creditable sequel to his offices for Hugh! So his mind wandered backwards and forwards.

Chaos lasted for a while, and it is not impossible that the tumult was so new that he rashly suffered it, believing in his own powers of self-government, and aware of a whirl, as of hot-headed youth, which he had thought the years had left behind. The day changed, brooding clouds gathered round the mountains, which closed in, rank after rank; nearer hills, heavily purple, swept up from the gloom of the valley. The road slowly mounted, the dust subsided, and the crawling carrioles in front looked as if an effort might overtake them. But Wareham checked the impulse, and his skydsgut's attempted spurt. He would not see Anne until he had resolved on a line of action. A resolution, carefully thought out, would serve as a guard against the rasher promptings of his heart, and between this and Stalheim he had to come to terms with this resolution. One was already there—not to give her up if he could gain her. Behind this his heart entrenched itself, grumbling.

Yet, in spite of such a reservation, carrying a good deal with it, Wareham hugged the delusion that the other was the more important. Conscience had much to say as to what he should write to Hugh, how wrap up the communication which was so abominably angular and assertive, that, say what he would, it inevitably presented itself in a repulsive form. Conscience harped loudly upon truth, yet was anxious to give truth what should have been unnecessary adorning. Finally he resolved to write to Hugh that night, and to tell him—? to tell him that he had met Miss Dalrymple. This decided, he was forced to admit that so much Hugh knew already. There must be a more expansive confession; he had to add—admired, liked her. And this written, in thought, appeared so significant to Wareham, that he imagined himself closing the letter here, and drew a breath of relief. But conscience, refusing compromise, cried out for something explicit, and here came the difficulty. All the sentences he revolved looked either inadequate or shameful. "Do you give her up?" Free she undoubtedly was, having herself asserted her freedom, but free to Hugh Forbes' chief friend?

Yet something he must write, and until it was written and answered, keep his feelings out of reach of betrayal. Here was a resolution which he grasped, for it belonged to the honourable instincts of a fine nature, too deeply rooted to suffer in the general upheaval. He added a rider, necessary if unpalatable. He would not avoid Anne to the extent of provoking her own or other remark, but he must avoid—well, such a walk *à deux* as they had taken that day, for instance.

The road grew steeper, and he jumped out of his carriole. Stalheim was perched above, a hotel, two or three scattered cottages, and a waterfall. He climbed through gathering clouds, and when he reached the door, was met by English tourists of the most noisy and offensive type. All his own people had vanished, and he saw no more of them until supper, which was eaten to the accompaniment of a band. Mrs Ravenhill confided to him that she hated the place, in spite of the magnificence of the scenery.

"And Millie and I have determined to go to Gudvangen to-morrow, and wait for the Monday steamer. I cannot stay here to see my own country-people making themselves so obnoxious—" She hastened to add with scrupulous care, "You don't expect me, I hope, to repeat that you are not in the least tied to us, and must not be influenced by anything we may do."

"Does that sentence mean that I am forbidden to accompany you?"

"Forbidden? Oh, no; but the others stay on, and this is one of the special places in Norway."

"I detest special places."

She warned further.

"Remember that we heard the little inn at Gudvangen was very primitive."

"That decides me. If you will allow me, I shall certainly go there with you."

Millie's face was all brightness. Wareham, indeed, was inclined to look upon the proposal as the reward of merit, to plume himself upon a sort of recognition of his having kept on the side of his conscience. It was a step out of his dilemma. Two days of voluntary banishment from Anne meant a sacrifice worthy of the altar of friendship. He would write his letter, avoid walks, avoid the smallest betrayal of feeling. All looked easy.

If love laughs at locksmiths, how much more at lovers' resolutions!

Chapter Seven
How a Letter got Written

So satisfied was Wareham with his ample precautions that, supper ended, he went in pursuit of Miss Dalrymple. She had vanished. Mrs Martyn engaged him, and Mrs Ravenhill and Millie joined in; presently a harp and voice struck up in the gallery round the hall. An hour later Anne appeared at the door, wet, breathless, but in high spirits. She said she had been paying tribute to the place, had gone down the Gudvangen zigzags to see a waterfall—two waterfalls. A beautiful sleigh-dog slipped in behind her.

"Anne!" exclaimed Mrs Martyn, disapprovingly. "In this rain!"

"Mountain-rain—mist."

"And alone!"

"Mayn't oneself be good company?"

She laughed as she said it. Wareham, looking at her, found delightful charm in her laugh. He felt that in breaking away he was giving Hugh an extraordinary proof of loyalty, and probably his face expressed this conviction, for Mrs Martyn said sharply—

"Mr Wareham may admire imprudence—I don't!"

Anne's face chilled. He returned—

"My opinion is worthless, or I should venture to suggest dangers in wet clothes."

"Dangers? Madness!" cried Mrs Martyn, jumping up. "Come, Anne, I have waited for you until I can hardly keep my eyes open."

"They are going to dance," Millie hazarded. "Let them. I go to bed."

"I am tired of the noise," said Mrs Ravenhill.

"And I have a letter to write," remarked Wareham.

Anne, who had recovered herself, looked back over her shoulder with a smile.

"Do letters ever come or go?" she asked.

The idle question gripped Wareham. The letter—the act of writing—had been his difficulty; now, with recollection of how long a time must pass before it could reach England, and bring back its answer, came a sinking of heart. Honour bound him to the lines he had laid down. If he remained near he must take no steps to win her until he heard from Hugh. If he could not trust himself, he must hold aloof. There was the situation—briefly put. Cruel! For every hour, every minute, now, was worth months, years! Now the days were strewn with opportunities, he was thrown into her society. If ever she was to be won, now was his chance. Impatience caught, shook him! It might be a fortnight before answer came from Hugh, and when he looked at the past week, and reflected that it seemed a month long, he found the prospect of two such periods intolerable. He endeavoured to detach himself from conditions, and to philosophise; but philosophy is old and scrupulous, while young love has no qualms in taking advantage of the first opportunity which presents itself, and tripping up the elderly combatant. Wareham gave up arguing with himself, and set doggedly to work to write his letter.

Step number one was difficult enough.

Nothing satisfied him in expression. More than one scrawl was tossed aside as inadequate, absurdly inadequate, or as expressing more than he meant. What did he mean? There was the mischief. In these early days, when he had only just begun to read his own heart, and might reasonably claim a little time for its study, it was detestable to have to offer it for a third person's perusal. He resented the position the more that he was unused to interference with his liberty. He lost his first flush of pity for Hugh, and wrote with a certain asperity—

"Circumstances have thrown Miss Dalrymple and me together; perhaps this will prepare you for what I have to say. In a word, I believe I am on the brink of loving her. The knowledge only came to me to-day; I imagine it will not please you. My dear fellow, I would have given a good deal for it not to have happened; don't reproach me without keeping that in mind. As it is, all I can do is to hold back—I don't say draw back, because I have done nothing—and let you make the next move. If you have any hope, if you desire to try your luck once more, telegraph through Bennett, 'Wait.' You can trust me to make no sign till word comes from you, whatever the cost to myself. So much I owe you, and perhaps you will think I owe you more, but I believe you are generous enough to forgive what could only be a wrong if I snatched your chances from you. At best, my own may be small enough, they appear to me so small that this letter becomes offensively presumptuous in even treating of them. Yet, lest you should ever think me treacherous, I write it, and repeat that I hold myself bound in honour and friendship to take no step in advance until you have told me that I am free, or let me know that you have not yet resigned your hope."

The wording displeased him, but it did not seem as if any thing he wrote could give him satisfaction, so that he hurriedly closed his epistle, and took it to the office. A heap of letters lay on the table, they had the appearance of having been seeking their owners for weeks, and of reposing at last with an air of finality. Wareham looked at them askance, as if each carried a threat of delay.

In the morning Anne sat next to him at breakfast. She said to him immediately—

"Why are you so cruel as to leave us? We are pinned here until Colonel Martyn and Mr Grey come back. Besides, I don't like being driven from point to point, without time to draw breath. I feel like a note of interjection."

He made a weak reply, to the effect that Mrs Ravenhill disliked the place.

"And you are bound to Mrs Ravenhill?" She hastened to apologise. "Of course you are. Forgive me."

If this was offered as an opening, it failed. After a momentary pause, she said—

"You should have been with us last evening."

"Us?"

"I had a companion; did you not see him? He came in with me."

"Oh, the dog!"

"I don't permit those contemptuous accents for my friends. He behaved like a true gentleman, and took me to the very place where I wanted to go. No one else offered." If this was coquetry, it was accompanied by a frank smile at her own expense. Wareham stiffened, looked away, and broke out eagerly—

"How long shall you stay here?"

"Until Blanche is tired of it. I suppose till Monday. Are you not coming out to see what you came from England to see?"

"Oh, we are all coming," said Wareham, raging at his fetters.

She looked at him with eyes surprised but twinkling, talked about London for a decent interval, and left the room. He scarcely expected to see her re-appear with the others in the hall, but she was there.

Whatever Stalheim may suffer from its visitors, it is magnificently placed, a height among heights. Straight in front the Naerodal cleaves the mountains, its conical Jordalshut dominating the rest, its lovely mist-drifts playing round the summits. Below, a silver flash darts through the greys, and slender falls leap down to join the river. Nor is this fine cleft the only outlet. As they strolled up a road to the left where was a broken foreground of shrub, boulders, and cut grass—made lively by magpies—the great valley through which they had passed the day before, opened, and swept away into purple gloom, until the eye reached the mountains behind, here shrouded in cloud, there uplifting snowy heights against the menacing darkness. There was a wildness, a grandeur, a savage desolation, such as they had not yet seen under the August skies of Norway.

At the end of the walk Wareham took credit to himself for his conduct. He was sure that he had been quite natural, had walked with Anne, talked with Anne, and looked at Anne, without betraying attraction. This satisfied his man's code, which, once alarmed, is minute in such matters. He even avoided wishing her good-bye—marked slight; possibly, too marked. When the Ravenhills started, he dispatched his portmanteau in a carriole, and followed on foot.

It was a day of broken lights and flitting shadows; waterfalls rushed down on either side, and the beautiful salmon river, beryl-coloured, milky white, indigo, raced along by the road, and offered its counteracting life to what gloom there was. Wareham gave eager appreciation to the green flashing world through which he walked, his conscience was light, he enjoyed the smell of hay, snatched from steep roof-like patches of earth— the slender falls, scarcely more than silver threads, which leapt incredible heights to escape from their ice-prisons—the sweet pure air, the spring of turf at his feet. Far away in front the little carriages with their dun ponies spun along; presently a wild unkempt figure, carrying a sickle, and clad in scarlet jacket, broad hat, and knee-breeches, strode from a bushy path, a dog as wild as his master at his heels. Then a cottage or two with flowery roofs came in sight, a glimmer of fjord, and he was at Gudvangen. Mrs Ravenhill and Millie were standing outside Hansen's primitive little inn when he reached it.

"I don't know what you will say," said Mrs Ravenhill, laughing. "Are you prepared to live in a deal box by the roadside? But Millie and I think it delightful."

"Then I shall think it delightful too," said Wareham. "One can always fish."

Millie inquired if he had seen the waterfall.

"That little thing!"

"Speak respectfully, please! One of the highest in Europe, two thousand feet, with a jump of five hundred, isn't to be dismissed in such a slighting tone."

"You are going to rival Mrs Martyn in facts. But I see you have taken Gudvangen to your heart. Shall we go and explore?" On the way he was struck with Millie's light-heartedness, and said to himself that here was one of those happy natures from which care rolls off. She spoke with almost extreme admiration of Anne, but Mrs Martyn she did not like. Her mother remonstrated that she had never been harmed by that lady.

"Padded glass," was all that Millie vouchsafed.

Wareham wondered a little at such unexpected perspicacity.

A figure in a long mackintosh ran joyfully up to the girl. It was the young Siamese prince, breathless with triumph, and a basket of twenty-eight trout.

"You are at Hansen's?" he demanded, his eyes sparkling.

"All of us—"

"Then they shall be cooked; we will have them by and by. Perhaps I shall even catch some more."

"We will live on trout," said Wareham. "I must have a try."

"Do," Mrs Ravenhill urged. "I promise you that Millie and I will bring appreciative appetites."

They did not meet again till supper, shared with three English fishermen, who bemoaned the dry weather, and two German girls, travelling on foot with knapsacks.

"What have you discovered?" Wareham asked. "But I can tell you. Another waterfall."

"Another? A dozen. We found a delightful walk which you shall see to-morrow. There is but one, so it is as well it should have charms. It leads to Bakke, where the pastor—whom we met with a pipe a yard long—has service to-morrow, and we can either row along the fjord or walk. Mother will walk, I expect; she sees sketches at every turn."

Wareham foresaw another *tête-à-tête* stroll, but on this occasion felt no disquietude, looking upon Millie as a soothing little companion, who might be induced, without suspicion, to discourse now and then upon Miss Dalrymple. So much depends on the point of view! Mrs Ravenhill's was not the same. She started, resolved to remain with the others, but a shadowy view of the fjord, with a group of infantine kids in the foreground, shook her resolution. The lights were perfect. Millie's little fancy, if it ever existed, had quite fluttered away, danger could not exist. She wavered, resisted, wavered again, and fell. They left her happily oblivious of everything beyond the purple and green splendour of the hills, and the absolute reflection of line and tint in the glassy waters.

"I never before realised how much happiness belongs to art," said Wareham, as they walked away. "It makes one envious."

"Is not yours art?" Millie asked.

"Nothing so graceful."

"You paint in words, and words are stronger than colours."

"No words could bring those reflections before you."

"But they could extract their inner meaning?"

Wareham looked at her with surprise, feeling as if he had been gravely addressed by a butterfly, but the next moment she had run lightly up the bank after strawberries. From this point of vantage she flung him a question.

"Has Miss Dalrymple a mother?"

"A step-mother."

She knelt down, the better to fill a small basket she carried, and the impulse to speak was too strong.

"You are not angry any longer?"

He paused a second, then his words rushed. "It was a misconception, such as comes from judging before one has heard both sides of the question." To talk more easily, he reached her side with two strides, and stood looking over the fjord. "He—my friend,"—the words stuck a little—"never blamed her, but, you know, in such cases, one takes forbearance as a matter of course. I knew he was generous. I concluded he must be wronged."

He paused. Millie, on her knees, leaned backward, but still occupied herself with the strawberries.

"The wedding was close at hand, was it not?"

"Close. Was she wrong?"

The question put, he blamed himself for asking it. It was offering up Anne's conduct to the world's judgment. Millie did not answer until she had dropped two or three crimson berries into her basket, then she said in a steady voice—

"If it was an escape from bonds, it was right."

The answer was unexpected, should have been welcome. Yet it seemed to push Anne or Hugh Forbes to the wall, suggesting that if she were not to blame, he was. Wareham uttered an impatient sigh.

"I cannot conceive what she could object to in Hugh!" he said, the friend uppermost again. Millie was silent. "And yet—women—?" he added tentatively.

She turned back some leaves, under which a cluster of fruit glowed.

"I believe that I am surprised you don't condemn her with the rest of the world," he said at last, in order to force an answer.

"How should I? I never saw your friend. Miss Dalrymple has been very nice to me, but I know nothing of her, or of her life." Millie's words were hurried. "You asked me if she were right or wrong. How should I know? But if she was ready to brave people's tongues, either she had never loved him, or she did not love him any more. In either case, when she found it out, she must have been right not to wait until it was too late. That is all I can see clearly, and I dare say, if I knew more, I should not see so much."

"I believe you are right," said Wareham admiringly. He was in the condition to find oracles in all that agreed with him. "When you know Miss Dalrymple better, you will be sure you are."

"Miss Dalrymple is not easily known."

"Not?"

"Not by women."

To this man does not object, and Wareham merely pondered over it. Millie moved a little farther off. He followed.

"I do not know that it is a disadvantage?" he said, ignoring her last words, and defending blindly.

"Oh, no! Why should it be?"

Wareham would have preferred something more combative, wishing for argument, which was unattainable when his companion only acquiesced. He stood meditating, and Millie started from her knees.

"At this rate, we shall never get to Bakke!" she cried. "But strawberries are irresistible."

"Do you really like them?"

There was a dissatisfied note in his voice. She thought with a pang—

"Already he can see nothing to praise where she is not," and then was horrified because she seemed to make this a reproach. To punish herself she went back to Anne.

"I suppose the Martyns and Miss Dalrymple start in our steamer to-morrow? Do they go to Balholm?"

Wareham imagined they would go where Mrs Ravenhill went. Her spirits sank. She could not chatter as freely as usual, yet made a gallant effort.

"What flower is that? I never saw any like it. Oh, thank you! Look, it really is odd, canary-coloured, and hanging by a sort of filament. We must take it back to mother, who loves flowers."

Hearing this, he gathered everything which came in his way. He was conscious that absorbing thought left him a dull companion, and wished to compensate for it by what small attentions he could offer. As for Millie, he looked at her only to compare her with Anne, and the small fancies which had crossed his mind during the first days they had spent together, had flitted into the unremembered past. He liked her, nevertheless, and recognised a sweetness of nature which, in the years to come, would make a husband happy. Perhaps he even liked her better than at first, when a certain air of alert agreeability had once or twice annoyed him, and pointed to fatigue in companionship. And as she walked in front, what seemed a sudden inspiration struck him. Here was the very wife for Hugh Forbes. He loved liveliness, and her very prettiness was lively; it was, indeed, the very word to use in describing her. And how admirably such an arrangement would fit the puzzle into place! Millie could not understand why he began to talk of Hugh. He grew eloquent. Hugh was the pleasantest fellow! Generous. Lovable. Amusing. Rising. The picture requiring to be toned down slightly, he admitted that he was inclined to be idle; but idleness is a sin a girl readily condones. Millie listened, under the impression that Mr Forbes was talked of that he might think of Anne. The subject was distasteful, but she said heroically —

"How strange she did not like him!" Then, as Wareham laughed, a smile dawned on her face. "Have I said anything odd?"

"No, but I have," he explained. "I have been trying to make one woman see Hugh's attractiveness at the very moment when she knew another woman could not bring herself to marry him."

"That might not have been his fault."

"Then it was hers?"

Millie felt disposed to cry out at this persistence. The talk had been full of pricks, yet was not without its tremulous pleasure, since she was nearer to Wareham than when indifferent subjects were discussed. He would not have cared to enlist her on Anne's side, if friendliness had not urged him. She said, after a momentary pause—

"Why not his misfortune?"

He was silent. It would have been difficult to have satisfied him at that instant, and Millie's suggestion quite failed. He dropped the bitter-sweet topic, and talked of Bakke and the curve of the fjord behind it, promontory overlapping promontory, every light, shadow, and colour reflected in the water. An ugly little church stood near the brink, round it nestled the living and the waiting dead, a few flower-roofed cottages, more black crosses. They stood and looked over the paling; grass waved upon the graves, the same flowery sorrel-tinted grass as scented the air; two or three children were in a boat, the oars splashed, otherwise not a sound broke the silence. Millie's spirits rose. In the midst of a great nature, she and Wareham seemed to stand alone, to be brought nearer. When she reached her mother, her eyes shone.

Wareham went up the Naerodal alone in the afternoon, but in the dusk all three again strolled together. Clear golden lights swept along sky and fjord; long shadows trembled in the water; two or three ponies scrambled like goats among heaped-up boulders, and the goats themselves, perched on inaccessible heights, sent down faint argumentative bleatings in response to the wild cry with which a girl was coaxing them.

What land is this, in which we have all once wandered? A land of shadows and sweet lights, touching everything with mysterious charm. Hush, dreamer! You know now, though you did not know it then, that this is Arcady.

Chapter Eight
Eden

The steamer was to start from Gudvangen at two. Wareham already felt as if he had offered up so much to duty that he might expect reward. To have left Miss Dalrymple to the mercy of possibilities in the shape of other men, for two long days, was in itself an assurance that he could trust himself; and if that were so, the reasons for avoiding her became ludicrously small, almost, indeed, offensive. He went to fish, but the point he chose commanded the road through the Naerodal, and when he saw the carriages broadening from specks into shape, and at last could distinguish clearly, he was not very long in making his way after them to Hansen's.

Mrs Martyn and Anne were standing in the porch talking to old Hansen, as well as limited vocabularies would allow. Wareham was welcome as an interpreter to three of the party; he hoped that Anne's smile meant more.

"You see, we are here," she said; "we have torn ourselves from Stalheim, wicked Stalheim!"

"Why wicked?"

"By contrast only. Here you look so pastoral, so idyllic, that our little crowds, and bands, and bad dinners, take quite an iniquitous air."

"We had a chaplain," put in Mrs Martyn. "To point out how bad we were!"

"Well, I am glad you have escaped," said Wareham. "Where's Colonel Martyn?"

"Thereby hangs a sad tale, for he has telegraphed that he will join us at Balholm, and Blanche is much displeased. And Mr Grey is left in the vortex at Stalheim. Don't look so reproachful, or we shall ask you to go back and rescue him."

"And miss my steamer? Forbid it, fates! Gudvangen is a charming spot, as you see—Eden, if you like; but to be left here without a companion, to live upon trout and biscuits, and amuse oneself with a jingling piano, and old photographs, would make one hate Eden. Besides, all my philanthropy is packed up in England. But what have we here?"

A larger carriage drove by to the other hotel, and was followed by a second. Both were filled with shouting parties of tourists, waving and yelling. Old Hansen set his face grimly.

"Now," he said to Wareham, "tell me, what people are those? They belong to your country. You can explain. We have nothing like them. They do not care about the beauty, or the history, or those who live here. They are middle-aged men, many of them. They shout, and sing, and laugh as loud as they can. What are they? Why do they come?"

Wareham muttered something to the effect that there were fools in all countries.

"Tell him it's the way we treat our lunatics," Anne said. "It's our new system of cure."

"The steamer does not go until two," Wareham said, in a low voice.

"Will your Eden bear looking into?"

"Come and see."

"Blanche, will you explore?"

"No. It is too hot. I hear there is a shop with rather nice furs, and I haven't seen one for a week. Mind you two aren't late."

"Late, when it isn't half-past twelve! But I can't sit on the steamer with those lunatics a moment longer than is necessary, and Mr Wareham's inn may be delightfully primitive, but I have never set myself up as a specimen of primitive woman, and I prefer Eden without its inn. Well, Mr Wareham, I am waiting." She stood erect, smiling.

"Where will you go?"

"What have you to offer?"

"A path by the fjord, where you will find Mrs and Miss Ravenhill sketching, and the road by which you have just come."

"You don't perplex one with the amount of choice. We will go back. Stalheim, wicked Stalheim, attracts me, I own."

They were walking along the road. Whenever he could, Wareham glanced at her, admiring the easy poise of her figure, her light strong step.

"Aren't you contented with having brought down a part of the world you admire?"

"They don't harmonise with Eden, to tell the truth," said Anne, laughing. "I'm not sure that any of us do. But I grant you all that you demand as to its charms. Look at the soft shadows on the hills. I can fancy it a very refreshing little place for a day; perhaps two,"—doubtfully—"if one was sure—absolutely sure—of getting away the day after."

"Is that all you could give to Eden?"

"Alas, alas!" Rather to his surprise, Anne was grave. "But when one has lived always in Vanity Fair? Do you not feel with me? Something else will be provided for us poor things, something more in accord with our heritage of ages?"

She gave him a look in which he read what she did not say, and they walked on silently, making their way at last to the brink of the river. The clear water rushed noisily past them.

"A chatterer," Wareham declared. "Pleasant chatter, don't you think? If you are sure we have time we might sit down here a little while, and perhaps grow cool."

"Plenty of time," he said, consulting his watch. "If we are back by a quarter to two, we shall do very well, for all your things will have gone on board."

Anne was already perched on a stone.

"I throw responsibility on you. I have come here to enjoy myself, not to fidget."

"What shall we do to secure your object?"

"Oh," she cried impatiently, "don't talk about it! If it isn't spontaneous it is failure."

"Then I mayn't even ask whether you prefer silence or—"

"Ask nothing. Tell me, if you like, what you did yesterday?"

"Walked."

"Here?"

"No, by that other path which you rejected, to a village called Bakke."

"Were you alone?"

"Oh, no, we all started together. Mrs Ravenhill fell upon a sketch, and her daughter and I went further and returned to her. There you have it all."

Miss Dalrymple scrutinised his face with a smile.

"There is something very attractive about her," she said, "though she does not like me."

"I have never heard her say so."

"No, she would not. She is good. I can quite imagine her in Eden. She would make Adam very happy. Don't you think so?"

"I believe she would make an excellent wife," said Wareham, keeping on open ground.

Anne said no more. She asked questions as to how the salmon got up these rivers, and announced her intention of trying to catch one when next she went to Scotland. At last Wareham looked at his watch.

"There is time enough to take it as coolly as you like," he said, "but perhaps we had better go back."

Anne sprang up.

"I am ready. As we cannot stay, I believe I shall be sorry to leave Gudvangen." Wareham's heart throbbed.

"I shall never forget it," he said.

"Never? Why? Was Bakke so delightful a place?"

"I leave you to imagine why," he said, in a low voice.

"Leave me nothing in the form of a riddle," said Anne; "I shall disappoint you."

He raged again. Were all his chances to slip by? There are moments when we feel as if we rode upon the wave, as if what we wanted was just within our grasp. This was such a moment, and he was bound—could not so much as stretch out his hand. His heart, submitting sullenly, would say something.

"Miss Dalrymple," he began, "is there absolutely no hope for Hugh?"

She paused for a moment.

"What right have you to ask?"

"None, except,"—he would have liked to have shot out, "that I want relief from a torment of doubt," but controlled himself to say—"except knowing that he has not given you up."

"You should not use the present tense. I can answer for it that you have not seen him for ten days. Doesn't that give time enough for a man to change?"

Wareham looked at her, his face hard.

"Yes," he said shortly. "That is not the question. How long does a woman take?" She made an impatient gesture.

"For pity's sake! When I came to Norway to escape Hugh Forbes!"

He was silent, suddenly conscious that he dared not probe farther. Womanlike she glanced at him, to read what she could in his face, but his eyes were on the ground. When he raised them, he stared before him at an empty fjord. He dragged out his watch.

"Impossible! It is not half-past one."

"What is the matter?" Anne asked.

"The steamer! Am I dreaming, or has she gone?"

"Certainly she is not there." Anne quickened her steps.

Wareham's face was very grave. He dashed into the inn, and hammered at old Hansen's door. Anne waited outside, reflecting on the situation. Wareham came slowly out at last, followed by the burly landlord.

"I am afraid it is too true," he said. "I shall never forgive myself for implicitly trusting a Norwegian time-table. They left at one o'clock."

He looked at Hansen, Hansen looked at Anne. It was she who first spoke.

"When is the next boat?"

"To-morrow afternoon."

Wareham hazarded the remark—

"If I were to take you back to Stalheim? There is sure to be some one you could join."

"I hate to be baffled," said Anne. "And you may have forgotten that all I have in the world—here—has gone on the steamer."

"Heavens, yes!" said Wareham, struck with this fresh complication. He looked so shocked that Anne in self-defence began to laugh.

"Did no one miss us? This is humiliating!" It appeared that Mrs Ravenhill inquired, and was told they intended to go on board without returning to the inn. Mrs Martyn stayed in a shop until the last moment, and had barely time to scramble on board; it was quite natural that she should suppose the others had been before her.

"So we have no one to blame but ourselves," said Anne.

"But me," corrected Wareham. "You disclaimed responsibility from the first."

"Oh, we will share. It is less dull to hold together. And what does the landlord suggest? We can't be the first castaways."

"He says that the last victims took a boat, and were rowed to Ulvik. But Balholm is a good deal further," Wareham said, after consultation.

Anne decided promptly.

"Very well. Please get a boat."

"You venture?"

"Why not? What else can be done?" Wareham could think of nothing. The misadventure meant more to him than it did to her, at least it seemed so beforehand. He had gone rashly near breaking his resolution in capturing that solitary hour with her, and was forced to reflect that he had not come out of the ordeal scathless. Fate was punishing him by prolonging what he had already found too long for his strength, and there was nothing for it but to accept fate. He said hurriedly—"I will see about a boat at once," and was going, when she called him back.

"We must have dinner before we set off."

"You put me to shame," he said. "I believe my wits have deserted me."

"Worse things have fallen to my lot," she laughed; "do you expect me to offer you, words of consolation? Bear your burdens with greater philosophy, Mr Wareham."

"If that were all!" rushed from his lips.

"I can't even lighten them by ordering dinner," Anne went on, taking no notice. "Bennett's Conversation-book is on the steamer, with everything else, and I can remember nothing but *mange tak*, which doesn't seem called for at this moment."

"At any rate, I can order dinner," said Wareham humbly.

"And you couldn't do anything better. Please have a great many trout. Who knows when we shall dine again!"

"I must find out how long a boat will take in reaching Balholm."

"Don't ask," Anne said quickly. "Don't you see that as the thing has to be done there is no possible use in looking at the difficulties? I, on the contrary, mean to treat it as something special. All the world and his wife—even those horrid tourists—go down the Nserofjord in steamers; how much more enchanting to be rowed dreamily, with neither smoke nor noise! Pray don't be so dismal about it. Do you know that you are paying me the worst of compliments? Endure your fate bravely, and order the trout."

Thus adjured, Wareham departed. Gudvangen was sleepily interested, and the misadventure had happened before. He chose a good boat and two rowers, and going back to the little saal, found Anne making an excellent dinner.

"When one is cast away, it is prudent to chose a place with shops for the event," she said. "I have made this an excuse for buying some delightful furs. Money I have none, but they trust me."

"I have money," said Wareham, hastily turning out his pockets, and unnecessarily ashamed of this fresh absence of foresight on his part. They could not reach Balholm before the middle of the night, and Anne's wraps were on the steamer.

"Very well. Then you shall pay as we pass, and I will owe it to you instead."

"Having brought you into the predicament, I think I might be allowed to provide the necessaries of life."

"Do you mean that you are proposing to present me with a set of furs?" said Anne, laying down her fork and staring at him.

"Something you must have to keep you warm."

"Mr Wareham, pray don't make me begin to regret this incident."

He saw that she was vexed, and dashed away from the subject.

"Poor old Hansen was mortally afraid we should want him to telephone something or other. I believe the telephone is sending him off his head. He would have sent out to look for us if a message had not come down from Stalheim just at the critical moment."

"Can't we use it?" said Anne, with a little more anxiety in her voice than she had shown hitherto.

"Only backwards to Stalheim, and then, I imagine, telegraph to Voss. That would not help us?"

"No, no; we are doing the only sensible thing. The trout are excellent, and I encourage hunger."

"We will take some food with us."

"And tea. I insist upon tea."

"But how to boil it in a boat?"

"We will land on a rock," said Anne, who was laughing again.

"A fjord picnic. By all means. Besides, of course there are villages."

"We don't want to be delayed, and I shan't agree to anything more sociable than a rock."

"You command the crew."

They were on excellent terms again; Anne's momentary haughtiness past, she was mirthful over their prospects. They went out and bought the gaudiest *tine* Gudvangen could produce, and packed it with what provisions they could find. Anne insisted, moreover, that there should be a packet of tobacco for the rowers. Then she went to fetch her furs, but apparently had changed her mind, for Wareham was not allowed to pay for them. That she would arrange in Bergen, as originally fixed.

"You have not forgiven," he said, in a low voice.

"Not forgotten," she corrected. "By this time to-morrow I may have done so."

He accepted the hint, and was silent.

They went down to the boat, and saw all their things placed, watched by the few interested spectators Gudvangen sent out, and by old Hansen, who took a fatherly interest in their proceedings.

"Can we sail?" asked Miss Dalrymple.

"There is not a breath. But the men are good rowers, and I can take an oar to relieve them. There will be beauty enough to please you."

"Provided expressly on my account," said Anne lightly. "You will expect me to be so prodigal of compliments at the end of the voyage, that I shall not praise your arrangements now. Are we ready?"

"A good journey!" called out old Hansen. Wareham waved his hat, Anne nodded and smiled, the boat moved smoothly along out into a world of reflected colours.

"Good-bye, Eden," said Anne.

Chapter Nine
Tongue-Tied

For a time neither of the two companions spoke. The hush of the place was upon them; the extraordinary stillness, unbroken by so much as the cry of a bird, or by any sound more harsh than the soft rhythm of the rise and fall of the oars. On one side the grassy path, along which Millie and Wareham had walked to Bakke, wound, clasping the rock with a green girdle; on the other was neither path nor habitation, only the bold sweep of the mountain side, clothed with verdure running up to the snow patches, and coloured by blue shadows, or cut by the slender silver line of a *fos*. Whatever there was, rock or trees, snow or leaping water, its double was below, with some strange charm added to its beauty; and so narrow was the fjord, that these reflections seemed to meet and fill it.

Anne sat with her head turned away from Wareham, looking over the side of the boat into the green mystery through which they moved. He would not speak, fearing to disturb her, but he was able to watch her to his heart's content. He was certain that she had grown younger since coming to Norway; he heaped scorn on himself for having detected hardness in her lovely face. And by what miracle were he and she together! Yet his position was cruel enough, for this day had already deepened his love, so that it was more and more difficult to keep back any outward sign which hinted at its expression; and although, placed as they now were, that would have been impossible, he told himself that if he were not bound by his duty to his friend, he might have put his fate to the test no later than to-morrow. To-morrow! That was an endurable date, but to be forced to wait, wait, wait, until the letter brought back an answer!—the letter which— He began to calculate. Saturday—this was Monday, and there was certainly no boat likely to leave Norway until the middle of the week. His letter was dawdling along, and at such a rate an answer would hardly reach him while he was in the country. And all these weeks to be tongue-tied!

Anne turned round at this moment. Apparently she was not thinking of him, and had but changed her position in order to look at the other side of the fjord; but every time her face came before him under a fresh aspect, he was conscious of a sweet surprise. Presently she looked full at him, and smiled.

"I want to say something and I can't express it," she said. "I suppose that is incomprehensible to you?"

It was so like his own case that Wareham dared not venture to say how like. He was forced to treat his own feelings as if they were a packet of explosives, and keep light away from them. Anne went on—

"I am perplexed with myself. This is so much more beautiful than I conceived, and it is so odd that I should think it beautiful!"

"Why?"

"Why am I, I?—I can't explain. I only know that my friends will tell you that I am insensible to beauty of scenery."

"Rank heresy."

"I don't know. It has been dinned into my ears so constantly that I have ended by accepting it. They assure me I have no eye for colour."

"I could confute them."

"Oh, once let me feel sure of myself, and I could manage the confuting," said Anne coolly. "After to-day I shall not go down before them quite so easily, for I believe it is the colour which enchants me. Was ever anything so exquisite as this crater!"

"I am glad you have extracted some compensation for my stupidity," said Wareham, greedy of assurance that she liked to be in the boat with him. She took no notice beyond saying—

"I still think they behaved rather meanly in deserting us."

"What are they feeling now, I wonder?"

"As little as possible."

"Do you imply that they will not be uneasy?"

"Blanche will say that it is Anne all over, and that she may be left to take care of herself. I dare say she is right."

"Do you like the woman?" he asked abruptly.

"No catechism, Mr Wareham."

"Miss Ravenhill described her as 'padded glass.'"

Anne meditated, and looked amused.

"That is a clever definition, whether it is she or not. I should have thought it more likely to come from you."

"It was all her own. Mrs Martyn seems to me rather forcedly rude than anything else."

"She has not a bad heart," said Anne. "Rudeness is to her mind an outward expression of honesty, but one which she does not appreciate in other people. It is astonishing what a different aspect our own virtues wear—transplanted."

"If she is kind—" began Wareham.

"I do not say she is always kind. She can hurt. She will not be kind about me to-day."

A thorn pricked Wareham. He said hastily—

"She will know it was not your fault."

"She will try to keep me from knowing it. You may be sure it will be long before I hear the last of it, from her or from—others."

"From others?"

Anne looked straight in his face.

"Mr Wareham, I imagined you to be a man of the world. If you are, you must know as well as I that people will chatter."

"The world is not always absurd," he retorted, with heat.

"When was it not a gossip? Now I will ask a question which I have avoided before. When shall we get to Balholm?"

"About two or three in the morning."

"And you flatter yourself that will not give a handle for talk!"

Wareham had been surprised that she had said nothing of the sort before; he was conscious at the same time that if it had been Millie, the fear would not have struck her.

"When they know the facts, they will see there was nothing else for us to do."

"They won't know facts. One fact will be sufficient for them, and to that they will hold on as a dog to a bone. Never mind. I have gone through as much before."

"When?" Wareham asked jealously.

"Oh, not with this sort of experience. This is new to me. But I have served as a bone so often that I am used to the worrying. Don't let us talk of it now. I want to drink in my new enjoyment, to develop my new sense. Look at the drifting shadow on that hill, and the splendour of the snow. But it is the water, the water that fascinates me. I am going to watch it."

He accepted this as a hint that he was not to speak, and the turmoil in him was not sorry for silence which left time for many voices to have their say. This hint of Anne's that the world would make her suffer for what his carelessness had brought upon her, carried with it an almost unendurable sting. Under other circumstances he would have said to her, if not that hour, to-morrow, "I love you. Be my wife." But his duty to Hugh? Doubly bound, as he was, by the promise of his letter to abstain from any step until the answer had come, could he fling it to the winds, and forswear himself? The letter to which he looked for deliverance was but tightening his bonds. He was swayed this way and that, now swung low by such fretting thoughts, now conscious of mounting to heights of bliss in the warm fresh air, with the mountains and the water around, and Anne sitting close to—touching him. She said presently—

"We are the only thinking creatures in sight, and the world looks very big. Does it make you feel small or great?"

"It dwarfs one, doesn't it?"

"It seems to me as if I had seen it all before, and I have been trying to think where. I believe now that it was when I was a child, and sat solitary, reading Sinbad the Sailor. Perhaps there was some old picture, for certainly this takes me back to that."

"Were you solitary?"

"Very," Anne said, smiling. "I brought myself up, and very badly. Look behind. The mountains are closing; now that they have let us out, they shut their portals."

She was silent again, and Wareham, quick to read her moods, humoured her. The boat moved slowly along, slowly it seemed, when the great surroundings filled the eye. The heavens were blue, but here and there a white cloud drifted lazily, or caught the mountain snow-beds, and curled round them, like a vaporous reminder of their fate. The lovely vivid green of the young summer crept up and down the mighty hills, softening the rude scars of centuries until they looked no more than delicate and shadowy indentations; the stern granite blossomed into tender rose and grey, and the water-world below gave back all this and more. Every now and then the men who were rowing exchanged a word: they had grave steadfast faces.

"Talk to them," Anne said suddenly at last. "Ask them about their lives." Wareham struggled obediently.

"My questions are obliged to be simple," he said. "And I am even more anxious the answers should be. A universal language. Is it a dream?"

"We are pleased to infer that it is our own which will serve the purpose, but by the time the idea has developed into fact it may be Japanese."

"To become a ruling nation they will have been forced to adopt ours."

"Oh, British arrogance! However, I do not wish it. Uniformity is always dull, and I would rather suffer shame from my own ignorance than have all the world patted down to one dead level. There is dignity in the unknown. When I hear these men talk, I can't help imagining that what they say would be worth hearing, if I could only understand, though probably it is about nothing more valuable than as to how many gulden they may get for their hay, if, indeed, any of them ever sell anything. Do ask them that."

"I can't," Wareham confessed. "My conversation is chiefly made up of nouns and notes of interrogation."

"Well, what have you extracted?"

"Both are married. One has four children, who walk five kilometres to school every day of their lives. The other has a son, of course in America. He is a wood-carver, and hopes by the sale of his work to lay by enough to take him to Chicago."

Anne's eyes sparkled.

"Tell him I will buy a great deal. As soon as I meet my money again," she added, laughing. "Am I not to be allowed to assist?"

"I have nothing to do with your purchases," Anne said quietly. "I dare say you want something for your friends at home. Have you a great many?"

Wareham blurted out—"I have no greater friend than Hugh Forbes." Why he said it he could not tell. He had been forcing himself ever since they started to keep Hugh's image in mind, and his name leapt suddenly to his lips. Anne did not look discomposed.

"He is a very good fellow," she said, after a momentary hesitation.

"Yet you would not marry him?"

"It has puzzled you? It puzzled no one else. Blanche Martyn will tell you she knew how it must be from the first."

"Why?" asked Wareham, leaning forward with his arms on his knees, and staring at the bottom of the boat.

"You should ask her, not me. The accused is not bound to criminate herself."

"The accused! Good heavens, do you suppose!" he began passionately, then by a great effort stopped. Anne was looking at him through half-closed eyes.

"However," she went on, as if he had not spoken, "I will let you hear her explanation. She thinks I am a flirt."

"She is a detestable woman."

"Oh, no; and I believe her to be right. I told you just now that I had no sense of colour; well, I have a worse confession to make. I have no heart."

"One is as true as the other," Wareham protested stoutly. She shook her head.

"Possibly it may come. But as yet I am without it."

"You forget. You gave me another reason."

"That I did not care for him sufficiently. It surprised you. It might be a proof that what I tell you is no more than the truth. For it would be difficult to conceive any one more lovable."

Wareham's own heart agreed, but refused to accept the conclusion.

"Really," she said, "it was this charm of his which opened my eyes to my own want. I meant to marry, and so long as I did not dislike the man, would not trouble myself to think I need give him more. Suddenly I discovered I liked him too much to let him find himself in that position, and released him. It was the best act in my life, and it has alienated the friends who were most worth keeping."

Wareham's hopes met this dash of ice-cold water with a gallant effort for his friend. He turned pale, but muttered—

"You do not know yourself. You may love him yet."

"Never. All that I felt was that I could not feel."

She spoke with conviction, and the conviction roused traitors in his own heart, who repeated the sweet assurance again and again. As for her saying that she could not feel, he laughed the notion to scorn. Had he but the chance, he would teach her to feel, batter at her heart till it awoke with an ache to find itself captured. The danger was that before this happened his honour might have to hang its head, disgraced, for the frank confidence she showed seemed to bring her nearer and nearer, and made waiting harder. He hoped he had strength to be silent, for he dared not attempt to argue with her. With an abrupt movement he motioned to one of the men to cease rowing, and took his place. The strong regular play of the muscles came like a relief, but the other man, forced to a quicker stroke, presently remonstrated. Wareham asked whether it were impossible to sail, quicker movement seeming imperative. He knew what the answer must be when he put the question, for not a breath of wind stirred the glass of the fjord. After he had rowed for one man some time he relieved the other; if it had been possible he would have liked to have had it all on his shoulders. Anne said to him at last—

"You are putting such energy into your work that it tires me to look at you. Does half-an-hour more or less really mean so much?"

He laid down the oars, and came across the boat to her side.

"It means nothing, except that I felt the need of a spurt. We are close to Utne, where we should find a decent inn. Had you not better stop there and rest? You want food by this time."

"I would rather not stop. I have been eating biscuits, and you might as well follow my example."

"Suppose Mrs Martyn has waited?"

Anne meditated.

"Let us row near the shore. If any one belonging to us is there, they will see and make signs. But there will be no one."

There was not. Wareham would gladly have hailed Mrs Martyn, yet was conscious of a throb of delight when the pretty little village lay behind them. They were by this time in more open water, and the depression which had fastened on him fled away.

"What are your commands about your picnic?" he asked, smiling.

"Find out from the men if there is any place where we can land and boil some water." This took some time and a little guessing. Finally—

"I believe they say there is an island," said Wareham.

"I am sure there is."

"We should reach it in an hour."

He spent the hour in blissful dreams which, having been once routed, now trooped merrily back. Anne was generally silent, but when she spoke it was with the same friendly ease she had shown throughout the day, and she made no complaints of fatigue. Indeed, he classed her as a heroine when he reflected that she had uttered nothing in the shape of a grumble. Would not most women have indulged in something of the sort? Wareham liked to believe that they would, and exalted her accordingly for her forbearance. It was evening by the hours, and they were well in the Sogne fjord, when Anne pointed out the island towards which the boat was directed.

"Do you see?"

"I see a rock."

"And what else would you have in mid-water? If we can but find something to burn!"

"I believe there is a hut," said Wareham, curving his hands into a telescope.

"A solitary! Only this was wanted." Anne's face was radiant.

"He may drive us away."

"A man? Oh, no!" she laughed serenely.

Her confidence proved well-founded, for the Sogne fisherman, who leaped down the rocks to give the boat a helping hand, gave them a grave welcome. He was a wild figure with his scarlet jacket, brown breeches, and light hair under a broad hat. Anne looked at him appreciatively.

"I could not have dressed him better myself—for the piece," she said. "How odious I am to say so! It is one of the snares of over-civilisation that, instead of the theatre suggesting nature, nature suggests the theatre. This is all so natural that I feel we ought to be applauding."

She was stiff with sitting. Wareham gave her his hand to help her from the boat, and the light touch of her fingers thrilled him.

The island was no more than a rock, with scant herbage; a few goats and a dog shared it with the man; a boat was drawn up at one shelving point, and the low hut was formed of heaped pieces of rock and roofed with waving grass. There was no chimney; a hole in the roof sufficed for the smoke to pass through. Anne was as excited as a child. She unpacked her *tine*, and spread their meal on a rock. Wareham had to act as interpreter, and ask that a peat or two might be set ablaze to provide them with hot water; the man's good-will did not reach the point of making him hurry, but he watched Anne's quick deft movements with amusement. When all was ready they sat down together. Anne had brought a little tea-pot and two cups, Wareham a bottle of wine, which the men drank out of a rough mug; he could not give up the pleasure of letting Anne pour out tea for himself. It was a very frugal meal, added to, though it was, by dried fish; and when it was finished, she dispensed tobacco to the three men. It seemed she detested the smell; Wareham suggested their walking round the island until the pipes had been smoked. She hesitated, finally agreed.

They scrambled round to the western side, a filmy glory spread over the heavens, interrupted only by the swoop of a grey vapourish cloud. As it had been all along, what the waters saw they gave back again, so that the golden suffusion reached to their very feet. The near reflections were now dark.

"To live here alone! Can you conceive it?" Anne exclaimed.

"Not for one of us; but with so thin a population, solitude probably is second nature."

"Solitude would require thought, and thought culture."

"Work might take its place. Work here must be incessant. Relax it, and you die."

"Why not? What makes it worth while to live? Would any one miss him?"

"Depend upon it, he has a world of his own, but, why—"

He stopped suddenly. Anne looked at him in surprise.

"Why?" she repeated.

He had caught himself on the point of rushing into more personal speech, and the jerk with which he pulled himself up made him awkward.

"Why should we not ask him? For one thing, I imagine he does not stay in winter. He is only here for the fishing."

"Oh, winter! The very idea is terrible. Yet I should like to see this country in its own snow and ice. Warmly wrapped, I can fancy it bearable, even enjoyable."

"Yes. Cold is the rich man's luxury." He answered her mechanically, his thoughts flying impatiently to Hugh, picturing him receiving the letter, answering it. Anne looked at him in surprise, reading trouble in his face.

"Never a luxury to me," she said. "And it is growing cold now. Don't you think we may start?"

The red-coated fisherman put aside all thought of payment. Wareham had difficulty in making him accept a very trifling sum. He stood watching them, and, for a time, as long as they looked back, they saw him blackly silhouetted against the clear sky. Anne had wrapped herself in her furs; the great open fjord gradually paled, the sound of the oars seemed to grow louder; it was like a dream to Wareham, with something of the bondage, the confusion, and the fret of a dream, yet with its strange delight as well. Once or twice he and Anne exchanged words, once or twice he took the oars again; outlines grew vague, it was not dark overhead, but they felt as though they were rowing on into the night. Suddenly Anne looked up.

"The bottom of the boat is wet. Is that right?"

Wareham bent down and uttered an exclamation, for water was certainly oozing in, and under cover of the dusk had been unnoticed, until Anne moved her foot and touched it. He called one of the men, who made an examination.

"Is it a leak?" she asked presently.

Wareham spoke quietly.

"There is a cork acting as a plug, and it appears to be rotten. But you need not be alarmed."

"I am not alarmed. What shall you do? Try to land?"

There was a consultation.

"The men say we should gain very little. It is twelve o'clock, and Balholm is as near as any other place, so that they advise our going on. Of course one of us will keep close watch, and bale out what water comes in; also have something ready to serve as a plug. But I am afraid it adds to your discomfort."

"Oh no, I shall be admiring your resources. Don't leave me useless. Would you like me to act like the boy at the Dutch dyke?"

"I am sure you would," said Wareham, in a low voice which silenced her.

It was not very easy to find materials for the plug. Anne handed him her gloves, and he abstracted one, but was afraid of discovery if he kept the other. A felt hat belonging to one of the men was rolled as tightly as possible, and held ready; at the same time the men insisted that the cork should not be removed until absolutely necessary, and one was told off to bale and watch.

"All the sensations I imagined are going to be provided for us in miniature," said Anne, with a laugh. "A desert island, and a leaky boat in mid-ocean. Mr Wareham, you are a conjuror!"

"May the conjuring land you finally and safely at Balholm!"

"After which!" She laughed again.

Silence fell on them once more. One man was scooping up the water in the tin mug; it gurgled under his hand, and the splash of throwing it over followed. The fjord, in the clear semi-darkness, stretched into infinite distances, a wisp of cloud sailed slowly overhead, a pettish breeze blew chilly against Anne's cheek. She called across to Wareham — "There is a little wind. Can't we sail?"

"These fjords are treacherous. I dare not. You are not cold?"

She was, but she would not let him know it. It seemed to her that the quantity of water in the boat increased, but they laughed at her offer to assist in the baling. At the end of half-an-hour Wareham changed places with the man who was dipping. The change threw him again close to Anne, and facing her; it struck him that she looked alarmingly white.

"You are exhausted?" he asked anxiously. "You don't know how strong I am."

"I can't get them to quicken stroke. They are steady, but slow."

"Patience, patience!" He saw that she was smiling at him.

"You need not preach patience to me," he said, in a low voice. "So far as I am concerned, I should be very well pleased to go on like this for ever."

"There might be worse things," said Anne dreamily, and his head swam. He was silent because he dared not speak; his thoughts leapt forward to the time when he might call her his own; meanwhile surely this was the very bliss of misery! It was she who spoke next. "It is lighter," she said. "I verily believe the day is breaking."

Wareham consulted his watch.

"Yes, and in an hour we reach Balholm."

"Cork and all?"

"I think so."

"Tell me. Have we been in danger?"

"Not since you found it out, and we have had something ready. If it had suddenly given way, matters might have been different; but as it is, we have nothing to fear beyond the discomfort of a wet boat."

"And I suppose there will be some one about. Mr Grey calls this the Land of the Always-up."

"I suppose so. At any rate, we will get them up at Kviknaes'. Perhaps Mrs Martyn will have thought of you sufficiently to order a room to be kept for you. You ought to see Balholm now."

"There is too much mist."

Gradually this light mist melted, light laughed out, a wind swept the mountains and left them clear; everything was bathed in silvery radiance, the colours were delicate, the air vigorous and keen. Anne shivered.

"It is like one's lost youth," she said.

Her lost youth! Wareham lifted a look of reproach, but circumstances had come to the aid of his faltering resolution, since scooping water from the bottom of a boat is fatal to the sentimental view. Anne at last began to laugh at him.

"I am sure your back aches," she said.

"You may be sure. There is lost youth if you like," he answered, straightening himself, and stretching.

She advised him to change with a rower, but he would not. It was something to be near her, though he suffered for it twice over. And the strong heart of the morning showed his hopes in stouter aspect. Hugh would see that his cause was desperate, and generosity would not suffer him to wreck another life with his own. Before he left, Wareham had treated his friend's crushed heart with severity or lightness as need arose, now he allowed it to have been serious enough, but as serious as his—never! Nevertheless, he could not indulge undisturbed in the wild dreams of happiness which flitted through his head, for with them Hugh's face intruded itself.

And—the letter!

They were near the landing-place at Balholm, and fronted by the mountain with the strange cleft in its snowy summit. Mountain, field, the few red-roofed houses, the outstanding pier, were bathed in the glory of the sun, now hastening upwards. One or two figures stood looking at the oncoming boat.

Wareham flung a glance over his shoulder.

"They are expecting us," he said, "you see."

A shout came to them across the water—another. A thought startled him, he looked eagerly at Anne. She had her eyes fixed on the shore, some agitation had crept into them, and for a minute she did not speak.

"Who is it?" asked Wareham hoarsely, without turning round.

"It is Mr Forbes."

"Impossible!"

"See for yourself."

Chapter Ten
The Inconvenience of Two Heroes

At its best, the unexpected is apt to come off awkwardly, and here was more than one awkward element. When hearing distance was reached, they found that Hugh was speaking volubly —

"Are you all right? No one suffered? What a nuisance for you both! Bring the boat a little further on, Dick, and Miss Dalrymple will land more comfortably. Are you all right?" anxiously again.

"My dear fellow, we're in a water-logged boat," Wareham called out, not sorry that his words were truer than they would have been five minutes ago, for with his attention elsewhere a good deal of water had leaked in.

"Horrors!" cried Hugh, pressing forward, and ready to jump in to the rescue. "Is Miss Dalrymple wet?"

"I'm afraid so." Wareham was cool again outwardly. "Here, take this rope. Now, Miss Dalrymple, your foot here—so. You are cramped? Do not hurry. We shall not be swamped just yet."

He managed to put his hand for her to tread on, while Hugh eagerly helped her. In another moment men and all had scrambled on shore, and Hugh was shaking hands violently with his friend.

"I never was more annoyed than to hear what had happened, but I felt certain you'd come on, and have been on the look-out all night. They shouldn't have left you. It was too bad. Miss Dalrymple, are you sure you are not cold?"

"I am sure of nothing," said Anne, speaking for the first time. "May I inquire what extraordinary chance brought you to this place?" She looked rather amused than vexed.

"I heard you were here."

"How?"

"Wareham, like a good fellow, telegraphed."

Anne darted a look at him. He stood helpless. Explanation was impossible. She said only — "Oh!"

"Of course I couldn't be certain where I should strike across you," Hugh went on, "so I came straight up in the steamer, and asked as I came along. Some other friends of yours are here. They seemed awfully cut up about you. But pray, pray come at once to the hotel. I have made them keep coffee and cold meat ready, and your room is all right. Dick will see about those fellows."

He swept her away. Wareham stared after them, dumb wretchedness gnawing at his heart. Complications gathered round him. Anne might naturally resent what had the appearance of an act of treachery; and was this the end of the fair dream which had floated with him along the clear waters of the fjord? He stood reduced, insignificant, before Hugh's assertive energy. Of her his last view as she walked lightly away was a side-face turned inquiringly towards Hugh.

Wareham's mood might be painted black — of the blackest. If virtue does not always meet with a reward, she expects it, and grows huffy at non-fulfilment. He felt he had behaved well towards Hugh; an occasional slip of the tongue should not count in comparison with the many times that he had bridled it, and each of these times was quick to multiply itself. By dint of looking back he convinced himself that Hugh's debt to him was great.

It was one way of discharging it to be waiting at Balholm, at three o'clock in the morning, to hand Miss Dalrymple out of the boat!

The men paid, and left to make the boat water-tight, Wareham walked slowly up the short incline towards the inn. He lingered, from an irritable disinclination to see Anne and Hugh together again; but before he reached the door, Hugh came out to meet him like a bolt. He seized Wareham's hand and wrung it.

"My dear old fellow," he cried exultingly, "was ever anything in the world so amazingly lucky! I might have knocked about the country for a week without tumbling up against them, and of all the blessed moments for a man to arrive, just when she was a bit sore at their want of care!"

As Hugh paused to contemplate his good fortune, Wareham thrust in a question.

"What on earth made you go in for such a" — he would have liked to have said "preposterous," but left it out — "hurricane dash across the seas?"

"What else would you have expected when I had your telegram? Wasn't I just wild to get word with her again? And saw no chance of it. Look here, what food there is, is waiting for you in there. Come and eat. I've got to talk to some one about it all, and I'm not so unreasonable as to harangue a hungry man."

"More sleepy than hungry."

"Well, you must eat before you turn in."

"Has Miss Dalrymple had some food?" Hugh laughed joyously.

"Do you suppose I didn't see that she had all she wanted? It's gone up to her room, of course. She's got to pay that tribute to Mrs Grundy. Here you are; now what'll you have? Here's the landlord himself. Beer, sausage, kippered salmon, marmalade, coffee?"

Wareham made a selection; Hugh rattled on, helping himself meanwhile.

"I believe I'm as hungry as you are. Meat in this country is uneatable—or was yesterday," he added, with an exulting fling at his own change of mood; "but I can't understand that it isn't the orthodox breakfast-time. I suppose one must go to bed, but I shan't sleep—not a wink. I say, old fellow, it was awfully good of you to send me that telegram—awfully. And now you've seen Anne—"

"Anne? Is she Anne again?"

"She's never been anything else in my heart. Now you'll understand. Enough to throw a man off his balance, wasn't it?—to think of losing her. She's splendid. And to tell you the truth, I've been fretting myself with the idea she might be annoyed at seeing me here at her heels."

"Well?"

"Try the salmon? No? You'd better. What was I saying? Oh, I believe she was rather pleased than otherwise. Women are not to be counted on. They'll fight you, but they like to be taken by storm."

Wareham agreed with a groan, thinking of himself in the boat. Hugh went on—

"She didn't seem a bit vexed. But as I said before, I couldn't have chosen a better moment if I'd waited a year. Selfish pig, that Mrs Martyn. I don't believe she cared one halfpenny. Those other people, Ravenstones, Ravenhills—what are they called?—were twice as feeling. The mercy was that it was you, old fellow, and no other man, who was with her."

It was impossible to keep back a sharp "Why?"

Hugh laughed.

"You've never seen me a prey to the yellows, but I can imagine myself in their clutches. Another man would have meant possibilities. No, I'm grateful."

Wareham had a horrible impulse to cry out, "Fool!" and this to his friend. Instead of it, he said—"You'd better bottle up your gratitude till you know it's due." He would have liked to let out more, but how?

"I'm not afraid. And I tell you what, I'm glad for another reason. You can't have seen her for all these hours without understanding something of her charm. Where are your prejudices now? But I won't reproach you. You've done me too good a turn. By Jove, it's hard work waiting, even if only a few hours!"

He had his elbows on the table, his chin in his hands. Wareham pushed back his chair and stared at him with something of the feeling of a man who, worsted, yet will look his fate in his face. He knew his age—eight-and-twenty—but never before had he seen him as the very incarnation of youth. It could be read in every line, in the twist of his shoulders, in the spring of his thick wavy hair, in the attitude, half comical, half petulant. He was tall, and his shoulders prognosticated size; fair as a northerner, and clean-faced; grey-eyed and wide-mouthed. Wareham, with thirty not long left behind him, felt an absurd envy of his three years' advantage. He stood up suddenly.

"Look here, Hugh, I'm done. I'm going to bed."

"All right, old fellow. You do look a bit seedy. Shall I come up and see that they've treated you properly? Say the word, and I will."

"For heavens sake, no."

"You'd rather tumble in at once? Good. I haven't said half there is in my head, but I dare say you think it'll keep. I don't know what I'll do. Lie down, I suppose; but there's a bath-house out there on the pier, and I feel more like a swim. You won't try that instead?"

"Bed," said Wareham laconically.

"Bed it is, then. I'd better show the way in this rabbit-warren. You're close to me."

"Kviknaes will come. He and I are old friends."

It was difficult to shake off Hugh's good-will. Wareham had no inclination for sleep, but imperative need to be alone, to meet these disjointed fancies which had neither sense nor sequence, yet threatened mastery. Kviknaes, smiling hospitably as though four o'clock in the morning were the usual hour for receiving guests, showed him his little room, the same as he had had there once before. It looked out on the great fjord, now lying in sunniest radiance. Evidently Hugh, from the next room, had spied the boat coming over the waters, and timed his own departure to the landing-place. Wareham decided, with a grim smile, that Anne doubtless credited him with a night watch on the shore.

This was the first consolatory reflection, and it was petty enough.

It allowed entrance, however, to others. His mind was like an American house with the valves for hot and cold air both open; cold and heat rushed in in brisk emulation. Out of sight of Hugh, out of hearing his transports, with the shining waters before him across which he and she had floated, he wondered at his own sudden dejection, and rated it as cowardly. The world's veriest fledgeling would have borne himself more bravely. Say that Hugh was there, say that Anne encountered him without displeasure, what did that prove? Did he expect her to frown, to hurl reproach? He eluded that second speech of hers in the boat, which had fallen icily; he went back to her confession that Hugh bored her. That had seemed to him decisive. A woman does not marry the man who bores her, except for cogent reasons, which he would not hold of possible weight with Anne. He bored her, she had flung up her engagement and fled. There was the long and short of it. Nothing was altered, and out jumped a hundred excellent little arguments protesting that nothing ever should alter.

But the worst of these Jack-in-the-box puppets is that a very little sends them in again. Opportunity—golden opportunity—had been his, when his hands were tied; would she ever come again? How was Anne to know what point of honour checked words, looks? If she did know—there was the rub!—would she accept it as valid reason? Down, dismally down, went the poor puppets, one after the other. She would not, she could not!

If that had been all! But he knew that he was turning his back upon the worst difficulty.

What would happen when the unconscious Hugh received that letter which was off on its travels after him, and which sooner or later must come into his hands. What should he do? Forestall it? Stand aside and wait?

Regrets, forebodings scourged him. If he had spoken he might have won her. Faith to his friend—which he could not have failed in without being false to himself—had probably lost her. And in spite of all, there was that in the situation which might cause Hugh to think him a traitor.

The varying sensations of the day had battered him into a condition more nearly approaching exhaustion than he knew. Sleep came before he had formed plans for his waking, and he was only aroused by Hugh thundering at his door.

"Slept well? So have I. Like a top. Come along down to the bath-house."

Wareham dispatched him with promise to follow. Waking, as often happens, had brought decision, so that he shook himself free of the foggy doubts which beset him a few hours before. There could be no question of Hugh's prior rights. He had nothing to do but to stand aside, and hold his tongue. As for the letter, it must be left to its fate. Long before it reached Hugh, that impetuous young man would have carried or lost the day, and Wareham had sufficient faith in his friend's warm-heartedness to believe that he would understand, too. That, for the moment, was of greater consequence. He walked slowly down to the pier of black piles, where a red-tiled building is picturesquely perched, revolving other people's possible actions. They are wheels which we can drive with fewer jolts than our own. And the pure fresh air, the sparkling gaiety of the morning had their effect. They intoxicated Hugh. Wareham, who had a stronger head, felt their influence more subtly. Thoughts of escape had fluttered before him; now he would have none of them. Stand aside he must, but from where he stood he could see and measure, and that alone was an incalculable advantage.

Chapter Eleven
Catechisms

Breakfast was going on, and merrily, to judge from the rush of voices which met Wareham when he opened the door. His friends were there together, and a place was kept for him next the Ravenhills; opposite were Mrs Martyn, Anne, and Hugh. As he took his seat, Mrs Martyn spoke across the table.

"Pretty proceedings, Mr Wareham!"

"They did not cause you disturbance?" he asked, with a simulated anxiety which sent round a smile.

"Nothing serious. I believed either of you equal to the task of looking after the other. Which took the lead?"

Anne's clear voice struck in—

"We shared. I claim the suggestion of dinner at Gudvangen. Mr Wareham was too much overwhelmed by the misadventure to preserve his presence of mind."

"But that was before starting. I can't conceive how you survived so many hours!" Wareham perceived that the incident of the island had not been offered to Mrs Martyn's consideration. His heart congratulated itself. Hugh's indignation rushed in pointedly.

"It's true enough that Miss Dalrymple wanted something by the time she got here." He muttered to Anne—"Much she had ready for you!"

"I think you were to be envied," Mrs Ravenhill said. "The fjord was so beautiful that I hated being carried through it at a rush. And night here is little more than a quiet day."

"Only too short," agreed Anne. "The sun was upon us before it seemed possible."

Wareham's prescribed attitude of bystander did not preclude his sucking in these little, sweets of comfort with delight. But Mrs Martyn had not done with him.

"What were the charms of Gudvangen, Mr Wareham, which made you so oblivious?"

"Poor Gudvangen! If you speak of it in that tone, I shall believe it was you who bribed, the captain to start an hour earlier than his right time."

Millie put in a fluttering word.

"It was a delightful place."

"To Mr Wareham's companions." Malice lurked in Mrs Martyn's sentences. Millie coloured, Anne sat indifferent, Hugh it was who answered.

"No wonder. But I get so called over the coals for want of punctuality that I vow I can't help being tickled that Wareham should be the sinner. How was it? Had a brown study got over him, Miss Dalrymple: Or did anybody fall asleep?"

"I think we were all to blame," said Mrs Ravenhill kindly. "We should have made sure that every one was on board. To tell the truth, I did not for a moment believe that we had really started."

Anne spoke again, languidly.

"Is not the subject threadbare? You will force Mr Wareham or me into invention of adventures, since there is nothing real to relate that we can flatter ourselves would interest you."

The we and ourselves fell delightfully on Wareham's ears.

"My dear Anne, you don't do yourselves justice. Mr Forbes is dying to know how you were occupied when you should have been at the steamer."

Anne lifted her eyebrows.

"Mr Forbes?" she said questioningly.

He hurried to disclaim.

"Not I. I am only glad you had Wareham to look after you." Under his breath he grumbled, "Confound her!"

Why might he not be left alone? His own resources would carry him like the trustiest steed through the tilting which he foresaw ahead, but to be forced into a position he had no mind for, to be treated as though he were a jealous ass, and so thrust against Anne's susceptibilities, was sure to irritate her. If a wish could have swept Mrs Martyn out of Norway, she would have found herself at this moment in England again. Wareham, equally irritated, knew that it was for him to speak.

"It was simple enough," he said. "We had strolled out of sight or hearing of the steamer, believing that she would not start for an hour and a half. At the end of an hour we found you had all flown. We wanted Colonel Martyn to look us up."

"Yes. Tom is always ready to undertake other people's business," said Mrs Martyn, helping herself to marmalade.

"Do you expect him to-day?" Mrs Ravenhill put in, conscious that her neighbour would prefer a change of subject.

"To-night at latest. Unless missing steamers should be in the air."

She looked meaningly at Wareham. He turned to Millie.

"Have you thought out any plans for to-day?"

"We meant to explore the place a little this morning, and go to Fjaerland by the evening steamer. It is a pity we can't sleep there and see the glaciers, but as it is we must just go up the fjord and down again. Mother was out early this morning."

"Sketching?"

"Yes. She likes it immensely here."

"And you?"

"Not so well as Gudvangen. But it *is* very nice, and"—regretfully—"it is so near the end!"

"How?"

Millie sighed. That he should have forgotten that they were to start for England on Friday, and this was Tuesday! But no ill-humour crept into her voice.

"You know we go to Bergen to-morrow night, then home."

"I had forgotten," said Wareham, staring at his plate. "Isn't it a very short stay?"

"Only a fortnight. But that I can hardly believe."

"Nor I."

"I suppose you will go further north, with the Martyns?" hazarded Millie.

He said abruptly, "I know nothing," and checked her.

Their opposite neighbours rose and departed, Hugh flinging an ecstatic look at Wareham as he went. Wareham's spirits sank to mute misery. Anne's side allusions had been kindly, but she had not dropped one direct word for him to live upon, and fear of letting honour slip must prevent his seeking it. He writhed under the thought that she yet believed him to have summoned Hugh, and a hundred voices within him seeming to clamour for the right to put this one thing straight, he found it hard to silence them.

Breakfast over, Mrs Ravenhill and Millie vanished, giving him to understand that the sketch had to be finished.

"But I dare say we shall soon meet again," Mrs Ravenhill said, "for here again there is not much choice of roads, and I am sitting humbly by the roadside."

Wareham went off like a moth to get close to what hurt him.

She was not to be seen, however, nor Hugh either, so that though he was not scorched, he suffered from another kind of smart, and it did not soothe him to drop upon Mrs Martyn seated in one of the many balconies. He would have escaped, but she saw and captured him.

"I want to speak to you, Mr Wareham; pray come and sit down. We shall all be starting out in an hour's time. Meanwhile, here we may have a few minutes' peace."

He could not excuse himself, and sat down reluctantly.

"I am not going to scold you about yesterday," she said, "although I think you will allow I might."

"You do not accuse me, I hope, of premeditation?"

She professed not to be certain, but glancing at Wareham's face, dropped her attempt at jocularity.

"I dare say it was Anne's fault. She is astonishingly wilful."

"I thought I had made it clear that the mistake was all my own. You must be well aware that Miss Dalrymple had the right to be excessively annoyed."

Mrs Martyn smiled.

"Anne would not trouble herself about talk, if that is what you mean. She has proved herself absolutely indifferent. She will do the same here."

Spite of himself, he looked up eagerly.

"Yes. Of course I speak of young Forbes. Her friends will not thank me when they hear that I have allowed him to tack himself on to us."

The traitor in Wareham mentally blessed these friends, though his better instincts forced him to say —

"Why? Hugh is an only son, his father a baronet, and he what the world calls a good match."

Mrs Martyn turned her large fair face towards him, and raised her eyebrows.

"Middling. No objection was made when Anne said she would marry him. But she let matters go too far, even for her, this time, and naturally they won't be pleased to have it all over again. Mr Forbes says you telegraphed to him. I wish you had left it alone."

"Pray don't think I telegraphed to him to come. It was the last thing I desired."

"I should have imagined so," said Mrs Martyn dryly.

Wareham bit his lip.

"One must keep a promise."

"Must one?"

"You will allow that the manner in which Miss Dalrymple broke off her engagement was maddening for my friend? Not an interview, not a word, only complete annihilation of all that had passed. Of course, from her own point of view, she may have been justified. I say nothing of blame."

Mrs Martyn smiled. Wareham had seldom found his own temper so tried as in this interview. He felt as if her great hat had an irritating personality, and crushed him.

"You may know, or you may not know, that the blow to him was so serious that it brought me back from India."

"Isn't there such a thing as a ricochet?" asked Mrs Blanche innocently, so innocently that the innocence tickled him.

"I am afraid there is," he admitted with candour. "Shall I go on?"

"Oh, by all means. You had just landed from India?"

"Miss Dalrymple allowed Hugh no communication. He could not even find out where she went when she left London. It seemed to me that he had a right to learn her reasons for dismissal, and I assured him when I quitted him that he should hear from me if I had any news of her whereabouts."

"I could not have believed that Lady Dalrymple's servants were so above suspicion." Mrs Martyn heaved a sigh at recollection of her own.

He went on to say that finding Miss Dalrymple had crossed in the same boat with himself, he telegraphed to Hugh from Stavanger. He knew of no other course he could have taken. And he descanted on it, intending all to be told to Anne. He finished up by repeating that no idea of Hugh's coming had crossed his mind.

"I dare say not. Magnanimity has limits," she murmured.

Thinking it well to turn a deaf ear, he added that he had written a letter of some importance to Mr Forbes from Stalheim.

"From Stalheim?" She appeared to meditate, looking at her own hands, which were very small. Then her question flashed out.

"Was it to say you were in love with Anne?"

Wareham had got himself in hand by this time. He bowed.

"That or anything else you please, Mrs Martyn."

She asked whether the letter had reached Hugh.

"How should it? He left England immediately after my telegram, and there has been no time."

Mrs Martyn looked out at the fjord, but Wareham saw her shoulders shaking. Tragedy was uppermost with him, and at this proof of heartlessness he thought appreciatively of Millie's padded glass. She turned round, however, demurely composed.

"Won't it be a little inconvenient, by and by?"

He gazed loftily over her head.

"I don't know that we are immediately concerned with my letter. That, at any rate, cannot be accused of bringing Hugh."

"I wish something would take him away again. I had not the smallest intention of being mixed up with one of Anne's complicated affairs," cried Mrs Martyn.

The speech jarred.

"If his presence is disagreeable to Miss Dalrymple, she can certainly send him off. He will have had his explanation. Perhaps it will prove the shortest way out of the difficulty."

This laid him open to an embarrassing question, "What difficulty?" Fortunately for Wareham, she did not wait for an answer before putting another. "Are you a writer of books?"

"I can't deny it?"

"Yet read a woman's nature no better! Anne will not send him off."

"Accept him, then."

"Nor accept him."

"Paddles!"

"If you had studied the genus as you should for your profession, Mr Wareham, you would not find the riddle hard to solve. Anne likes Mr Forbes enough to like to have him about her, but she would not marry him, because she could not endure fetters. Now she salves her conscience by thinking that she has done her best to give him time to recover; you and fate have baffled her, and she—will enjoy herself."

He forced himself to say quietly—

"You describe a—"

"Flirt. Anne would not deny it if you charged her."

Her words in the boat were recalled by a reluctant memory; with them came the charm of her voice, her smile, more powerful than words. He started up, and stood leaning against the railing of the balcony.

"It comes to this. You and I read differently. I think you unjust to your friend, you hold me a fool. Of the two, I prefer the *rôle* of fool. But whichever turns out right, I don't see that we can do anything except wait, for it is certainly Miss Dalrymple who must tell Hugh to go or stay. Unless you have that authority?"

"I!" She shook her head. "Anne's chaperons are dummies, they don't interfere. Besides, I couldn't be bothered. I don't even know why I have talked to you, except that A one and Mr Forbes will not be amusing companions this morning."

Wareham was cheered by the touch of feminine spite in this speech, the more so as he had seen Hugh cross the garden forlornly. He inquired what might be Mrs Martyn's plans for the future.

"I suppose my husband will return to-day, and then I shall insist upon going as far as Vadheim to-morrow night. Do you mean to come with us to the Geiranger? You had better, for I can't be responsible for your friend."

"Thanks. But I shall get back this week." Decision had stepped in so promptly that there was no time for regret to interpose, although she hung helplessly on his skirts. Mrs Martyn raised her eyebrows.

"You go with the Ravenhills? They mean to secure berths in the *Ceylon*, which is expected here to-day."

"I dare say that will suit me."

When he left her he would not seek Hugh, but went to the little office from whence letters are dispensed, with a feeble dream of lighting upon his own. Failing in this he betook himself to the road, and presently came upon Mrs Ravenhill sketching, and Millie enticing half-a-dozen small children away from her mother by means of barley-sugar. The girls hushed themselves with awe and delight, the boy, all one broad laugh, flourished sticky fingers, and threatened to descend upon the paper, in spite of reproachful cries of "*Daarlig Olaf!*" At sight of Wareham he fled.

"And I breathe," said Mrs Ravenhill.

"But he was much the nicest," declared Millie. "All the grown-up people are so grave, that it is a comfort to see one having a good time while he is young. He was not really so very naughty, though his sisters were dreadfully scandalised. Think of their all living in those lovely cottages!"

And indeed the group of houses which Mrs Ravenhill was drawing made a perfectly harmonious note of colour. The sky delicate broken grey, the hill behind, grey also, running down in fine outline; against this a group of houses, red-roofed one or two, timber-pitched another, gabled, white-plastered, jutting out, running back, and set in waving emerald rye. Where the rye ended, long flowery grass began, and grew down to the foot of the bank where the children were playing. A woman with a white handkerchief on her head, and carrying two pails with a yoke, came down the little path which the thick grass hid from view; the swift-driven clouds cast swift soft shadows, the air was sweet with hay-making.

Wareham was in the state of mind when this soothed, because it seemed apart from the world of men and women, as represented by Mrs Martyn. He had gone to her feeling that the dearest part of him was sacredly wrapped up and invisible, and with shaking shoulders she had plucked it forth, and given him to understand that she knew all about it. The man must be more than usually magnanimous who does not chafe at insight from which he suffers. Here were women who made no pretence at insight. With them he felt healthfully at ease. And so scaly-strong is the coating behind which we flatter ourselves we are entrenched, that nothing could have more amazed him than to know that Millie, simple soul, read through him as easily as, and more truly than Mrs Martyn. He said suddenly at last—

"How do you return to England, Mrs Ravenhill?"

"Not as we came." She shuddered. "The *Ceylon* tourist steamer will be here to-day. I am told that she is an old P. and O., and very comfortable, and that we can get berths in her."

"But you don't go on board to-day?" Brace himself he must, but hardly to the extent of leaving so abruptly.

"No. We shall meet her at Bergen on Friday."

He asked to be allowed to take their berths, and let fall something to the effect that if there was another to spare, he might secure it for himself.

"You will have had a short holiday." Mrs Ravenhill added a little vermilion to her roofs, and sighed hopelessly over the flowery grass. Millie tried to check her heart's throb.

"You come to Fjaerland to-day?" she hazarded.

They were all to go, it appeared, and Wareham agreed eagerly. What did it matter so long as he refrained from a word? Of course he would go. He sunned himself in the anticipation.

Chapter Twelve
An Air with Variations

The day had passed with little to mark it to Wareham, to whom events meant a word from Anne. They met at early dinner as they had met at breakfast, and again he had to content himself with indirect speeches. In the afternoon the *Ceylon* came in and anchored; Wareham went off and secured three berths. He felt himself a model friend, but this did not prevent his looking forward eagerly to the evening. Colonel Martyn was the next to arrive.

At six o'clock came the Gudvangen steamer, which was to take them to Fjaerland. Anne and Colonel Martyn were the last to come on board, Hugh fuming impatiently until they appeared. He surrounded her with solicitude.

"I almost gave you up. I thought you had changed your mind."

"If I had?"

She tossed the words at him as she passed.

"We might have taken a boat and repeated yesterday," said Hugh daringly.

"I hate repetitions."

Wareham heard and chuckled. But where is your woman's consistency? The next moment she had given her young lover a smile which put the other man's blood into a fever. Hugh looked round at him radiantly. Mrs Martyn eyed him with an experienced glance expressive to Wareham of "You see!" He walked away.

When he came back the group had been enlarged by several of the other people from the inn, who were making the same little voyage. An elderly man, with a keen clever face, held forth to Mrs Martyn, and Wareham was not ill-pleased to note that the lady showed signs of discomfiture. He interrogated her closely, would have chapter and verse with her statements, and ruthlessly fastened on the futility of certain vague expressions in which she took refuge. Wareham stood for a minute receiving broken sentences from the group, except when Anne spoke, upon which the other voices faded into indistinctness.

"Nothing in Norway to compare with Scotland."

"Well, I don't know. There's good—"

"Didn't you hear? She is expected to-morrow, and great preparations—"

"Horrible food!"

Then a voice like a bell.

"I half wish we were going home in her, she looks so big and so roomy."

Only the foolishness of love could make music out of this every-day remark, but to his ear it sounded in sweet relief to the clatter of the others. So sad is the eclipse of friendship before the greater light, that he was conscious of a wish to swing Hugh out of his place by her side, and stand there himself. Had not he had his chance and failed? To be swaggering round, and playing dog in the manger, was an unworthy solace. To be compelled to hover near with a heart full of yesterday, was to munch ashes. For let philosophers say what they will, the past is at best unsatisfying food, but a past which has no more substance than hope unfulfilled, chokes you with its dusty remembrances. Wareham went restlessly about the vessel, talking to the red-faced burly captain of the *Kommodoren*, to any one: wherever he went he saw Hugh's spirited figure, Anne's pale clear-cut profile, and these two only. At last, as he was speaking to an elderly lady with a sweet kind face, he surprised her by quitting her suddenly. Opportunity had come, and he flew to Anne's side.

"At last!" he cried, and had to check his exultation. "I thought I should never be allowed to speak to you alone!"

"After yesterday you could scarcely complain of that difficulty." Anne was smiling, her eyes were half-shut.

"Yesterday!" He made an impatient gesture.

She asked whether it was so long ago?

"Half a lifetime," he answered boldly, and had a wild fancy that a tremulous colour just crept into her cheek. But she hastened to inquire whether he did not find the scenery very fine?

"I have not seen it."

"Where have your eyes been?"

"On my heart," would have been a true answer. He pressed it back and muttered, "I have been wanting to say a word, but Hugh monopolised you."

"Your friend. You should have been satisfied. But tell me what you wanted so much to say?"

"You heard his greeting. Did you imagine that I had told him to come out?"

"It surprised me."

"Pray let me hear that you thought better of me than to believe it."

"Better? Do you not present yourself as a symbol of friendship? And friendship is held to condone blunders." She spoke teasingly.

"No, no. I telegraphed—" Suddenly he found it hard to explain why he had telegraphed. "He had a right to an explanation." The words came out apologetically.

"And you were the *deus ex machinâ*. I told you you were a symbol of friendship."

Coldness was in her voice, and Wareham, reader of hearts, believed he understood why she was dissatisfied.

"I have offended you. I read it in your eyes when you saw Hugh," he said dismally.

"Oh, Hugh, Hugh!" She made the exclamation with impatience, and frowned.

He would have given worlds to ask why, if she were displeased, she did not dismiss her young lover, but dared not. Then she slowly let drop four words which set his blood leaping in wild bounds. "You might help me."

Heavens, what did the words, the look she turned on him, mean? Reproach, encouragement, were both there. He stood stupidly, stunned by the delicious shock; conscience faltered, passion rushed to the attack. This appealing to him, this, as it were, holding out her hand—bliss!—ecstasy! Conscience panted out desperately, "And Honour?" and, once having thrust in her word, stood firm.

Wareham felt as if in that minute he had lived a year. When he spoke his voice was hoarse, his face white.

"I cannot," he said. "It rests with yourself."

She was looking at him, and her face did not change, nor did she speak. They stood silent, fronting the mountains, and presently Hugh's voice sounded cheerfully behind them.

"I can't find your parasol, Miss Dalrymple. Mrs Martyn thinks you must have left it behind."

"Ask her whether it is not her umbrella she wants," had been Mrs Martyn's exact words, for neither sun nor rain was likely to trouble them.

These he did not repeat. He was sharp enough to guess that he had been disposed of for a motive, but hugged the thought that it was merely caprice which had served this purpose. For caprice he was prepared, resolved that it should not put him out of countenance. An indefinite presentiment kept Wareham on the watch. It was a nothing, yet it had fallen on a crucial moment. How would she behave to Hugh? The next moment, Anne turned, smiling carelessly.

"I am ashamed to have troubled you, and for what seemed an absurdity. Who wants a parasol at such an hour? It is that I am a baby, and like something in my hand." Hugh was for starting off again. "No, no, no more errands. You may sit here and tell me about the Standishs'. When did you see them? Have they gone abroad? Mary wrote a line to me before we left England, but she told me nothing of their plans."

"And they knew nothing of yours," stammered Hugh the happy, afraid of uttering anything which carried the ghost of a reproach. Mary Standish was to have been their bridesmaid.

Wareham would hear no more. He wheeled round and departed, with not a word of thanks to cast at conscience, though she had saved him from a scrape. Going forward, he stood moodily watching the pallor creep over the vast snowfield which runs along the western side of the fjord, and from which glaciers like pale ghosts crawl down to the water. At Fjaerland itself there was a short stoppage, people came on board who had tramped to the Suphelle glacier, and were enthusiastic over its beauties to those who had not seen it.

And now, in going back, the glories of the sunset touched each opening fjord with strange variety of effect and contrast. One had wild and menacing clouds sweeping on with threat of storm; in another the mountains lay in indescribable calm against a clear daffodil sky; a third again was radiant with light, and crowned with floating rosy clouds. Voices hushed themselves, the ripple of the water grew more insistent, lovely reflections trembled downwards. By and by a green promontory was passed, and Balholm stood hospitably alight.

"Nine o'clock," sighed Colonel Martyn, with disconsolate acceptance of his fate, the high tea which he hated. Meantime the professor had asked Mrs Martyn—who piqued herself upon her facts—if she knew the number of square miles covered by the snow-area at which they had been gazing.

She had an impression it was five hundred.

"An impression!" He was scornful. Women's knowledge invariably consisted of impressions. Mrs Martyn, who liked to be rude herself, was always crushed by retaliation in the same coin. She escaped, and clung to Mrs Ravenhill.

"My dear, protect me! That man is a bear. He can never have been used to any society at all. Everything that I say to him he contradicts flatly, and comes out with the most disagreeable speeches! I daren't say a word. He frightens me. And why does he choose me—poor, inoffensive me?"

Anne, as she walked up from the landing-place, got hold of Millie.

"You are really going to break away to-morrow? I envy you."

"I am sorry," Millie said simply. "There is so much more which I want to see."

Anne answered her abruptly—

"It is like everything else. Life is just an air with variations, and you get sick of the air. I am tired of mountains and fjords. More tired of hearing people cry, 'How beautiful!'"

"When they say it of yourself?"

"Most of all. Yet when it doesn't come, I miss it." She laughed.

"Ah, I can't help you," Millie returned.

"What is it you want?"

"To be what I am not—what I never shall be."

They were at the door. Anne ran up-stairs, Millie dropped her defensive armour with a sigh. She had somehow expected, and dreaded, that when Anne spoke of their leaving, she would allude to Wareham. Now that she had not done so, she was disappointed.

Wareham was caught by Hugh Forbes as he went out of the saal.

"Come for a turn, old fellow," he besought. "There are a hundred things I want to say to you."

"Hadn't you better go after Miss Dalrymple?" said Wareham sharply.

"She won't let me. Says she's had enough of me for to-day."

Hugh laughed, and Wareham hesitated. Self-flattery murmured that possibly she had intended this half-hour for him, and the thought fell sweet as honey drops. But away from her charm, her beauty, conscience was not to be beguiled. Avaunt, tempter! Step forth, honour! Dull paths are safest, and the dullest of all dull paths appeared this walk with Hugh, Anne left behind in a balcony overlooking shining waters.

They were out, with Hugh anxiously asking why he must go to-morrow?

"Its an awful nuisance," he burst out, "and I do think it's hard on a fellow to be left unsupported just at this ticklish point. You could be of untold good—you have been already, of that I'm certain. Anne likes you, and likes to talk of you. Now a great blundering fellow might have done a lot of mischief. Crammed me down her throat, or tried to cut me out. I vow I wouldn't have trusted any one but you yesterday in the boat. When I heard that she was coming along with some man, I was awfully cut up, I can tell you; and Mrs Martyn never let out who it was. Just like the woman! It was Miss—what's she called?—Ravenstone who cleared me up. Why don't you take to that little girl? A good soul, with a heart of gold, and a dimple. I've heard you say you loved dimples, and, upon my soul, I never saw a prettier."

Wareham's irritated exclamation was restrained by the recollection that here was the very suggestion which he had intended for Hugh himself, presented topsy-turvily. He was forced to laugh.

"Arrange matters for yourself, only leave me out of the pattern, for I don't harmonise."

Hugh rushed into farther confidences, but owned that he was in a funk.

"If I could but imagine what upset the coach last time," he complained, "I'd take good care to avoid it again; but I give you my word you know as much as I do. She won't speak of it, won't listen, won't so much as drop me a hint; and to think of her bolting again puts me in such a devil of a fright that I daren't hold on to the subject. Now, Dick, if you'd stay and sound her a bit, I should be awfully obliged to you."

That or any other subject. His heart jumped like a hungry dog, grateful for a bone. He had to recall himself to his resolve.

"Can't."

"Don't tell me you're not your own master."

"No man is his own master that has set his shoulder to the wheel."

"Well"—Hugh walked on, revolving—"there are twenty-four hours yet; you may get a chance in that time."

Wareham was stung into exclamation.

"You don't know what you're asking!"

"I know exactly; and it isn't much for a clever fellow like you. You can understand that when I go pottering round, she sees exactly what's coming, and shies. As likely as not, she doesn't want to hurt my feelings—"

"Oh, your feelings! She didn't show much regard for your feelings when she flung you over!" cried Wareham savagely.

"No, but look here, old fellow, you mustn't be so prejudiced. It was natural enough when you didn't know her, and I shan't forget what you did for me in those black days, but I did think that once you were thrown with her you would have your eyes opened, and appreciate her."

Wareham looked queerly at him.

"How do you know I don't?"

"Because then you wouldn't blame her. And I believe you'd stick to me now. At first I could think of nothing but that I was near her again, and could look at her; but finding out how gingerly I've got to move, makes me uneasy. If you were here you'd give me a wrinkle or two. Come, Dick, think better of it." Hugh decapitated an inoffensive ox-daisy as he spoke. "You needn't expect to put me off with talk of business. Don't I know most of your affairs?"

"Not all." Wareham's voice had grown gentler. "Hugh, do you remember my telling you that I had written a letter?"

"To me?"

"Yes."

"I recollect. It had slipped my memory."

"I wish I could prevent its ever reaching you."

Hugh burst into his cheery laugh.

"That's what I feel sometimes when I've sent off an epistle to the pater. But you don't suppose anything you said to me would make me cut up rough?"

"When you've got it you'll understand why I go," the other went on, unheeding.

"Mysteries, mysteries!"

It must be owned that Wareham thought his speech would have thrown a little light. He breathed hard, and his face flushed. Hugh went on—

"I know you've thought hard things of Anne. But, old fellow, you've never failed me yet; and that's why I want you now. You could say what I can't say myself."

"What one can't say oneself had better remain unsaid." Something in the tone penetrated, and gave the young man a tinge of uneasiness.

"You don't mean that you think—" He stopped aghast.

Wareham answered with a hand on the valve. If his words were to fly, it should not be on a wrong tack.

"What?"

"That, after all, I've no chance?"

"Heavens, man, how should I think such a thing! I know nothing of what you have said to her, or she to you. You've got your opportunity—what more do you want? Go in, and win."

"All right, old fellow," Hugh said good-humouredly. "May you be a true prophet. Anyway, don't be put out about your letter. I've a thick skin, as you've proved before now. And if it bores you to stop, go. Only if you do get the chance before leaving, and if you can get her to give you a bit of explanation, it may make matters smoother. Isn't there some old Viking or other buried about here? Well, we'll go back."

As they returned they found signs of festivity about the rival inn; Balholm sat round the walls of the saal, and in the centre a picturesque musician played the Hardanger fiddle; the wild piercing sounds, half savage, half plaintive, penetrated the night. Wareham stood at the door after Hugh had left him, held by some spell for which he could not account. The music conjured up strange imaginings—the silence of the mountains encompassed lonely fjords; pallid snowflakes chased each other into clefts, where they lay shrouding the rock; winds whistled through cowering trees, and in a moment the cruel howl of a wolf rose menacingly above the other sounds. The tragedies of the country had found a voice in the wild, almost discordant, instrument. Wareham stood absorbed, staring at the ground. When the music stopped, he looked up uncertainly. Hay sweetened the air, golden light still lingered in the sky, yet he shivered. The landlord came out. Wareham gave him a gulden for the musician, and walked slowly back to his own quarters.

Chapter Thirteen
Persuasion

The next day the wreathing mists which lightly swept the mountains had gathered moisture enough to descend in thick rain. It fell continuously, but was still so vapourish that there was as much white as grey everywhere, and the sun behind the clouds suffused them with dazzling light.

The broad fjord presented enchantingly ethereal and aerial effects. A grey veil blurred the heights on its other side, but here and there a mysterious gleam of whiteness shot out from their snowy summits, radiantly piercing the gloom. Silvery lights fell across the faint grey of the waters, which changed to opal nearer shore, and took in places a clear transparent emerald-green. A rough ridge of stone walled in a small harbour, and here were boats drawn up, black, green, white, sharp points of contrast to the delicate half-tones beyond.

The covered balconies of the inn were thronged with dissatisfied travellers, casting gloomy glances at the falling rain.

"Detestable climate," muttered Colonel Martyn, pulling up his coat collar. He added to Wareham, "You're a lucky fellow to be getting out of it. I wish I could."

"Don't be absurd, Tom," his wife retaliated. "The weather at home is infinitely worse."

"I don't see it."

"You are like the ostrich. You bury your head."

The professor lifted his from a newspaper, with the sniff of a war-horse.

"My dear Mrs Martyn, you don't credit that ridiculous fable?"

She raised her hands imploringly.

"Take it. I yield. The professor has got possession of a hundred harmless illustrations, which he puts to the torture, and then gibbets."

"To be worth anything an illustration should be accurate."

Anne went to the rescue.

"We may struggle after truth, but accuracy—! Half-an-hour hence, and unprepared, I defy the professor to repeat this conversation without an error."

"Facts, facts!"

"Facts come to us thick with paint. Who will describe the view before us? One person says 'Beastly weather,' another is eloquent on the loveliness of silver-grey. What, then?"

"The fact remains that it rains," said the professor, with a bow. He was forbearing to Anne.

"Not a drop." Hugh turned round from contemplation, his laugh vigorous and infectious.

"The ostrich is forfeit," confessed the professor gallantly. "To some eyes it appears that he buries his head, others behold him running upright. He is gone, and science with him. Am I forgiven?"

"You never asked me that question," said Mrs Martyn.

"My dear lady, you never gave me the opportunity."

While they laughed, Anne made a scarcely-perceptible sign to Wareham. He came close.

"What takes you back in such a hurry to England?"

He hesitated.

"Is it business which I should not understand?"

"Business which I can't explain, would be nearer the truth."

She leaned forward, dropping her eyes.

"Mr Forbes says that all his endeavours to keep you have been in vain. Are you inexorable? I believe we are going to the finest part of Norway. But perhaps you are afraid of another *contretemps* such as that of Monday?"

His head whirled; he dared not look at her. In an odd, strained voice he muttered something which sounded like "Perhaps." She took no notice, but went on lightly—

"You need not have any fear. You will be amply protected. With Colonel Martyn of the party, I defy any one to be late for anything."

He kept his eyes fixed on the opal waters, and stood up as stiffly as if he had to receive the shock of a charge. Who to look at him would have guessed that he felt as if all were lost? The ages have at least taught man to keep his face like a mask.

"You are very good. Hugh will—will look after you. It is impossible for me to stay."

He stammered, he did not know what he said, but he had not yielded, he was sure he had not yielded.

The victor is too often represented as a fine fellow, marching away self-contentedly to the sound of his own trumpets. Much more frequently he is bruised and battered, nobody giving him so much as a cheer; while his own discontented ideal scornfully holds up a mirror that he may not deceive himself with vain imaginings. This a hero!—Poor mud-bespattered figure! Just scraped through a conflict without utter overthrow, standing upright, it may be, but in what condition! Nothing to be proud of here. No subject for triumphal arches or laurel wreaths, which, indeed, became ludicrous even in imagination. Fit only to creep away, bind up his wounds as best he may, and cleanse himself from the mud-stains, and say as little as possible of what has happened. And yet a victor.

Wareham wandered about that day, seeing little of the others, and especially avoiding Hugh. The misty rain continued, grey and silver predominated everywhere about the fjord, but the mountains behind the little village reared purple glooms into the cloud regions, and the greens were vivid. The whole party were to go on board the steamer which came in at seven or eight in the evening, and to separate at Vadheim at one in the morning.

By the time they started the rain had ceased, and there were clear lights about, though no gorgeous pomp of sunset. A chill was in the air, suggesting wraps, and if adventurous spirits made excursions to the upper deck, they soon retreated to the heap of luggage which offered seats and comparative shelter. Anne had taken up a position between the professor and the elderly lady. Hugh could not get at her, and mooned about disconsolate. He went to Mrs Martyn, at last, in sheer despair; she laughed at him.

"How many days has your satisfaction lasted, Mr Forbes? And do not copy-books assure us that happiness is a shy goddess? Be indifferent. That is your only chance of cajoling her to stay."

"As well say, be some one else. Won't you help me?"

"I would not if I could. Anne is charming as she is. Married, I don't know which would be the most miserable—she or her husband."

"I would risk it."

"Of course. Because you have lost your head. I should not wonder if the professor would risk it too."

Hugh began to laugh.

"You will be saying as much of Wareham in a minute."

"Do you mean that he owns to it?" asked Mrs Martyn innocently.

His laugh grew hilarious.

"No, no, no. The bare idea is too comic. I have never known him smitten. He will not even consent to stay on with us, though Anne asked him herself."

"And you have asked him also, no doubt?"

"In vain, though! I have never known him so stiff. If it had been any one else, I should have suspected the attraction of Miss Ravenhill's dimple."

Mrs Martyn gazed at him admiringly.

"How clear-sighted you men are!" she cried.

Hugh disclaimed modestly.

"Not we, for you women often puzzle us. But if I didn't know Wareham, I don't know who should. He's been better than a brother to me, stuck by me, and pulled me through a lot. Oh, hang that old man! If he's going to monopolise Anne, I'll have a smoke meanwhile. You're coming down to the feed, Mrs Martyn? May I choose your places?"

"Leave that to Mr Wareham," she called after him, with a laugh.

Wareham sat with the Ravenhills at the other table of the narrow cabin. Anne's voice behind him sounded in his ears, so that he heard little else, and gave himself the luxury of silence that he might listen to the dear sounds. Mrs Ravenhill found him a dull companion, and raised her eyebrows to Millie to indicate her opinion while she praised the salmon. Youth had ousted age, and Hugh was at Anne's elbow, with irreverent jests upon the professors dread of the cabin. The steamer had anchored off a little village, to disembark a company of unkempt soldiers, and was rolling steadily, to the discomfort of more than one.

"I looked into the ladies' cabin," said Anne. "It is not to be faced, and I shall spend the night on deck."

"I too. But the night is not very long."

"True. I had forgotten. We land at one. Are you really coming with us?"

"What else on earth should I do?"

"That is easily answered. Go home with your friend. Are you not his *fidus Achates*? Don't you think it base to desert him?"

He dropped his voice into rapture.

"You don't expect me to prefer his society to yours!"

Mrs Martyn, who had quick ears, bestowed a mental smile on the one-sidedness of friendship. Anne looked at him calmly, and remarked—

"You are an extraordinary boy."

He flushed and asked her not to call him a boy. She answered that she thought him younger now than ever before. "It is only a boy that would have shown so much rashness."

"How?"

"In hurling yourself upon us, as you have done. Unasked, except by your faithful friend."

Threat lurked in her voice, and terrified him into instant humbleness.

"Forgive me."

"If I do, it is because you are what you disclaim, and not quite responsible. The real offender should have remained to take care of you."

"I don't need him, if you won't laugh at me too cruelly. Besides, do you know that Dick is only three years my senior! Upon my honour, that's all."

She made no remark on this, but changed her note to one more serious, and therefore more alarming.

"Your coming with us is certain to revive talk—hush!—and I do not wish that to happen. While you were here with another the fact was not so pointed, but I did not realise that Mr Wareham proposed to leave you altogether on our hands, and I do not like it."

"He will go," Hugh said gloomily. He began to see Wareham's departure in a menacing light. "You know he told you so!"

"Oh, me, me!—Am I his friend? When he gave you wise advice, did he not treat me in the light of a baleful ogress? However, there is no more to be said, for if he will not make so small a concession for you—"

Her tones betrayed annoyance. Hugh's heart descended to his boots, and he mentally resolved upon another and stronger argument with Wareham.

His path would not be strewn with roses, he began to see; at any rate, if the roses were there, thorns also gave plentiful promise. And he could not understand Wareham, on whom he would have counted for staunch support in these prickly ways. Poor Hugh, whose lights were steady but not brilliant, felt himself unable to comprehend either his friend or Anne. At times she suffered his hope to sail like a kite, straining at its cord, then with a jerk down came the poor flutterer, and dragged helplessly on the ground. Up again, he forgot the downfall, and was as unprepared as ever for disaster.

It was cold, sharply cold, on deck. People began to prepare for sleep. Mrs Martyn betook herself to the ladies cabin; Mrs Ravenhill and Millie stretched themselves on the ground in a small corner at the head of the companion ladder. Anne barricaded herself amongst the small luggage, and warned off Hugh, who wandered round disconsolate.

There was still clear light in the sky, though the horizontal layer of clouds had grown dark, almost black. Black, too, were the low hills which rose on either side of the broad Sogne; here and there a single light gleamed out of the solitude; now and then a bubble of laughter broke from a group on the deck. Hugh went in pursuit of Wareham, and found him in the forepart of the vessel talking to a Norwegian gentleman on the politics which were causing upheaval in the country. When he at last walked away, Wareham remarked to his friend—

"Individually they are a strong nation, but our overgrown world now requires quantity at the back of quality. Besides, they have no young men."

"Why?"

"Emigration. The passion for their country remains, but only as a sentiment. It does not bring them back to starve for her."

"They would be fools if it did," commented Hugh.

"True. But it requires fools to do great things. However, my Norwegian is not quite of my opinion. He thinks the struggle with nature's physical forces so tremendous that it exhausts the energy of the people. In old days it flung them southward to conquer more promising lands. This is no longer possible, and he holds that they must for the present content themselves with crossing the seas and growing rich by the work of their brains. The worst is that the men who return do not bring back the fine qualities they took."

"You are interested in them?"

"They seem to me among the best people in the world."

"But you have seen so little!"

"One day I must come back."

"Look here, Dick, what a fellow you are!" Hugh exclaimed remonstrantly. "There's nothing to take you home, and you won't stop, when you might be of the greatest possible use to me. Anne is beginning to cut up rough, because she thinks my staying on with them alone looks marked. Do think better of it. You're not tied to those other people."

"I can't be uncivil to them."

"I claim you before them."

Wareham sighed wearily.

"Haven't we gone through it all? I tell you I know what I am about."

"That letter. It has something to do with that letter, I'll swear it has! And what rubbish! As if anything you said could ever come between us. Out with it, man; let's hear this mighty matter. Then perhaps you'll stay and study your Norwegian in peace."

"My Norwegian must wait. The *Ceylon* has me fast booked."

Hugh was put out.

"I never knew you so stiff!" he cried, with vexation in his tone.

"You must take my word that I have reasons."

"At any rate, you might give me one." Wareham was silent. Hugh kicked at a rope.

"What on earth can I say to Anne?"

"You might be satisfied with your position," the other man went on, disregarding. "A week ago you would have thought it bliss."

"So it is." Hugh rose on wings. "But if ever you'd been in love, you'd understand that the uncertainty is awfully trying. After what happened once, I shan't have a minute's peace until we're married. Now, when she might have let me say something, she has sent me off."

Wareham was understood to mutter that no one could assist Hugh but Hugh himself.

"Oh, I know, I know! Only I want to keep her pleased."

Three weeks before his friend would have flung out that if he couldn't effect this preliminary he had better step aside and leave the lady to please herself. Three weeks, however, had changed, if not his opinions, at least his power of advancing them. Silence was again his refuge. And Hugh meandered on.

"Perhaps old Martyn will say a good word for me. Suppose Anne says I am not to go on with them!"

"Can't you take your dismissal?"

"*No!*" Hugh flung out the word with such energy that a passing sailor looked round to see whether the quarrel was serious. Wareham recognised and admired the tenacity.

"You've grip," he admitted. "It would take less to put me off."

The young man made no answer. They were nearing a landing-place, the usual group stood there, only that at this hour they were dark shadows, now and then flashed upon by a moving light; two boys in fur caps carried great plates of wild strawberries. Hugh bought a couple, with promise that the steamer should bring back the plates. He dashed off with them to Anne, and was back in a moment.

"Happy hit, she likes them! But she wants you to come, too."

Wareham hesitated—went—with a shrug at his own weakness. Anne pushed a camp stool in front of her.

"Sit there. Mr Forbes, please carry some to Mrs Ravenhill. They are delicious."

As he went off obediently, Wareham said—"You are unkind."

"No; he is pleased. He thinks you are sure to say something in his favour, and jumps at the opportunity."

"Is that why you sent for me?"

"To hear your counsel—yes. As it is you who have planted me in this quandary, you had better at least tell me what you would advise?"

"That I leave to your own heart." He was conscious that prudence would have touched the string more lightly.

"You are so uncomplimentary as to have forgotten what I told you, and not so long ago. I don't own the thing. At all events, it is of the smallest."

"So is what we see of the moon," said Wareham, pointing to a slender crescent.

Anne smiled, for a woman who talks of heartlessness does so to be contradicted.

"Well, it appears to me that you put forth little on behalf of your friend."

"One doesn't praise the people one loves." He dared not look at her, but her nearness thrilled him, and he had not thought to be thus together again in the mysterious dusk of a northern night. She was silent for a time; when she spoke it was to say slowly—

"If you tell me that you honestly wish it, I may—perhaps—"

But he had started up impatiently.

"Good heavens, am I your guide? I have nothing to do with it. I wash my hands of all!" He added with a strong effort, "Let me say that you could not choose a better fellow, and that he loves you with his whole heart."

"How big is that?" Anne demanded, in a mocking tone.

The question jarred. He loved, but did not like her so well as before. "You, at any rate, have no reason to doubt its generosity," he answered gravely. "And one thing I will ask of you—do not cause unnecessary pain."

"The situation is none of my creating. Give me credit at least for having done my utmost to avoid painful positions. You, or fate, have baffled me, yet now you refuse to interfere, and I do not pretend to answer for myself."

She pushed away the plate of strawberries, and leaned back among the rugs and furs, her face pale in the half light, her voice cold. Wareham was still standing, when Hugh came back and glanced from one to the other.

"Have you persuaded him?" he inquired.

"Mr Wareham?" said Anne carelessly. "I should not venture to attempt it."

"Time's nearly up," Hugh announced. "In a quarter of an hour we shall be at Vadheim, and Colonel Martyn wants to know if you have seen the brown rug?"

"Tell him it is here," she said, with a little eagerness; and Hugh was turning away when Wareham stopped him.

"Stay," he said. "I will go."

He did not return. Lights shone out ahead of them, and there was a stir in the vessel, and an uprising of sleepers, for this is the point where those bound for Northern Norway leave the Sogne. The professor's voice was heard, acutely insistent. Colonel Martyn came to look for Anne and his rug. The lights resolved themselves into illuminated windows of a square inn, and, with no movement about it, this midnight illumination had an almost spectral effect.

A procession of good-byes followed.

"Good-bye, Mr Wareham," said Mrs Martyn, with a laugh. "High ideals may be very fine things, but they don't pay, and you had better have stayed."

"Lucky man, with a tender chop in sight!" muttered her husband.

As Anne passed out she turned a smiling face towards Wareham, but if he had feared or hoped for a farewell word, he was disappointed. She said no more than "Good-night," and put a warm hand into his. He had prepared himself for words, but silence knocked aside his defences.

"We are friends?" he asked eagerly.

She lifted her eyebrows, still smiling.

"I should never reach your ideal of friendship. Keep it for Mr Forbes."

Hugh pressed in from behind, laden with bundles.

"Here's everything, as far as I can see, but if you find anything, Dick, leave it with Bennett in Bergen. You're a villain, not to come along with us." Then, in a whisper, "Wish me well, old fellow!"

He had only time to spring on shore, the vessel backed slowly away from the pier, the figures faded into darkness, the spectral inn presented its squares of steady light. Wareham stood watching, then, with something like a groan, turned away, and flung himself down where Anne had sat among the luggage.

Chapter Fourteen
"Over the Water wi' Ane"

As the fjord widens into open sea, the hills sink into insignificance, and the steamer makes her way between clustering islands, rocky and barren; but on nearing Bergen the scenery again gains dignity, and Bergen itself, lying on a promontory between two harbours, and overshadowed by fine mountains, is strikingly picturesque. There is an air of vigorous life about it; oddly-rigged and brightly-painted vessels scud along before a wind which catches the waves, and tears them into foam; against the beautiful shadowy hills stands a jumble of red-roofed houses, pierced, as it were, by a forest of masts.

Mrs Ravenhill, sitting on the upper deck, swept the scene with what Millie called her air of hungry enjoyment.

"She sees points, effects, and is perfectly happy. What I foresee," added the girl, laughing, "is a struggling crowd, from which I shall have to defend her."

"Norwegians are never rude," announced Mrs Ravenhill.

"Not often. But what of that girl at Stalheim, who demanded money because you had sketched her cottage?"

"Oh, Stalheim! Stalheim is a spoilt place. I do not count Stalheim."

"You will find points enough and to spare," said Wareham, "and if you can get on board a steamer, you may have peace also. I suppose Smeby's will do as well as any other hotel?"

So it was settled, only, as Smeby's was full, Mrs Ravenhill and Millie went across the street, and had rooms at the house of a kindly, funny little woman, who told them long Norwegian stories, which she found it impossible to conceive were not understood. The days were bright, but chilly, with a spirited wind blowing in from the sea, and ruffling the harbour. The Ravenhills attempted no demands upon Wareham's hours; he was free to come and go, join them or leave them alone, whether Mrs Ravenhill sketched or made regulation purchases of spoons, furs, or photographs at the shops. This liberty pleased him, it allowed him to live with Anne in thought, and to be miserable over the combinations he foresaw. When two and two must drive together, would not Hugh contrive to be with Anne? No one would prevent it if Anne suffered the arrangement. And to be near her—to look into her eyes! Now that the victory was won, he gave himself the luxury of imagining what a defeat would have brought him: he might have been in Hugh's place, and his heart leaped with the conviction that he would have been preferred. He walked hurriedly, urged, goaded, by this thought; over his head clouds were flying, gulls screamed to each other, flashing white wings against the grey. He walked long, seeing nothing; when he wheeled round at last, it was more from instinct than intention, and after supper he went out again.

Mrs Ravenhill was not quite pleased.

"No one invited Mr Wareham," she said to Millie that night. "If he chose to come with us, he might take more trouble to be entertaining."

Millie stood at the window, her back to her mother.

"Never mind," she said at last. "You have earned his gratitude."

"Why?"

"He is not very happy, so he likes to be alone."

Mrs Ravenhill laid down the photographs she was examining, and stared.

"Not happy? Millie, you catch up absurd fancies! The man eats, drinks, talks, as usual. He has not been confiding in you?" —quickly.

The "No" came with a sigh.

Her mother heard the "No," and not the sigh, and took up the photographs again.

"Then I wouldn't waste my pity. I will tell you what I think. Mr Wareham has lived in his own interests till he has grown selfish; the large party and the little rubs did not please him, and he came away. He is welcome to go where he likes. All that I complain of is that he seems to think he owes nothing to us. You see what I mean?"

"Yes."

"And don't you think he was glad to break away?"

"Perhaps," said Millie untruthfully.

"Oh, he was." The mother was persuaded that Millie never flung a thought in the direction of Wareham, yet, mother-like, would not believe that he could have been attracted by another when her girl was there.

Descent such as that ranks with the incredible. Yet if—if Millie were not so entirely heart-whole as she believed, she yearned to offer comfort. She said, with a smile—"Miss Dalrymple has too much of the bearing of a conqueror to please a man not easily subdued."

The girl's heart was trembling lest the secret it held should escape. She praised Anne on purpose to be quit of all suspicion of jealousy.

"She is one of the women who has a right to such a bearing. If I were a man, I should fall in love with her a dozen times over."

Mrs Ravenhill's momentary suspicion fled.

"He could have stayed if he had wished it, I suppose," she said cheerfully, and slipped into other talk.

A newspaper had given them moderately late news of their country, and when they met at breakfast, Wareham alluded to it.

"At home, if you miss the *Times* for a day, you become a hopeless laggard in the world. It is amazing how soon the feeling wears off."

"By the way, I see the professor mentioned for an appointment," said Mrs Ravenhill. "Our professor?"

"Mrs Martyn's." They laughed.

"Whatever it may be," said Wareham, "he will not be troubled by the misgiving that a worthier man might have been found."

Millie remarked that he had a very accurate mind.

"From which he shoots out poor Mrs Martyn's facts as rubbish."

"But in Miss Dalrymple's hands he is a lamb," said Mrs Ravenhill. "I think she might even venture on a statistic unquestioned." Wareham made no answer, he turned to ask something of the long landlord. Millie spoke to a pale-faced girl, who was still shuddering from the crossing she had just gone through, and unwilling to believe that anything in Norway could be worth its preliminary horrors. Mrs Ravenhill got up.

"Which is the way to the fish-market?" she asked.

"I will go with you, if you will allow me," Wareham answered.

"Don't let us trouble you."

Millie was conscious of a touch of stiffness in her mother's manner, but he showed no signs of noticing it.

"You should have gone earlier," he said. "Seven or eight o'clock is a better time. However, you will gain some idea of its picturesqueness even now, and from there you can have a look at the Hanseatic House. There is a general museum, too, and a good one."

The one important street in Bergen runs directly through the town. Here and there desolate open spaces break away, the safe guards from the ever-dreaded enemy fire; here and there cellars yawn, heaped with gaily-painted *tine*; here and there again you catch sight of the dancing waters of the harbour, and a jumble of shipping. It is at the end of the harbour that the fish-market is held; the boats are jammed together, the buyers stand and lean over the railings; women in thickly-plaited black dresses with close black caps, a rim of white round the face, and one spot of white behind, are sprinkled among the more ordinary costumes. More remarkable were the fishermen in the boats. Old and young, the hardy faces caught and held attention; you looked at men. As Wareham had said, the great throng was over, but even yet there were plenty of purchasers, and a penny would gain a plateful of little fish.

And here, in the heart of old Bergen, is the house of the Hanseatic League, unchanged since the time of the traders. It is the past, fossilised, for some; for others it is the means by which to drift back themselves into the past, and join the ghosts. Away with the crowd of laughing sight-seers! here sits the merchant in fur cap and gown, his account-book before him. Check the entries if you will, it lies open. Here is the eating-room for the apprentices, lads who, taught to sweep and cook, should make good husbands by and by. But as their dignities would not put up with bed-making, and woman was not admitted, all the beds are provided with a sliding panel, whereby that useful but dangerous appendage, standing outside, could insert her arms and head—no more!—and arrange for masculine comfort. And here is the great lantern which, fixed on a pole, the trader carried in the funeral processions of his guild. From youth to old age it is all here.

"The outer circumstances of life, outliving life," said Wareham, as they emerged. "Now, will you come to the other museum, and plunge still farther back into the age of flint implements?"

Mrs Ravenhill shook her head.

"Any stone would do as well for me. My mind refuses to leap those distances, and I look at them foolishly unimpressed."

"Is it only flint implements?" Millie asked. "I don't object to them, but I believe it is because I am so ignorant that I can't gauge my own ignorance."

It appeared that with many other collections, there were old Norwegian curiosities, and a fine set-out of wooden bowls, which attracted Mrs Ravenhill, bent on taking home trophies of that description. Passing the fish-market again, Millie bought a basketful of cherries from a boat laden with nothing else. The small events of this day came back to her afterwards with a curious distinctness, and yet there was nothing especially to mark it to her, nor at the time did it seem blessed. Certainly not deserving the golden aureole which set it apart. She said little, but let her thirsty heart drink in what tasted like delicious draughts, and thrust aside the consciousness that soon thirst would be on her again. Whatever Wareham had done the day before, to-day he was all kindness. Mrs Ravenhill, never, indeed, exacting, had no reason to utter a complaint. Five o'clock saw them in the launch of the *Ceylon*, red-roofed Bergen curving behind them, and it was not long before they steamed out of the harbour. The wind was fresh, but for a long time they were under the lee of the shore, and even through the next day most of the passengers kept fairly on deck. But by Sunday the vessel was rolling heavily, and Millie appeared alone. The usual service could not be held, and only one or two ladies left their cabins. It was natural that Wareham should be much with the girl. They talked of Norway. From that they fell to talking of those who had been their companions, of all, at least, except Anne. But a question was so close to Millie's lips, that at last it flew out.

"Was it Mr Forbes of whom you once spoke?"

"Did I speak."

"At Stavanger," she said reproachfully. He had forgotten the confidence. "Before you knew Miss Dalrymple."

"Ah, yes, it was before I knew," he acquiesced, and went off in a dream.

She supposed the "Yes" was intended for an answer to her question, but it was not clear enough fur her burning longing to be certain.

"They were once engaged?"

"Yes." He forced himself to add with a smile—"The sphinx was a woman."

"To have followed shows that he must love her," said Millie thoughtfully.

"Why not?"

She hugged her pain.

"Why not, indeed! But if she is as unchanged as he, will he not suffer?"

"Fortunes of war," returned Wareham briefly, and dropped the conversation; from which, however, he drew the consolation that Millie's pity showed what she thought was in store for the young man. For this he forgave her the questioning which he might otherwise have resented. He had not a suspicion that she saw any further than her words told him, the childish dimple in her cheek belying such a thought. What he read was as much curiosity as belongs to a daughter of Eve, joined to a kindly sympathy for the young fellow whose perseverance perhaps touched kindly romance. If adverse fate could have flung these two together! He talked to her, reaching further into her mind than ever before, and the more he probed its innocent depths, the more he blamed fate for its dilatoriness. And Millie, all unconscious of this dream, suffered a lurking fancy of possible contingencies to brighten her eyes and deepen the pretty colour in her cheek. The sun shone, but the wind was cold. Wareham felt that he was responsible for her comfort, and saw that her deck-chair was placed at a right angle, and moved when necessary; he helped her when she moved, and sat next her at meals. On his own account he was glad of the companionship, for to be alone was to think, not of Anne, but of Anne and Hugh.

By the next morning they were in smooth water, and Mrs Ravenhill came on deck. She thanked Wareham for his care of her daughter.

"I was helpless myself, and I couldn't condemn her to the cabin. But I am glad to be up again, if only to see the mouth of the Thames."

"A yawning mud-bank. Our coast doesn't compare well with Norway."

Mrs Ravenhill's patriotism led her to declare that one looked for something beyond beauty in the Thames, and Wareham owned, in spite of his speech, to ardent cockneyism.

"Which means that you will soon be out of London."

"In a few days. And you?"

"We shall stay. This has been our holiday. When you come back, I hope you will find us out."

"I shall come, and ask you to show me your sketches, so as to be carried back again." He said it warmly, and Millie's heart beat. Afterwards came landing, train, and a grimy plunge into London. At the station they parted.

End of Volume One.

Chapter Fifteen
The World is Stuffed with Sawdust

The Ravenhills kept house economically in South Kensington. True it is that the economies of life are among its heaviest expenditures, but necessity had not forced them into that dismal position. They lived prettily, and cared little for what they could not have. The house was charming, though the furniture might not have fetched much at a sale, the transforming genius, taste, not being marketable. Fresh chintzes and flowers, with old white Dresden, and Mrs Ravenhill's watercolours on the walls, kept brightness even in the land of fog. The very morning after their return Millie came into the drawing-room and dropped a handful of flowers on a tray where glasses waited. She flitted about, setting a glass here and a glass there, until the room began to recover the homelike aspect which had been wanting. Millie from time to time contemplated it, her head on one side. Darting out of the room, she returned with certain Norwegian treasures, for which room had to be found. A queerly-painted old wooden bowl with horse-head handles was whisked from table to table, until it rested on a high stool. A small model of a spinning-wheel went to live under a minute palm. Spoons joined a silver family. All was arranged when Mrs Ravenhill came in from more prosaic domestic duties, and smiled at Millie's haste. Looking at the bowl, she admired the arrangement, but begrudged the stool.

"So few things as there were in the room vacant for emergencies!"

"It was made for it; and it looks happier already. I have always felt for the poor thing waiting for stray uses; with only once a week a cup or a book bestowed upon it."

"Well—!" Mrs Ravenhill resigned the point. "And soon we shall want a reminder or two, for once again under the shadow of the butcher and baker, I doubt fjords and mountains being real."

Millie allowed this to pass. "They will be turning homewards by this time," she remarked.

"Who? Oh, the Martyns. And they have the crossing before them. There we have the advantage."

"I liked the *Ceylon*," said Millie.

"Do you mean you would go through it again?"

The girl was bending over a flower-glass: she closed her eyes, a throb of warm blood filled her veins.

"Oh, yes," she said fervently.

"You must go without me, then. I thought going and coming both horrible. And I don't consider that we were very lucky in our companions."

A disclaimer sprang to Millie's lips, though she forced it back.

"Don't you?"

"Mr Wareham improved, but he was absent-minded and oblivious. However, they will all seem nicer looked at from a distance, and we are not likely to meet any of them often again." Mrs Ravenhill's cheerful prophecy pierced her child's heart. Millie's humble little desire reached no further than to the joy of seeing him now and then, but its roots ran deep, and to have them wrenched at so cruelly was sharp pain. It would have been worse had not her faith in Wareham flown to arms at this attack upon his word, for he had said he would call and see them, and nothing would have induced her to doubt him. Why should she? Mrs Ravenhill's enmity—too strong a word—was due to an unacknowledged fear which now and then invaded her motherly heart. She imagined that in flinging a small dart at Wareham she was taking a wise precaution, unconscious that every attack sent Millie running to his side, eager for defence. He had been in her thoughts as she made the room look its prettiest that morning; she imagined this and that catching his eye, and provoking a smile of association. At the idea she smiled herself.

"We managed very well with our holiday, I think," said Mrs Ravenhill cheerfully, "for by coming back early we shall have a beautifully peaceful time. We will enjoy ourselves, Millie, and do a number of nice things for which one has no leisure in summer and no weather in winter."

Millie agreed.

"I suppose really there is no one left in London?"

No one, her mother earnestly hoped.

The bell at this moment seemed to tinkle a satire on their hopes, and Millie's heart gave such a throb that she sent a guilty glance at Mrs Ravenhill, feeling as if she had betrayed herself. Mrs Ravenhill lifted her eyebrows by way of asking who it could be; they heard a quick step, not the step of a servant, the door was opened impetuously, and the next moment a girl was kissing Millie, and uttering disconnected interjections.

"Fanny!" cried Mrs Ravenhill, "I thought you were in Scotland."

"And I thought you were in Norway, and came just to find out your address. The luck of it! When did you come? Where do you come from? Do you stay?"

"Yesterday, from Norway, and to stay. Put you? You in London in August!"

"For my sins, I said as I came along, but with you here it has already lost its penitential aspect, and I don't think half so meanly of myself. That's the worst of goodness. A reaction comes."

She dragged Millie down beside her on a settee, both hands clasping her arm; she looked a child, not quite what is called pretty, but sparkling with fun and life, her eyes grey Irish, with a fringe of dark lashes. These eyes eagerly devoured the other girl's face. It was an old habit, and Millie used to present herself smilingly for inspection.

"Well?"

"Well,—oh, you needn't tell me you've enjoyed yourself, for of course you have," she said musingly.

"In spite of horrid crossings," put in Mrs Ravenhill.

"Were they horrid?"

Millie observed that her mother found them so.

"Yes, you've enjoyed yourself, you needn't tell me, and yet—"

"Yet what?"

It was Mrs Ravenhill who put the question. "There's something. You're not quite the same."

"To be always the same one must be carved in stone," remarked Millie. "I'm sunburnt, which proves I am not a statue. But you? It is our turn to ask questions. How came you in London?"

Lady Fanny sighed and folded her hands.

"Because the world is stuffed with sawdust. Imagine Milborough having the baseness to throw me over when he had promised me a cruise in his yacht! I was so cross that I felt I must do something disagreeable in order to keep up my position of martyr, so I proposed to come and spend a week with my old governess, Miss Burton. If I talk like a lesson-book, forgive me. I ask questions because I am sick of answering them."

"You will come here at once," said Mrs Ravenhill, with decision.

"May I? Delightful. I had meant to go into Shropshire to-morrow, but I will send Ward by herself, and joyfully stay. By the way, where do you think that Milborough is gone? To Norway. I intended to telegraph to Bergen and tell you so. And of course that added to my injury, for I had counted upon meeting you round some corner in the most unexpected manner."

Her spirits rose, she flashed fun upon them, and told stories to her own discredit with mirthful mimicry. Then she fluttered round the room, noticing what was new, and discovering all manner of similes for the stool which at last had found a use.

"It has a little the air of Milborough taking the head dowager in to supper. But I'll never pity Milborough again. He has behaved too ill!"

Millie asked why he had failed.

"He was snubbed by a certain young lady, and revolted against women. This is an attempt to break away, and have only men on board; and how dull they'll be! I picture the poor bored creatures stretched about on the deck, sleeping and eating, their wits in leading-strings. What can they talk about, with not even a newspaper to suggest topics? I shall be revenged."

She must hear everything at once, and everything meant especially whom they had met. Mr Grey she knew, but her interest in Anne Dalrymple was shown impetuously by a burst of ejaculations and questions. She had heard so much, admired, blamed, wondered in a breath! Anne's last engagement and its abrupt ending had brought a chatter of tongues upon her. Lady Fanny's admiration for the way she moved forbade her to condemn what certainly required excuses; she laughed at her own illogical reasons, but clung to them.

"To see her dance is a dream," she declared. "I could forgive anything for the delight of watching her. And you looked at her for a fortnight!"

When she had Millie up-stairs alone she returned to the subject.

"Tell me more about Miss Dalrymple. They say men find her irresistible."

"I dare say," said Millie, with a little reserve. But the next moment a smile stole into her face. "Who do you think we left with her?"

"Who?"

Lady Fanny sat on the edge of the bed, her sparkling face eager with animation.

"Mr Forbes."

"No!"

"True, I assure you. He was going further north with them."

"Then it will all come on again. It must. She could not have allowed him to join them if he was to be dismissed again."

"So I fancied."

"So you know, I should think. The very idea would be preposterous. They will come home re-engaged. Such an odd position!" Millie's heart joyfully echoed the conviction. She did not venture to talk about it to her mother, who might guess too much, but to her friend, with whom no fencing was necessary, she might play round the subject at her pleasure. Wareham's name had not as yet been mentioned, but Lady Fanny had a curious interest in Miss Dalrymple, and her persuasion that now she would be captured and led to marriage, Millie felt to be so reasonable that she was not troubled with misgivings as to the pleasure with which her heart responded. To most of us persuasion is another word for doubt, but Fanny was young enough to be convinced of her persuasions. She wished to hear more, all that Millie could tell her, and drew her conclusions with swift security. If ever she had been disposed to blame, she forgave her sister-woman amply.

"Of course she liked him throughout, she did not know her own heart!" she cried with enthusiasm. "Poor thing, how I can feel for her!"

If there was a certain incongruity in the epithet as applied to Anne, Millie did not quarrel with it.

"And I like him, I like him too! He has shown himself above the common herd. Men are so petty in their unforgivingness, so vain of pretending to be marble! He is the more of a hero, for not setting up to be other than flesh and blood. He will win her, you will see! unless—"

"Unless what?"

"I was going to say unless there should be any one she likes better, but there can't be, or she would not have allowed him to remain with them. No, no, it is going to be the romance of the year. Lucky Millie, to have been let into it!"

She looked at her enviously. Millie laughed and feared she had not sufficiently recognised the romance when face to face with it. Fanny's questions were not at an end.

"The first meeting! That would have told one, that would have been delightful to see. Where was it?"

Millie hesitated, but not even to her friend would she relate what had actually happened.

"I believe he met her as she landed. She missed the steamer, and had to follow in a boat."

"Alone?"

"No. Mr Wareham was luckily with her. *The* Mr Wareham."

"Oh, and Hugh Forbes' friend. That explains. Of course he had something to do with bringing them together again. I could not think how it had been managed, and, my clear, your stories always wanted detail. When it was your turn to tell one, do you recollect how invariably I had to come to the rescue?" She kissed her. "But it's a blessing to see your dear little face again. If I'd stayed on at Miss Burton's, she'd soon have had me in the corner. And now that I'm here, I'll forgive Milborough. At least, I'll forgive him if he falls in with all your people, and brings home a report of how things are going with Miss Dalrymple and Hugh Forbes. He's such a dear boy!"

"Lord Milborough?"

"Hugh Forbes. It's unselfish of me to wish him to marry her, but I do."

Millie joined in the aspiration, liking to remember what her mother said of Fanny's quick penetration, and forgetting that here only a part had been offered for her inspection. Such as it was it gave an interest to Norway which their visitor might not otherwise have felt, and Millie was ready, not only to harp on the theme, but to play as many variations as she pleased. The weather changed to wet; in London this is scarcely a drawback, but it may be turned into an excuse. Millie made it an excuse. Her mother grew uneasy at such want of energy; where was the use of imbibing draughts of Norwegian air if the after-results came to no more? Lady Fanny pleaded for indulgence in laziness, the most fascinating pursuit in the world, when you gave yourself up to it.

"Give yourself up to it when you are as old as I am," cried Mrs Ravenhill, provoked, only to be told that nothing could be thoroughly mastered which was not learnt young.

Lady Fanny, indeed, had by this time gathered more than Millie suspected. She had been sharp enough to note a change, and once that had struck her, would not rest until she had got to the bottom of it. When she expressed a wish to see Mr Wareham, whose novels she liked, Millie remarked indifferently that he had talked of calling while he was in London, and the hint was responded to by a fervent hope that they might not have such ill-luck as to miss him.

"I dare not tell your mother, she would despise my weakness. Support me, dear, when I protest against being trotted out. London is unwholesomely stuffy, the only fresh air to be met with in August is in one's own house, and I can't live without fresh air."

She was more open in her confidences than her friend, and enlivened the time by description of more than one admirer. According to her, she had met with instances when their affections had shot up with a growth as amazing as that of Jack's beanstalk. One meeting sufficed, then the proposal followed like a flash, with not even a decent interval for appearances' sake.

"Milborough thinks they are afraid of losing a dividend."

"And you have learnt all this at twenty!" groaned Mrs Ravenhill. But she had to own that Lady Fanny's warm-heartedness had not suffered. What was most to be feared was that experience would have wrecked her faith in genuine liking, and that the jests she caught up for defence would be turned against her own heart.

Millie believed that her penetration would extract the real from the counterfeit.

"For another," Mrs Ravenhill agreed. But she feared horror of shams would make her suspicious where her affections were concerned. An old playmate would have the best chance, or possibly a man like Mr Wareham, who, she was ready to allow, had sterling qualities.

"Perhaps they will meet," said Millie demurely. "He spoke of coming here."

"Oh, he will have other things to think about. No, I am only using him as a type of the man Fanny might respect and trust, poor child! It's a terribly trying position with her fortune, and no father or mother, and Lord Milborough not so steady as he should be."

As the first days passed, Millie felt each evening that the chances for his coming were by so much doubled, and her spirits rose, but when five had slipped by, they sank in waters of dejection. She fought heroically to prevent their loss being discovered, and succeeded fairly, helped by Lady Fanny, who loved fighting of any sort, especially on the side of woman, and was firing her soul with blame of Wareham. She flung herself into the breach with chatter of brilliant nonsense, for which a laugh was sufficient answer, and Millie, who was so ashamed of the unreasonableness of her suffering, that the idea of its being observed was agony, comforted herself with the assurance that she had joined gaily in the conversation, and betrayed nothing.

Chapter Sixteen
Straws

By Sunday Millie had given up all thought of seeing Wareham. He had told her that his stay in London could not exceed a few days, business might keep him there so long, but he had even talked of a quicker escape, and laughed at his probable solitude and discomfort at a club where workmen would be in possession, and he'd be hunted out of his favourite corners. The difference in comfort between a train on and off the line, he declared. "Women manage better in their worst domestic emergencies, but man is a helpless animal."

"From what you have told me, though, you have liked to rough it in other places?" Millie remarked in wonder.

"To rough it—yes. That is easy enough. To be uncomfortable in the midst of luxury is quite another matter, and there I rebel. If the best cook in London is in the kitchen, why should I dine on a burnt chop?"

He laughed as he said it, and she consoled herself for what seemed the blemish of self-indulgence in her hero, by the conviction that he spoke in jest. But it came back to her, and she reflected with a sigh that he had probably found his conditions irksome, and fled from them. She was spared shock to vanity, for she had never thought of her own attractions as strong enough to influence his staying, and it had only been a modest hope that they had become so friendly that he would keep his promise to see them which was disappointed. When Sunday afternoon came, it was not expectation which held her at home, but a dislike to Miss Burton, to whose house Lady Fanny, accompanied by Mrs Ravenhill, had dutifully betaken herself. She sat with a book on her lap, languidly idle, when Wareham was introduced. Pleasure leapt into her eyes.

"We thought you were gone!"

"Only delayed and busy."

"You have been able to endure your club?"

He laughed. "I have not had the time to consider my miseries. I dare say they have been of the worst. How is Mrs Ravenhill? Your maid said that she was at home, and I hoped in this weather!"

"I expect her every moment. You know she never minded weather, for as to that we seem to have left all that is delightful in Norway. You have not heard from them?" Wareham laughed.

"I see you have already forgotten the fate of letters, how slowly they get out of your delightful country! Besides, I expect none." He looked healthy and in good spirits. Millie's own rose. She pointed out all the treasures to him; he had seen them before, but already they had acquired memories, which is but another word for history. This came from Stavanger, that from Odde.

"But nothing from Gudvangen, which was the nicest place of all," she cried.

"Pity that strawberries are not solid reminiscences," he said, laughing, whereupon she ventured a bantering remark upon his own experiences.

"You nearly had too much of my nicest place."

"Very nearly."

His tone did not encourage her to continue, and she was sensitive to all its changes, yet the subject attracted her inevitably. If she left it, it was only in appearance. Wareham, on his part, was always freshly struck with the fact that she was prettier than he imagined, and as he wanted to forget Anne, he carefully impressed the discovery upon himself. A heart which had suddenly grown restless was something new to him, for many years he had declared that it would trouble him no more, and from its quiet vantage-point had discoursed philosophically and wisely to Hugh and his fellows. It is bewildering to conceive yourself standing on a solid hill, and to find yourself shot into the air by a volcano, and Wareham was annoyed both with the volcano and with Anne. Away from her, her power waned; he admitted her charm, but could weigh it against this or that, and face probabilities. What he told himself was, that it was, after all, probable that Hugh would win the day. His youth, his impetuosity, and the liking she acknowledged, would all stand him in good stead. Vanity might whisper that she had shown decided marks of preference for himself, but if he had had the chance, it was very certain that he had put it behind him. Even—and here there came another restless throb—even if Hugh were once more dismissed, she was not likely to forget what almost amounted to rejection of her overtures.

He did not repent. He thought of her as a splendid woman, dwarfing others, but at any cost to himself he was glad to have been true to his friend. What he did writhe under, and heartily wish he could undo, was the letter, the pursuing letter, by this time probably in Hugh's hands. His first act, on reaching London, had been to go to Hugh's club and ask for his letters, hoping that he might thus intercept his own. All that he learnt, however, was that those that had reached had been already forwarded. Vexation— more than vexation—he might feel and did, but for the letter there was no recall.

Therefore, nothing remained but to wait and leave matters as they were. And his blood had cooled. Away from her, he could even imagine obeying wise dictates, and resigning her, though she might be free; nevertheless he was conscious all the while that once remove the restraint, and his heart might again astonish him by independent action.

Meanwhile he was glad to find that he liked being with Millie. Towards her he felt calm friendliness, and the sensation was as refreshing as cool air to a fevered head. He thought of her as some one to whom he could talk without dread of misconception, the idea that she liked him had never entered his mind; the companionship which might easily have proved irksome had not chafed, because she and Mrs Ravenhill were careful to avoid anything which had the appearance of a fetter.

The two were chatting gaily when Mrs Ravenhill and Lady Fanny returned. Fanny had pointed, in dumb show, to a man's hat in the hall, and lifted her eyebrows interrogatively. Questions in a small house were to be avoided. Mrs Ravenhill shook her head. Fanny had already guessed, but the mother had no more thought of Wareham than of any other accidental acquaintance, and expressed her astonishment upon seeing him.

"I hardly thought you would have found us out, or, indeed, that you would have stayed on in town."

"You have not flown yourselves?"

"Oh, women, women! They do not require all that a man demands; besides, a house is an anchor, and we only occasionally drag ours. Let me introduce you to Lady Fanny Enderby."

The ground was gone over again, and the possibility of Lord Milborough falling in with the friends they had left discussed. Lady Fanny promptly showed her interest in Miss Dalrymple.

"And I hear that Mr Forbes is of the party, so now one knows what to expect."

In spite of philosophy, Wareham felt keen inclination to fall foul of this assurance. Mrs Ravenhill said briskly that she hoped things might turn out well for the young man, for there was something very attractive about him. She asked Wareham whether he would dine with them on the following day, with a sort of apology.

"We don't give dinner-parties, but we have shared a good many indifferent meals together of late."

"Thank you—I am afraid I am leaving London to-morrow," he said hesitatingly. The next moment he added—"After all, I don't see why I shouldn't afford myself the pleasure. I will put off going until Tuesday."

Lady Fanny drew her own conclusions, and they were favourable. For a man to stay in London for the sake of dining with three women, she felt, spoke volumes. Her own experience in signs was so much more extensive than that of either Mrs Ravenhill or Millie, that she looked on them from heights as a professor would look at a tyro, and smiled at the mothers unconsciousness, and at Millie's—to her—evident perturbation. She longed to cry at her—"Dear, don't be a goose! Take your due, or you will never have it!" but comforted herself with the reflection that perhaps Wareham was used to women who expected much, and that Millie's absence of assertion might constitute her charm. The censor thought it bad for him, and her fingers tingled with the wish to teach a lesson, but it must be remembered that she judged him as an incipient lover; and that her haste for the happiness of her beloved Millie led her to jump at unwarrantable conclusions. They would have amazed Wareham, who felt that here he was free from the heated atmosphere in which he had lived of late.

Prudent Fanny avoided comments, of which she knew the danger. She contented herself with remarking that evening to Mrs Ravenhill—

"I am so glad you asked Mr Wareham to dine. I am sure it was a tribute to my curiosity."

"To be candid, I believe it was because I thought I must, after having seen so much of him in Norway, but I am glad if it pleases you. Were you really curious to meet him?"

"Of course I was. Ever since I heard that you had travelled with Miss Dalrymple and Mr Wareham, I have felt that life had been unfairly generous to you for a whole fortnight, and I was so dull all that time! The most humdrum people you ever saw were collected at Thorpe. Whatever wits I possessed before were sat upon, and the poor things don't yet know whether they may peep out again."

Millie remarked that she appeared to have amused herself.

"No, no, no such thing! Neither myself nor any one else. And there were you with an author, a beauty, and a revived romance. How could you come away?"

Mrs Ravenhill laughed.

"We didn't feel necessary."

"And you brought the author."

"Yes. If Millie's ideas were correct, the poor man had nothing for it but to fly."

"Why?" Lady Fanny pricked her ears.

"She fancied he had lost his heart to Miss Dalrymple. I don't know, I am sure, if she was right, but it is quite possible. According to you, Fanny, such matters don't take long, now-a-days."

Lady Fanny had received a shock, though she carried it off stoutly.

"Oh, no, not long. But *his* heart is safely buttoned up under his waistcoat; trust me! Admire her, he would, he must—that doesn't include loving. Besides—his friend! Why it would be base, dishonourable! Millie, you are an uncharitable little ignoramus, to take such ideas into your head."

And Millie was content to think so.

The next day was brilliantly fine, and they were to go to tea at the Tower, and as Lady Fanny had never seen it, the sights were to be pointed out to her beforehand by a special warder. They went by Underground, and on the way to the South Kensington station, a gentleman doubtfully crossed the road, and was struck by amazement at finding himself before Lady Fanny. Mrs Ravenhill perceived that he was a clergyman, tall, and, at this moment, pink. He began to stammer vague sentences, mixtures of pleasure, astonishment, apology, Lady Fanny surveying him with a frown.

"What could bring you to London at such a time?" she exclaimed severely, and introduced him as Mr Elliot, Mrs Ravenhill gathered that he came from the neighbourhood of Thorpe, and inspiration led her to see in him a supporter for Mr Wareham that evening, with the want of which her mind had been troubled. She asked him to dinner, as an acquaintance of Lady Fanny's, and increasing pinkness did not prevent his absolutely leaping at the proposal. But when they had left him, Fanny fell upon her.

"What possessed you? The idea of being saddled with Mr Elliot! He will sit mute."

"He might do worse. But I am not afraid. You will make him talk."

"I? Not I! I have no patience with him. He is the most preposterous man!"

"Fanny, you're not really vexed?" whispered Millie, as they went down the steps. Her friend darted a look at her. They had to fall into single file, and there was a rush for the train.

On a fine autumn afternoon there is no more delightful spot in London than the Tower. The great river flows by, alight with sunshine, crowded with life; and here as elsewhere, privilege leads to pleasant paths. They strolled where they pleased, and lingered. The river front held them long. Transforming sunshine softened stones and the old tragedies which clung to them; as for the green, it was so inviting a spot that Fanny declared it made her wish to be beheaded there. She flashed here and there in her most fitful mood. Millie could not make her out; she herself declared that the sun intoxicated her, yet once the other girl imagined that she caught a gleam of tears in the grey eyes, swept out of sight the next moment. Something was amiss. Perhaps she would rather go home. Millie did not dare put the question, but she flung out a rope.

"This tea? Must we go to it?"

"Must we! How soon may we? was in my mind," said Fanny promptly. "Sympathy with Guy Fawkes has exhausted me, and my ideas drop greedily to the level of tea-cakes. Come, Mrs Ravenhill."

No more suspicion of a tear. Millie, happy herself, believed she had been mistaken, and amused herself by watching how the young men of the party drifted to Fanny's side. She flung sparkling sentences about, and told one or two stories with irresistible mimicry. The Tower was talked of, and the old traditions which are not permitted to live on, even there; history was compared to a captive balloon, kept floating before our eyes till a prick collapses it.

"More like an old picture, gaily painted over. We bring our turpentine and away flies the decorative colour, leaving truth dingy," said Lady Fanny.

"The warders of the Tower are placed there to prevent either catastrophe," said young Sir Walter Holford. "They have strict orders to admit neither dynamite nor Professor Winter."

"Is he dangerous?"

"Destructive. If any man can pull down Church and State, there you have him."

"And he looks so amiable! Once I met him, and he fascinated me with the history of our own village, until I saw it in all its developments."

"Yes, he can be graphic, when he is not shy," remarked an old gentleman.

Lady Fanny instantly inveighed against shy men.

"They spoil conversation," he agreed.

"Their own lives, and other people's."

Millie thought of the pink clergyman, and was sorry that her mother had been so precipitate, but could not understand rancour on the part of her friend, whose heart was so kind that she would have expected pity. Going home, Fanny was silent, and Mrs Ravenhill openly wished they had a quiet evening before them instead of two gentlemen to entertain.

She delivered this sentiment as they reached the door. Fanny murmured to herself—"Dear blind woman!" while she went wearily up-stairs. She wanted to be alone, she was afraid that Millie would follow her, but she did not. Each girl was on the defensive, conscious of something in her heart, which she was pressing back, and inclined to avoid the other. Lady Fanny did not come down until the two guests had arrived; her greetings were formal. She swept the room, and discovered that Millie had been at work with dainty touches, which somehow vexed her. As for Mr Elliot, he became hopelessly embarrassed in his attempts to explain what had brought him to London, until Mrs Ravenhill took pity on him and engaged him gently, while Wareham was left to the two girls.

He was conscious of a curious dual feeling, as if he had two natures, the one persuading the other against its will. He almost believed that his short sharp fever was at an end, and encouraged the pleasure he took in Millie's society as offering proof of returning reason. It was true that the sight of the girl, the sound of her voice, now and again recalled some incisive remark of Anne's. He recollected, for instance, that she had called her "an embodied conscience," but the remembrance was free from disturbance. Once, however, quite unreasonably, for the talk was of a lately written book, a vision of Anne, radiant as the morning, standing between walls of rye in the rocky little path at Haare, flashed upon him, and for the moment he saw nothing else. It cost him a wrench to come back, and he turned almost eagerly to Millie. Metaphorically, she was the shield to present between himself and distracting memories. Fanny was neglected, and smiled.

"Talk, talk," she said to herself, "for the more you get below the surface, the better you will appreciate her. But if I thought Miss Dalrymple was a rival, I should try to crush poor Millie's incipient liking."

She was uneasy, but there was nothing for it but to keep on the watch for the blowing of straws. And her other side engaged one ear. Mr Elliot was talking, and talking coherently, to Mrs Ravenhill. Fanny caught a sentence and smiled.

"Sense, thank heaven!" she went on. "Why on earth can't he keep to it?"

She was forced, presently, into closer contact. Mrs Ravenhill became a little annoyed at having the stranger so persistently thrown on her hands; dinner, and Fanny's near neighbourhood, gave her an opportunity for insisting upon her sharing in the conversation.

"You did not tell me, Fanny," she said, "that Mr Elliot was so near a neighbour of yours at Thorpe."

"It is difficult to believe it, at times," said Fanny demurely. She flung him a glance through her long lashes, under which he became incoherent.

"Not—not near enough, and the road is de—delightfully muddy," he stammered.

"Delightfully, when you are in search of an excuse! I did not know that men were so afraid of mud. No, no, Mrs Ravenhill, if you want to know the truth, it is that one must be a pauper to be worthy of Mr Elliot's friendship. With parish pay and a craving for grocery tickets, you might hope to be the object of his warm regard, but other people are not even believed to possess souls."

Mrs Ravenhill was surprised. The words jested, but there was a sting at their back unlike Lady Fanny, who never wilfully hurt.

"She is giving you a good character." She smiled at Mr Elliot, by way of offering consolation, and Fanny tossed out her next words in a sharper tone.

"Why? For supposing that incomes preclude souls? That's the way with your clergymen. Rich people have pockets, but no souls; or if they do possess any poor shrivelled little things, they can be left to take care of themselves."

"No, no, Lady Fanny," protested her victim, pinker than ever. "You forget. They—they have other opportunities."

"Do you mean being sat next to at dinner?" Her eyes smiled at him an invitation to say more, to use his; as he was silent, she drummed the table with impatient fingers, and dropped her voice. "What brought you to London?"

"There was—there is—question of a living."

"Offered?"

"Yes."

"And accepted?"

"I—I hardly know—I believe it may be."

Silence. Then—

"Where?"

"In Oxfordshire."

"And good? I mean good as we mercenary people weigh goodness?"

"Oh, yes." He ventured to look directly at her. "You—you think I should take it?"

She turned her head away. A smile was on her lips, and she mimicked his hesitation slightly.

"I—I think that's a matter you must decide for yourself."

His voice gained confidence.

"Laugh at me as much as you like, if only you will advise me. That is why I came to London."

It was Lady Fanny's turn to look discomposed.

"Hush!" she said, under her breath, and glancing at Mrs Ravenhill. "I do think that you shy men, when once you speak, become absolutely audacious. Pray how should I advise?"

"Am I fit? You know me."

This time she laughed out.

"I don't indeed. You must go to your old people for a character. Very possibly they might give you one."

"And if—if that question were answered," he went on hesitatingly, "there are others—"

She cried impatiently—"I don't believe you ever would be without them." But by this time Mrs Ravenhill, thinking that Lady Fanny had had enough of her silent neighbour, struck in with an observation.

Wareham and Millie were in full tide of talk. Released from the usual daily remarks of travel, they had touched on many subjects, and reached books. He found she had read a good deal, and with delicate observation. Miss Dalrymple's taste was of stronger calibre, and she admired what Millie shrank from; but he recognised that this was not so much from the timidity he expected, as from finding what was bad, ugly, and unsympathetic. Millie steered carefully away from Wareham's own books; he caught himself, however, reflecting gratefully that he had never written anything he should be ashamed for her to read.

Lady Fanny played in the evening, wishing, as she said, to promote conversation. Perhaps it was also to afford a cover for Mr Elliot's silence; certain it is that he subsided into a chair which commanded a view of the piano, and uttered no sound. Mrs Ravenhill asked Wareham where he was going when he left London, more for the sake of saying something than from interest. He named Wales, as a place where he had never been and which seemed to offer advantages, among them that of being easily got out of.

"Failure can be remedied in an hour," he said, with a laugh at himself. "I dare say I shall drift back to London before I have long been out of it."

Mrs Ravenhill did not even say, "Come and see us." She was indifferent, little dreaming how hopefully Millie hung on the suggestion.

When Wareham left, Mr Elliot, by a superhuman effort, managed also to take his leave. He had said no more to Fanny, but his eyes must have expressed entreaty, for she remarked, on shaking hands, that if chance brought him in that direction again, she would be there a few days longer.

"Fanny!" cried Millie, reproachfully, as the door closed.

"Yes—terrible, isn't it? But the poor man is lost in London. One must do what one can. How hot it is!" And she went singing to the window, and out on the balcony.

The night was fine. Wareham and his companion walked the length of the park instead of calling a hansom. Away from bewildering woman Mr Elliot could talk quietly and sensibly; he told Wareham that a living was awaiting decision, and Wareham honoured the young fellow for the manner in which he discussed it, half envied the enthusiasm with which he spoke of his work. They parted friendly, Mr Elliot to strike off to the Marble Arch, Wareham to make his way slowly down Piccadilly, twinkling with lights even in August.

He felt more at peace than he had felt of late; hailing the return of common-sense as a sick man hails convalescence. Anne Dalrymple had filled his mind so that other women were dwarfed by her to nothingness; now he was able, he thought, to relegate them to their true proportion. The longer he reflected upon the state of affairs he had left behind, the more fully he was convinced that Hugh would regain his lost position, the two would return to England engaged, and Anne would not descend to another fit of freakishness.

To have broken his own chains by that time would be to regain his self-respect, to look Hugh frankly in the face, laugh, if he laughed, at a transient folly. Now and then, it is true, thought glanced off to the other possibility, and dizziness warned him of danger. For, if Hugh were rejected—Wareham found himself once more at Anne's side; with a flutter of Love's wings, away went the defences he had built up round his heart, tumbling into pitiable ruin, and the traitor heart rejoicing. This was not like the victory of common-sense; he pulled himself together, and dragged back his scattered forces, marshalling Millie in the van, praising her delicate unobtrusiveness, and applauding himself for appreciating it. The dimple, even, was hauled up to the rescue. Nothing was more charming, more womanly than a dimple. By the time he slept, he was satisfied to have regained his position. He slept well, too, another proof of foolish Love defeated. Avaunt, teasing boy, too feeble to overthrow real resistance!

By morning a capricious rain was falling, washing the blackened leaves. Wareham was not leaving until the afternoon; he took a turn in Saint James's Park, to have a look at the wood-pigeons there, before going to his club for letters. A telegram awaited him. The name of Martyn as sender awoke no association until he read—"Forbes ill. Some one should come. Bergen, August 17th."

He had scarcely finished before he remembered that Hugh's sister was in Germany, and old Sir Michael incapacitated from moving by rheumatism. Another reflection, as instantaneous, reminded him that the Hull steamer started that evening. There was no question. He sent a telegram to Sir Michael, drove to his rooms, where fortunately his man had his things ready, and caught the train for Hull.

Chapter Seventeen
The Result of Incoherence

Millie, with shame at her own appropriation, which, looked back upon, appeared excessive, decided that Fanny had been bored that night, and no wonder, with so floundering an acquaintance thrust upon her! She admired her friend, penitently, for that last offer of a plank of refuge, and hoped that bashfulness might prevent his accepting it.

"Why were you so kind, Fanny?" she remonstrated. "I am sure you had done all that could have been expected of you!"

"Oh, and more. He never expects," said Lady Fanny, musingly. "One ought to do something for the helpless. You, at any rate, might be obliged to him."

It was Mrs Ravenhill who asked why?

Lady Fanny considered that he made a second centre of conversation, and, cried out at, maintained her assertion.

"First you have to discover what he has to say, and then to help him to say it. It is very absorbing."

"I think you might have been more helpful, then," Mrs Ravenhill remarked, smiling. "For a long time you left him to me, and what did I know of what he had to say! And I don't approve of your laughing at him, for he is a good man, and carries it in his face."

"Is goodness pink?" asked Fanny, with an innocent air. The next moment she cried out, "Oh, don't listen to me! Good? He is better than all of us put together. The poor love him. You don't know how he has changed the place where he has been working. Even Milborough hasn't a word to say against him. There was a young fellow at Huntsdon going to the bad as fast as he could, and Mr Elliot got hold of him and never let go again—that's the only way of describing it. It was splendid. And then one makes much of these little trifles, as if they mattered! as if they could compare with the real thing!"

And once more Milly caught a gleam in the grey Irish eyes, which, if it had been possible, looked like tears.

Mrs Ravenhill, suddenly enlightened, was beginning to say something in praise of such a character, when Fanny interrupted her.

"No. He's absurd, ridiculous!" she cried, and tore him to tatters.

This was at breakfast. Afterwards, when Millie was alone with her mother, she flew at her with questions. What did she think? Was it possible? Mrs Ravenhill was as much at sea as herself. Everything pointed to unlikelihood, yet nothing else seemed to explain those rushing words with which Fanny had painted a noble nature. They talked amazedly. The last person they would have expected! Mrs Ravenhill was more quickly reconciled than Millie.

"If she respects him, I have no fear; and what else can have attracted her? I hope he does not think of her fortune, but I should not suspect him."

"No, no! But a man that she laughs at!"

"It is her revenge on her own heart. I can hardly fancy Milborough approving, still—in a year she will be her own mistress. And, after all, Millie, we may have gone too far. It may be no more than girlish enthusiasm. You know, as well as I, how quickly Fanny is stirred by what she admires, and, poor child, Thorpe has not too much of that! If I were you, I would say nothing to her until she speaks herself."

Not a word did Fanny breathe, and perhaps was unconscious of having betrayed feeling. A suggestion made that she might not care to accompany Mrs Ravenhill and Millie for some shopping, she set aside, declaring that with fashion changing every week, she must make the most of being at head-quarters. Mrs Ravenhill satisfied herself by leaving word, unknown to her, that if Mr Elliot appeared they would be at home for tea. However, the precaution was useless, for he did not come, and Fanny made no remark.

By the next day, Mrs Ravenhill, now on the look-out for signs, convinced herself that her guest was restless, and earned off Millie. Fanny, left to herself, wandered about the house, and peeped over the stairs when a hesitating ring sounded, declaring that it must be his.

"He cannot even ring like other people, he turns it into an apology," she cried, angry with every shortcoming. But when only a card followed the ring she grew uneasy, beginning to fear she knew not what, wandered on the landing, watched from the balcony. "This living?—he is in the tortures of doubt; so am I. It would make all the difference; perhaps provide him with a tongue, at least give me an excuse. An excuse! Now, Fanny the coward,

Fanny the worldly"—she scourged herself with scorn—"what excuse do you want? You know him—that he is worth a hundred of those butterfly nonentities who are suggested as appropriate husbands—yet you have not the courage of your convictions." Then, with a laugh, she relented from her fierceness. "When the courage of convictions includes something extremely like having to offer oneself, one may be forgiven hesitation—"

At this point Mr Elliot was announced, and Fanny coloured as furiously as if she had been caught in the act she was contemplating. She even descended to an untruth by implication of surprise.

"You are the most surprising person! Who would have expected you to be still in London!"

"Did you think I had left?"

Mr Elliot was no longer shy, and his look, fixed on hers, was as frank and open as a child's. Lady Fanny fidgeted, and confessed—

"No, no, I did not."

"I could not have gone without seeing you. Do you recollect what I said I wanted?" Fanny nodded, and remarked that it could only be a question of what he wished himself.

"Scarcely that," he said, without looking at her. "But circumstances have forced me into decision without asking your advice."

She leant forward eagerly.

"I am very glad. I hope you asked nobody. Why should you hesitate? It was offered to you because you were the best man. The best man should have it. Yes, I am glad, for it shows that they can appreciate—"

She stopped, fearing to have said too much. He fingered a paper-knife on the table, and eyed the floor. When he spoke, it was with a certain stiffness.

"I shall always be sensible of the kindness—the undeserved kindness. It has made me more ashamed of my own failures than ever before—"

"Oh, no," cried Lady Fanny, happy enough to jest once more, "I forbid your growing more retiring. Go on, please, go on; never mind the failures. I dare say your letter of acceptance was as full of apologies as if you were a fraud."

"I—I—" he became nervous again, but recovered himself. "I have refused."

"Refused!" Her voice was tragic.

"I could do nothing else."

"Why, why? What possessed you!"

"There was another."

"Another? What other?" She grew ashamed of her eagerness, and sat back in her chair trying to look unconcerned. "Of course I have no right to ask."

This roused him. He looked at her like a man who had been struck. "You are the one, the only person—forgive me, I don't know what I am saving."

She looked away. "If you were kindly to explain what you have done, and why?"

"Yes, yes, I came here to do so. When—when I had seen you on Monday night, I thought—I fancied—yes, I determined to accept the offer. There seemed no reason against it, except the doubt whether I should not be filling the place of another man who would be better fitted. But—one may carry that fear too far—"

Fanny played with a flower. "Is it possible!"

"I thought so," he said humbly. "The offer came unsought, and it did not appear to me that I should be right to reject it until to-day. To-day I had a letter."

"From the Duke?"

"No. From the wife of a man who, it appears, hoped to have had the living."

"Men hope easily."

"He had grounds. The Duke replied to him that if he had not offered it already to me, he should have been glad to have assisted him."

"He had applied for it! What becomes of your scruples in such a case?"

"They belong only to myself. Heaven forbid that I should judge a man who has worked on a pittance, and is saddled with half-a-dozen children."

"Oh, of course!" cried Lady Fanny pettishly. "I wanted to hear that conclusion. Are you certain there are only six?" He went on, unheeding.

"There can be no doubt that he wants it more. And he is a good man. I know him. He will work the parish well."

"Pray, are you aware that the Duke never offers a second living to a man who has refused one?"

"I should not expect it."

"And you do not care! It is nothing to you that—"

So far Fanny's words rushed, then she suddenly stopped and crimsoned. He drew a hard breath, and was silent, and with him silence said more than speech. She interpreted it as a declaration that he knew what he was renouncing.

After what seemed to her a long time she forced herself to say—

"Have you absolutely decided?"

"I could do nothing else. You—you disapprove?"

"I? It concerns yourself only."

"Yes—of course!"

He sighed and stood up. Lady Fanny's foot impatiently patted the carpet. She turned her head away, and remarked that he had probably consulted his friends before making a wreck of his prospects.

"There is no one to consult," he returned. "If my father had lived, he, I think, would have bid me do as I am doing. It has helped me, to remember that."

"I don't think you appear to require consolation," said Fanny airily, and hated herself for her cruelty. She used it as a spur, wanting him to say more, but he only answered—

"One should not."

"You prefer to be a curate all your life?"

"Prefer? No. I am dishonest if I give you that impression, but in this case there was nothing else to be done."

"I wonder how many people would have thought so! Well, as I have said more than once, you must please yourself. For the sake of a man whom you have never seen, and on account of a few quixotic scruples, you give up your own advancement, and disappoint all—all your friends."

The words were indignant, but the voice trembled. He made a step towards her, checked himself, and drew back. The hand with which he grasped a chair tightened its hold as he said slowly—

"Try to think of me kindly."

"You go back to Huntsdon?"

"For a time, a short time. Afterwards I shall look out for work in London."

"Oh!"

She turned away her head, then, as he offered his hand, remarked, "You will not stay to tea?"

He would not. Something was murmured of an appointment, and before she quite realised that he had said good-bye, she heard the front door slam. She flew to the window only to see a black back disappearing, rushed up to her room, bolted the door, and sobbed on her bed, scolding herself the while. "He has behaved splendidly as usual, and I not a good word to throw him when I love him better than ever. I would not have had him do differently, no, not for all the livings in England, but I haven't the grace to say so, and have sent the poor fellow away with a sore heart. What does Milborough's opinion matter? In a year I can do as I like, marry a chimney-sweep, I suppose, if it pleases me, with only a chorus of protesting uncles and aunts to fear. Be honest, you stupid little thing, and own that it is your own pride, your own odious contemptible pride which stood in your way! For Lady Fanny Enderby to marry a curate without prospects, for no better reason than that he is a good man, and she loves him, when all the while, only a finger lifted, and there you have a budding Duke at her feet, certainly not the best of men, and certainly not beloved!"

To be fair, she trotted out this youth before her judgment, and tried to credit him with what virtues might charitably be hoped to be his. Opposite, she set up John Elliot, at his pinkest, when she thought she hated him, and looked at the pair with coldly discriminative eyes. To the eye, goodness would have kicked the beam, but that her heart flung its weight into the balance, and was big enough to carry the day. She sat up, sighed, bathed her eyes, and dismissed the young lord, frankly owning that she wished he and the other could have changed places. Heigh-ho! and the worst of it was, that after that day he might have no more to say to her.

When Mrs Ravenhill and Millie came home, Lady Fanny sat with her back to the light, and asked questions with an immense show of interest. She laughed immoderately over the slenderest materials for mirth, avoiding allusion to her own visitor until suddenly dragging in the subject.

"By the way there has been a visitor—Mr Elliot."

"His card is down-stairs," said Mrs Ravenhill. "You saw him?"

"Saw, and quarrelled with him."

"Why?"

"He came to London to accept a living, and some man's wife has written to say she wants it for her husband."

"Well?"

"You needn't ask," said Lady Fanny, with asperity, "or, you wouldn't need to ask if you knew Mr Elliot. Of course he means to hand over the offer to him."

There was silence, then Mrs Ravenhill said gently—

"I think your Mr Elliot must be a very fine fellow, Fanny, and I'm beginning to be proud of knowing him."

"That's the only pride left to me." She broke down, and buried her face in a sofa cushion. Millie was by her side in a moment, with her hand in both hers.

"Dearest, clearest Fanny!"

"Idiotic Fanny!—Say anything you like—Nothing would be foolish enough.—And I do detest shy men"—with a gasp between each sentence, and a laugh at the end.

Mrs Ravenhill slipped out of the room.

"There! Now I have spoilt your mother's tea."

"She had finished. Fanny, tell me, are you going to marry him?"

"Oh, I suppose so,"—sighing. The next moment she had pushed Millie aside, started up, and stared blankly at her friend. "Good gracious!"

"What is it?" cried Millie in alarm.

"I had forgotten! He has never asked me. Isn't that necessary?"

"Perhaps words aren't necessary?"

"Oh, they are—unfortunately—for now nothing will ever work him up to say them. I'm not sure that he could have done it with a living at his back, but now, not a word! Martyrdom, self-denial, all the discomforts of life! Perhaps if I were to have small-pox, or to tumble into the fire and be horribly scarred—otherwise!—Oh, Millie, when you fall in love, avoid excellence. The inconvenience of it!"

Millie murmured something consolatory, but Fanny broke in with a quick shake of the head.

"My dear, I know all you're feeling, wondering what I find in him to like—attraction of opposites, isn't there such an expression? There ought to be. I don't expect you to sympathise, I only ask one thing."

"Anything!" Millie kissed her.

"Don't call him worthy. That's what they'll all do, I know, those of them who try to approve. 'Fanny has chosen a very worthy man.' To hear that, I really believe would make me hate him."

She had the promise. Satisfied on this point, she began to talk about him, his simplicity, earnestness, unworldliness. "So unlike us all. And now, what he has just done, though it has driven me distracted, isn't it splendid? Tell me, do you know any other man who would be so disinterested?"

Challenged, Millie flung a mental glance at Wareham, but finding it impossible to set the two men side by side, signified her admiration, thinking it unnecessary to allude to its qualifications. After Fanny had glorified her idol for a little, she fell back upon the difficulty. He would never, never propose. What was to be done? Somebody must move.

"Somebody must," Millie acknowledged. "Can't he take a hint?"

"Never."

"Would you like mother to write?"

"And get her into a scrape with Milborough and all of them? No."

"She might ask him to luncheon—to breakfast?"

"He would arrive at eight. Besides—oh, no, no!"

Her head was buried again. When she lifted it, it was to remark—

"The morning is so cold-blooded! If there was only some excuse!"

"I dare say mother has a paper to be signed before a clergyman," said Millie hopefully. "And they're all taking holidays. I'll go and see."

Fanny called anxiously after her—"Not a word of me!"

Reluctantly Mrs Ravenhill consented, though she declined to offer the bait of a signature. She felt that Fanny's love must be real, since it could not have sprung from imaginary causes.

"And the man is a gentleman," she said.

Millie sighed and owned amazement.

"So that no one has really the right to object. I have long wished her to marry, and her own heart is more to be trusted than Milborough. He shall be asked to luncheon, and shall have his opportunity. Whether he'll take it!"

This communicated to Fanny by Millie, she was dolefully certain that he would not come.

"Don't you think he may read encouragement?"

"Dear man, yes! But he'll think himself bound to quash encouragement. And if he should come, and turns pink—I shall inevitably be cross. This is your doing, Millie! I'll—"

She threatened.

"What?"

"Do the same for you some day."

There was a pause before the answer came, and Fanny prophesied disaster. At first he had left London; when that idea was abandoned it was for the certainty that she had so disgusted him at the last interview that he would have no more to do with her.

"The more right I thought him, the more disagreeable I became. My dear, depend upon it, he is blessing his stars for his escape. And his mind once made up, no little inveiglements of luncheon will move him. Millie, what possessed me to be such a wretch?"

Her presentiments were unfounded. Mr Elliot wrote to accept, and Fanny's mood varied between mirth which sparkled sometimes through tears, and a dignity which her friends found comic. When he arrived, she was in her room. Millie went to fetch her, and was told that it was no use, she should not come down.

"Two shy people will be ridiculously unmanageable, and you shan't be saddled with them. Besides, I suppose he is roseately triumphant?"

A happy inspiration made Millie assure her that he looked as if he had not slept for a week. Lady Fanny fidgeted.

"Absurd!"

"I only answer your question."

"Well, go. I will see about it. But don't expect me," she called after her, warningly.

Luncheon was announced before she appeared, with dignity in the ascendant. She hardly glanced at Mr Elliot, and her embarrassment was greater than his, for he carried the look of a man who had been through the worst, and has nothing to fear. Ice all round and about. Mrs Ravenhill and Millie made heroic efforts to warm the chilly atmosphere, but do what they would, it enveloped them Fanny without a tongue had changed to lead and to a stranger.

The dreary meal ended, Mrs Ravenhill rose. "Millie and Fanny will take you up-stairs, Mr Elliot," she said, "for I have to go out." Up spoke Fanny.

"Mayn't I come with you?"

"Oh, certainly," said Mrs Ravenhill, provoked. Then, to her amazement, Mr Elliot's voice was heard.

"There is something I should be glad of an opportunity of saying, if Lady Fanny could give me five minutes."

And, "Certainly she will," interposed Mrs Ravenhill again. "The drawing-room is at your service. Come, Millie."

Fanny's feet dragged all the way up-stairs. She marched into the drawing-room, and sat stiffly on a seat by the window; tried to say something jesting, and failed. All that she got out was—

"Well?"

"Forgive me if I speak of my own feelings. It is for the first and last time," he said hurriedly.

A slight movement of her head.

"I—I am quite aware that they have no excuse, except in the law of our nature; one must love what is lovable, however wide the distance. Your kindness, your sweetness—"

His voice shook, but he controlled it, and she was aware of the effort. "I don't want to talk of anything except just to tell you what, even with the gap between us hopelessly widening, I think you should know. If I could have fairly accepted this living, without harming another man, I had a wild dream of trying whether my love could have won some crumb of hope. I would have waited years, a lifetime, but I meant to try to win your heart at last. That is at an end. Since I have been in town I have made inquiries— to stay at Huntsdon would be impossible—I—I am not strong enough—I have accepted an offer of work in London. Forgive me for troubling you. It seemed to me that this much I might say. You may trust to my giving you no more annoyance. I am very grateful to you for letting me speak."

He stood looking down upon her, and all Fanny's composure had returned, and with it her powers of teasing. She leaned back in the chair, and glanced up at him with a wicked smile in her eyes.

"Oh, don't thank me. If you only knew how glad I am to hear your plans!"

"They please you?"

She evaded the question.

"I admire your rapidity. It is all settled then? Perhaps you don't return to Huntsdon at all?"

"It is necessary until my successor comes." He spoke quietly, but his face was that of a man braced to meet strokes. Suddenly he put out his hand. "Good-bye, Lady Fanny." She rose, without taking his hand, and leaned against the window.

"You have decided so much that I should like to know if you have fixed upon a house?"

"A house? Where? In London?"

"In your new parish, of course."

"I have not thought of it."

"And that's lucky," she said, with a smile which sent his head spinning.

"Why?" The word broke from him.

"I should hate a house I did not choose for myself."

"You!—Fanny!" He made a step nearer, but checked himself, gripping the back of a chair, and breathing the words—"You are cruel!"

She darted a look at him.

"Do you want me to retract?"

He became incoherent.

"You—you know I daren't think of what I want—"

"You might."

"Fanny!"

She leaned forward a little, her lips curved into a smile.

"Well?"

For answer he caught her to him with a cry, and another "Fanny!"

When she was released, she put an anxious question.

"Tell me the truth. It was really you who proposed?"

But he had grown audacious.

"What does it matter?"

"It matters a great deal, for I had been screwing myself up to do it, in case you were too shy, but I really believe it would have killed me. Didn't you see how uncomfortable I was?"

"I, you mean. I was wretched."

"Cool enough to speak. And of course when you said that if only this and that had happened, you would have asked me to marry you, it was exactly the same as asking me to do it now."

"Was it?" His tone was blissful. Then a cloud swept over him. "Poverty—can you face it?"

Lady Fanny shook her head dolefully. He stepped back.

"No? But I am poor. No, of course not. I have been very wrong."

She put her hand shyly on his arm.

"Dear, we shan't be poor, unless—" Her smile returned. "What do you call poverty?"

"I suppose we ought to have some hundreds a year?" he said, with gloom.

"Oh, more."

"More? Then indeed I have done wrongly. My income will not reach four."

Her tone mimicked his.

"And you give away three-quarters. You must be the worst match in the country."

"Oh no," he said simply. "Till now I always thought that I was rather rich. But I see now that of course you want more—coming from Thorpe and its luxuries, and—I am ashamed at my selfishness."

"I don't wonder. But let us see. You know I have something."

"Have you? Enough to give you a little of what you have been accustomed to?"

"That, and a few pounds over for you, which you may spend on beef-tea and flannel." The murmurs which followed were incoherent. Lady Fanny said afterwards to Millie—

"For pity's sake, let no one tell him I have three thousand a year. If he doesn't fly from England in dismay, he will want me to build two or three cathedrals at least. And now to prepare for the family wrath. At any rate Milborough can't say much. He should have taken me to Norway."

Chapter Eighteen
Bergen Again

A telegram from Sir Michael, thanking him for his promptitude, was put into Wareham's hands as he stepped on board the boat. It told him no more than he knew before, that no other person was available for poor Hugh, but it gave his conscience an imperative excuse for his present action. Undoubtedly some one had to go, and as undoubtedly that some one was himself.

Two days and nights of forced quietude give ample time for reflection. Wareham tried to attach his thoughts exclusively to Hugh. So sudden an illness was strange. He remembered now, and with compunction, that during their short meeting at Balholm he had once or twice thought him looking ill, but there had seemed reason for it, in the hasty, anxious journey he had made, and Hugh himself had uttered no complaint of physical suffering. Wareham wondered whether any accident had happened.

It was again the *Eldorado* on which he found himself, and the *Eldorado* inevitably carried back his thoughts to Anne standing on the deck. He remembered the repulsion with which he had first seen her, and yet, as he knew now, the involuntary admiration against which he had battled. One short month ago! It appeared a lifetime. How inexplicable she had been, but how enchanting! Memory went lovingly over the days, the hours, made dear by her presence, and he awoke with a start. This was not thinking of Hugh.

He tried to extract assistance from his fellow-passengers, but they were not many. It was late for people to betake themselves to short-summered lands, and it was the homeward vessels which were crowded. He found a few Norwegians his pleasantest companions, but spent a good many hours alone, looking at the long green sweep of the waves, and growing increasingly impatient. At Stavanger he went on shore, avoiding the Grand.

The low islands and rocky coast were singularly familiar, so was Bergen, its hills grey, its red roofs insistent. Among the crowd on the landing-place

Wareham quickly recognised Colonel Martyn's thin length, and perceived that he was expected.

The greeting was unemotional.

"Had a good passage? But I needn't ask. You are only half-an-hour behind time."

"You have not spent it in waiting, I hope?"

"Not I. That long fellow, Smeby, sees to all that, and sent word when your boat was in sight."

"How is Hugh?"

Colonel Martyns face took an added gloom.

"Bad, I fear."

Wareham glanced quickly at him.

"Danger?"

"Afraid so."

Silence. The grey stones at Wareham's feet grew for a moment indistinct, then he put a question in an unchanged voice.

"I'm in the dark, remember. What is it, illness or accident?"

"Oh, illness—in fact, typhoid. They say the seeds were in him when he came, then everything aggravated the attack. I felt doubtful about him from the day after you left, but one couldn't get him to knock off. At last he collapsed at Molde, and the only possible thing was to put him on the steamer and come down to Bergen, where he could be better seen to. We got here on Monday."

At the end of a few steps, Wareham remarked—

"I wish I had brought a doctor."

"Well—for your own satisfaction. But on that point we've been lucky. An English doctor turned up at Molde, and came along with us. He keeps an eye on the Norwegian fellow, and is satisfied."

As to nurses, too, they had been fortunate. Not only had one been found who spoke English, but an English nurse, going home in attendance on a lady, had been captured, and installed.

By the time all this was told, they had reached the door of the hotel. Colonel Martyn looked into a room.

"Blanche and Anne are out," he said. "What will you do? Go up?"

"At once, if I can."

But Wareham had to curb his impatience for half-an-hour. Colonel Martyn left him, and at the end of that time a nurse, who astonished him by her youth, came to tell him that he might see Mr Forbes.

"You will be careful not to excite him, sir," she said warningly.

"Does he expect me?"

"Yes. He was certain you would come." He asked no more questions. To see and judge for himself was his thought. The dark room gave him his first pang, it was so unlike Hugh's love of light and life. Then he began to distinguish eyes gazing at him from hollow depths, and his heart sank. A weak voice—not Hugh's surely—said,—

"Here you are, old fellow!"

"Come to look after you," said Wareham guardedly. "You've been tumbling into mischief."

"Is Ella with you?"

"She's playing about in Germany somewhere, and there was no getting at her in time. So Sir Michael approved of my coming instead."

"Poor old dad!"

"I'm going to telegraph to him presently."

"Lie to follow by post," quoted Hugh, with a weak smile.

"No. I expect to tell him that the sight of me has given you a start."

No answer came. Wareham perceived with a pang that Hugh's boyish jollity had left him, and found himself wondering for the hundredth time whether disappointment had—not caused, but fed the fever. He dared put no questions, each one that suggested itself seeming to threaten excitement. At last he remarked that, considering the stones of Bergen, the room was fairly quiet. The nurse answered that this bedroom had been specially chosen on that account. She came and stood at the bottom of the bed, looking at her patient; and Wareham inquired in a low voice whether there were anything he could get?

She thought nothing. Colonel Martyn and Miss Dalrymple were careful to carry out all that could be suggested.

"He dozes a good deal."

To the uninstructed mind, that seemed the most hopeful thing yet extracted; yet something in Hugh's face, dimly seen, and even in his attitude, gave his friend a sharp pang of uneasiness. The nurse went back to her place, her patient's eyes were closed, and Wareham's presence seemed to be unnoticed. All was silent except for the sound of breathing, the buzzing of a fly, and the occasional drip of melting ice through flannel. Wareham sat like a statue. His thoughts fastened themselves upon Anne Dalrymple's name, and wondered impatiently how he was to learn the relations in which she and Hugh stood to each other. Except from herself, it seemed unlikely that he would learn anything. And how much did Hugh know? Had the letter overtaken him?

Restlessness came at intervals, and Wareham would have been sent away, but that the name of "Dick" was audible more than once in the wandering, and the nurse fancied that his presence had a quieting influence. It was quite an hour and a half before he stole out of the room and down to that which had been got ready for him.

After a bath, he had an interview with the doctor, a fair-haired young Norwegian, sensible, and, Wareham thought, clever. It was not reassuring. The disease had laid hold with great force, and there were grave fears as to the strength holding out. Still youth was on the side of hope. The doctor thought he had battled too long at first, when he dragged himself about, though feeling ill. Now, all was being done that could be thought of. If Mr Wareham wished for a third opinion, he could call in the head of the hospital; perhaps before doing so he would like to have a conversation with his compatriot? To this Wareham agreed, and after sending as favourable a telegram to the old father as conscience allowed, crept up to Hugh's room again to learn that there was no change, and went down to wait for Dr Scott to return to the hotel.

The small salon had little to offer beyond a piano and some loose pieces of music. Wareham drew a chair to the window and sat there, watching the passers-by in the street. He had waited for half-an-hour before the English doctor came in, a sallow keen-eyed man, with spectacles.

"Mr Wareham?"

"And you are Dr Scott? Mr Forbes' friends are greatly indebted to you."

The other wasted no time in disclaiming. "I am glad you are come. Mr Forbes is very ill."

"So I gather." He had meant to have pushed the question of hope home to this doctor, but something within him revolted. Why insist upon a form of words?

"Of course," the other went on, "you feel that he is at a disadvantage among strangers. But there are clever medical men here, and from what I have seen, you may have perfect confidence in young Sivertsen." He spoke quickly. "Were I you, I would make no change."

"I don't dream of it, and what you say is very satisfactory. The utmost I thought of was the advisability of another opinion in consultation. If the case is so grave, it might be desirable for his father's sake."

"Certainly. I agree with you. Sivertsen thought this would be your wish."

"I hope you are not leaving?"

"Not necessarily at once. My holiday is longer than usual, owing to its being a recruiting after illness, and I can remain another week."

Wareham expressed his pleasure. The doctor took up an old illustrated paper.

"If it had been practicable for him to have gone straight to England from Molde," he went on, "it would doubtless have been better for his family, but it is unlikely that it would have made any difference in the disease."

"I suppose no steamer was available?"

"No. Though Lord Milborough's Yacht arrived just after we had got him on board, and followed us here."

"Lord Milborough! Is he in Bergen?"

"You may see his yacht if you go round to the harbour. I rather think that Mrs Martyn and Miss Dalrymple may be on board."

This struck strangely on Wareham's ears, though, after all, there was nothing very strange about it. He asked if he might go up to Hugh, and was advised not. Quiet was, of all things, necessary, for the temperature rose as the day went on, and with increase of fever came delirium.

"I'm not a bad nurse," he pleaded. "Can't I relieve guard?"

"Oh, you will be useful, but not in that way," said the doctor inexorably. "Will you come out for a turn? I have been over the leper hospital, and shall not be sorry for a whiff of fresh air."

The day was grey and colourless; the water had grown leaden. Wareham found himself longing to look at the yacht, but too much ashamed of the wish to express it. It was, however, in the doctors mind, and they found themselves gazing down from the Frederiksberg. There in the broad harbour lay two or three yachts. Wareham inquired which was Lord Milborough's.

"She lies behind. The *Camilla*. White."

"Oh, the schooner."

"Beautifully fitted up, they say."

Wareham kept his eyes fixed upon the yacht, where fancy planted Anne, dispensing smiles. He did not listen while his companion talked of novel inventions introduced into his *Camilla* by Lord Milborough. He heard, however, that he daily sent the ice wanted for Hugh. By way of saying something, Wareham at last remarked that he had never met Lord Milborough.

"You have seen many others of his pattern. He is emphatically the young man of the age; kind-hearted, indifferent, self-pleasing. His inclination is towards refined pleasures."

The description sounded too tolerant to Wareham, who had adopted a rapid distrust of Lord Milborough, for which he would have found it difficult to account. He believed that his companion was merely quoting stock phrases, which had done duty until they had lost the freshness of a sketch from life. He painted his own picture of the subject, working out that word, self-pleasing, until the likeness was chiefly shadow. An intuitive sense of unfairness, however, enabled him to keep the portrait to himself.

Dr Scott's energy soon began to fidget for exercise. He wanted to walk a mile or two. Wareham would have chosen rather to wait and see whether Anne put off in one of the boats buzzing round the yacht; to see her especially from his vantage height. But he became aware that folly was fighting for the upper hand, and walked away discontentedly.

He was taken briskly through the town, along streets of white-painted, red-tiled houses. Lofoden boats were in the harbour, laden with *klipfisk*, or oil. The greyness turned to drizzling rain, and the view from the Floien, which was the object of their walk, had vanished into mist. Dr Scott advised his companion to come early one morning.

On the way back, Wareham put a question. Had Hugh seen either Mrs Martyn or Miss Dalrymple since they reached Bergen? Dr Scott's answer came after a momentary hesitation.

"Once. To say the truth, we have not encouraged their visits. Mrs Martyn—well, Mrs Martyn was not intended by nature for a sick-room, and though Miss Dalrymple showed extreme tact and kindness, the sight of her sent up his temperature." He added dryly—"I imagine she not infrequently has a disturbing effect upon heads and hearts?" and without waiting for an answer, went on—"So far *we* have succeeded in warding it off; it is, however, highly probable that he will insist, in which case—"

"He is to see her?"

"Certainly. The irritation of refusal would be more harmful than the other sort of excitement."

"One question. When do you expect a crisis?"

He was answered that this was difficult to say, owing to their not knowing the time that he was attacked. Things pointed, however, to a day early in next week. Dr Scott hoped not longer, then turned the conversation.

They were met at the door of the hotel by Colonel Martyn.

"Just back from the yacht," he announced. "Milborough wanted us to dine on board. As we wouldn't, he's coming here. I've been up, doctor, and seen one of your dragons. No change."

The doctor nodded and began to mount the stairs. He turned to say to Wareham—"What's your number? I'll send for you if I think it desirable."

Wareham told him, adding, "I'll be there or in the salon."

"You'd better look in, and see my wife and Miss Dalrymple," suggested Colonel Martyn, flinging open the door. "Any one here? No—I suppose they've gone to rest, women always make out they're tired with doing nothing. Well, we shall meet by and by."

Wareham acquiesced, and went off to solitude. Before long a nurse tapped at his door. Mr Forbes had called for him so often, the doctor thought he should come, under strict injunctions of quiet. He found him restless and wandering, and as his presence seemed to give a certain ease, remained there until late, when he went down for a solitary meal. The dining *saal* was deserted, but he was provided with a small table by the window, and with what could hastily be heated again. He had drunk his coffee, and was thinking of returning to Hugh, when there was a rustle of silk in the doorway, and there stood Anne Dalrymple.

Chapter Nineteen
Will She Leave Him?

"Have you finished? Am I disturbing you?"

Wareham sprang up.

"I believed I was never to see you."

His voice said more than he intended, more than he had known he felt, for he had imagined himself cool as a frosty morning. But in the moment of her entering his glance had devoured her, he saw her grave, not a smile curving her lips, and her dark eyes weighted with what looked like sorrow. He told himself that to see her otherwise would have killed his love; the pictures of her which he had summoned up, amusing herself on board Lord Milborough's yacht, he had made perhaps purposely repugnant, calling on them as part of his defences. After all, he perceived that he had wronged her, his accusation of want of sympathy was cruelly unjust, and he flung shame on himself for having encouraged it. Under whatever circumstances they were to meet, down with pretences! She sat throned in his heart.

She hesitated for a moment before she spoke. "Why did you leave us, Mr Wareham?"

"It seemed best. Besides, my leaving could have had no ill effect on poor Hugh. You did all that was possible for him."

Would she sit down? He did not venture to ask her, but she drew a chair into the corner, and for the first time smiled, perhaps at a flickering idea that she was shocking the traditions of Mrs Grundy. She said, alluding to this—

"They are all up-stairs, and chattering so hard that there would be no getting in a word. I wanted to speak to you in quiet. You have been with him?"

"As long as they would let me."

"Well?"

"He is very ill."

"Oh, poor fellow, poor fellow, I know it! I believe I could soothe him, but those nurses are mechanically scrupulous in carrying out whatever idea has been worked into their heads, and they will not let me go near him. If at any time you think it would be well, promise to send for me."

Her eyes pleaded. Wareham promised, remembering that a condition guarded the pledge.

"Tell me, if you can, how soon he complained of illness," he said.

"After you left? He never actually complained, but he looked ill, and allowed that he had headache the next day—the day we left Vadheim. At Sande he seemed better. Then came—let me think—yes, it was from Sande that we found the heat rather tremendous. After that he flagged, I am sure. What should we have done?"

He read real trouble in her eyes.

"I can think of nothing. I know Hugh. He would not give up."

"Give up? No. He knows how to hold on."

There might have been a double meaning in his words, but at such a time Wareham could not so much as glance at it. He said only—

"The time must have been difficult for you all."

"Hardly. There was so little choice. The only question lay between remaining at Molde or coming on here, and then we had Dr Scott on whose shoulders to slip our responsibility. I bless him for his decision. What should we have done without nurses!"

She stopped and looked out of the window, her mouth half open, and the breath coming lightly and quickly between her parted lips.

"From what I have seen he is being admirably cared for," said Wareham, "and I should think the risk of taking him to England would have been too great."

"To England?" She turned and looked at him. "Oh, in Lord Milborough's yacht! Did Colonel Martyn tell you that was discussed?"

The name of Lord Milborough pricked him. He replied that his information came from Dr Scott, and went on to say that he had lately seen Lord Milborough's sister.

"Lady Fanny? Is she like her brother?"

"To know that, you must describe him. I have not the honour of his acquaintance."

She smiled.

"I never describe friends, only generalise. I am in love with his yacht. We were on board this afternoon. To-morrow you must come for a little sail."

"Thanks. I mean to stick pretty close to this house."

Anne seemed not to have heard this rejection of her offer. She leaned back, her eyes fixed on her hands, clasped lightly on her lap. Wareham's look followed hers, to see whether her rings told a story, and read none. Presently she said reflectively—

"It would be difficult to get sufficiently fast hold of Lord Milborough to describe him. Where did you meet his sister?"

For some reason the question was not welcome. He answered, however, without hesitation—

"At Mrs Ravenhill's."

"Ah, the Ravenhills! We live in a kaleidoscope ball. A shake, and the colours change, and quickly! After seeing so much, it is heartless not to have thought more of them. But they and you were fast friends."

She gave the effect of a question to this assertion. He parried it with—

"You liked them too, I fancy."

She paused, and repeated softly—

"They were your friends."

Wareham made a movement. He caught at another subject as a drowning man at a rope.

"I have written to poor old Sir Michael, and shall telegraph every day, for everything may have changed before my letter reaches him."

Anne stood up, her tall figure dark against the window.

"Freedom from letters has been a boon, absolutely I had had none until two or three followed us to Molde. And, by the way,"—she turned to him smiling—"I gave Mr Forbes his, and one of them, which had been much re-directed, he greeted as coming from you."

Wareham felt himself redden. He said, shortly—

"Yes. I wrote."

She glanced at him, and moved towards the door.

"If you have a few minutes to spare, do come and see the others."

He had not intended going into the salon, but she drew him irresistibly, and he followed.

The small room seemed full, but no one was there except the Martyns, Lord Milborough, and a couple of other gentlemen. The windows were wide open, and the gas turned down. Anne went quickly in.

"Blanche, I have brought Mr Wareham."

Mrs Martyn gave him a hand without heartiness.

"We did not expect to meet again so soon, Mr Wareham. It has been a most anxious time."

He bowed. "I have come, I hope, to relieve you."

She motioned him to sit by her on the sofa, but Anne stopped him.

"First, let me make you and Lord Milborough acquainted. I believe you already know Mr Burnby? But not Sir Walter Paxton?"

Each man looked at the other with disfavour, as is the habit of men. To avoid speaking to them, Wareham dropped into the seat Mrs Martyn had indicated, and she immediately bubbled into whispered confidence.

"Yes, it really has been terrible, having that poor young man so entirely on one's hands, and so awkward, too, after what had happened! You remember I told you how very foolish I thought his coming?"

"I remember. But this could hardly have been in your thoughts."

"No, of course not. Not this in particular, but I felt sure some unpleasant complications would arise, and Anne is absolutely enigmatical. You never know where to find her. I dare say you want to know in what position the two stand. Well, I can't tell you. I know no more than yourself."

Wareham repudiated curiosity, and felt himself disbelieved. Mrs Martyn waved a white hand and smiled.

"Oh, I don't suspect you of such a weakness. It is one that man cherishes in secret, and you might be obliged to me for answering questions without forcing you to put them. I own frankly myself that I wish to find out, and cannot. But, poor fellow, however it was, this—"

She stopped and sighed expressively. Wareham felt a grip of fear.

"I have known men pull through far worse illnesses," he said doggedly.

"Oh, of course! So have I."

"But you think in this case—" The words seemed forced from him against his will.

"Oh, I don't forecast. I have no reason for my opinion beyond what all know, but I hear the doctors daily report, and it—well, no one can call it encouraging. Oh, most sad! Extremely sad! The only son, I think?" Satisfied on this point, she went on—"Now that you are come, I have been telling my husband that as we can leave him in good hands we must see about getting home. Of course, on no account would I have gone when there was no one here to take charge, but poor Tom is hard to hold, Mr Wareham, now that we are in the middle of August."

He implied understanding, and asked whether they thought of leaving by the Saturday steamer.

"Not a berth to be had. No, Lord Milborough is most kind. He will engage some woman here as a sort of stewardess, and will take us all. I do think it a delightful arrangement, and so would you if you had seen the yacht."

Wareham thought his approval so unnecessary that he remained silent, and let her talk on, while he, half unconsciously, watched Lord Milborough and Anne. The doctor's description rose in his mind, but of indifference none was apparent with Anne near. She had gone to the other end of the room, and sunk into a chair, Lord Milborough and young Sir Walter attaching themselves conversationally to it. Colonel Martyn and Mr Burnby, who was older than the other men, discussed salmon-fishing at the table. Wareham caught words which implied that Anne was being reproached with having left them.

"Why on earth you should stop in this awfully stuffy hole at all, I can't for the life of me conceive!" urged the owner of the *Camilla*. "You might as well come and live on board at once, and if you're anxious, I'll keep a service of messengers running between the inn and the harbour. Come, consent!"

Anne shook her head, smiling.

"I've a weakness for feeling the ground firm under my feet."

Lord Milborough flung an inimical glance at Wareham.

"You needn't be tied, now that fellow's come."

"That fellow! You deserve to be gibbeted by him for the mockery of generations! Show a little respect, please, for wits, even if you don't appreciate them."

Sir Walter came to his friend's rescue with a request to know what Wareham had written, and one or two names having been quoted under Anne's breath, acknowledged that he had seen them lying on his club table.

"Fame indeed!" cried Anne, with mock enthusiasm. "Mr Wareham will be cheered." In spite of her adoption of his cause, she made no movement when Wareham rose and left the room. He ran up the stairs, telling himself that he was glad to get out of her presence, and opened the door of the sick-room softly. The door was out of sight of the bed, and the nurse made him a hasty sign to remain unseen. After standing for some time, he sat down, burying his face in the cup of his hands. Hugh was talking rapidly and incoherently, every now and then Anne's name broke out with a sort of cry; then his voice sank again into the same quick senseless murmur. Pity swelled within his friend; he reflected harshly on Anne, lightly laughing down-stairs, while here a young heart was beating out its life, with thoughts of her uppermost. That she could leave him in this state, he told himself, was inconceivable.

When he came out, an hour later, he retracted, for Anne met him on the first landing.

"I thought you were never coming," she exclaimed impatiently; "how is he?"

"You are on his lips," said Wareham.

"He does not know what he says?"

"No. The fever runs high."

"Oh, poor fellow, poor fellow!" she murmured, a line of pain cutting her forehead. "If he really wants me, remember your promise."

He could not refrain from saying—

"Mrs Martyn gave me to understand that you were leaving at once!"

Anne flashed round upon him.

"Mrs Martyn talks, but you might know better! Pray how are we going?"

"In Lord Milborough's yacht, she said."

"Thank you." Her tone was contemptuous. "Wait till we are gone!"

His heart grew soft once more under renewed faith in her.

"I hardly thought you would desert him," he said, in a low voice. "Mrs Martyn, however, spoke as if all were settled."

"If she goes, I stay," was Anne's answer, and he could have wished for nothing more resolute. It was the last word he got, for she vanished.

Before her, he believed in her implicitly; once out of sight, doubted. He was ready to admit that she would go unwillingly, but with pressure put upon her by all the others, it seemed to him that she would scarcely hold out. The following morning, however, when he went down to breakfast, he found Mrs Martyn engaged in cracking an egg. She presented him with a few perfunctory questions as to Hugh's welfare, only to turn eagerly to her own grievances.

"I must say that this suspense is intolerable, for Anne has got it into her head that we ought not to leave until we know one way or the other, and I really can't see why. If one could do the smallest good to the poor fellow, it would be quite a different matter. I would sacrifice anything, anything! But you are here, and he has everything that can be thought of, and, of course, his coming out was really a most wilful act on his part. Anne should never have allowed him to join us. I foresaw nothing but difficulty. And I must say it is a little hard on poor Tom, who has his moor waiting, and is naturally longing to get there. For myself, of course I should not care, but I think of him, and am seriously annoyed. Besides—the yacht! Such an opportunity!"

Wareham did not feel himself called upon to answer. It appeared that she only required a listener, until she turned to him and said—

"Pray assist me."

Upon that he inquired how he was to do so?

"Persuade Anne. When I talk to her, all that I extract is that I can go, and that she will remain behind. Of course, that is not to be thought of."

"Hardly."

"No, but she is capable of carrying it out. And it really is absurd! After throwing him over as she did, she cannot pretend to have very strong feelings."

He perceived that Mrs Martyn was seriously annoyed, thus to give rein to her speech. It drew him the closer to Anne.

"If Miss Dalrymple is resolved, she has probably thought the matter out thoroughly," he replied, ignoring Mrs Martyn's last remarks. "And nothing that I could say, even were I disposed to say it, would influence her."

"What good can we do! I suppose Anne does not propose to nurse him?" she said sharply.

"I imagine not."

She stood up.

"I might have known there was no use in asking you. Take care, Mr Wareham. Anne is inscrutable." This was a parting shot as she whisked out of the room.

Whether inscrutable or not, he cared not a rap, for the caution set his blood tingling until he forced himself to turn aside from weighing it.

Up-stairs he was not wanted; he sat in solitude for some time, and the young Norwegian doctor was his first visitor. He brought information of a consultation later in the day, said he thought Hugh was holding his own, and spoke hopefully; there was a telegram to be sent, a letter to be written, then a visit to the sick-room, where Hugh knew him, and smiled satisfaction.

That day and the next passed without his having a word with Anne. Once or twice he fell in with Colonel Martyn, who gained in his regard, and whatever his feelings might have been as to the waiting moor, kept them heroically out of sight. Wareham perceived that it would have gone against his instincts to have left Bergen, while poor Hugh's fate was in the balance; further than this, that he took pains to find advantages in Norway, where before he had only grumbled. Of Lord Milborough he spoke with respect, as the owner of first-rate shootings and one of the best yachts afloat. And more he did not touch upon.

Chapter Twenty
Not for Two Months

Beyond the hotel the street is intersected by a wide space, at once a convenience and a provision against the fiery power which threatens Norse towns. The houses are irregular, an atmosphere of shipping hangs about, vessels are moored alongside the pier, seafaring men stroll. When Wareham wanted a breath of fresh air, he went there.

Monday was an anxious day; the fever showed no signs of abatement, and Wareham would not leave the house until late. It had rained all the previous night, pools lay in the broken ground, overhead white shreds of clouds sailed gaily across sweet depths of blue. All was ruffled movement in the harbour, dance of water against the bigger vessels, and a toss from right to left of the smaller boats. Splashes of scarlet, of emerald green, struck out boldly against the black sheds which rose sharp from the waters edge. Red-roofed houses curved round the wood of masts, and the dominating mountain rose in a grand sweep behind.

Here Wareham carried his unquiet spirit. He feared for Hugh, he hated himself for the penetrating dreams of Anne which haunted him. Honestly, he had tried to avoid her, had chosen Dr Scott for his companion, and declined invitations to the yacht, of which Colonel Martyn was the bearer, with scant civility. But she was in the air. He heard the rustle of her dress on the stairs, Hugh babbled her name, he was in the house with her, and the effort to shut her out of his thoughts made him the more conscious of her influence, and kept her always before him.

He strolled along a short pier, where a steamer was unloading, sat down on a coil of rope, and faced the water. Only a few minutes had passed before he caught the sound of voices, and a group bore down upon him, Mrs Martyn and Sir Walter in front, Anne and Lord Milborough behind.

"You have gained a nickname. We call you the Invisible," Mrs Martyn began, and rained reproach upon him for his love of solitude.

He made no effort to excuse himself.

"Will you come with us now? We are only to be out two or three hours, and I assure you, Anne keeps Lord Milborough to time."

Anne spoke gravely.

"Why tease Mr Wareham? I admire him for his friendship. If I were allowed to be of use, I should leave you all to amuse yourselves by yourselves, but my offers are invariably rejected."

"I'll fall ill at once, Miss Dalrymple, if only you'll nurse me," said Sir Walter. He had a small languid face, and an unwholesome skin. Wareham wondered how Anne could tolerate his company and smile upon him as she did.

"Don't flatter yourself you'd be permitted the choice. Now-a-days a sick man lives under an iron despotism. It is not what he likes, but what he is allowed."

"Luckily for us," Lord Milborough remarked, in a low voice.

"I detest those nurses," broke in Mrs Martyn. "One must submit to them, and all that. Still, I shall always believe that they delight in exaggeration. I'm sure one hears enough of such an illness as Mr Forbes', and of course it must run its course. But I do not see why one should be alarmed as to the result."

Wareham looked without answering. Anne shot him a glance which meant, "Do not mind her." She chattered on—

"And you won't be tempted? It really is a pity. Well, come in to-night and hear our adventures."

Anne lingered a moment behind the others. "Let me hear from yourself. Such garbled reports reach me! I am so sorry for him!"

"He shall be told that."

"And for you. But that I dare say you don't believe."

He was too ready. She sighed.

"All this going about does not look like it, but what can I do? We live in a world in which poor women can't speak or act without remark fluttering about them like harpies. If one could only be oneself!"

With that she was gone. Wareham paced up and down his stones. What did it all suggest? If her words were for Hugh, vanity was scarcely answerable for the conviction that something was meant for him. He hastily pushed away the thought, which at such a time seemed brutal, and looked round him in search of assistance for casting off meditation. The energy of movement presented itself invitingly; he saw a boat near, and signing to its owner, rowed for half-an-hour with purposeless vigour about the harbour, coming in stiff, but braced. As he reached the hotel, Dr Scott met him, and answered his unspoken question. "Very ill."

"Worse?"

"With the fever so high he must be worse. It saps the life of a man. Poor fellow! I suppose no one can come?"

"No one. I gather you have little hope?" Silence answered the question. All the hours seemed to have been leading up to this moment, yet Wareham was unprepared for its shock. He turned white. Dr Scott went on to soften his unpronounced doom.

"I may be mistaken. One is never absolutely without hope in these cases, where youth is on our side, and I think Sivertsen is more sanguine than I am."

Wareham went slowly up the stairs, heaviness in his heart. The turmoil about Anne which had filled his mind was suddenly swept into nothingness. Until this moment, it appeared to him he had never realised what hung over them, and all tender recollection of past years surged up like an overwhelming wave. Opening the door, he heard the babble of words rushing incessantly, not loud, but unintermitting. Hugh had grown so accustomed to his presence, that there was no longer a dread of added excitement, and he was admitted at all hours. Sometimes he sat by his bedside, openly in view; sometimes, when the fever ran high, placed himself behind the bed, an unseen watcher. He dropped there now, on a sign from the nurse.

Eyeing the floor, remembrances flitted across it. Hugh the school-boy, as he first recollected him, a fair curly-headed young giant, blue-eyed and open-faced, fighting an older and bigger fellow with indomitable pluck, and at another time taking a punishment which should not have been his. Once on the track, a dozen such memories of acts which had first drawn the two together, upstarted. Times down at Sir Michael's, where Wareham, a lonely boy, was always welcome. Older life, when Wareham's intellect had taken him to the front, and Hugh's idleness hobbled him. Then the days he did not care to think about even now rose up; no words could have made them clearer; he recollected his misery and the young man's patience, and the recollection thrilled him, striking, as it did, across the mutter of delirium. In natural sequence followed Hugh's own trouble, which Wareham looked at now through cloudy remorse, impatient with himself that at first sight of the syren he did not fly, that he had been so dull in reading signs, that he had not waited, repressing the hateful letter. Imagination conjured up reproof in Hugh's hollow eyes; at times, when he caught them fastened on his face, mute reproach, a hundred times more pathetic than words. His ear was constantly on the alert to catch something bearing on it in delirious sentences, he had an insane notion that then he might have quieted him with assurances. Every now and then something struck on his heart with a sound like a knell.

He spent the greater part of the night in the sick-room. Anne's request that he would himself bring her news of the patient, he ignored. The morning showed a change, but one enemy retired only to make room for another, for which indeed it had been working, and doctors and nurses gathered all their resources to meet deadly weakness. That morning came a request for which Wareham was prepared. Could he see Anne? The doctor had to decide, and gave unwilling permission, fencing it about with limitations of time. In answer to Wareham's questioning eyes, he said—

"We have not the right to refuse."

What passed, his friend never learned. He absented himself, and took care not to go up till all fear of meeting with Anne was over. He knew only that the interview had not lasted more than a few minutes, and that the nurse was cross, admitting no right to human nature in a patient. Love, of all disturbing forces, should be shut out of a sick-room. Not venturing to snub the doctor, she snubbed Wareham, while nursing her charge devotedly. But in the course of the day, Hugh looked at him and said "To-morrow," and he understood that something was to be said to himself. It relieved him, for he had the longing of a woman for a word out of the silence of darkness which he foresaw.

"He wants to speak to you alone," Dr Scott said the next morning. "The interview won't be so disturbing, I imagine, as that of yesterday?"

Wareham had to intimate that it was not unlikely it would.

"Bad," said the other. "However, as I said, I couldn't consent to prevent a man from saying what he wished at this stage of his illness. You must do your best to keep him quiet."

"And when?"

"In ten minutes."

Ten minutes passed, and Wareham was at Hugh's side. His heart sank at the alteration, and his voice, when he tried to speak cheerily, had a false ring which he fancied audible to all. Hugh looked at the nurse, who retired reluctantly, showing Wareham as she went out that a restorative was on the table.

"I waited," said Hugh.

Wareham forced his face into a smile.

"Wait longer, old fellow, if you're not up to talk. I'm here, night and day."

"I know. You've been awfully good."

His friend did not answer, except by laying his hand on an arm which shocked him by its thinness, and for a little while there was silence which Wareham did not dare to break. What lay beyond it? Hugh's next words touched the sore.

"The letter."

The answer was in a shaken voice.

"I would give my right hand never to have written it!"

Fun once more gleamed in Hugh's eyes.

"Poor old Dick! Odd, wasn't it? I couldn't help laughing to find you'd been so bowled over!"

His voice was little more than a slow whisper, broken by pauses, sometimes sinking so low as to be almost inaudible. Wareham felt that the time had come for him to speak.

"Don't try to say anything, but just listen. On my honour, the thing was on me before I knew where I was, and, while I flattered myself—like a fool—that I detested her for the way she treated you, I never thought that all the time she was slipping into my very heart. At last, one day, I saw myself and her. Hugh, that very day I wrote that letter. And, look here—though I said just now that I would have given my right hand not to have written it, I don't know how I could be facing you now if I hadn't." He reined himself back into slow speech. "I never spoke a word to her. The secret rests between you and me. She hasn't an idea. Get well, Hugh, and God knows whether I will not stand aside and be thankful that you have her!"

Silence, and the ticking of the clock. The nurse looked in at the door, but retreated at a sign from Wareham. Hugh said at last—

"I urged you to stay."

"And now you know why I refused?"

"Yes. Poor Dick!"

His look made the question superfluous, yet Wareham said—

"There never will be bad blood between us?"

Hugh's hand sought his in pledge.

"Never. I want to make it all right."

"Wait for that, Hugh."

"For what? For my ghost?" He breathed the words. "When you saw me that morning—what a sell!"

"Nothing had been said," repeated Wareham doggedly.

"I know. *I* couldn't have been so straight—with Anne before me. But you can't laugh now at my madness."

"Not I."

Silence again, and another spoonful at his dry lips. He whispered. "I'm glad I came."

His friend had no words for this.

"Yes—glad. I know her better." His voice gained strength, and his eyes turned again to Wareham. "I could have made her love me."

"I have seen all along that you were the only man she liked," the other said, with confidence.

"I don't know." His feeble hands beat up and down, as if he were indicating balance. "She's not easy. If I'd lived, I couldn't have given her up. Now,"—a sign stopped Wareham's protest. "Yes, but I'm dog in the manger still."

Wareham felt a cold clutch at his heart for which he loathed himself.

"Be what you like, Hugh," he said quickly. "No one has so much right to speak as you," and whatever his heart might say, his will would have bound itself irrevocably to his friend's bidding.

"I want—you to have her," Hugh sighed, turning away his face.

Once more the nurse looked in at the door, signifying disapproval. Wareham hastily nodded, and she withdrew her head. He had to put down his ear to catch Hugh's next words—

"Don't let us pretend—I'm dying—win her, Dick."

It was impossible for Wareham to speak. He pressed Hugh's hand, and he was thinking more of Hugh than Anne.

"Only—"

A pause.

"I told you I was a dog in the manger."

"Tell me what you wish, old fellow."

"I want to be remembered—just for a little. I don't want you to speak just yet."

"I couldn't."

The dull eyes brightened.

"You promise?"

"Sacredly. And, Hugh, I've no right to think she ever will consent."

"Ask her in—" He paused. "Is two months too long? Remember, I held her mine once. I can't set that on one side. You promise? Not a word till two months have passed?"

"You have my promise," said Wareham quickly, the more quickly for shame at the murmurings of a greedy heart.

"When you've got her—you won't mind having waited. I've said my say, Dick. Yesterday—"

"Yes?"

"I asked her to kiss me, and—she did." His voice grew stronger, and he smiled feebly. "That other lean-souled woman wanted to come, but I wouldn't have her."

"Mrs Martyn?"

"Yes. She's curious. Say nothing to her, Dick."

"Nothing. Old boy, you've talked enough."

"Well—" Hugh acknowledged.

A silent pressure, and Wareham went. He wanted to be by himself, and though there were only half-a-dozen people he knew in Bergen, the place seemed full of them; there was not a corner round which they might not appear. He might have walked off out of the town, and been safe, but he would not leave the house for more than half-an-hour. For that time the museum struck him as a safe refuge, and he made for it.

Turning up a broad street to his right, a sailor crossed the road and touched his hat.

"Beg pardon, sir, but ain't you Mr Wareham?"

He signified his right to the name.

"I've a message for you, sir, from the young lady on board the yacht. I was to say as we ain't going out of harbour to-day, sir, and that if she was wanted, you'd only got to send a boat for her."

He was told to carry back the answer that Mr Wareham would take care to act upon her wishes.

"You've a fine yacht out there," he added, in order to gratify the man.

"If you saw her sail, sir, you'd say so. But she hasn't done nothing here, and it seems as if we were going to be too late for the regattas. Never knew that happen afore."

He departed, and Wareham walked on quickly to the museum, ran up the broad staircase, and wandered into a world of arctic creatures, where he was secure from interruption.

For the last three or four days his hopes of Hugh's recovery had been low, now some conviction told him it was all but hopeless. "Hugh, old Hugh!" he kept repeating to himself, as the past years of their friendship trooped up again. Always he had been, in thought as well as fact, the elder, the supporter; now in the shadowy twilight of the Great Unseen, Hugh had passed to strange heights of experience; the careless words he used to rattle off, dropped now, changed, as coming from one whose feet were near the eternal shore.

The special thing which Hugh had to say had scarcely presented itself since. It seemed a matter of no moment; something perhaps to be considered in the far future, but not yet. Dying, Anne belonged to Hugh; Wareham's only dread was lest she should disappoint him, a vague uneasiness about Lord Milborough was in his mind, and he did not think Hugh had any consciousness of this new disturbing element. He asked few questions about her, and it was impossible to say what had passed between them in their last interview, except that he had appeared satisfied. But Anne herself? She had refused to leave the place, had, but half-an-hour ago, sent a message that she was at hand, yet Wareham had his doubts. Did she feel? Did she care? Her own words came back, when she had called herself heartless, and under the intoxication of her presence he had indignantly refuted the accusation. Admitting it even, how was he to blame her? since a vessel can pour out no more than is in it. But with those eyes! Was it possible that no heart reigned behind them? If it were so, Wareham, suddenly stern judge, acknowledged that it was well Hugh should go while yet he loved her, and clung to the dream that she might yet love him.

Chapter Twenty One
Farewell

There was no shutting out from Hugh's room after that day. A silent figure stood at the door, waiting, its very shadow mighty enough to sweep away bolts and bars. Whoever Hugh cared to see, came—except his sister. He asked often for his sister, but Wareham knew that there must have been difficulty in finding her, more difficulty in her reaching them. Besides, Sir Michael's health was very precarious, and a telegram had mentioned increased illness. Hugh listened, and apparently understood, but weakness prevented his brain from grasping it except for a few minutes. When he wandered now, it was feebly.

Spite of persuasions, Anne went no more on the yacht. More than once Wareham found her on the landing; outside Hugh's room, her face drawn, her eyes red-lidded; she flung him imploring glances, yet he fancied that when a call drew her inside, she went reluctantly, and came out quickly.

Once she cried to Wareham—

"This is dreadful!"

"As gentle as it can be," he answered.

"Don't talk of gentleness—it is horrible, inexorable! To see him lying there, a grey shadow, when he used to be so splendidly living! It was that magnificent vitality of his which gave him his power. When he liked he could dominate. I am pagan, pagan, if you will. Death the friend? Not it. Death is the enemy, the hateful enemy, and we all tremble before him, like cowards!"

She flung back her head, and her red eyes looked defiantly at Wareham. He said—

"I am not a priest."

"No, but you are a man. Say what you feel."

"Enemy, then, yes. Conqueror, no."

"Oh!" She flung out her hands impatiently.

"You are like the rest. What do you *know*?"

"You tell me that is the end." He pointed to the door. "I see in it a beginning. 'The power of an endless life.' If hope were a phantom, it would fade before the face of death. Instead, it strengthens."

A great yearning looked at him from her soul through her sad eyes. He had never before seen such a look. She turned away.

As she went down the stairs she said, hurriedly—

"Call me if I am wanted." Then she came back a step or two. "Not unless I *am* wanted, mind."

He took this as a further hint that she dreaded these visits to the sickroom, and would avoid them when possible. As it fell out, she never went again. Hugh drifted into a semi-conscious state, the presence of Wareham appearing to give him a certain satisfaction, but no desire strong enough to require expression. Doctors, nurses, chaplain, friends, watched. Wareham wrote to his father—

"He does not suffer. I do not think he wishes for anything. If I mention your name to him he smiles, but makes no attempt to speak more than an occasional disjointed word. The people here would do anything for us; his illness has confirmed my idea that the Norwegians are among the kindest people in the world, and the least mercenary. Comfort yourself with the thought that he could not have been better cared for even in his own home than here with strangers—but I know what you are feeling, 'If only I could have seen him!' More than once he has asked for his sister; he accepts, however, all that we tell him of the difficulties of getting here. Indeed, nothing appears to disturb him. There is an English yacht in the harbour, belonging to Lord Milborough, and he is as ready as others to be of use.

"You will want a word as to Miss Dalrymple, for whom, I know, you have no kindly feeling. You would retract if you saw her now. I am sure she suffers. Whether she ever really loved Hugh, I cannot tell. Had she—but it is impossible to theorise. I am also sure that she liked him, and he is happy in the conviction that he would have won her. This parting is quite without the bitterness of the first. She is at hand to see him if he desires it, and this, though the friend she is with is urgent to return to England.

"I am writing my letter in Hugh's room, where there is something already of extraordinary peace. If the border-land of death were always so restful, it seems to me that half our dread would vanish.

"An hour later. I have wondered more than once whether he realised his own position, or whether weakness permitted no consciousness beyond the consciousness of the moment, but he has just asked that he might be taken home. I told him there would never have been any question of this, and it seemed to satisfy him. My letter cannot go before to-morrow, and by that time I may have more to add."

What he added was written the next day in his own room.

"He passed away at nine this morning. The peace of which I wrote to you has not been broken, and dying seemed as natural and simple an act as living. I feel that you will long to be told about the hours before, yet there is nothing for words. It was like a hand slackening its hold in quiet sleep, and no more.

"I was with him throughout the night, and, of course, always one of the nurses; but I do not think he recognised either of us for many hours before his death. The doctors say that unconsciousness usually comes on at an earlier stage. Neither of us knew the exact moment at last; once or twice before we had thought him gone, and afterwards fancied that he breathed.

"Now you will want to know what arrangements can be made, and I must tell you hastily, lest I lose the mail. To-day is Saturday. I am ignorant as to whether there are stringent rules as to the time of burial in Norway, but I do not doubt to arrange somehow, for no steamer leaves before Tuesday, when one goes to Newcastle. I do not telegraph to you until Monday. I should not do it then, were it not for the fear that Ella might be meaning to leave Hull on Tuesday, for, unless absolutely necessary, it always appears to me cruelty to inflict that length of waiting which lies between a foreign telegram and the details of a letter.

"I wish you could see him."

Wareham spent a good deal of the day with Dr Sivertsen, going through necessary formalities and making the necessary arrangements. He was not sorry to accept the young man's invitation to his house for supper. They talked of Hugh. Dr Sivertsen spoke of his frank simplicity.

"Something in him," he said, "resembled the best type among us Norwegians."

"That is for you to say, not me," Wareham answered. "If we have learnt nothing else from your late revelations of yourselves, we have been, at least, taught not to classify so glibly as has been our custom."

"We have thought more than we have written," mused Sivertsen, puffing at his cigar. "And when I was in England, some years ago, it appeared to me that English conception of the northern character was principally based upon the tales of Frederika Bremer and the stories of Hans Andersen. There they saw one side, and of the moral character, I allow, the best. But they can hardly be said to draw a complete picture. Moreover, you are a writing nation; perhaps are not without danger of writing yourselves out?"

"Perhaps," sighed Wareham wearily.

"We have the charm you thirst for—novelty. Novelty stands with you for originality, especially when united to daring."

"Which you have never lacked."

"In action. Of old our habit was to send the deed before the word. We are changing. I do not say it is for the better; but I dare say we offer greater interest to the world. Your young English lady is of quite another type from Mr Forbes."

"Miss Dalrymple?" asked Wareham, with curiosity. "I hardly knew you had seen her."

"Yes. I was interested, understanding from Dr Scott that she was to marry him. Was that so?"

"Hardly. It might have been so in time."

"It surprised me. She is much more modern, much more subtile. Is she greatly grieved?"

"I cannot tell you. Probably I shall know to-night."

He rose. The young doctor walked with him as far as the head of the harbour. Lights twinkled here and there, people strolled about, and Wareham was perforce reminded of that evening in Stavanger, of Millie's pleasure, of what now seemed like the beginning of all things; for what is the day when a man first sees the woman he loves, but, to him, the day of creation?

He walked slowly. No need to hurry back. No one was waiting, no night-watch lay before him. Dr Scott had hurriedly packed, and got off by the Hull steamer, taking the English nurse with him. Wareham felt that he must see the others, and hear from them their plans; Colonel Martyn was the only one he had spoken with, and he had said they would at any rate make no movement that day. As Wareham came near the inn, a party of gentlemen turned out and came towards them, and an instinct of avoidance thrust him into the door of a shop. There he waited until they had passed; what gratitude it was necessary to express, he had a preference for enclosing in a letter. Laughter broke out as they came near. Sir Walter spoke in a drawl—

"Clear deck for Mil at last. Worth waiting for, eh, Burnby?"

"You're an unfeeling dog," muttered Lord Milborough.

Wareham, within, saw that he alone was not smiling.

"Wants condolences—" was all that reached Wareham's ears, with a retreating laugh. He felt angry that even so much had been forced upon him. There was nothing astonishing in the words. Reason might have told him that the *Camilla* would not have furled her white wings in Bergen harbour unless some pretty strong attraction had influenced her owner. And further, that it was unconscionable to expect regret for Hugh from men to whom he was only a stranger and a rival. But many people, perhaps unconsciously, embody abstract qualities when they present them to their mind, and Wareham, the most reasonable of men, turned reason into an old woman with a shrewish face and an uplifted finger. There were times when he hated her.

He looked into the salon at once, and would have escaped when he beheld only Mrs Martyn, but that young lady had her eye on the door.

"Ah, Mr Wareham, we were expecting you," she cried, in an injured voice. "Tom has been to look for you more than once, for really, with so many dreadful things happening, and so much to be thought of, I am *most* anxious to get home."

Wareham refused to accept the responsibility of their stay. He merely asked—

"When do you start?"

"I hope you will induce Anne to leave at once. She is quite unnerved, unstrung—I do think she might show a little more consideration. But really, this has been the most unfortunate tour I ever made! Poor Mr Forbes ought never to have come out, ill as he must have been from the first. And, of course, Anne behaved very badly to him. I don't wish for a moment to defend her, only it seems a little hard that Tom and I should be made to suffer for it, doesn't it? Now the only thing for us to do is to go home as quickly as possible."

He expressed a hope that her wish would be carried out.

"If Anne is sensible—"

His heart went out to Anne. No, she was not heartless.

"But, as I said, pray tell her that you quite agree with us. I must say I think her wishing to stay here is not, not quite—well, of course, it was all broken off, and it *will* so attract attention again, just when it was to be hoped it was dying away. I am sure I don't know how I shall face Lady Dalrymple, she will be so extremely annoyed!"

It appeared to him unnecessary to offer either argument or consolation, and the only remark available was—"You go in the yacht?"

She looked shrewdly at him, and withdrew her plaints.

"How else? Besides, Lord Milborough is very pressing. But as we can't expect the poor man to stay here day after day, Tom is anxious we should be off to-morrow. They have all just been here. Didn't you meet them?"

"They passed me in the street."

"I forgot. Of course you have been too much occupied to see anything of them. Besides, men rarely like each other. Don't go. Anne will be here in a moment. The comfort that it will be to get back to properly-proportioned evenings and late dinners! You really wish to go? Then I will fetch Anne." Remembrance of Hugh made it easy for him to beg her not to do this with an earnestness which perplexed her, but she was keen to carry her point.

"You can't refuse to see a lady, I suppose?" she said, jumping up. "I want you to tell her that she can do you no good by staying."

"Me!"

"And herself harm. But that—"

She rustled out of the room, with an air of filling space, which belonged to her. Vexed at this special interview, Wareham walked restlessly about the room, turning over fragmentary literature. Two Germans came in, stared at him, went out again. Then, to his relief, appeared Colonel Martyn. His sympathy was unaffected, and Wareham had never liked him so well; but at this moment his merit was the merit of being a third person.

"I went to look for you a couple of hours ago," he told Wareham, "thinking I might be of some little use, but you weren't to be found. Sad time this, for you."

"Thank you. It is. But Sivertsen has been most useful, and in this country the officials don't go out of their way to be overbearing, as I have found them in Germany. I believe that everything's arranged. Mrs Martyn talks of your leaving to-morrow?"

A gleam of unmistakable relief irradiated Colonel Martyn's face. He hesitated over his "yes," however, and added—

"Unless you want any one?"

Wareham hastened to repudiate such a need, looked at his watch, and yawned.

"Turn in," Colonel Martyn suggested benevolently, and spoke of the wakeful nights the other had spent.

"Mrs Martyn asked me to wait for her." He avoided Anne's name.

"I'll go and hurry her up."

In spite of this fresh propelling force, long minutes passed before Mrs Martyn rustled back alone, but in high spirits.

"I am really so sorry, Mr Wareham! Anne is such a strange girl, one never knows how to take her, and she says she can see no one more. But, after all, she has come to her senses about leaving, and agrees to go to-morrow. Congratulate me."

"I am only sorry my name should have been intruded on Miss Dalrymple," said Wareham gravely. "She understood, I hope, that you imagined she had something to say to me?"

"I dare say. It really does not matter," Mrs Martyn returned airily, and he began to discern where the intention had lain. It annoyed him both then and when he afterwards thought of it.

In the room of death, his last look at Hugh's boyish quiet face made his promise take the form of a most willing offer. Nothing more remained that he could do to please him. Friendship and sympathy were closed for ever here. Only this was left, and it had already become sacred. The look in Hugh's eyes, the touch of his hand, rose up before him—witnesses.

He was determined to avoid so much as a word with Anne the next day, and as it fell out, had no difficulty in keeping his resolution. The start was made early, and Colonel Martyn, his face verging on cheerfulness, ran up to wish Wareham good-bye. The word said, he asked whether he would not come down to see the others, but men were waiting, and Wareham's excuse natural. They had quitted the house some fifteen minutes, when he followed, telling himself that to see Anne leave the shores, himself unseen, would do no one harm. For three days past the weather had been heavy, and the coast colourless; now the sun shone out, a roughish wind was blowing, the water danced and sparkled, and the yacht looked like some beautiful creature straining to be free. The launch was on its way. Wareham's eyes held it as it slipped over the bright waves, until he lost it round the vessel. Presently, almost imperceptibly, masts, lines, sails, began to move with the moving clouds, and—a white cloud herself—the *Camilla* glided swiftly out towards the open, carrying Anne.

He and Hugh were left.

Chapter Twenty Two
A Name in the Air

A fortnight later, Lady Fanny, having meanwhile paid a rapid visit to an uncle's house, was again at Mrs Ravenhill's. She had flung over her engagements in Scotland, remarking, and with reason, that until she could get hold of Milborough, and have things started on their proper lines, she would rather not encounter the rush of autumn country-house gaieties. She professed herself to be occupied in the study of economy, as although her fortune would be large, she declared that it would be all given away except a fragmentary residue.

"I mean to shock him by my trousseau, though," she announced one morning when she sat on the carpet in Millie's bedroom. "I shall show him just a few of the bills, and see his face!"

Justice to Mr Elliot obliged Millie to remark that she believed he would like Fanny to have the very best, but she was scouted.

"The best, yes, but if you knew his ideas of what the best costs! Now, Millie, I'll be quite fair, I'll say nothing, and the next time you see him, get out of him what he supposes would be the expense of a wedding-dress. If his imagination conjures up a sum beyond five or six pounds, I'll give you a silver frame for his photograph. There, is that comfortable?" She patted Millie's ankle.

"I'm sure it's too tight. I couldn't walk."

Lady Fanny consulted a small book on her lap, and began mournfully to unfasten a roller bandage.

"I suppose it *is* too tight, but I really don't see why you should expect to walk about when you're done up in strips. And that was my best figure of eight. However, of course if you insist upon such trifles—oh, *what* is it, Millie? You shouldn't shriek!"

"Not with a pin running straight in? Oh!"

Lady Fanny began, with shaking fingers, to search for the offending instrument. Found, it was discovered to have punctured a hole from which a small drop of blood was oozing. The girls looked at each other. Fanny got up and walked to the window. From that refuge she remarked—"You'd better bathe it."

"Aren't you coming to assist?"

"You can manage that by yourself."

Millie laughed.

"You won't do for the hospitals yet, Fanny! There! A bit of sticking-plaster is on, and I am quite tidy. Suppose we give up the bandaging, and try something else?"

Lady Fanny came eagerly back.

"Yes, something else. Will you have a broken collar-bone, or shall I take your temperature? Only—" with a sigh.

"What?"

"The thermometers do break so easily! This is my third. Please be careful."

Millie promised. The thermometer was inserted under Millie's arm.

"Now we can talk," Lady Fanny remarked with satisfaction, stretching herself in a basket-chair. "Oh dear, oh dear, don't you think it a little hard that I can't get proper attention from Milborough? This waiting is horrid."

"Oh, horrid!" Millie agreed. "But you must hear soon. I suppose the fact is that he has been so busy since he came back, that he has not had the time to go into it."

"Busy! Milborough busy! Little you know him. Too idle to read his letters is more likely. But I do think he might take the trouble to open mine."

"I wonder whether he met the Martyns?" Millie said reflectively.

"If he has, and if I know Milborough, he has fallen in love with Miss Dalrymple." Fanny was too much concerned with meditation on her own affairs to notice that Millie made a quick movement before she said—

"You forget—poor Mr Forbes! I do think it is so terribly sad!"

"Ah, but I did not say that Miss Dalrymple had fallen in love. No, no, I think better of her. Even if she had not—but she must have cared! She would never have let him join them after all that had happened, unless she had intended to marry him. Her face is not like one of those horrid girls who lead men on just to throw them over. No, Millie. If you and Mr Wareham thought that of her, you were both shamefully unjust."

"He did not think so." She spoke with difficulty. "Fanny, I don't think you understand. *He* would never blame Miss Dalrymple."

A string of undecided questions ran through Lady Fanny's mind, quick as lightning. "Shall I? Shan't I?" She gave way, and inquired carelessly—

"Do you mean to tell me, seriously, that Mr Wareham was smitten?"

"Yes. The more I look back the more I think so."

Millie spoke in a low voice. Her friend jumped up and kissed her.

"Goose!" A cry followed. "Good gracious! Millie! The thermometer!"

"Safe, safe, where you put it."

"Oh, you're a dear. You're made to be experimented upon. Now let us see."

With heads close together, hair mingling, and the thermometer on a table before them as if it were something which would go off if meddled with, it was studied. First Millie said she could see nothing. Turned delicately, a thread-like line revealed itself.

"Normal is 98 degrees—about."

"This looks like degrees!"

"Then you must be very ill."

Lady Fanny turned a tragic face upon her friend, and Millie shuddered with a feeling of preliminary collapse. The practical instincts of her mother, however, came to her rescue.

"What was it when you began?"

"That!" Fanny pointed mournfully.

"It hasn't moved?"

"It never does!"

Suspicion began to twinkle in Millie's eyes.

"Which end do you put in?"

Fanny pointed again, this time with dawning hesitation.

"And the other is the bulb! Oh-h-h!" They fell upon each other, as young creatures do, with bubbling laughter. Fanny screwed up her thermometer vindictively, and tossed it into a basket; then, to get out of the reach of Millie's mockery, skilfully turned the conversation to the point from which it had broken away. She produced Lord Milborough's letter, and, for the twentieth time, took opinion upon its meaning—"Dear Fan—Don't be a baby. I'll write by and by,"—on her dignity as to the baby, and perplexed by being, as it were, set on the shelf, at a moment which for a woman is the one moment to which all time has been leading up.

"It is so strange, so strange!" she repeated. "A whole week ago!"

Millie, turned to sympathy at once by the droop of the mobile mouth, uttered her consolations.

"Dear, you couldn't expect him to like it *very* much, and perhaps it is better he should not write at once. Now he will have time to think it over, and be sensible."

"John has had no answer either, for I told him to telegraph." She released herself from Millie, and sat up, fun sparkling in her eyes. "Though I knew that was asking too much. If I'd been an old woman to be got into a hospital now! But just for ourselves—oh, the extravagance of it!—he couldn't, he couldn't, he couldn't! So perhaps Milborough's had the decency to write to him."

"And, anyway, you'll be your own mistress in a year."

"Yes." She made a face. "A whole year! Besides, I want Milborough to be nice. And here he leaves me, not even telling me when he is to be at Thorpe again, or whether I'm to ask any one, or—I tell you what, Millie, perhaps we can see something in the *World*. I'll run down-stairs and get it."

The *World* gave the required information. Lord Milborough's name figured in a list of visitors at a big Yorkshire country-house. There, it also appeared, were to be found Lady and Miss Dalrymple; and after the girls' surmises, the names had a certain significance.

"He has actually left the yacht! There is something, I am certain there is something! At another time I should write and ask him," cried Lady Fanny. "Now, where is Mr Wareham?"

His movements were not recorded.

"Not there, at any rate. Millie, I told you you were a goose. But I have no patience with Miss Dalrymple! That poor man just dead, and here she is, amusing herself. Oh, yes, that explains! I know Milborough. But how can she turn from one to the other? Tell me quickly, Millie, is she the girl to marry him just for the position? Because—a marriage without love—I never before knew how horrible it must be! And poor Milborough, he isn't very good, I know, but I do hope he will never have that fate." Millie felt faithless to her friend—cruel—for the glad throb in her heart, and the instantaneous wish to extol Miss Dalrymple. She briskly argued that with the choice which lay before her, there was not the temptation to snatch at this world's prizes which might beset an older or less beautiful woman. Besides—she smoothed over the fact of their being in the same house as possibly a mere coincidence. Fanny listened, shrewd enough to see something of the forces which pulled her friend's reasons, and set the active puppets dancing, yet with her imagination captivated, as it had been all along, by dreams of Anne Dalrymple.

Elsewhere the notice in the *World* was remarked and commented upon. Wareham was still at Firleigh, with old Sir Michael. There he had taken Hugh, and there the young heir was laid by the side of old forefathers, youth stepping in to sleep between them as quietly as they. For centuries Forbes' had lived and died there; they lay, cross-legged and mailed, in niches; knelt stiffly on brasses, with children in graduated rows behind; their names stared down from marble tablets, vaults held them closely; a few, Hugh's young mother one, had prayed to be laid under the daisied grass of the churchyard, where the larks sang, and showers and sunshine fell. Wareham often thought of it as the most peaceful place he knew.

The Hall itself had suffered many transformations. It stood, as always, in a cup of land, sheltered by ground and trees, but the demon of damp had only been exorcised by late generations at the cost of architectural beauty, and instead of the fine old red stone house, up rose a solid, substantial square. On one side a terrace flanked it, while the garden was out of sight of the windows, lying behind, and a little higher than the house. Through it the family passed to church, always on foot, for weddings and funerals alike; through it, with the summer flowers massed in gorgeous colour all round, Hugh was carried, three white wreaths lying on his breast, and Sir Michael watching from a bedroom window.

The old man was very ill, so ill that they all knew there would be a second, what—from the ancient custom—the people round Firleigh called "carrying," before long. But his spirit was still masterful, and his fingers clasped the reins he could not use. He was keen that Wareham should stay.

"When you're gone, I shall think of twenty questions I had to ask," he said. "There's no one but you, Dick, to answer them. Your room's always kept for you. What d'ye want? Paper, ink, books? Miles will order down anything. And you'll never need to come again. Stop two or three weeks, till—till it doesn't all seem so raw."

Of course Wareham stopped.

A sister of Sir Michael's was there, a kindly woman, but a little precise, and Ella, Hugh's only sister, a girl who required to be well-known before you could even in thought extract her from a crowd of other girls. Anything distinctive she appeared to shun. Hugh she adored, and Wareham admired the self-command which crushed back outward manifestations of grief, but it made conversation difficult, since one subject was uppermost in their hearts, and that Ella shrank from, as from a touch on a wound. Sir Michael tolerated no other. Wareham sat for hours in the window, the old man in a great chair by the fire, for fire was necessary for his chilled blood; long silences between them, then perhaps a dozen questions strung on end, each harping on the same note. Miss Dalrymple's name was like a match to powder.

"She's the cause," Sir Michael would violently burst out. "Without that woman, Hugh would have been living still. She should be branded as a jilt. Mark you, Dick, so sure as there's a God above, it'll come home to her one of these days. I shan't forget my poor boy when he came down to tell his old dad that he'd got her to say she'd marry him. I heard him on the stairs. Up he came, three at a time, and into my room with a whoop." He rambled away into details, where failing memory lost itself as bewilderingly as a traveller in a wood. But he never let go his clutch upon Anne's sin. Wareham, whose heart smarted to hear her blamed, tried in vain to soften judgment.

"Remember, sir, that if she had made a mistake, she went the best way to mend it."

"Mistake? What mistake?"

"That of supposing she loved Hugh well enough to marry him."

Sir Michael smote his thigh weakly.

"She would have, if she'd had a heart as big as a pea. Do you tell me he wasn't the boy to make a girl love him? Why, there wasn't man, woman, or child could stand out against Hugh when he set himself to win them. A heartless jade, Dick, a heartless jade!"

Wareham eyed the carpet with a frown. Sir Michael's anger was unreasonable, because based on imperfect knowledge, and its daily repetition irritated him. One argument, and one only, sometimes availed to check it.

"He loved her to the last, sir. It would have cut him to the quick to think you hadn't forgiven her."

The old man covered his face with his hand.

"That was the boy all over. He had his mother's kindly nature, sweet as sunshine. Never bore a grudge. If he and his cousin fell out and fought, Hugh would lend him his pony an hour afterwards, without a backward thought at his bruises. However badly she'd treated him, he'd have smoothed it over to you. Would she have married him?"

"He thought so."

"Ay, ay, he would make the best of it. But what did you think, Dick?"

The question he had never yet been able to answer. He muttered something to the effect that principals knew best in such a matter. It seemed to him likely.

"Wrong, sir, wrong. Hugh has told me one thing, and you another, and my own sense, if it isn't what it was, may be trusted for the rest. She's one of those creatures that like to keep men dangling round them. Tell you what, Dick. When you write a book about them, call it *The World's Curse*."

When Wareham read the notice in the *World*, he tried to persuade himself that it was with an indifferently critical eye. If Anne could turn so swiftly from one to the other—let her! He even smiled over it, acknowledging the aptness of the possible marriage. If love were out of the question, as well one man or the other, the betterness consisted in the income, and he mentally took off his hat, and stepped aside. His persuasions, however, were open for his heart to argue with. Lord Milborough might love, but women such as Anne do not invariably carry out what the worlds judgment insists must be their action; the Anne he believed himself to have discovered was too complex to be counted upon. His heart wandered in meadows where hope sprang and budded, for if she held a thought of him, she would not be unfaithful to it, and in a few weeks' time his lips would be unsealed. Free to love her—free to woo. Wareham's blood leapt at the thought! Hitherto he had never seen her except in bonds, in fetters; a passion of wild words flew to his lips at the bare dream of permitted speech. Once he caught himself muttering, "I love you, I love you!" when Sir Michael was uttering his usual tirade against her, and something hasty which he uttered in defence gave the old man a suspicion. He thundered out—

"You're not playing the fool too, Dick?" Wareham pulled himself together.

"I hope not, but if you saw her, you'd understand her charm."

"Saw her? Don't let her come here. I couldn't trust myself. D'ye hear?"

There was difficulty in soothing him, and his suspicion died in the greater disturbance.

Two or three large estates covered the neighbourhood, so that of actual neighbours Firleigh had not many. The houses had shooting-parties filling them, with whom the Forbes' in their trouble had, of course, nothing to do; the ladies of the houses drove over to see Ella, who escaped from them as much as she could, clinging to solitude.

Wareham used to take a gun and a dog and go across the fields, more by way of pleasing his host, who believed that here was enjoyment, than because he cared about it himself. He was not in the mood for sport; what, however, he did like was the rich ripeness of the time, the filmy cobwebs glittering on the grass, the pale yellow of the reaped corn-fields against the earth-brown. To sit on a log, and let fancy weave other cobwebs, blue and white smiling down upon him from above, had its pleasantness, and, what was more, its peace. Report of the birds he brought back did not satisfy Sir Michael, who was always wanting to bribe him into staying by the best inducements he could offer.

"We must get Dick a day with Ormsleigh," he said to his daughter, one day. "Pottering about here is miserable work for a young man. He'll be off before we can look round."

"Catherine will be here to-day. I'll tell her what you wish, father."

"Ay, do. Catherine, now," he muttered. "There would have been a girl!"

Ella vanished.

The invitation came. Wareham would have refused, but that he saw old Sir Michael had set his heart upon the matter, for Lord Ormsleigh's shooting was the best in the county.

"I'll go," he said to Ella, "since your father won't believe that I like sport better as an excuse than a pursuit."

"Dear old dad! His imagination is not strong enough to conceive that any one can find enjoyment except in the ways he liked himself."

She had overtaken him as he was strolling home across the park. Ella had been to the village, and had just turned in from the road, which at this point sank into a cutting, so as to be out of view of the house. They walked slowly, now and then standing still to look at an opening between the trees, revealing blue depths. For a woman, Ella was tall, and carried herself uprightly. Looking at her, you gathered an impression of force in reserve. To the outer world she was cold. Wareham knew her better, a medium intellect, but a strong true heart. He saw now that she had something to say, and waited. She said it as they stood still.

"Dick," —she turned and faced him, breathing hard—"let me hear about Miss Dalrymple."

"I expected you to ask."

"And I couldn't before. I've been afraid."

"Of what?"

"That I might not be able to go in and out to father without distressing him. I've been keeping everything back, pressing it down with a leaden weight. There, that will do. Don't let us talk about myself, but—tell me—how was it between them? Would she have married him?"

He had to fall back again on the same answer.

"He thought so."

"And you thought not? I see it in your face."

"Then my face lies, for I cannot tell. Remember, I did not even see them together. A woman might have got to the bottom of it all, but I felt myself hopelessly floundering on the surface. He was content, isn't that enough for you to remember?"

Her eyes met his gravely.

"Don't think that I am like father in blaming her," she said. "I believe I understand. And I am glad that Hugh was spared suffering, for he loved her with all his heart, and she would not have married him."

Wareham looked at her in surprise. Just then they heard steps and men's voices coming along the hidden road: here and there a detached word or two reached their ears. Was it a trick of fancy which made two of these words sound like "Miss Dalrymple"? As the tramp died away, he looked at Ella, and lifted his eyebrows inquiringly.

"Lord Ormsleigh's party going home from shooting," she said. "They sometimes cut across by the road when they have been at Langham."

"Did you hear a name?"

"No."

"I could have sworn that one of them spoke of Miss Dalrymple."

"That is very unlikely. More probably she was in your thoughts just then."

He felt guiltily conscious that she was seldom long out of them. But whether his companion had heard or missed it, the more he thought about it the more positive he felt that those were no phantom words which had crossed his hearing. What should have brought her name into the men's mouths? Common-sense, which sometimes becomes a very imp of mockery, burst out laughing in his face. Why not, as well as any other name? In these days, beauties unseen and untalked about hardly count as such, fierce lights beat everywhere, tongues discuss familiarly, a serenade is not the gentle tribute of one lover for one ear, but a whole band, drums, trumpets, waking the silence, banging, flaring, calling all men to listen. He had to own this, for he had often moralised upon it. But to feel and to moralise are different conditions, and he resented that careless twitter of Anne's name in the road.

Chapter Twenty Three
A Walk

The next day Wareham spent his afternoon by walking into the small country town where was the nearest railway station. Something which Sir Michael wanted gave him the excuse without which a solitary walk becomes a burden in spite of conscientious evokings of the joys of solitude. And he undertook the further office of calling at post-office and station for letters and newspapers, to the disgust of the groom, who had his own Saturday afternoon diversions in view, and felt himself defrauded. In happy ignorance of his displeasure, Wareham whistled to Venom, Hugh's fox-terrier, and started.

The day was dark and still, life dragging heavily, as it does in September days, yet not without a sombre beauty. Masses of firs here and there relieved the monotony of foliage, and the gorse spread a burnish of gold on broken ground. In the road it was duller. Mud prevailed, and withering grasses coarsely fringed the mud, while autumn had not yet flaunted its yellows and reds to hide decay. Wareham, generally quick to notice nature, walked on unheeding.

Reaching the town at last, it struck him as usual, as an ugly expression of man, varying between squalor and dull respectability, bare brick and slate in rows. The station was uglier, but more attractive in spite of blackness, something of magic still lingering about the sharp bright lines, the rushing monsters that whizz along them, the flaming eyes that glow in the night. Wareham turned towards it.

He was too early. The London express was not due for ten minutes, and he went off to execute Sir Michael's errand, promising to return later. It had been market morning, and farmers and farmers' wives yet lingered in the streets, enjoying weekly greetings. One or two carriages drove about, and Wareham noticed the Ormsleigh brougham at the door of a shop. He went to the post-office, and stayed to send off a couple of telegrams in answer to the letters he found there. Then he walked round by the church, for the pleasure of looking at the noble lines of its tower, and, having by this time completely exhausted Venom's patience, betook himself again to the station.

Newspaper in pocket, he started for home. As dusk approached, the day cleared, and, facing the west as he walked, he noticed signs of preparation in the heavens, as if a pageant might presently disclose itself. The road was inextricably connected with thoughts of Hugh: as boys they had often ridden home under the oaks, and the absence of change in immaterial things is no less oppressive than its presence in material. Hugh's vitality was so amazing that it was next to impossible to think of his life having gone out from among them.

He was still a little distance from Firleigh when, with a curve of road beyond him, sounds reached his ears, remote, yet carrying something in them which hurried him forward. Venom in front was plainly puzzled; he had halted, and was considering matters with cocked ears and head on one side. A few moments brought Wareham within sight and quickened his steps to a run, for evidently there had been an accident.

The brougham, which he had recognised as belonging to Lord Ormsleigh, was reclining angularly against the hedge, the horses were disengaged and held by a hatless groom, while a couple of other men, one of them the coachman, had apparently just succeeded in extricating two figures from imprisonment in the overturned carriage. It caused Wareham not the smallest astonishment to recognise in one of them Anne Dalrymple. He was by her side the next moment.

"Tell me that you are not hurt!"

Anne, who was very pale, showed more amazement.

"Mr Wareham! Have you sprung out of the earth?"

"Good fortune brought me here. My question first, please."

"I haven't a finger-ache, but I am frightened to death, and poor Watkins is worse. Watkins, open your eyes, the danger is over, and the coachman is dying to get to the horses."

But Watkins insisted upon uttering short cries of terror, and requiring man's support. Meanwhile Wareham questioned the coachman.

"A broken pole? How's that?"

"*I* don't know, sir. I could have sworn it was sound, but the off-horse gave a bit of a shy, and it snapped like a twig. Never saw such a thing."

Further explanation put the credit of seizing the horses' heads upon a young farmer who was passing, and showed all the necessary presence of mind. Anne's exhortations at last induced Watkins to struggle to the bank, where she shut her eyes tightly to avoid seeing the horses.

"Now, what's to be done?" said Anne. "We were on our way to Oakwood."

"And you are two miles from the house."

"No more? We will walk."

"Would it not be better to send on the groom with the horses, and let a carriage come back for you?"

"Thank you. No more carriages to-day. I had a momentary expectation of being kicked into splinters with the brougham. Come, Watkins, you are not really hurt, and I am sure you would rather walk. Think of the tea that waits for you."

But Watkins' protestations became piteous. She described herself as all of a tremble, and as unable to stir. Anne tried arguments to no purpose until her patience failed.

"If you like it best then," she said, "you must stay here until we can send for you, for I am going to walk, and the coachman thinks they can get the carriage home by leading the horses."

"What, stay here by myself, ma'am, in this dismal road!" cried Watkins, roused to protest.

"If you can't walk. Unless you prefer to get into the brougham."

This she declared to be out of the question, and was melting into tears, when the young farmer, moved to compassion, stepped forward with a suggestion. A little way from the road, it appeared, there was a house. If the young lady felt herself able to walk so far, he would be happy to show her the way, and she could stop there until they sent a trap from Oakwood. Watkins, taking a good look at him, and recognising a preserver in a very personable young man, closed her eyes again, sighed, and consented.

"The young lady being provided for, now for the young woman," said Anne, turning with a smile to Wareham. "I am not so helpless as Watkins, but to walk in the rear of this melancholy procession is not particularly inviting. Is there no shorter way across the fields?"

He glanced at her from head to foot.

"You don't look fit for walking," he said, "except in the park."

"I don't dress for the lanes," she answered coolly.

"And your shoes are absurdly thin."

"When you have finished your criticisms, perhaps you will answer my question. One no more expects criticism from a novel-writer than pepper from an oyster."

"Thank you. I accept the simile."

"One good turn deserves another, so will you tell me whether you are going to show me a pleasanter way than the road in company with a broken-down brougham? Or shall I ask the coachman?"

"Certainly not," said Wareham hastily. Anne's question was by no means such a simple matter as she imagined. The shortest way to Oakwood took them, beyond a doubt, exactly in front of the house at Firleigh; it would, indeed, be necessary to pass directly before the window. And he dared not cause Sir Michael such a shock. Firleigh lay in the region where little events are chronicled. The appearance of Mr Wareham and a strange young lady, beautiful and beautifully dressed, would reach Sir Michael with the rapidity of an electric shock, and, require explanations. This, at any rate, must be avoided. He must take her into the grounds, but a circuit through a wood would have to be made. He explained that they need not follow the road for more than a quarter of a mile.

"Come, then," said Anne, "let us get over the quarter of a mile."

She was in high spirits, disposed to laughter as he had never before seen her, rippling with fun over Watkins, her preliminary look at the young farmer, and evident appreciation of his civility.

"I shall hear so much about him to-night that I hope he may drive all that she felt and did in the carriage out of her head."

"You were not frightened yourself?"

"Oh yes, as much as I had time to be. But as to nerves, Watkins usurped the display. The bump against the bank reassured me at once."

"I bless the farmer."

"Yes. Without him," — Anne turned paler, she was perhaps more shaken than she knew.

"I suppose that you?"

"I," said Wareham, deliberately uttering the last thing that he desired to say, "I was, as usual—too late."

She looked at him inquiringly; their eyes met, naturally she expected more. His mouth grew rigid, under a sudden impression of his own weakness, when he had thought himself absolutely safe, and he added hurriedly—

"Do you see that gate? There we turn off." Anne's voice was a little colder than it had been.

"I have not apologised. I may be taking you out of your way. Are you staying in the neighbourhood?"

"At Firleigh."

There was a momentary pause before she asked—

"And are we near Firleigh?"

"We are going to cut across part of it now." He opened the gate as he spoke, and she walked by his side for some minutes in silence. Then she said—

"It is curious that we should have met. Of course, I knew that Oakwood and Firleigh were near each other, but—it seemed unlikely that you should be here. Poor Hugh!"

"He would like to know he was remembered."

"He asked me to think of him sometimes. If that were all—it would be easier to satisfy the dead than the living, for who can help remembering?"

"Not I," said Wareham, with a sigh.

"His grave?"

"You must see it."

"And his father—?"

"Sir Michael is too ill to receive visitors." Wareham spoke hastily.

"Ah, poor old man! But I must drive over and see his sister." A touch of hesitation reaching her, she said sharply, "No?"

"Remember that they were irritated, rather, I should say, Sir Michael was irritated, by your dismissal of Hugh. Something of displeasure you must expect."

They faced the west and a fir wood as they walked. Grey clouds covered and contracted the sky, but at the horizon lifted sufficiently to show a fiercely burning line of red, cut by the stems of the fir-trees. Anne stared before her, with her head thrown back. Wareham let his fancy skip to possible futures when they two should walk together, side by side, with no shadows between them. But he would keep faith with Hugh, control voice and look.

"They are unjust," slowly said Anne, at last, and he started, brought back from rapturous dreams.

"He is an old man, very feeble, and had but one son," he pleaded. "Ella, I am sure, judges more fairly."

"Unlike a woman, then. If that is their feeling, I wish I had not come here. I assure you, though you may not believe it, that there was some— sentiment in my visit. I believed I should be welcomed. I should be, if they understood. That was the one time in my life in which I acted unselfishly. And if I had been left alone—if you, for instance, had not taken upon yourself to set poor Hugh upon my track—it would all have died gently away. Friends meddling. When has it not brought mischief!" Anger suited her, and the darkening of her eyes. Wareham felt no uneasiness from her wrath, so lost was he in admiration. "And for a man to meddle! As if his fingers were delicate enough for the task of dealing with our vanity!" She laughed shortly, disdainfully. Suddenly she flashed out—"What did he tell you?"

"He?"

"He. Hugh." As he hesitated, she added impatiently—"He must have spoken of me?"

"He told me"—Wareham spoke measuredly—"that he believed he should have won you."

Her face softened, she turned dewy eyes towards him.

"I am glad, I am glad. He deserved to be happy. It is so dreadful to die, and, poor fellow, I have thought since that I might have given him more comfort. Dear Hugh!"

"You loved him!" Wareham exclaimed involuntarily.

Anne flung him another glance.

"Almost," she said.

"If he could only hear you!"

"Ah," she said, with a movement of her head, "almost would not have satisfied him or—" She paused.

"Or?"

"Or me."

There was another silence, silence more significant than speech. When Wareham spoke, his voice was hoarse.

"You have given up, then, that fiction that you are heartless?"

"I do not know," said Anne quietly. "Was it not you that tried to argue me out of it?"

"You must learn it by something different from argument," he replied slowly.

She made no answer. In one hand he carried a newspaper, unconscious that he held it in a grasp like that of a vice. They reached the wood at this moment, and stepped under the firs. Anne asked whether they could see the house.

"By coming a little to the right. It lies in a hollow."

She stood still and looked.

"And I am not permitted to go there?"

"Illness excuses everything. I assure you Sir Michael's condition is such that we don't know what a day may bring. That has kept me here."

"One hears of nothing but death," said Anne restlessly. "I do not like the house. I cannot fancy Hugh in it. It is gloomy."

"You see it on a dark day, and saddened. It may be fancy, but I always think that old family places share the feelings of their owners."

"Then Oakwood should be cheerful?"

"It is."

"You come there sometimes?" Anne asked. She had turned her back sharply upon Firleigh, and was walking on.

"Sometimes. I shoot with Lord Oakleigh on Monday."

"That will not be of much use to us women."

"But I shall venture to call, and inquire for—"

"For Watkins," Anne broke in with a laugh. "Hers will be the sufferings. We mistresses are made of sterner stuff. Well, we all have what we ask for, and depend upon it, Watkins will get her sympathy."

He inquired whether her stay would be long. She smiled at the idea.

"You know what these autumn campaigns are like. A flying two or three days, then, bag and baggage, away to the next station. A 'prest' day no longer exists. You would discomfit your host and hostess very much by staying."

"Where has the change come from?"

"From superhuman efforts to exorcise the fiend—dullness. He is the only evil power which the century has not whitewashed, and he takes advantage of his position to keep us all in thraldom. The very flutter of his shadow is enough."

She lapsed into silence. The wood by this time lay behind them, and before, a rich country of broad outlines. The sky had lost its fire, heavy clouds menaced, once or twice Wareham thought he felt a drop of rain. Saying this to Anne, she turned her face upward. "Have we much further to go?"

"A quarter of a mile to the lodge, half to the house. You can just see the red chimneys."

"By walking fast, I dare say we shall escape it." She did not, however, increase her pace. Her next remark was to suggest that he should turn back. "Aren't you afraid that Sir Michael may hear that you have been walking with me? And through part of his own land!"

"It is very probable that he will hear of it," said Wareham quietly.

"And you will be in disgrace!" She aimed at light ridicule, but there was a touch of sharpness in her tone, which told him that the old man's ill opinion had stung her. The next moment she owned it. "If only I could see him! He must have got a distorted notion into his mind. Perhaps you share it still?" Gladly would he have accepted these invitations to the personal. All he dared say was that it was not unnatural that Hugh's father should have brooded over his son's disappointment.

"And his death has fixed it indelibly in his mind."

Anne moved a little faster.

"Perhaps he *lays* that also to my charge?"

"He could not be so unjust."

Suddenly she stood still and faced him, soft entreaty in her eyes.

"Mr Wareham, are you my friend?"

Was it the pallor of the gathering clouds which whitened his face? He stammered—

"That—" "And more," was on his lips, when he succeeded in turning it into, "That I think you know."

"The only one, then, that I have here. Try to make them feel more forgivingly. Once, I know, you felt as they do; now, if my heart is to be trusted, you are kinder. After—what has past, it hurts to be so harshly judged. Please be on my side."

Pride, worldliness had all vanished. She spoke like a child, and looked at him beseechingly—so beseechingly that his heart rose in a wild clamour of desire to take her into his arms. The force with which he had to hold back this desire left him staring stupidly, only able to stammer out—

"You need not ask me!"

Perhaps Anne read the turmoil in his face, for her eyes smiled at him, but the next moment she turned away, and walked on silently. When she spoke it was to say—

"Here is the lodge, and your labour ended."

"I can't leave you till we reach the house."

"Oh, very well." Her tone was indifferent, but presently she put an unexpected question—"You remember Lord Milborough?"

"Certainly," said Wareham, wondering what he was to hear.

"He hopes you will come to Thorpe next month, when he has some big shoots."

"Big shoots are not at all in my way."

"So I supposed. Still, as Lady Dalrymple and I and many other delightful people will be there, your highness may perhaps condescend to find attraction, if not in pheasants?"

Her tone was bantering, but did he dream when he read in it a touch of pressure? Prudence shook a warning finger, Love laughed.

"It is very good of you to suggest it," said Wareham, "but I really think you must be mistaken, for Lord Milborough and I only exchanged a few words, and—"

"He is even less in your way than big shoots, you would like to say," broke in Anne, with a laugh. "Well, I own one may have too much of his society."

"Then why go there?" asked Wareham bluntly.

"Can one choose just what one likes? When I can, I do." She quickened her pace. "Here is the rain at last."

"And in three minutes the house."

The door was open, lights streamed out; evidently another arrival had just taken place, and there was some amazement on the face of the servants at seeing Miss Dalrymple appear in the dusk, escorted by Mr Wareham.

"You will come in?" she said.

"Thank you, no. Sir Michael will be expecting me. I hope you won't be the worse for your misadventure."

From the hall she waved her hand without answering. Wareham turned away.

His walk back was mechanical, and he was scarcely conscious of the rain. It was as if Hugh was by his side, asking if his promise had been kept, demanding an inquiry into words and looks. If thoughts had been in the compact, miserable failure would have been the verdict; as it was, Wareham did not believe that he had betrayed himself. But was ever man so hampered! From first to last since he had known Anne, Love and Honour had struggled; there never had been a moment in which he felt himself free to say, "Dear, I love you!" and yet all the bonds were unseen, some might even say, fantastical. And now, at last, when Death had stepped in between the combatants, even Death could not avail. What must Anne think, if Anne thought at all about the matter? He counted the days. A month had passed.

Nearing the house, he resolved that Sir Michael should hear from him who it was to whom the accident had happened, for chance mention of her name, which might very well occur, would give him a distrust of Wareham. But he found that there had been an increase of illness which made all speech impossible, and Ella was so much occupied with her father that he did not see her until late, when she came in to the drawing-room to find him sitting there with Mrs Newbold. The rain had increased to a wild storm, and a log fire was burning. Ella slipped into a three-cornered chair, close by the hearth.

"Better," she said, in answer to her aunt's inquiry, "and asking for you."

Mrs Newbold bustled off. Wareham said something about the storm.

"And you were caught in it?"

"That was no hardship. I simply walked home and changed, and it did not come on till late."

"But tell me about the accident."

"Ah, you've heard of it?"

"We hear everything," and she laughed. "If you would like to know how, in this particular case, understand that the stable-boy's father lives at a house where the lady's-maid was taken to rest, and she related that her mistress was walking to Oakwood with a gentleman, whose description Jem recognised as yours. He brought home the lady's name, and my maid conveyed it to me."

"It is all true," Wareham said gravely, "and I should have taken Miss Dalrymple by the short cut in front of the house, but that I was afraid of annoying Sir Michael. We went round by the wood instead."

"And she was not hurt?" asked the girl, spreading out her hands to the blaze. "I should like to see her—to talk to her."

"That is what she wishes very much. What do you think? Can she come?"

Ella shook her head. It was impossible.

"Perhaps," she said, "she may be at church to-morrow, and if father is well enough I shall go. Did she speak of—Hugh?"

"And of Hugh's family. Evidently when she came here she meant to have seen you all. But—as you say—it's impossible."

Wareham had also thought about the coming day, its delights and its dangers. Dear delight to look at her, danger lest he should fail in his promise. But here, he told himself, that could not happen; here, where Hugh's face met him everywhere, here, where Hugh himself lay at rest, neither friend nor love could forget him. When the day arrived it was blustering and wet: Ella and he walked to church under drenched trees, and she wondered whether Miss Dalrymple would be there. Wareham could not doubt it. Nature would draw her to look at a grave. He felt it. He had a curious desire, too, for her to see the lines of old Forbes' linking past centuries to present, from whom Hugh drew his brave blood. The Oakwood estates doubled, trebled the Firleigh ones, but Oakwood was a mushroom compared to Firleigh, and Lord Oakleigh's a new title, while the other belonged to the soil.

Anne, however, was not there. He was disappointed, but excuses tripped promptly up. No other ladies came from the house, and to have seen Hugh's grave in company with her jovial host would have been like sitting with a jester to view a tragedy. He was sure that Anne had done well to avoid it. Could he have taken her there! And a whisper suggested that Anne could generally arrange what she liked. He flung it from him. Here, after all that had passed, she must have walked warily, or have attracted curious eyes. Ella, too, Ella would have been jealous if Hugh had not his due. And the due meant much.

What Ella thought she did not say. The girl had a curiously reserved nature; it seemed so impossible for her to express her feelings, that she was not credited with many. Their walk back was silent; wind-driven rain beat in their faces, and splashed heavily from the trees, sodden flowers lay prostrate in the garden, an old grey dial turned its weatherbeaten face vainly upwards. Wareham tried to shake off the gloom.

"You don't mind rain, Ella," he said. "Come for a stretch this afternoon."

"Perhaps, if father keeps better. But he may want me to sit with him."

"You don't get air enough."

"I find one can live very well without it."

"Live, but not thrive. We'll take the dogs, and get to the top of Slopton ridge." The next moment she stopped, all the colour out of her face.

"Dick—look!" she cried with anguish.

For all the blinds were down, and one more Forbes had joined his forefathers.

Chapter Twenty Four
Doubt and Pride—Which Wins?

For a week Wareham stayed on at Firleigh, walked with another funeral through the garden and along the church path, and laid old Sir Michael down by the side of his young son and younger wife—ashes to ashes, dust to dust. There was much to arrange, much that a friend—a man—could do to spare poor women. Death, like life, has its routine, which must be gone through, though tears proclaim it heartless; and when the head of a family steps down from his place, another waits to climb into it, all of which needs moving out of the way for some, advancing for others, and filling of vacant space.

Here the heir was a nephew, a young lad of fourteen, hastily sent for from Eton, and present at the funeral with his mother. The boy was a fine fellow, but the mother had that capacity for irritation which is by no means the exclusive property of the ill-tempered. Words, kindnesses even, grated. If it is ourselves that reveal others to us, Wareham found himself reflecting that she presented the world with a likeness of herself, painted blackly, when least she intended it, for she seldom spoke of any one without a depreciatory remark. He resented, too, the airs of ownership she had already assumed, and her benign patronage of Ella. Talking to Mrs Newbold, he let fly his dislike.

"The woman fingers everything as if she were appraising it," he said. "Her hand crooks involuntarily."

"I wish poor Ella could have her last days in peace," sighed Mrs Newbold.

"Do you mean that she intends to stay?" Mrs Newbold nodded emphatically, and sighed again.

"Ella said something, and Amelia jumped at it. She said it would be as well to look round her. Said this to Ella, and not a thank you with it!"

"If I can prophesy at all, this will quicken your own movements. What do you think of doing?"

"Ella will come to me in Monmouthshire for the present. That will give her time to look round, instead of deciding hurriedly." When things had so far advanced, Wareham felt that he might leave. It annoyed him to see Mrs Forbes already in possession, and hinting at this or that change.

"Ella is young, very young," she remarked to him one day. "She does her best, but I should never allow the coachman to order what he chose," and the "I" was imperial. The day before he left, Ella came to Wareham in the library, Venom at her heels.

"You really must go to-morrow, Dick?"

"I must—to avoid war. I can't be decently civil to your aunt for twenty-four hours longer. You can. That's the wonder."

"Worries have shrunk into pin-pricks, I think," she said simply. "But I am sorry for the servants, who will all leave the place, and who have been here, some of them, as long as I have. Their hope is to return to me some time, but when the dragging up is going on, one feels as though one could never take root again. However, I didn't come to say all this. I came to thank you, and I can't."

"I should be ashamed of you if you could. Look here, Ella, I suppose this plan of yours about going with Mrs Newbold is the best just at present?"

"Don't you think so?"

"Hum," said Wareham ruefully. "She's a kind old soul, but body and mind made up of cotton wool. The finest quality of cotton wool, that I allow, still—"

Ella smiled.

"There's a time when cotton wool is just what one wants."

"I've never met with it, then."

She did not go on to tell him that he might. What she said was spoken with hesitation.

"Dick, I've been thinking about Miss Dalrymple."

"Yes?" He drew his breath.

"Shall you see her again?"

He was conscious of the weakness of his answer.

"Perhaps. I hardly know. She spoke of our meeting at Thorpe—Lord Milborough's—next month. I may or mayn't be there." She took no notice of these carefully expressed doubts.

"Please tell her that I should have liked to have seen her. She mustn't think that I reproach her—I know it made Hugh happy at the last."

"Yes," cried Wareham eagerly. "Thank you, Ella. You can be generous."

"If he had lived, perhaps I shouldn't have been," she said quietly. "But he loved her dearly. I believe it would hurt him if we bore a grudge. You don't, do you?"

He said "No" with fervour, thinking that our own pre-occupations serve as a thick bandage for the eyes, for once or twice he had suspected Ella of reading his secret. It appeared, however, that she was absolutely unsuspecting. She talked on for some time, and he saw that hers was a strong soul, facing the inevitable undauntedly, and without murmurs, strong enough not to refuse tears, but to control them. He said to her once—"You have learned to live," to which she answered that one hasn't got to learn that lesson by oneself. It seemed that she feared for the people in the village, who might lose Firleigh advantages, but she meant to talk to Catherine Oakleigh about them.

"And Reggie is a nice boy," she went on. "I am not afraid of things by and by."

So, on the next day, Wareham turned his back on Firleigh. For ever, he told himself, though Mrs Forbes had expressed a gracious hope that they might often see him, and was contentedly unconscious that he went away raging at her, and comparing her to a tremolo stop, to the scrapings of slate-pencils, and to many other sources of irritation; calling her, to himself, the trumpet of deterioration, that belittling woman! Relief at escape from her balanced the real grief it cost him to quit a place which had been like a home so long.

When he left Firleigh he had hardly made up his mind where to go. Restlessness was upon him, but travel was impossible, when he was like some tethered creature, bound not to go out of call, of reach, and hobbled, as he told himself. Not much more than a fortnight of this uncertainty remained, yet the time appeared portentous in length. He had a vague inclination to bury himself in London, and write, but experience warned him that, pre-occupied, his brains would not answer to the call. The impulse, however, was strong enough at the station to lead him to take a ticket for London.

Before he had been there two days he was sorry he had come. Writing was not for him; the sentences yawned at him like bald-headed idiots. But here his will stepped in and brought discipline, commanding that so much should be done at any cost, even probable future consignment to the fire. Something might be saved from it, at any rate his self-respect.

Wareham ground away at his work, and in the afternoon plunged into street labyrinths, walking, walking, walking, without care where he went, so long as it was where he was not likely to meet his fellows. Oftenest he found himself down by the river, standing by black wharves, watching the river life with unseeing eyes, the river itself moving slowly, like the burdened thing it is. But sometimes he wandered round old city churches, quaintly named, lonely protests against the mammon around them, echoing emptily on Sundays, when the great human tide had flowed away from their walls. He passed up a narrow passage one day, and came full upon a lady sketching in a corner. It was Mrs Ravenhill, and escape was out of the question. Besides, his better nature was ashamed of the impulse. They greeted each other without astonishment, for no one is surprised to meet an acquaintance in great London, and Mrs Ravenhill explained that she was taking advantage of a fine day to finish an old sketch.

He remarked—

"And alone?"

"Yes, I can't condemn Millie to be my companion here. Have you come from Thorpe?"

"No," said Wareham, with wonder.

"Lady Fanny certainly said in a letter that you were expected," said Mrs Ravenhill, a little vexed with herself for a slip which appeared to prove them interested in his movements. She added rashly, "Or perhaps I made a mistake."

"I have not received any invitation to Thorpe," returned Wareham, reserving the fact that one had been talked about. "Has Lady Fanny gone back?"

"Yes. There were to be large shooting-parties, and her brother wanted her. You had a sad time after we saw you. It shocked us greatly to hear of Mr Forbes' death, and now his father."

Wareham entered into particulars. She listened with interest, saying at last—

"I am glad the poor young fellow had friends. The seeds of illness must have been in him when we saw him, and yet he seemed so full of life!"

He wanted to find out whether Miss Dalrymple was at Thorpe, and could not bring himself to put the question. But the certainty that they would know led him to propose calling, which he would have fled from but for this inducement. He left Mrs Ravenhill to finish her drawing, and went to his club, a couple of hours earlier than usual, to ascertain whether any letter had arrived from Thorpe. The question of accepting or not accepting the invitation, he flattered himself remained in the balance. The fact of its arrival would prove to him that Miss Dalrymple was there.

Nothing came. He read the evening papers, impressed by their dullness; dined, dropped in at a theatre, and was immeasurably bored. What had come to the world that it could do no better?

Another day and no note. Now he wandered into wonder whether his reticence had for ever disgusted Anne, knowing nothing of his pledge. She had given him openings enough, he saw them the more clearly when he looked back at them; her verdict must have been either indifferent or stupid.

The Ravenhills, with that link of Lady Fanny, began to look so attractive that he grew anxious for the time to arrive when he might pay his promised visit, and took many precautions to find them at home. He chose five o'clock, and was rewarded by hearing that both Mrs and Miss Ravenhill were out. The delay added to his determination. He left word that he would try his luck again at the same time, and went through another restless twenty-four hours, scourging himself with contempt that it should be so, and amazed to find his cool control swept away by a surging tide of passion.

This time the Ravenhills were at home. Millie greeted him charmingly. The curves of her face had grown softer, her eyes had gained depth, the alert air, which sometimes annoyed him, was absent. Each time that he saw her he thought her prettier than before, but now no dream of comparing her with Miss Dalrymple crossed his heart. There Anne sat supreme.

The talk of course fell upon those last days at Bergen. They sat near the fire, with the tea-table in a cosy corner and the room cheerfully lighted, while Millie plied him with questions. Both thought, and thought truly, that their interest lay with Hugh, yet with both the figure of Anne stood always in the background; he wanted Millie to speak her name, she was secretly relieved that he had not yet mentioned her. Then another lady came in, to whom Mrs Ravenhill devoted herself, and Wareham and Millie drew off a little.

She said—

"Directly we heard that sad news, we thought what a shock it would have been to you, but we did not know you had been there until Fanny told us."

He pricked his ears, and asked mendaciously—

"The Lady Fanny I met here?"

"Yes. You know she is Lord Milborough's sister. Do you remember the clergyman, Mr Elliot, who was also here?"

"Yes. I thought—perhaps—?"

Millie laughed.

"It is wonderful, but true. He is the last man I should have suspected Fanny would have chosen. But do not speak of it, for nothing is settled yet, and Lord Milborough will not say anything definitely."

"He can stop it?"

"Only for a year, but Fanny would hate to go against him."

He was willing enough to talk about Lord Milborough and Thorpe.

"So that, after all, it may come to nothing. Poor Mr Elliot!"

"No, no, there is no fear of that. Fanny will not change. She will be quite independent when she is twenty-one. Indeed, she is in terror lest Mr Elliot should find out how large her fortune will be."

"Is Lord Milborough like his sister in character?" asked Wareham carelessly.

She repudiated the notion. "You saw him at Bergen?"

"I saw the surface. He was described to me as indifferent to most things."

Millie hesitated. "I think he will take trouble to get what he wants. I don't know whether you will put that down to his credit or not? But I do believe that in his own way he is fond of Fanny, and perhaps—"

She stopped. Wareham would have given a good deal to know whether the "perhaps" had remote connection with Miss Dalrymple. He had time to reflect, for Millie was called upon to provide another cup of tea for the visitor. When she came back he put a leading question.

"Do you often go to Thorpe?"

"Very very seldom. The house is generally full at this season, and just now there is a big party." She hesitated again, reproached herself, and added, "The Martyns and Lady and Miss Dalrymple are there."

He looked up quickly, and his eye met hers. Something in it told his secret, and Millie turned pale. The thought was not strange to her, perhaps, although latterly it had withdrawn; it was always standing at hand, ready to step in; but withdrawn it had, and to see it again, and to have it advancing so determinedly that she could never any more treat it as a figment of her imagination, gave her a sharp stab. He, all unconscious of his self-betrayal, thought his remark, "A drifting together of Norwegian travellers!" diplomatic; and he ventured to add, "I have heard that Lady and Miss Dalrymple are not sympathetic."

"Fanny does not say. I believe they had only just arrived," murmured Millie.

The visitor was departing, and she was glad of the interruption. When it was over Mrs Ravenhill drew her chair near the others.

"Millie," she said, "I fancy Mr Wareham gives me credit for romancing, but surely Fanny in her last letter mentioned his name as among the people they were expecting?"

"I think she said he was invited, or was going to be invited."

"Ah, then, that was it."

"And perhaps they have thought better of it," returned Wareham, a little awkwardly.

To this there could be no answer, and Mrs Ravenhill turned the subject. Wareham lingered as long as he thought decency required, and rose to take his leave. Mrs Ravenhill reverted with a smile to her supposition.

"If you had been going to Thorpe, I should have asked you to put Lady Fanny's gold thimble, which I only discovered this morning, in your pocket. But now I will send it by post."

"A safer plan," Wareham agreed. "Even if I had received this visionary invitation, it is improbable that I could have accepted it." The fiction served as indemnification for pricks which judgment administered when his mind flew to Thorpe, and beheld himself with Anne, rashly venturing within reach of temptation, while his promise still held him dumb. Walking away in the darkness through Sussex Place, he flung not a thought behind at poor Millie, all his dreams fluttering round Anne. He had succeeded in the object of his visit, and had discovered where she was, a knowledge which he would have been happier without, as the vague uneasiness which Lord Milborough's name aroused became more insistent when he learnt that he and she were actually again together. It was in vain that he told himself it was, no doubt, the fulfilment of some promise made in Norway, that the same party which had foregathered in the yacht should meet again at Thorpe. Suspicion, thoroughly awakened, assured him that more lay in it. And why was he to be asked? This, he knew, must be Anne's doing. Lord Milborough and he had scarcely met, certainly had shown no inclination for each other's society, and although he was not unaccustomed to being sought as a literary lion, that would not be the explanation now. Perhaps Anne desired him to see her.

An impulse led him to strike upwards to the Park, for the jangle and the fret of the streets became insupportable, and, more than this, it appeared that he had a companion at his elbow whom he loved, yet longed to dismiss. If not, why were Hugh's words sounding—reverberating—in his ears? Above wheels, and underground hiss of train, louder, far, than when the dying man spoke them—"You promise? Not a word for two months." And then again, again, the same words, the same voice.

Wareham paced impatiently. Why this repetition, which seemed like doubt? Honour fretted under the imputation. But ten days remained of the trial time, then came free speech, at least the power to ask for what he wanted. If, as Love whispered deliciously, Anne loved him, she would not so quickly sell herself to another man. His heart plucked courage from the "No" which he shouted at it. And, during that time, it was better that they should not meet, for it was intolerable bondage to be tied hand and foot, yet be by her side. Count days and hours, but count them out of sight of her. He resolved to decline, and slept more peacefully that night than he had of late.

The next morning he was half ashamed of the past evenings disturbance, and would have been amazed if any one had informed him that cool reflection is sometimes as much to be watched in love as a sudden drop of temperature in a fever. Among his letters were two which he looked at without a throb, although by the post-marks he knew that they must be from Thorpe. The first he opened was a brief invitation from Lord Milborough, asking him from Monday to Thursday. As he read, Wareham framed an answer of refusal in his mind. The other was from Anne, as short, but different. She underlined a hope that he would come.

And now cool reflection stepped briskly forth. Go or not, let him choose which he deliberately preferred, only avoiding the cowardly fear that he might not be master of himself. Pledged he was, and pledged he must remain, since no thought of evasion could be honourably entertained for a moment; but he was not therefore bound to give false impressions, or to allow Anne to suppose that he by choice avoided her. His refusal would make her think so? Then let him go.

Wareham wrote and accepted. As a compromise, he left Anne's letter unanswered.

Civility, he thought, required that he should go and ask for Lady Fanny's thimble. He went on Sunday afternoon.

"So I was right, after all," Mrs Ravenhill said, with a laugh. "I hope you will get good shooting."

Millie chiefly talked to a boy about postage stamps. She and Wareham scarcely exchanged words until he rose to leave. Then he said —

"Have you any message?"

"For Fanny?" She looked surprised. "My love, please."

"I meant for Miss Dalrymple."

Her "Oh!" was abrupt. She added, immediately, "No, I shouldn't venture. Miss Dalrymple has probably forgotten that we ever met."

In his hansom Wareham reflected that women were difficult to understand in their dealings with each other. Anne had always been charming, why should Millie turn a sharp edge towards her? It was the more astonishing because Millie had nothing of the angular about her. As little would he have imagined that she had the heroic soul. Yet one may call it so when a woman bears the quenching of her hopes without complaint or bitterness. Millie went cheerfully about her daily occupations. Her mother imagined her a little pale, no more. She preferred silence, but talked as usual when it was necessary. Altogether there was nothing to call for remark. Yet in that look she had read Wareham's heart, the more quickly, perhaps, for the quickening in her own, and before it all the budding hopes which were gently unfolding themselves shrivelled and died. To believe that Miss Dalrymple might reject him would have brought her no comfort, for there still exist women to whom love is so delicate and wonderful a thing that they can only look upon it as eternal, and she was ready to stake her faith upon Wareham's constancy. One night Mrs Ravenhill unconsciously fell into the channel of her thoughts.

"Fanny has not written?"

"Not a word; so I suppose she waits until she can tell us that something definite has been said or settled."

"It is too bad of Lord Milborough. I am afraid he is going to object strongly, and *yet* wishes to avoid upsetting Fanny while he has this large house-party. Or is he really taken up with thoughts and wishes of his own?"

"I wonder," said Millie.

"If there was ever any truth in that fancy of yours about Mr Wareham, he will add another complication! But I don't believe it. I think you were determined to create a romance."

The girl laughed, with successful hiding of the effort.

"Well, we shall hear what Fanny thinks."

"Poor little Fanny!"

"She will have to fight her own battles and his too."

"Oh, I am not so sure. He has fighting blood in him."

"Is it the glow of the Berserker?" asked Millie wickedly.

Doubt had not left Wareham. It laid a hand, healthfully cold, as he had to own, upon the visions of Anne which crowded before him. It suggested a telegraphed excuse as a means of escaping the ordeal. But it found itself confronted determinedly by a strong man's pride. Now that he had agreed to go, pride assured him that to shrink was disgraceful, and before pride, stepping robustly forward, doubt looked a poor shadowy thing. Wareham ordered it out of the way, and Monday saw him in the train which would take him to Thorpe in time for dinner. He had a drive of some miles from the station, and from the length of road which lay between the lodge and the house, perceived that the park was very large. A slight descent led to twinkling lights. Here stood the great house, planted solidly as a castle, of which, indeed, it only wanted the name.

And here was Anne.

Chapter Twenty Five
Fire and Cold Water

Wareham was met in the hall by Lord Milborough—thanked for coming. They went up the broad staircase together.

"The first gong has sounded, and there's nobody in the drawing-room," his host explained. "You'll find friends here, I hope. Colonel and Mrs Martyn."

He paused. Wareham did not feel the necessity for speaking.

"Lady and Miss Dalrymple, and half-a-dozen others."

The half-dozen others multiplied before dinner. The great drawing-room with its fine Gainsboroughs looked cheerfully full. Lady Fanny welcomed Wareham warmly, and put a dozen questions about her friends.

"You saw them yesterday?"

"And am the bearer of lost property."

"My thimble! Thank you a thousand times. Sad to say, I had never missed it; but I must not let Millie know that, or I shall be scolded for my idleness. Oh, if you had only persuaded them to come with you!" She hoped that Wareham's heart echoed the wish, and would have been mightily disappointed could she have peeped at it. Where was Anne? Not yet in the room. Mrs Martyn, however, smiled at him from a sofa, and he was obliged to seat himself by her side, and to endure a characteristic greeting.

"I hope you don't object, Mr Wareham; but it almost gave me a shock to hear you were coming. I knew the sight of you would bring back that nightmare time at Bergen."

"Did you mind it so much?"

"How can you ask? I tell Lord Milborough he saved my life, for if the yacht had not been there, I might have hung myself. That poor young man! You never ought to have told him to come out. It wasn't fair on us."

Wareham sat mute. She glanced at him, and played with her great fan.

"And now you have arrived, I suppose, to see the next act of the play?"

He inquired what that was to be.

"You don't know? Then I shan't enlighten you. This is a good house, isn't it? with capabilities. And the pictures are good. There are one or two smaller and extremely choice in the boudoir opening out of this room. Ah, Anne is coming from it at this minute."

Anne it was, followed by Lord Milborough; Anne in soft draperies of white and yellow, here and there flash of diamonds, brilliant as Wareham had never seen her before. She came towards him, and he rose.

"You are to take me in to dinner," she said smilingly.

"Fortunate I!"

Another man presented himself.

"Not to-night, Mr Orpington. Go and ask Lady Fanny to effect an exchange between you and Mr Wareham."

"It seems that I am indebted even more than I knew," said Wareham, in a low voice, as they proceeded to the dining-room.

"It is my rule to resist tyranny. What can be so odious as to be handed over for two hours to a man with whom you have nothing in common?"

Others noticed the act. As they passed Lord Milborough's chair, he murmured—

"Queens command."

Anne took no notice. As soon as they were seated, she said to Wareham—

"Now for your apology."

"My apology?"

"I wrote, and you did not bestow upon me so much as a line. Were you afraid that I should trade with your autograph?"

"Folly is not yet quite rampant in man. I answered by obeying."

She turned a little towards him.

"It is not a bad house to stay in. One has one's liberty." The next moment she added—"Do you know my step-mother?"

"No."

"She is there—in black and green. Black hair as well. You need not murmur inarticulate admiration, for we do not love each other."

"That does not make her the less handsome."

"To women it does. Where a woman dislikes she cannot admire. Probably you know most of the other people?"

"No. I see Lord Arthur Crosse next Lady Dalrymple."

Anne let her eyes rest reflectively upon the two persons he named, without answering the remark except by a slight nod. Presently, however, she said—

"Do you think he will marry her? The question interests me more than it should, for you know that we are in a measure bound together. My father ruled that I was to be dependent upon her until I married—or she. I believe our old lawyer got that last clause put in out of sheer good-will to me, for my father had faith in her perpetual tears. He loved me, too, but he tried to see too far. I am not sure that a will is ever a just thing. The dead, should they control the living?" She was unconscious how closely Wareham's thoughts flew with hers. He said—

"They must, while men have hearts. Made as we are, it is impossible to refuse what the dying ask."

"What they ask?" repeated Anne, lifting her eyebrows. "I was talking of what they command. The most undecided of men becomes an irrevocable force by the mere act of dying."

"There are other forces besides that of law," Wareham persisted. "A wish may bind as tightly as a will."

He was reminded of an old trick of Anne's which he had almost forgotten, when she threw him a glance between half-closed lids. But the lady on his other side addressed a remark to him, and Anne took the opportunity to talk to her neighbour. Wareham saw Lady Fanny looking at them with what he supposed to be surprise at the audacity which had changed the order of the dinner, or, rather, the diners; of other thoughts of hers he was unsuspicious. By and by Anne addressed him again.

"Are you the typical Englishman, only happy when you are killing something?"

He broke into sturdy disclaimer.

"You mean because I have come to shoot? I like the open air and the walking; as for results, I am absolutely indifferent."

"But you go out with them to-morrow?" He said yes, and added quickly, without looking at her—

"Why else am I here?"

"True. Why else?" Anne said, speaking deliberately, and nibbling an almond. "To tell the truth, I thought it probable the inducement might not be sufficient. That was why I wrote."

The answer "Your summons brought me," rushed to his lips, and had to be driven back. He only ventured on, "And I have not thanked you," and dashed in another direction. "Colonel Martyn looks almost happy. I expect this life is very congenial to him."

"Nothing could be more so. He is out from morning to night, and can tell you the history of every hit and every miss, chapter and verse. Norway was wasted time in his life."

"He has more heart than his wife," said Wareham bluntly.

"You were speaking to her just now. Has that caused your criticism?"

"Not that more than another, but it did not change my impression."

"I suspect that to change would always cost you something," said Anne, smiling.

He was on the watch against a personal note, and held himself woodenly irresponsive. But the fretting consciousness of being tongue-tied whenever he was with her, of being forced into the condition of a surface against which a match was struck in vain, worried his nerves into irritation. More than once he thought that Anne glanced at him with surprise at his dullness, or might it be his coldness. This seemed hardly possible to him, conscious as he was of a fire within which had to be kept down by liberal sluicing with cold water. It was delight to be near her, yet torture, and he told himself that he had been a fool to come. Yet when the men were left in the room after dinner it had become a desert.

The evening might have been blissful.

Opportunity was there, could he have grasped her. Once or twice, it is true, Lord Milborough succeeded in monopolising Anne; but there was scarcely a minute when Wareham was not aware that the privilege might have been his, had he sought it.

Anne's extreme beauty, the brilliant beauty which belongs to night, the attraction she undoubtedly was bent on exercising, made his brain dizzy. As they parted in the hall, she said reproachfully—

"So you desert us for the whole of to-morrow!"

"Thank goodness!" said a voice behind.

"Discontented men hanging about the whole of the day would be unendurable."

It was Mrs Martyn. Anne laughed good-humouredly.

"I don't know your discontented men."

She was told to wait until experience had been broadened by marriage, and rated with prophecies all the way up the stairs. At Mrs Martyn's door she lingered, and finally entered, dropping into a deep chair near the fire. Blanche dismissed her maid, and stood by the mantelpiece, unfastening her bracelets.

"The house has capabilities," she said, "and you may make it charming."

Anne stared.

"My dear, you don't suppose that I am blind and deaf? Of course, we all know that you can marry Lord Milborough when you please. Why pretend?"

"What do you expect me to say?" said Anne coolly.

"Not the usual stock commonplaces."

"It is hard to be original when one has nothing to say; harder, perhaps, when one has. I give it up. Commonplace or not, I assure you Lord Milborough has not asked me to marry him, so that I have had no opportunity of—"

"Accepting him?" said Mrs Martyn eagerly.

"Giving him an answer."

"You are an adept, my dear, in holding a man at arm's length, or drawing him nearer as you please!"

Anne's eyes were charged with anger.

"Blanche!"

"Can you deny it? Every now and then you land yourself in a scrape, as with that poor young fellow. Anne, tell me"—with a change of voice she leaned forward curiously—"if he had lived, what would you have done?"

Anne glanced at her, and did not at first answer. She lay back in the chair, her dark head resting against the cushion, the flicker of the fire catching a diamond cluster which nestled in her hair. Presently she said slowly—

"I don't know. I believe he might have swept me into marrying him."

"Is that the secret?"

"I feel like Samson—as foolish perhaps in breathing it—but the man who marries me must do it quickly, give me no time to find out that I hate him, or to change my mind. If I see him hesitate, he is lost."

"You want a stronger will than your own?" Mrs Martyn said in surprise. "What a dangerous wish!"

"I want my eyes bandaged, like a shying horse," said Anne, smiling at her own simile. "Then I might take the leap. Otherwise I see too much, and imagination refuses to trot along meekly gazing at the one side of the subject which is presented to me."

"It is a pity you did not live in old days. A border raid or a swoop of pirates might have given you the wooing you desire."

Anne agreed.

"No time for hesitation."

Mrs Martyn remarked that Thorpe would be more to her own liking than an old Scotch stronghold. Anne got up.

"Ah, don't weary me with talk of it!"

"I believe, after all, you are like Samson, and have not told me the truth at all. What you really want is a struggle. You conquer too easily."

Anne stood considering.

"That is only the first act of the drama," she said at last. "I hold to what I have said. No more questions. Good-night."

As her maid was brushing her hair, she asked whether the Mr Wareham who had arrived that evening was not the same gentleman who had come to their rescue in that dreadful accident when they were so nearly killed? Anne laughed.

"Your memory is so creative, Watkins, that you add fresh horrors whenever you allude to that day. Yes, it was Mr Wareham with whom I walked to Oakwood."

"How you could, ma'am! My legs wouldn't have carried me."

"They must, if the young farmer hadn't been there. Did he tell you Mr Wareham's name?"

"Yes, ma'am. And that he was staying at Sir Michael Forbes'."

"Anything more?" asked Anne indifferently.

"He was a great friend of the family, Mr Smith said, and down there a great deal. There was some talk of he and Miss Forbes making a match of it. But people are so ready to talk!"

"They are!" Anne agreed with a smile. She sent Watkins away, and sat before the fire staring at a cheerfully blazing log, and bent on investigations. Mrs Martyn's rather broad statements were not required to enlighten her as to the fact that a crisis in her life approached, and for once she did not know how to deal with it. A year ago—six months ago—she would have known very well; then there came a hitherto unknown stirring in her heart, not love, but liking, for Hugh. It amused her so much to find herself at last the sport of fancy, that she caught at the diversion, meaning to break away from the mischievous elf when she pleased. But that strange weakness of her nature which she had confessed to Mrs Martyn, that yielding to a dominating impetuosity, carried her further than she intended. She was on the verge before she knew, she did not love him well enough to take the plunge, yet liked him so much that her retreat had to be cowardly.

Moreover, she had shocked her world, and felt her kingdom totter. To meet Wareham at this moment was to be irresistibly impelled to charm. Conquer him, and she was once more queen—at least in her own estimation. She found balm to her wounded vanity in re-asserting power.

Then she was puzzled. Convinced that to a certain extent she had succeeded, she was met by a wall of reserve, tried to get round it, to break it down; failed, and stood piqued and revolving. Even when she had to her own satisfaction penetrated the cause, it displeased her, for though she had never felt a deep love, she insisted that to be true it must over-ride friendship. Difficulty and displeasure together attracted her to Wareham the more, and when Hugh died, her thoughts crowned him for his fidelity; the more readily, since it could no longer hamper her. The verdict upon her that she was heartless she had accepted with a jest, and quoted the world, but it had secretly stung her, because she was suspicious of its truth. But her feelings towards Wareham relieved her, for something had awakened in her different from what she had hitherto experienced. She told herself that to marry him she might be ready to give up a good deal—Thorpe, for instance—and she closed her eyes, recalling his face, his voice, the strength of his mouth, which had always fascinated her. Meeting him at Firleigh, she had expected more than he gave: as it did not come, she supposed that he was waiting for a decent interval to elapse, or perhaps trusted to that second interview which Sir Hugh's death frustrated.

But now, now she had cast her die. Only by dint of ingenious management of Lord Milborough had she gained the invitation. Nothing at Bergen had raised his suspicions, and when he consulted her as to the people who should be asked, Wareham was indifferently suggested. A man of note.

"Not much in my line," said Lord Milborough, whereupon her "But perhaps in mine," alarmed him, lest she should think her tastes would not have full play. He was asked and was there. The next two days must decide. For that time she believed she could hold back her host. In that time she would take care that Wareham had his opportunity. She did not acknowledge herself to be won, but owned that he might win her. If he did not—then farewell, hearts and lovers. There remained Thorpe.

Chapter Twenty Six
On the Watch

Wareham was an early riser; he went out to take a look at Thorpe before others were stirring. The house was a large block, flanked, except on one side, by four corner towers, each finished by a cupola dome. On the differing side an addition had been built out beyond the towers. A dome resembling those at the corners sprang from the original centre of the house. The windows were square Tudor. A large projection marked the porch, entered by carriages under an arch; a background of fine trees, their foliage thinned but gorgeous, made a fitting setting for a stately building. Wareham pushed his researches into the park. The morning glittered with frost and keen beauty, the air was still and clear, a white sky overhead, and blue distances disclosing; after a time he reached a wood, civilised by a well-kept path running through it; seeing a gleam of water beyond, he told himself that he would come there the next morning, and went back to the house, braced by the fresh air after a somewhat wakeful night.

He had finished his breakfast by the time the ladies appeared, and had no more than a greeting from Anne before the shooting party set off. This, judgment told him, was well, since certain restive impulses of his heart warned him of danger.

The home coverts were to be shot, and before starting Lord Milborough gave some emphatic directions to his sister. She nodded impatiently—

"Oh, I understand, I understand. Mil, you never will give me a word."

"Is this the time for it?"

"Your time is never! You don't consider that I am breaking my heart. I declare if you are not quick, I'll stand up when dinner is going on, and insist upon an answer."

"And you're capable of it," he said, with a laugh. "Well, I'll tell you this, Fan. You're nothing short of a goose, but if I get what I want, you shall have what you want. There?" She shook her head dubiously.

"If you don't?"

"I am serious this time, and I mean to. Help me, and the better for you."
He was gone.

"And for Millie," Lady Fanny reflected with a sigh. She had read danger
in Anne's manoeuvre of the night before. And she already knew enough of
the world to gauge pretty accurately the power of Anne's charm. Spirits
bubbled too persistently with her to be checked, and she had nothing to cause
her serious uneasiness as to her choice of John Elliot, but she wanted every
one dear to her to be happy, to which end it appeared that Anne's marriage
with Lord Milborough would most effectually minister. Her present task
was to induce Anne to go out with the luncheon for the shooters.

"Bring as many as you can," had been her brother's directions, so
unwonted, that she perceived he feared too general a buzzing round Anne.
She went in search of her aunt, Mrs Harcourt, Irish, impracticable, and
witty; but she would have none of it, and shivered at the very idea of the
neighbourhood of wet turnips.

"As if you were afraid of turnips, Aunt Kathleen!"

"English ones, my dear, and chilly. Take that Mrs Martyn."

"You don't like her?"

"No better than the turnips, and for the same reason."

Others were not so impracticable, Lady Dalrymple agreeing with
alacrity, Anne too; in all, six or eight met in the hall when the time for starting
came. A pony had gone on with the provisions, and when they reached the
spot, the gentlemen were there, and luncheon spread. The neighbourhood
of a wood-shed had been chosen; faggots and logs formed seats, servants
were on the watch to anticipate every want. Lord Milborough fastened on
the place next Anne, Wareham sat where he could see her. He noticed that
she was silent, though smiling. What he failed to see was the quiet ingenuity
with which she baffled Lord Milborough's attempts to draw her away from
the others when the luncheon was over. She was assured that the finest
view in the county lay within twenty yards of where they were standing,
a whispered entreaty implored her to let him show it to her. Anne refused,
laughing.

"Our part is done, we vanish!" she cried. "I hope I have been better
brought up than to interfere with that more important part of creation
which was provided for men to shoot. Go to your birds."

He was heard to mutter—

"Hang the birds!"

"Come, come!" she called to the others. "Lord Milborough's patience is failing him so completely that he is on the verge of bad language. We are in the way."

Wareham had neither smile nor word, but a look in place of them in which he blissfully fancied reproach lurked.

The wood-shed was nearly a mile from the house, and in the nearest curve of road two or three carriages were waiting; one was Lady Fanny's pony-carriage. Miss Dalrymple asked to be taken in it.

"I am obliged to drive to Risley, not an interesting little town for a stranger," Lady Fanny demurred, but Anne held to her wish.

"Are you two going off together?" Mrs Martyn asked discontentedly, only to be answered by a laugh from Anne, and a gesture which pointed out Lady Dalrymple to her as a companion.

"Blanche detests my step-mother," Anne explained as they drove away. The remark jarred on Fanny, who thought only close friendship excused family criticisms, and read them in the speech. She expressed civil regret that the carriage would hold no more.

"Don't regret it," Anne said contentedly. "This is the first time that you and I have been alone together. But you are a very princess of hostesses."

Fanny flushed, pleased with the praise.

"You should have been with us in Norway. Why did not your brother bring you?"

"He thought better of it."

"And you would have come in for a sad time." She went on to speak of the sadness. "It was a great shock to Mr Wareham to find his friend so ill."

"Terrible!" cried Lady Fanny, impulsively. "I saw him the day before he had the telegram."

"Yes?"

"At the Ravenhills'. I was staying with them. Of course, then he knew nothing." Anne felt as if cold fingers had touched her.

"Ah, you made acquaintance with him at the Ravenhills'?" she remarked carelessly.

"Yes, he came there two or three times," said Millie's friend, glad to put an emphasis on the acquaintance. "They know him well, I think; I suppose from having met in Norway. Yesterday, he brought something I had left at their house."

Anne pondered. She was sure that she was the preferred, but was it not probable that with Wareham, who succeeded so admirably in repressing his feelings, cool judgment might stand arrayed against her, and carry the day? A peep-hole to his heart. What would she not give for it! At that moment she felt as if all that she wanted was—to know.

"Miss Ravenhill is your friend?"

"The dearest!" Rash Fanny added quickly, "I would give a great deal to see her happy."

"And what does that mean?" asked Anne, her lips tightening, though she smiled.

Fanny caught herself back.

"I suppose only Millie could tell us."

"Or one other."

No answer was given. Lady Fanny whipped up her ponies, they went flying down one hill, swung up another. A wind had risen, a grey squadron of clouds scudded overhead, out of the yellow trees came rustle and fall of leaf. By way of a safer subject, Fanny prophesied change of weather and rain.

"That will affect to-morrow's shootings," remarked Anne. "Poor Lord Milborough!"

"Oh, he'll not mind. I don't think he was keen about it to-day."

Her companion sat reflective. She said at last—

"I did not see much of your friend when we were travelling together."

"Millie is shy. And I think one must know her at home to know her at all. Once known, once loved!"

"You are a warm friend," said Anne, with a smile. "For a true estimate I must go to some indifferent person. Will Mr Wareham do? Or is he, too, bespoken counsel?"

A glance at Fanny showed her red, she did not like the word bespoken.

"I have never talked to Mr Wareham about Miss Ravenhill," she said stiffly.

"Oh, I have!"

It was irresistible.

"And what did he say?" asked Lady Fanny, with eagerness.

"Well, not quite so much as you. Could you expect it?" There was a touch of malice in Anne's voice, which Fanny resented.

"What did I say? That to know her was to love her? Oh, no, I couldn't expect that! Do you see that ugly little clump of houses? That's the beginning of Risley."

On the whole, Anne had gathered enough to make her thoughtful. She kept on indifferent subjects the rest of the afternoon. As they drove back it was evident that rain was at hand, the sky had grown wild, the country had that ragged look which thinning leaves give in a high wind.

"If I dared prophesy on my neighbours' clouds, I should say there would be no shooting to-morrow," Anne said.

"A house full of bored men instead," sighed Lady Fanny.

For their misfortunes Anne cared little. She had meant to find opportunity somewhere, and this promised freely.

That night she dressed for dinner with care, the white satin setting off her rich dark beauty, and if she had perplexities, no sign betrayed them. To see her lightly talking would have been to disbelieve that she could be keenly on the watch, eye and ear together heedful. She had to keep Lord Milborough pleased and yet doubtful, to ward off for another thirty-six hours what he was burning to say at once, to read Wareham's mind—if possible, to bring him to her feet. Then and not till then would she decide. But meanwhile she could not, would not, cease to be charming.

There was no repetition of her movement of the evening before, and thought for Millie led Lady Fanny to plant Wareham at a safe distance from the dangerous Miss Dalrymple. Anne submitted. That night she had foreseen would offer no chance of the words she wanted.

She was not mistaken in the effect she produced on Wareham. Her beauty was of the kind which is set off by rich surroundings; she seldom looked at him, but when her dark smiling eyes rested upon him for a moment, he was conscious of the same dizzy thrill which had seized him that early morning at Haare; and the greediness with which his ears drank in every tone of her voice, made him a dull companion to a young lady in awe of a well-known author, and prepared to treasure words. Anne did not fail to note his silence, nor that she held his attention.

After dinner he came to her, encouraged by her look, but Lord Milborough was there as soon. Would she prefer the billiard-room? Anne shook her head.

"Listen to the rain, and keep billiards for to-morrow, when you will be wandering miserably about the house, wretched examples of the unemployed."

Lord Milborough protested that there was no fear of his finding the house miserable. He would have given up shooting that afternoon, could he only have gone with her and Fanny to Risley.

"You would have been terribly in the way," he was told. "Only two should drive together. Besides, we amused ourselves by discussing some of you."

This piqued him into curiosity, as she expected. Wareham sat indifferent, caring nothing whether he were discussed or no, but conscious of imprisoned words beating wildly at the bars behind which he had set them. He knew now that he had been mad to come.

Ordinarily Anne and her step-mother exchanged as few words as possible; this night, as the party separated, Lady Dalrymple announced that she had something to say, and was bidden to Anne's room at a later period. When she swept in, attired in a flame-coloured wrapper of softest silk, Anne flung her a glance of reluctant admiration. She was under thirty-five, tall, and sufficiently dark to annoy Anne, who hated to hear of likeness; a too important nose stood in the way of claims to beauty, but perhaps gave weight to the verdict of handsome. A high voice had rasping tones in it, and the line of her eyebrows was so unpleasantly even as to suggest pencilling.

She sank into the chair which was pushed forward for her, and put her question.

"May I ask whether anything is decided?" Anne's eyes darkened, but she answered briefly—

"Nothing."

"And we leave on Thursday. I go to the Sinclairs' as settled, after that my plans are changed."

Anne did not turn her head.

"You mean to marry?"

"Lord Arthur Crosse."

There was a few seconds' silence before Anne said—

"I imagine you would like me to congratulate you. I hope you will be happy."

"Thanks. I might not have spoken of it for a day or two, but that I thought it might influence your own decision."

"Hardly." Both voices were cold, but Anne's the coldest, and she spoke with a sweet modulation which irritated Lady Dalrymple, conscious of her own harsher tones. Her next words were more hasty.

"Hitherto, at any rate, you have had a home with me."

"By my father's will it was provided for, I think?"

Lady Dalrymple's fingers tapped the arms of her chair impatiently.

"Certainly. But alone, you will not find that you can live in the same comfort. If you could, General Hervey is not likely to permit it."

For the first time there was a trace of uneasiness in Anne's repetition of the name.

"General Hervey?"

"Have you forgotten that in case of my marriage he was to act as your guardian?"

She had.

"Probably he will wish you to live in Eaton Square with them, and I scarcely think you will find this agreeable."

Anne's refuge was silence and a smile. Lady Dalrymple wished to wound, but not to break with her, for the Thorpe shooting was dear to Lord Arthur, and having been made aware of Lord. Milborough's wishes, he had impressed them upon his intended bride as requiring her co-operation. She therefore made haste to add—

"But of course you will marry, and quickly, and I have only said this because, if Lord Milborough's proposal has not come, it is undoubtedly imminent."

Anne listened, and said no more than—

"Is Lord Milborough the one man then in the world?"

"There are not many like him and available. That, I suspect, is the best answer to your question. Seriously, he is a magnificent match."

Anne sat mute. Lady Dalrymple glanced at her, and grew impatient.

"You are not in any doubt as to your answer?" she demanded quickly.

"I always doubt until the thing is said, and long afterwards," said Anne.

"Afterwards as much as you like. You can hardly toss over Lord Milborough as you have less important people."

"What an argument against accepting him!" There was angry light in her eyes, though she kept her voice cool.

Lady Dalrymple could not resist a taunt.

"It is an amusement, let me add, of which the world wearies in a woman. It forgives once for the sake of having something to talk about, the second time palls, and the third is wearisome and unpardonable. However," she went on, remembering her instructions, "the point is not whether Lord Milborough shall be thrown over, but whether he will be accepted?"

Anne sat upright.

"I do not know," she said coldly.

"He will ask to-morrow."

"He has said so?"

"Pray do not waste your indignation. Would he be likely to say so? But I can see."

"If he does," —she leaned back again, —"he will be refused."

"Anne!"

"Refused."

"You are mad."

"Perhaps. At any rate, that is what will happen to him if he puts his question to-morrow."

"But," said her step-mother with a gasp, "you have just said that you are undecided?"

"I am. I may veer round. I protest nothing, except that to-morrow shall not bind me."

Lady Dalrymple rose, feeling that the situation was more critical than she had imagined, so critical, indeed, that she began to fear she had said too much. She had never understood Anne, for which she was not to blame; at this moment she felt herself face to face with a sphinx, and looked askance. Luck, rather than tact, led her to add —

"Well, it is your own concern, no others," and to wish good-night.

Anne sat still where she had been left, thought busy. She smiled at her own clear understanding of the position, and perceiving Lord Milborough working through Lord Arthur upon Lady Dalrymple, recognised that this interview was intended as a probe before he ventured on the momentous question. Her fencing of the past two days had doubtless left him uneasy. She herself had foreseen fresh difficulties the next day, and was proportionably relieved by the conviction that after what she had just announced she would be left unmolested. Would Wareham speak? He should have the opportunity, and if—if—he succeeded in carrying her heart captive, she believed herself capable of marrying him, and renouncing more brilliant prospects. No one, it was certain, had attracted and piqued her as he had.

But Anne's heart was guarded in its impulses. It made no rash resolves. It looked to circumstances to determine choice, not by any means suffering itself to be swept away by a dominant emotion, nor disposed to hang too long in the balance. Anne was the world's pupil, and the world teaches the value of outer casings, with a side sneer at romance. The outer casings belonged unmistakably to Lord Milborough. This was not to be forgotten, though she was ready to make concessions to her heart. But there, too, uneasiness lurked. Millie's name had given substance to vague fears. Her love for Wareham, for love it was, in its degree, prevented certainty. Before him she was no conqueror, but shy, unconvinced of her own power. Did he love her? If he did, what shut his mouth? Was he uncertain, hesitating between her and Millie? Anne sprang to her feet, and stood breathing hard, hands clenched, eyes dark with scorn, face flushing with the thought. Weighing all that she would resign, she demanded a mighty love from him as an equivalent, not a jot would she yield, and understood nothing of the inequality of the bargain. Had she but known it, her unconsciousness was pathetic.

She went to the window, drew aside the curtain, and flung back the shutter. Rain drove wildly against the glass. She closed her defences again, and came back to the fire.

To-morrow she would know.

Chapter Twenty Seven
The Hour—and the Woman

Rain persistent, violent, drowned all thought of shooting. Colonel Martyn, it is true, with unconquerable energy, professed himself ready to make the attempt, but no one seconding him, he found consolation in a gymnasium which Lord Milborough had set up for the use of the household. Lord Milborough himself was moody. Anne perceived that her decision had been already made known to him, and that it did not please. This did not trouble her. It was Wareham who was on her mind that day—a day of days, did he but know it! a day with an aspect of finality about it, which made the chiming hours sound like a knell. Once, early, opportunity fluttered round her. They lingered in the hall, Mary Tempest, the girl whose organ of veneration for authors and beauties was largely developed, by Anne's side, when Wareham, seeing her thus safely guarded, approached.

"I will not class you with the unemployed," said Anne, smiling, "but I pity you, for, as you took care to tell me, you came here with one object, and that fails you. Charity obliges me to assure you that in the library you will find, I believe, a fine collection of books, and,"—looking round—"absolute quiet. I can speak securely as to the quiet."

"Thank you. But the picture-gallery? The pictures, I know, are famous."

Anne's brain was spinning questions. Here was the opening she desired. Should she accept it? Two or three hours later there would have been no hesitation, but the morning, the cold-blooded hours of the morning, when caution walks by man, repelled her. She objected that the light would be bad, besides, three or four of them had promised to go over the stables with Lord Milborough.

"That offers you no inducement?"

He owned that she was right.

"Let me hear how you have amused yourself at luncheon," she said, as she went away.

Mary Tempest's head was almost turned by Miss Dalrymple that day. She was invited to accompany her wherever she went, stables, conservatory, billiard-room. Lord Milborough fretted, once murmured "Cruel!" but Anne made no sign of having heard, and as the hours passed, his spirits rose. Hope had been delicately conveyed to him by the engaged couple; this day of delay was, no doubt, a whim of Anne's; humour it, and please her. It was proof of Anne's power that a young earl, with sixty thousand a year, was forced to contemplate the possibilities of a refusal, and dared not risk it.

At luncheon it was acknowledged that the wind had fallen, and that the rain was not so heavy. Lord Milborough proposed to drive Colonel Martyn to a neighbouring place in a dog-cart. Would any one else come?

"I don't mind," said Wareham.

Anne's fingers closed on her palm.

"If you are prepared for an hours wait?"

"Oh, I'm not." He laughed. "I avoid courting patience, the most annoying of virtues."

"I agree!" cried Lord Milborough. "Let us each throw a stone at her." He looked at Anne significantly. She sat smiling.

"No stones, please."

Colonel Martyn turned a gloomy face towards them.

"Of all places for patience, commend me to Norway, where they wheel you in a perambulator by the side of a salmon river," he said. "No newspapers, and your dinner at one o'clock off stewed whip-cord."

His wife put in that it had made another man of him. She thought it charming, except for the people you met, shuddering at remembrance of the professor. Lord Milborough considered it a fair yachting country. Anne pronounced in favour of the inland scenery and carriole driving. "Colonel Martyn's perambulators."

As they left the dining-room she contrived to be near Wareham, and to say, in a low voice, "You do not drive with Lord Milborough, will you condescend to a walk in the park? In this weather we cannot go far, but Miss Tempest and I pant for fresh air, and start at three."

The name of Miss Tempest set him at ease. He hesitated to trust himself to walk alone with her, his lips yet sealed; but with another, a third, what was there to fear? He showed his pleasure.

"Be in the conservatory at three, then," said Anne; "we will join you there. And bring no companion, for it is insupportable to have a troop at one's heels." She nodded and passed on. To Mary Tempest she said, "Come to my room at three," and sent her away radiant by adding, "There is something I want you to do for me."

Punctual to the moment Mary appeared. Anne kissed her.

"I know I can trust you not to talk," she said, smiling at her.

She was answered by a look of devotion. "The truth is, there is something I want to say to Mr Wareham."

"And you would rather I did not come?"

"No, no, not quite that. If you would start with us, and after a little time remember something which has to be done?"

"Oh, yes! I really ought to write to Horace."

"And your mother will not mind your coming home by yourself?"

"Mind? No, no!"

"Then I leave it to you."

"Oh, you may! Only—"

"What?"

"How am I to know when you wish me to take myself off?"

"I'll say—what shall I say?—I'll ask what Mrs Tempest is doing with herself this afternoon."

"That will do perfectly, and I can easily bring in my letter."

Anne saw that she had provided her young adorer with a problem which would occupy her thoughts throughout her part of the walk. To have something to do for Miss Dalrymple, and to do it intelligently! On the stairs they met Mrs Martyn.

"Going out in this weather! Well, perhaps you are right, perhaps I'll come myself."

"I am not in the humour for waiting," Anne said. "It is now or never."

"But I should not be long."

"Too long. Come, Mary."

Mrs Martyn was left reflecting, and suspecting a purpose. From no window, unfortunately, could she command the four sides of the house. She flew to her own, and stood glued to the pane. Nothing met her sight, but the dreariness of grey rain corroborated her suspicions, since she was sure that to walk through it with only Mary Tempest as a companion would have no attractions for Anne. Looking at last brought its reward. Three small figures emerged on a path; two she knew, the other she recognised by the ulster to be Wareham, and promptly admired her own powers of intuition.

"I knew it, of course I knew it, if only by Anne's manner!" she cried, and meditated upon the nature of woman as exemplified by Anne. With everything she could wish for in the world at her feet, she perceived that she wanted more, and would not be content unless Wareham walked behind to grace her triumph. More than this her friend would have laughed at, but so far she decided upon with easy security. Wareham offered a greater puzzle. She had been certain, petulantly certain, of his liking for Anne, and had drawn a rather spiteful amusement from the awkwardness of his position as Hugh's friend. Had he changed? She had kept him well under a microscope since he had been at Thorpe, and minute observations had on the whole confirmed her first opinion. Yet he had not to all appearances advanced one jot in his wooing. Why? Why not, now that his road was open? And if resolved against it, why was he here? Why, above all, was he walking in the park with Anne? As for Mary, Mrs Martyn tossed her to the winds. "The girl will be sent home, of course," and when half-an-hour later she beheld her whisk across the hall she again appreciated her own acuteness.

Wareham, blind man, permitted himself blissful thrills of delight. The fact that Anne had asked him to accompany them counted for much. He had the charm of her society, the defence of a third person. A few days now would end his ordeal, and happy the augury of this kindness! Strangely, perhaps, Lord Milborough's evident admiration troubled him little. Fear did not easily touch him, except the lately born fear that he might be caught by dishonour, and the time for this was almost passed. It did not require vanity to perceive that Anne encouraged him; and his mind, once possessed with the idea, went straightforwardly to the end to which happy paths lead.

Her presence by his side made him say—

"It is an insult to Norway to be reminded of it by storm and rain, but I could fancy myself back there again. Why?"

Anne laughed.

"Which part of Norway?"

He answered promptly, "Gudvangen"; adding, meaningly, "And that was a day of sunshine."

"Weather failing, you must be content with a frivolous association," she said mirthfully; "it is merely that I am wearing the same hat and coat."

"You remembered, then?" he asked, gathering delicious assurance from the fact.

"I don't think it is *I* who have shown forgetfulness," said Anne, in a low voice. In the same tone he returned —

"Certainly I cannot be accused of it."

It will be seen that matters were proceeding merrily, and unchecked — rather, one might say, assisted — by the modest presence of Miss Tempest. She being there, Wareham knew that he could not go to the point which was as yet forbidden, and, feeling himself safe from that temptation, had the delight of dallying round it, and venturing more closely than he yet had dared. Anne, on her side, saw the advance, and not realising that it was really favoured by limits, felt herself in the mood to be swung along, and resolved as to the moment when her companion should receive a hint to go. Meanwhile she flung her a crumb or two.

"The rain has grown harmless. You are not sorry I enticed you out, Mary?"

"Sorry! I think it delightful."

It appeared that she was almost as rapturous as Wareham. Anne told him of her step-mother's engagement, and found that he had guessed something. He asked whether it affected her unpleasantly.

"Oh no, I am glad. We have never pulled together." She stopped abruptly. "Pray where are we going?"

"Yesterday morning I came this way, and seeing a delightful path through a wood," said Wareham eagerly, "I set my heart upon showing it to you."

"Well —" She walked on, holding her umbrella lightly poised, really wondering whether Mary Tempest could be trusted to carry out her directions naturally. "We escaped from Mrs Martyn when we came out," she said, laughingly. "I suspect they are all finding it rather dull, shut up in the house. What is your mother doing, Mary?"

"She was writing to father." The girl came to a sudden stop. "Oh!"

"What is the matter?"

"Horace! Horace must be written to, and I have not done it!"

"The post goes out so early here, still — surely you will have time for a not very long letter?"

"Oh, but this is to India, this must be a long letter. Dear Miss Dalrymple, I am so sorry, but I am afraid I must go back!"

"Yes, I see. Well, we will all turn."

"No, no, I should never forgive myself; please go on, please don't think of it! See, it is nothing for me to go so far by myself."

"You are sure?"

"Certain."

"Well, what do you say, Mr Wareham? Will you put up with but one companion? I confess your wood attracts me."

He exclaimed—

"Don't let us miss it," and then felt a grip of terror at his heart. He had been content to go to the brink of a precipice and lean over, trusting to a barrier; here was the barrier withdrawn, and he left, dizzily attracted by his danger, and already making a step nearer. It seemed, indeed, as if he were two men, the one pushing, urging towards it, with taunt of cowardice, the other stiffening into resistance, and stammering—"Unless Miss Tempest would like us to return with her?"

Anne glanced at him. This second thought did not please her, though she knew enough to be assured that there would be no hesitation with Mary, who hurried shy protestations and fled. The others walked on. Anne was sensitive, and marked a change in Wareham's manner; he talked of books and impersonal matters, she listened unheedingly, occupied in reflecting why, with Mary's presence withdrawn, he ceased to be expansive. "He is afraid," she said to herself, and set womanly wits to find out the why. It was possible that he believed her to intend to accept Lord Milborough. Some remarks on the beauty of the park set her inveighing against overgrown places.

"I can understand Alexander's sigh for worlds to conquer," she said, "but not the joy of possession. Persons may be found, I suppose, who look at Lord Milborough with veneration because he is lord of half a county. That is inconceivable to me."

"You are not ambitious of power?"

"Of power, yes. What woman is not? But brains before acres, and the owners of acres are apt to cultivate them and let their brains lie fallow."

Wareham was indifferent to his rival. He said—

"I dare say you are right. Lord Milborough does not seem to me to be wanting in brains, but rather in finding occasions to use them. Politics—a national crisis—might develop them."

Anne shrugged her shoulders. "He is wearisome. Is this the wood?"

She expected Wareham to take advantage of her depreciation of their host. He merely answered the question.

"This is it, with such a broad path that I hope you will not get wet."

"Oh, the rain has stopped," said Anne, and shut her umbrella impatiently.

"I see water. Some one spoke of a lake, beautiful with rhododendrons in spring, and a house by its side, where Lady Fanny and her friend Miss Ravenhill spent a month together last year."

"That sounds very romantic. I wonder what they talked of all the time."

"I heard they were very happy," said Wareham.

His voice was under control. Anne, walking a little in advance, did not know that his eyes, fastened on her, gathered torturing bliss from watching her swift graceful movements. She pictured him for a moment thinking of Millie, then conviction rushed over her again and checked her steps.

As they reached the lake rain once more fell heavily, honeycombing the glassy water with an infinite number of tiny depressions. The lake was bordered with slopes of grass, and with magnificent clumps of rhododendrons and kalmias. Sweeping down in noble curves, they formed an island, and sent deep purple and green shadows into the water. On the left, and close to the water, stood a long low house.

"Let us wait there until the storm has passed. It is only a storm," urged Wareham.

Anne hesitated. But they were as secure from interruption there as anywhere else, and her umbrella hampered her. They went, and were made instantly welcome. The house was kept always in order in case visitors came from the big house, and a pleasant room received them—pleasant now, it had to be owned, rather by right of a blazing fire and comfortable chairs than from the situation which gave its charm in finer weather. Wareham, accustomed to take note of all around him, observed so much; Anne, absorbed, thought only that fate had brought them to the best possible place for her purpose. He pulled a chair near the fire.

"Sit here, and get dry. That last downpour was wetting."

She motioned to another opposite. "You there, then."

"Thanks." He walked restlessly to the window. "I do not think it will last."

"What does it matter? As well here as anywhere else. But man is a discontented being, always desirous of being where he is not."

The Swing of the Pendulum | 255

The reproach brought him back smiling to the chair she indicated. But something in his attitude laid him open to her next remark.

"You have the air of an unwilling victim. What is the matter with you?"

"It must be sheer inability to look as I feel. Do you think this can be anything but delightful?"

"Confess that you have not tried to give the impression. Or, no, confess nothing, let bygones be bygones, and let us pick up our friendship where you let it abruptly drop in Norway. Where were we then?"

She spoke jestingly, but his heart thrilled at the under-meaning her words indicated.

"To remember would be to go back," he muttered.

Her face changed.

"And you would not?" she said amazedly.

He burst out—

"Who would, when hope lies in front? To exchange hope for remembrance!"

Anne's dark eyes smiled contentment.

"No, you are right," she said. "We are all fools in our idle talk about the past; wreathing it with flowers which never grew, and turning it into a fetish. It is pathetic, after all," she added musingly. "And I don't think that the future holds me as it does you. Perhaps I am too unimaginative—"

"With your sympathy? Never!"

"But I believe I find more satisfaction in the present."

The words were spoken gravely, with a quiet which pleaded against any accusation of coquetry, had such an accusation crossed his mind. But he would have flung it from him as an infamy. Was ever man so tried!

The hour was there, and the woman; he, close to her, heart leaping to meet her heart, and no word permissible, possible! The trial was, as he had dreaded, almost beyond his strength. To have to answer her with cold words. And what woman would not resent such an answer! He dared not even look, since the look he must have given, wanting words, would be an insult. He sat mute, downcast.

Anne waited, expectant.

When no answer came her breath quickened. Her glance flew to Wareham, and she beheld only a wretched drooping head. Had she so utterly deceived herself that the passion she had imagined was but a sham, a mockery? Here, when no obstacle stood between, were they parted by his own want of will? She had felt that with him by her side, urging, sweeping her along, she might have yielded and turned her back upon her world's prize, but—a reluctant lover!

Pride stormed, yet something softer held it back. She looked intently at him, trying to pierce to the truth. That he was moved she saw. He could not be indifferent. What withheld him? She sent out another feeler.

"Mr Wareham, you look as if what I said had displeased you. What is there at fault? One must know one's sins to mend them."

He said in a voice strained because it tugged for freedom—

"Still more, one must know them to tell them."

"You are sitting there, and not accusing me of something?"

"I am heaping dust on my own head for a fool," he groaned. "Give me time, and you shall know."

She leaned back and stared at the fire, conscious of a thrill, but not the thrill she expected. Wareham's words hinting at a wall between them raised immediate discontent, for obstacles should be cleared when she was wooed. And she had set herself this day as the limit of the time accorded him, believing it possible that she might yield to impetuosity. To this sluggish demand—never! It was not for this that she could give up what she felt it was heroic to reject. She was colder now than five minutes ago.

Wareham, not yet enlightened, and imagining himself to have told only too much, leaned half across the table which was between them.

"Will you wait?" he breathed. The words, "Only a few days," almost choked him.

Anne's "I cannot," was inexorable, stunning. She rose up directly and went to the window, expecting to have raised a tempest, and for a moment again, perhaps irresolute. He stood, but did not follow her, and she felt angrily indignant that her power was not equal to breaking the silence. To hide the humiliation, she said lightly—

"Let us go before another storm begins."

Had she looked at him, pity might have stirred, but she went out of the room without turning her head.

Wareham followed.

She began to feel the position ludicrous. A walk of a mile with a man whom her impatience was ready to imagine had rejected her by his obstinate silence, was so hateful in anticipation that she would have been ready to bless Mary Tempest if she had brought a whole posse of spies upon them. Moreover, she foresaw that the weight of conversation would fall upon her, the woman, and therefore expected to keep conventionality in the front. Wet rhododendrons and dripping beech-trees suggested nothing beyond a passing remark, inane as it was safe. The dullness of Mary Tempest's home-life lasted longer, in the midst of it she fancied a desperate "Anne!" was breathed in her ear, and quickened her steps. Her coldness now had reached the pitch of a shiver at her own foolishness; above all, she wished to avoid the promise of an explanation. Luckily for her, the heavy drops falling from the trees allowed her the shelter of an umbrella; she kept it at her ears, and shot flying remarks from underneath, careful to avoid any which took the form of questions. Her endeavours did not prevent an angry acknowledgment that if he had anything he burned to say, he would have said it.

They were near the end of the wood, and her heart sank at thought of the long stretch which still lay between it and the house, when, to her joy, she heard voices. The gate was reached simultaneously, she and Wareham on one side, the other Colonel and Mrs Martyn with Lord Milborough.

"Are you surprised to see us?" asked Mrs Martyn, serenely smiling at the situation, which she believed to be disconcerting to more than one. "I was at my window when you crossed the park, and as Lord Milborough and Tom came back long before they were expected, we all started forth in pursuit. Have you been far?"

The question was put to Wareham, and he answered it by saying that they had taken refuge from the rain in a house by the lake.

"Where we admired your provident hospitality," Anne added, with a smile to Lord Milborough. "To be met by a cheery fire where one expected bare shelter, was such a delicious surprise, that I feel as if we ought to go back and do the honours to the owner."

"Oh, no, no," objected Mrs Martyn. "It is growing dark, and tea will be ready by this time."

Colonel Martyn announced that he should give himself a stretch, as he wanted exercise.

"You won't come, I suppose?" he said to Lord Milborough, who excused himself.

Mrs Martyn went on with Wareham, from whom she hoped to find out something; the other two followed, Lord Milborough's face clearing like magic.

"Stop, and let those people go ahead," he said.

"Shall we hurt them?" Anne asked demurely.

After the humiliation of the past hour, it was balm to feel herself again. Never had she liked her companion so well.

"*I'm* in the humour to do any one a harm who comes in my way," he muttered. "Anne!"

She lifted her eyebrows.

"Isn't she a new person?"

"Look here," he said, disregarding, "I got a hint that if I bothered you to-day my chance was up. I've tried, 'pon my soul I've tried, to keep off, and I can't. When I'd driven Martyn a few miles, I had to make an excuse and turn back again, and here I am by your side, and—"

He tried to possess himself of her hand, but she drew it away. Not so, however, as to show displeasure. The very audacity of ignoring her commands pleased her, since she flattered herself he found the task impossible, and contrasting the two, she scourged Wareham in her thoughts.

"Anne, will you marry me?"

"What were you told?"

"That you were to be left in peace. I vowed I would. But when I heard that you were with that fellow Wareham—"

"You broke your vow?"

"Like a shot—."

He was in earnest, she had never seen him so much in earnest. Some good elf had surely whispered in his ear what she craved for at that moment—perhaps always—a forceful impetuosity of wooing, which should snatch decision from her. Her hand was in his again, and not withdrawn. She begged him to have some thought of eyes from the house.

"Say yes, or I'll not answer for myself."

He was told to give her five minutes for consideration, and at the end of two was vowing that they were more than past, and pressing for his answer. To punish him, she lengthened the time, declaring that he should hear nothing until they had reached a certain tree near the house, and thus kept him fuming, at one moment uttering sincere vows, at the next denouncing her cruelty. Anne was in the mood to like inconsistency.

"Now!" he exclaimed, when they were a hundred feet away.

"Do you call that reached?"

The Swing of the Pendulum | 259

"If the sun were out, you'd be in its shadow. Give me my word. Just yes, Anne—yes! Such a small one!"

"No, is smaller." Then she repented and looked at him. "Yes, then."

"You are mine!"

"If you can keep me."

Wareham walked back with Mrs Martyn, for the first time in his life grateful to her satisfaction with her own babble. At intervals she tried to catch him with an astute question; indifference protected him, for his heart felt like nothing so much as an empty husk, and at this moment there was nothing to show or conceal. It was all over, for Anne's manner had conveyed to him that he would never be forgiven. In place of sweet Love he hugged Honour, a prickly substitute! Yet he breathed thankfully.

Of Lord Milborough he was not thinking, Mrs Martyn's hints not even reaching his ears. Half-an-hour ago Anne, he believed, would have been his, could he have claimed her, and to imagine that she was already won by another, would have been to degrade womanhood. He went mechanically with his companion into the house; all the women and some of the men were in the hall, where a big fire blazed cheerfully, and tea stood on a table where Lady Fanny chatted. Mary Tempest looked wistfully at Wareham.

"Where is Anne?" murmured Lady Dalrymple languidly.

"Behind us."

And at this moment she came in and stood a central point for the fire-light. As she drew off her gloves, her eyes, softly brilliant, wandered round the group, and passed Wareham unconcernedly; her beauty had the effect of eclipsing all the other women. Mrs Martyn touched Wareham's arm.

"Look at Lord Milborough's face."

He looked, uncomprehending.

"Oh, men, men," said Mrs Martyn impatiently. "Of course it is settled."

Chapter Twenty Eight
A Note of Interrogation instead of a Full-Stop

The Milborough marriage was the event of the winter. It was generally conceded that Miss Dalrymple was rewarded for those contrarieties in former love affairs which the world now forgave, but kept stored up for future use—or chastisement. Meanwhile it was at her feet as the most beautiful of brides, and the splendour of her lot made Lady Fanny's choice the more amazing. Lord Milborough's consent flew out readily enough when he was in the rush of his own triumph, and might have found wife and sister difficult to harmonise. Since his marriage, and since he finds Lady Fanny quite content to pass her days with her aunt, Mrs Harcourt, or the Ravenhills, he is disposed to grumble at her engagement to a curate. Anne takes her part.

"If she knows her own mind, for pity's sake let her go after it," she said once.

As to that wedding, one may prophesy.

But as to other possibilities, on which the last chapter is expected to pronounce, I can only express ignorance. All that this story professes to do is to take a few months out of the lives of certain men and women, and, very imperfectly, show what the months did for them. Now comes the future, as to which I know no more than you do. What do you think? Will Wareham, as the past recedes, read in it confirmation of Anne's verdict on herself—a heartless woman? If he does, will it affect his own heart? This is certain, that the first effect on him of hearing of her engagement was stupefaction. And Anne contrived, perhaps in good faith, to let him feel that she considered him to have behaved very ill. Possibly—but guesses are like the rootless flowers with which children deck their gardens, by to-morrow they may be worthless; and I am sorry, for I should like to group them as I want my flowers to grow, and Millie Ravenhill would make any garden fair.

What Wareham thinks he will do is to fling himself heart and mind into his profession. Certain, rash man, that he now knows a great deal about women, his new book deals chiefly with their characteristics. Cynicism is unwholesome in the body, and one may pardon its victim for spitting it out; since, thus got rid of, it often leaves the patient open to sweeter influences. One thing is certain, that whether his love for Anne is dead or not, his respect is gone, and that when he read the account of the great wedding in the *Morning Post*, he broke into laughter to think how clever a fooling hers had been.

A week ago, Colonel Martyn overtook him in Piccadilly.

"I've just left Blanche in Grosvenor Square—Lady Milborough's, you know. By Jove, that young woman has done well for herself!"

"She was made for her position," Wareham remarked.

"She climbed for it, you should rather say. She was a rare flirt."

"Stop," said Wareham suddenly. He was not the man to belittle the woman he had once loved.